Flashman Rides Again

(1966 – 1978)

By

Charles Pack

ISBN: 978-1-915768-53-7

Having paused, seeking some easier, shadier route, he shuffled out along the path, head down as if each footfall marked the end of his failing vision. Eventually, he reached the forest on the other side and disappeared, only to re-emerge some moments later, surprisingly agile, without his sack and weaved back the way he had just come before disappearing again.

The long grass at the edge of the clearing from where he had just come parted to reveal a younger man. He wore a green cap, of the type commonly seen on the heads of Mao Tse Tung's young revolutionary guards, and a ragged khaki tunic. Across his chest was stretched a canvas bandolier, stitched to carry four of the curved magazines that fitted the AK47 assault rifle that he held loosely at waist level.

Stepping out confidently, he walked at a brisk pace, following the old man's route along the path. After he had progressed twenty or thirty yards, a file of seven more young men followed him out into the open. Closely bunched, they wore a variety of ragged clothes, and most of them carried an AK47 too, and weighty-looking rucksacks, but two stood out. These two were dressed in dappled combat overalls, a pattern which the knowledgeable onlooker would know had originated in the East German DDR.

They carried themselves with a certain authority. Not for them the swift nervous glances that betrayed the youth and inexperience of their colleagues. Their leader walked at number two in the file. He seemed to stalk through the cleared grass on the track, and his expert eyes quartered the threatening edge of the forest. He seemed to miss nothing.

Unlike the others, he carried the bulkier RPD light machine gun with a fifty-round drum magazine firmly locked to the receiver. Instead of a cross-chest canvas bandolier sported by his colleagues, he carried eight spare drums in a canvas sack, looped like a blanket roll across the top of his rucksack.

This was both a boast and a testament to his strength. The drums weighed nearly thirty pounds, and the four anti-tank land mines in his pack weighed a further sixty pounds. Added to the extra grenades, water bottles, and civilian clothes in his pack, the total weight that he was carrying came to nearly one hundred and twenty pounds. He knew it, and the men knew it. They respected him – for he was a Commissar.

The second man was slighter but showed the same ease of movement as his colleague, like a beast of prey, and at home in an environment in which he was wholly confident. He marched at number four in the file. He also demonstrated his stature with his weaponry by carrying a rocket launcher. He carried it on a strap, slung from right to left across his chest. Charged with a projectile, the pointed head poked out over his head. He carried four spare projectiles in a canvas sack on his back. Each of the younger recruits also carried a spare. He was the Commander.

As the leading man approached the edge of the forest, he paused, peering at the dark line of the trees as if sensing some alien presence, and shifted the stock of the AK to his shoulder. He looked nervously back at his Commissar, who was just passing a small anthill in the middle of the vlei. As he looked back, the anthill disintegrated like a great pink puffball, and a jet of black smoke shot out of the base. The Commissar and the two men on either side of him seemed to lift as, almost simultaneously, there was another puff of smoke in the grass at the rear of the column, which felled two other colleagues.

The Commissar heard the explosion at the same time as the plated point of a 7.62 millimetre round slammed into his chest. It ripped through the ragged material of his blouse and through the skin behind and, building up a huge pressure cone in front of its line of travel, it shattered the rib in front of his heart, tore into the heart before exploding through the man's back in a pinky froth.

The man, called Comrade Knife, knew nothing of this.

The roar of the Claymore anti-personnel mine explosion that Comrade Knife had neither heard nor survived was then drowned by the harsh thunder of twenty Belgian-manufactured rifles and three machine guns. The weight of fire poured into the little column from three directions, and the tracers from the machine guns formed a crazy arrowhead that seemed to dance up and down the line of twitching figures.

A whistle blew sharply, and the firing stopped. It had all taken a mere ten seconds, and the noise was now replaced by the shrieking of birds, startled out of their midday somnolence by the hideous din. After a few minutes, the vlei settled down to quiet again, broken only by the muted crackling of the tinder-dry grass, which had been set on fire by the scurrying tracers, and the odd clicking around the perimeter, which told of new, full, magazines being fitted.

The whistle shrilled again, and from the sides of the track, about a hundred or so yards from it, six figures rose warily from the grass and approached the shattered column at an angle, three from behind and three from the front. When they reached the still figures on the ground, they started a little ritual that looked like a dance. Working in groups of three, one man would kneel by one of the dead, checking for life, while another stood beside him, pointing his rifle at the supine figure. The third, slightly to one side, seemed to sway as he kept his rifle trained on the bodies that had yet to be searched.

They worked quickly and efficiently, and after a couple of minutes, one of the searchers rose to his feet and called, "All clear, boss." From the middle of the vlei, a small group of four men rose up and walked to the killing zone. Like the searchers, three of the four were Africans. The fourth was Roly Flashman. Tall and not yet bronzed, his firm mouth and strong, cleft chin, spoke of a determined character. Deep crow's feet around his eyes indicated a maturity beyond his 27 years. As he moved through the grass, he talked rapidly into the green plastic handset of a radio strapped to his webbing harness. All four were dressed in the green, brown and khaki camouflage of the Rhodesian army.

Far away from the vlei, high in the hills above an escarpment, a young European wearing the chevrons of a corporal on the arm of his shirt sat at a desk in a tent facing some radios, earphones clamped over his head. He rapidly jotted down the message being relayed to him. When the message finished, he stood and left the tent, threading his way between the guy ropes and camouflage netting of the larger encampment. He entered another structure more akin to a marquee. The walls of this tent were covered in

5

wooden boards which held up maps marked with pins and tape. Three officers sat there.

The Corporal handed the message over to one of the officers, a grey-haired man with a leathered face who wore the three pip insignia of a captain on his shoulders.

"Message from A Company, sir. They've had contact."

The Captain read the flimsy message as the Corporal left the tent. He stood up and walked towards the map board, reading as he went.

"Call sign One has had a contact at Uniform Sierra one seven nine, three eight five." His fingers rapidly traced the coordinates to a point on the large map board. "They report seven 'terrs' killed and one wounded, captured. They've also got one local who was apparently acting as guide and porter. No friendly casualties, and they want a chopper to lift David in and the floppies out."

One of the other officers looked startled.

"Seven! That's a bloody good hit, Eric." He turned to the other Captain. "Get on to the Blue jobs and sort out a chopper, would you, Pete? You better get down with the Special Branch guys to see what the prisoner has got to say. Who's got One One?" he asked, referring to Lieutenant Roly Flashman's call sign.

The adjutant, called Eric, looked up. "That's Roly Flashman, sir."

"Christ!" The Colonel looked startled again. "He's only been on patrol for two days. For that matter, he's only been in the country for a week. Where did this contact happen, Pete?"

"Near Chimanimani, sir, north end of the Save River," then pensively, "'Roly Saves' – it'll have been a bit different from Belfast!"

They all laughed, but the name would stick, and the tall, dark haired, young man in a blood-soaked vlei in the middle of a Mopani forest became, instantly, a firm part of that extraordinary anachronism called the Rhodesian African Rifles, the last of the Askari regiments.

In the vlei, Roly Flashman stood looking over the shattered bodies of the men they had killed. A tall, slender black man, wearing the insignia of Warrant Officer Second Class on a band on his wrist, stood with him and an African soldier stood behind them, facing the direction they had come from, covering them. A fourth, a Sergeant, had strolled over to make sure that Comrade Knife had truly lost interest in life. An African soldier stood behind, watching their rear.

Roly bent over each of the bodies in turn, softly feeling the left side of each man's jaw, exploring for a trace of their pulse. When he reached the Commander, he looked up.

"Sarn't Major. This one is alive; get the First Aid kit."

A soldier ran over with a small rucksack containing the basic materials needed to keep a wounded man alive for the vital minutes it took to get an evacuation organised. The man's back was a bloody, sticky mess where it had been penetrated by dozens of the little pellets from the Claymore, but his pack had protected the most vital organs. His head had been grazed by one of the bullets, concussing him immediately.

Roly cut away the shredded material of the Commander's combat overall, swabbing down the entry holes with a cotton ball doused in disinfectant. He cut a sleeve away and, using the old cloth as a tourniquet, created enough pressure to find a vein in the man's arm. Hesitantly, he pushed a needle into the vein, attached it to a plastic tube and rigged it to one of the plastic bottles of plasma carried in the kit. Providing there is no haemorrhaging, he thought, he should be alright. Morphine could wait until, and if, he came round.

He lifted the man's head and took out a field dressing to bind the livid gash on his head. As he did so, the soldier who brought the medical pack, whose name was David Kumalo, started as he saw the man's face for the first time and called to Sergeant Nkala in Matabele, not the Shona that was the normal language of the African soldier.

The big Sergeant looked at the face of the wounded man and turned to Roly.

"Nkosi (Boss). This is a dangerous man. We must kill him now."

Roly had been born and brought up in Africa. The unthinking cruelty of many Africans was not new to him, but even so, he was startled by the demand. He had only known the Sergeant a couple of days, and he was not going to allow that sort of behaviour to start.

"Absolutely not, Sergeant Nkala. I have called for a chopper, and the police will want to talk with him when they can."

"No, Nkosi, he must die now," said the Sergeant as he lifted the butt of his rifle to his shoulder.

Angrily, Roly struck the muzzle of the rifle to one side and physically pushed the NCO backwards. His angry eyes looked into those of the African as if daring him to continue. Slowly, discipline took over and, dropping his eyes, the big sergeant turned on his heel and stomped off to where the group of soldiers were gathered round the old man.

Roly looked around the clearing, and a great sadness came over him. He had only been back in Africa for seven days.

It was likely to be a long wait for the chopper, and Roly allowed his thoughts to contemplate how he had got here. Inevitably he also thought of the gorgeous Kate whom he had met in England 11 months earlier. She was the daughter of a bank chairman, 4 years younger than Roly, and the eldest of four sisters. Weekends spent at her parents' home in Norfolk were a far cry from his current circumstances, and the spell of leave that he would be due, 3 months away, could not come fast enough. Why he did it, he didn't know, but it was there, staring at him on the hall table at Kate's father's house as he left one Sunday evening to go back to London. Roly had just picked it up and left without thinking. He had only heard about the BankAmericard, a first-generation credit card, and here was one staring at him. He didn't even understand how to use it.

He knew he had done wrong within 5 minutes of being on the A11 heading south in his white MGB. But how could he go back? There was no explanation to be made for such appalling stupidity, and Kate was unlikely to forgive him easily. He would just have to cut it up, forget the matter, and hope that no one suspected him.

Unfortunately for Roly, Kate's father, being who he was, had high-level security systems installed at their lovely Norfolk home. Roly's actions were recorded on CCTV. Dad knew where he had left his card, the same place as always, and the tape was rewound to reveal Flashman's stupidity.

A telephone call awaited him on arrival in London. Kate's father preferred to keep things low-key. Otherwise, it would be the involvement of the police and the unwelcome attention of the press. So Roly was told, in no uncertain terms, to get out of the UK and not come back. He was given 24 hours.

There was no arguing the toss. He would have to give up his job in insurance fraud investigation, or the stigma would be known and on record. But 24 hours was a challenge, and for once in his life, at 27 years old, he had a real attachment to a girl. Kate was precious, but there didn't seem to be any option. Africa was a spiritual home, and all he knew about was soldiering. Rhodesia was recruiting anyone with military experience, and a number of former colleagues were already there, and he could still see Kate between operations if she would have him back.

Saying goodbye to Kate at Heathrow had been difficult. They hugged each other, knowing that it would be a while before circumstances would bring them together again but also that each, being the individuals that they were, would not tie the other into any lasting commitment. True to form for the good 'bird' that she was, there was humour in her parting words, "I love you, Roly. And you enjoy yourself, please. At least I'll have had an advantage over my girlfriends."

"What's that?" replied Roly.

They kissed, and she murmured into his ear, "An intimate relationship with a white officer who has black privates!"

Simply put, Roly Flashman 'understood' Africa. His parents had lived near Nanyuki. Dad had been a District Commissioner in Kenya who had gone there, in part, to escape his own father's reputation, but people who had more than just a jaundiced view of Flashman's grandfather had had a funny habit of turning up rather regularly. Living through Mau Mau had made two significant impressions upon Roly; his love for Africa and its people and a close association with the British Infantry Battalion stationed there at the time.

In Kenya, the Kikuyu had been young Flashman's friends and the instincts that were now serving him well, lean, hard and sweaty, in the Rhodesian bush were developed in those early days, as well as the native language that he could speak.

Flashman was shaken from his reverie. His tiredness had nearly got the better of him. Swarms of flies were buzzing in this cauldron of a location after their brief but deadly exchange with the ZANU terrorists.

He looked around the vlei. Earlier, just after they had laid the ambush, a herd of Zebra had wandered into the meadow, seeking some moisture, some residue of the heavy dew on the long grasses. They had smelled the men and trotted off, snorting their disapproval of the intrusion. Later, a pair of secretary birds had landed gracefully, stalking between the anthills with long-legged dignity as they sought the rodents that provided their diet.

Now there was only death, and Roly felt a sense of sadness. He wondered if he could ever recapture the effervescent crusades of his youth when, careless of risk, he and his cousins had sallied down escarpments and walked, unfettered through the forests, sometimes hunting but, mostly, just watching the game that proliferated there.

He looked across at the Sergeant. He did not know him yet, but Roly had felt an immediate affinity for the big Matabele. The two of them were of much the same size and build. Well over six foot three inches with broad shoulders and tapering hips, the African moved with a fluid grace and economy of effort that spoke, not just of great strength but perfect co-ordination. Roly had already noticed his ready humour in the way he treated his soldiers, but the incident with the wounded man troubled him.

"Sarn't Major Yangeni," he called. The Warrant Officer left the wounded man and came over. "Why did Sergeant Nkala do that," Roly asked. "He is an experienced man. He should know better."

"Hongu Ishe*" the Warrant Officer replied. "I was surprised too. Nkala likes to take prisoners to get information. I asked Kumalo because he is of the

12

Ndebele, and he knows the family of Nkala. He says the man is Nkala's brother. Nkala will be shamed."

Roly looked up at the sky as he heard the fluttering notes of the incoming helicopter's rotors drumming against the heavy air.

"Oh God," he said to himself. "It's just like bloody Belfast."

*"Yes, sir."

July 1978

Rhodesia: 60 Days on Patrol

The four-bladed rotor thrummed in the hot air as the Rhodesian Air Force Alouette IV helicopter settled noisily into the burnt grass of the vlei. The first man to exit was the craggy-faced Captain called Pete from the battalion headquarters, who had taken the contact message. He was swiftly followed by a short, stocky, dark-haired man wearing a camouflage shirt, green shorts and heavy-duty desert boots with epaulettes on his shirt bearing the insignia of a major.

Behind him followed a slim, wiry man in his early thirties, who looked like a refugee from Height Ashbury. He wore a pink floral shirt with large collar wings loosely tucked into bell-bottomed hipsters. The hippy image was rather spoiled by the folding stock AK47 assault rifle that he carried, dangling from his right hand.

Uncertain of the protocol in this new army, Roly saluted David McNair, the stocky Major, who was his Company Commander, and briefly nodded to the Captain whom he had met only once when arriving in the battalion three days earlier.

"Good Morning, sir," he greeted the Major.

That was a new experience as well. In the 11th Hussars, the British Cavalry Regiment in which he had served, officers had not recognised rank between themselves and used Christian names when addressing each other.

The only exception had been the CO, who was either addressed as 'Colonel' or, under pressure, 'Sir'.

He led the newly arrived over to the ambush site and outlined the sequence of events that had prompted the action, provoking nods of approval from the two officers. The hippy lookalike, who was, in fact, a Detective Inspector in the British South African Police Special Branch, was more concerned with a minute inspection of the dead bodies of the terrorist group. He spent a particularly long time checking over the body and effects of the dead Commissar before attending to the wounded Commander. He was helped by a slender African police sergeant, also in civilian clothes.

"Sarn't Nkala," Roly called. "Wuya Pano*,"

The big Matabele managed to look disdainful of the command at the same time as obeying the order.

"The Sarn't Major says that this man is your brother. You must tell 'Ma Jonni' (police) how he is here."

Nkala glanced towards McNair for approval. He wasn't sure about this new Lieutenant with the funny accent, and McNair had not only been his Company Commander for the last 18 months but with the Rhodesian African Rifles ('RAR') for the eleven years before that.

*Come here

When Kumalo had called, and Nkala had seen Jacob's, his brother's, face lying in the dirt, he had nearly cried out. His brother had left the Tsholotsho district to come and join him in the RAR but had never arrived. Friends who had been on the same bus had described how a bunch of young hoodlums from Bulawayo, working

15

for the ZAPU party, had boarded the bus and forced all the young men off the vehicle a few miles west of Bulawayo. None of them had ever been seen again, and there had never been any doubt in Kumalo's mind that Nkala's brother had been taken to be trained as a 'Freedom Fighter'.

Nkala was shocked that Jacob had attained a seniority in the terrorist movement equivalent to his own and that it could have been he, himself, who had shot him. He turned, reluctantly, to speak to the police officer and the African Sergeant who had come with him.

David McNair was not a subtle man. His attitude to life was about as straightforward as you can get, but it was this and his experience that appealed to the African soldiers. He appreciated Nkala's stress as a successful Matabele amongst a majority of the Shona tribe in the RAR and having a brother who was a terrorist represented a degree of shame, a dent in the pride of a Matabele warrior, a direct descendant of the fearsome Zulus whose dreaded Impis had humbled the British Empire at Isandhlwana in 1879.

McNair recognised his discomfort. He motioned to Roly and the Special Branch officer.

"Roly, it looks like we've got quite an asset here. I'm going to take this bugger back with me but we'll be needing Nkala in due course to help turn him. You agree, Terry," he said, looking at the Special Branch officer, who nodded.

"You've done bloody well here, Roly. Meantime, what you have to do is mend a fence. This isn't your Pom army, and you've got the rest of the patrol to do it. What you have got to do is shake out all that British crap that you were taught and then learn what this war is about. At its crudest, survival. If you want to do that, Nkala can help you."

"Hardly effusive praise," thought Roly wryly, but there wasn't much place for heroes here, and he was happy that way. This war had already been going on for eight years and wasn't going to end tomorrow simply as a result of one successful action. He was going to have to earn the respect of his men.

The circumstances in Rhodesia at the time were such that the RAR were pretty much on active service the full time, a punishing rota of patrols with intervening spells of compulsory leave and training.

If Roly had any misconceptions about what lay in store, the next two months were to dispel them. He had been given, and it seemed, an impossibly large area to patrol – over six thousand square miles, demarcated by a series of rivers, including the great Zambezi to the north – on maps that barely showed any detail. So Roly did not know that his patrol would also be operating in Portuguese East Africa – Mozambique. Rations and re-supply would be parachuted in to him every week on the basis of one day's fresh food and six days' ration packs per person. The patrol would criss-cross the area responding with fast, forced marches to intelligence reports of suspected terrorist movements. There would be few roads, no artillery support and only emergency medical backup. If needed, only limited reinforcement would be available at likely four hours' notice.

The first thing for Roly was to adjust to the reality of living in the bush. He was lucky that the necessary skills of bush craft, observation, flora, fauna, and animal recognition were latent talents developed during his boyhood in Kenya, plus his basic knowledge of the Shona language was a big head start.

Getting through to Sergeant Nkala would be no mean feat, but he was helped by a couple of embarrassing but highly comical incidents.

The first occurred two weeks later. With dusk approaching, a campsite with good all-round fields of fire had been chosen, a clearing patrol sent out to check a perimeter of about a one-kilometre radius, and an evening meal had been prepared. Sometimes the whole platoon would then move after nightfall and set up an ambush for anyone seeking to take advantage of knowing their position.

On this occasion, the rota of sentries had been established, but just after midnight, Roly was woken by a scuffling noise and the sound of loose rock bouncing some twenty-five metres in front of him. Mentally cursing the guards for going to sleep, Roly nudged Sergeant Major Yangeni sleeping beside him. Behind him, he heard the faint rustle as the rest of the platoon became awake and alert.

Roly gripped his pen flare in his left hand, and gently, with his right, he eased the safety catch of his rifle to the 'Fire' position. The scuffling sounded again, closer, and Roly popped the trigger on his flare to send a red fireball to arc into the sky, illuminating everything in front.

The sudden bang of the flare going off and the burst of light led to a cacophony of outraged shrieks and barks as a troop of baboons scattered in front of him, babies clinging fearfully to their mothers. A big dog of a baboon, the paterfamilias of the troop, stood his ground on a large rock, snarling and barking, baring his huge yellow fangs. When he was sure his tribe was safe, he turned and strutted away, lifting his tail and showing his large pink bottom to Roly and his men.

Roly felt like a complete idiot. Around him, the platoon started to pack up their equipment, knowing their position to be compromised. The whispered word 'Murungu' reached Roly through the darkness, a disparaging Shona word for Europeans, almost the equivalent of 'nigger' in reverse. It was as if they had been expecting such an incident, and it hadn't taken long in coming. Roly knew he would have his work cut out over the next few weeks.

The second incident came a further three weeks on, some 45 days into the 60-day duration of the overall patrol. Roly had received intelligence that a small terrorist group's presence had been identified, trying to exit the country to the northeast with a group of youths that they had kidnapped. Roly was ordered to take the platoon due north in an attempt to intercept them, a task that, if they had any hope of achieving, meant a twenty-five-mile trek in less than five hours. They would be marching across the baking earth in temperatures well over 100 degrees, carrying full equipment and rations with depleted water rations.

Roly was under no illusions that it would be a severe trial for him. Only six weeks previously, he had been drinking and eating in London, saying goodbye to Kate. He was now feeling the pace and hardship of the patrol badly. The first few weeks had been bearable. He had been able to plan each leg of the route from water source to water source. But now he gave the orders to move, and the platoon marched very fast through the trees. As the heat built up and the men started to sweat, the little black Mopani flies settled in swarms on their faces, seeking the moisture around their eyes, noses and corners of their mouths, and Roly had no doubt that this was going to be a formative experience for his time as a soldier in Rhodesia. It was also going to teach him a wealth about the African soldier and his abilities. From the time that they set off, neither Nkala nor Corporal Adonis, in charge of the point section, consulted either map or compass and not one of the soldiers touched his water bottle. Nkala knew that Roly was suffering and yet forced a pace only just short of the mile-devouring jog that was the trademark of the Impis of his forebears.

The pace was killing, and it became a test between Nkala and Roly. Even some of the bush-hardened Africans were finding the going tough, particularly the two machine gunners and the radio operator who provided Roly with an excuse to call a short rest after the first hour. But it was only a short relief. As the second hour drew to an end, Roly could feel the hard, uncomfortable straps of his damned pack digging mercilessly into his shoulders. Always it came back to the heat and thirst, and with one or two of the Africans themselves showing signs of fatigue, the third hour became a grim battle for survival for Roly. His mouth dried out, and his tongue began to expand. He was fighting his own battle, and he was unaware of the Sergeant Major and his batman on either side of him as he began to stagger.

Ahead of them, Nkala seemed unaffected. After four hours, they were approaching a small ridge, and it was Yangeni who decided that he would halt the platoon and rest them before they went down the other side. He would persuade Roly that it was wise to send out a sweeping patrol to search for tracks. From the ridge, Roly could now see the bend of a river in front of them and a small trickle of water that meandered between the rocks and the sandy bed.

Gasping with relief, Roly almost tore his water bottle out of its pouch and gulped greedily at its tepid contents. At least he could speak without croaking, and he watched as Yangeni deployed the platoon in a semicircle to cover the four soldiers who were sent down to fill up the platoon's canteens. Roly's legs were shaking, and his whole body shivered as though he had a fever. He was happy that Yangeni was taking the lead in organising the sections and preparing the men for their lunch.

The men returned with full water bottles, and one of them gave Roly a big plastic cup into which he mixed a sachet of the powdered orange juice that the African soldiers loved. He seemed barely capable of thanking him before burying his face in the cup, seemingly finishing it before he had placed his lips to the mug, but his body began to slow its trembling as the moisture worked its way through his system.

He drank another half bottle before taking stock as the men boiled theirs for a midday meal and tea, infinitely more refreshing than pure water in that heat. Yangeni had joined Nkala and the trackers. They seemed to come to a decision before Yangeni walked over.

"Ishe," said Yangeni. "As we crossed the last river bed, our lead man thought he saw some spoor. But he wasn't sure; it could be that the terrorists were anti-tracking."

Roly had been about to radio in to report no joy but decided instead to check further and stated simply that he would be back on air in a couple of hours. Accompanied by Nkala and two of the trackers, they backtracked the mile or so to the place where the signs of the terrorist group might have been seen. The three Africans had started to cast along the stream bed, and quite quickly, there was a quiet cry of triumph. One of the trackers had located the clear imprint of a tennis shoe in the soft sand around the looser rocks of the stream bed.

Roly looked at Nkala and asked, "So how many and how long ago?"

Roly could sense the excitement that Nkala wasn't going to show.

"Ishe. We don't know how many, but they are going very, very slowly. They are doing their anti-tracking very carefully. Look."

He gestured to the stream bed. Roly could see nothing, and the big Sergeant explained in exasperation.

"Ah, Maiwe. Here, Ishe. See, the sand has been brushed. And here, where they have pulled the grasses to keep balance, they have then pulled down the big branch to cover where the grass was pulled."

Looking closely, Roly could now see the minute signs that they had picked up. He turned to the big Matabele and said

"And how long ago?"

Nkala turned to the two trackers, and they squatted around the big footmark. There was a great deal of knowledgeable muttering, head-scratching, hawking, spitting and, when a particularly pithy point needed making, a ruminative finger would come up to investigate the furthest caverns of one or other nostril.

Eventually, Nkala looked up.

"About five hours, Ishe," he said firmly. "The water was still here, but it began to dry very soon." He meant the light morning dew and then pointed to where the grass had been pulled and how it still looked comparatively fresh.

Roly first called Yangeni on the radio, indicating that he and the rest of the platoon should join them, and then got on to McNair to inform him that he would leave one section of his platoon where they were whilst he and the rest of the platoon would adopt light order and head off in pursuit.

Everywhere they came across the dropping of antelope, particularly Impala, of which they spotted a great many, bounding away with great graceful leaps at the approach of the men. There were also plentiful signs of bigger game, Sable and Kudu and, increasingly, elephant. They left great mounds of dung everywhere, and the tracker pointed to where they were fresher than the spoor of the gang that they were following.

As they moved closer to the great waterway of the Zambezi, the tracking became more difficult. During the rains, this part of the valley became a vast floodplain, but the soil was now baked to the consistency of tarmac. Only occasionally were the trackers able to detect the faint scuff marks that the group had left, although they were convinced that the gang was now a mere three hours ahead of them.

Roly radioed McNair with his position. Dusk was approaching, and it would be impossible to continue tracking after dark, but it seemed possible that the gang would continue to try to get to the river at Tete and cross during the night.

McNair signalled back that he would be deploying a stop line along the Portuguese road this side of the Zambezi. He wanted Roly to continue to track until the last light and then signal back the latest direction before the light failed completely. He would take that line for deploying ambush parties, and Roly was then to stop for fear of walking into one of those ambushes himself.

Despite zigzagging, the gang always seemed to come back to the same general direction, north and east, and about an hour before dark, Roly thought they had got lucky. The gang had had to cross one of the large, dry vleis, and their tracks through were clearly marked by trampled grass. The trackers were able to confirm that there were perhaps twenty-one personnel in the group. Roly radioed in the information and the platoon, despite their weariness, began to jog along the lines of the tracks.

With such clear direction, there was a chance that they could catch the gang before nightfall, but it was not to be. The vlei had given way to a forest of Mopani trees, following which the trackers were confronted by thick thorn trees, Jesse Bush, armed with vicious spines. The trees grew very close together, and the gang had split up as they dodged and weaved their way through. Following them became a slow, tiring and painful process as the thorns tore at their webbing and clothes and lacerated their bare arms and faces.

The Jesse thinned out, and the head tracker began to cast for the spoor of the gang again. Suddenly, he stopped dead and held his hand up, signalling for the platoon to stop and be quiet.

"Ishe," he whispered to Roly and, pointing to his left, "There."

He had spoken at little more than a whisper, but it was too loud. All around the platoon, there was a great rustling, and on all sides, elephant trunks popped above the bush, testing the air. The platoon had stumbled into the middle of a browsing herd and, despite their size, had not seen them. Furious trumpeting began, and the ground trembled as the herd stampeded away, the huge grey bodies barging through the trees and thickets. All except one vast bull, itself trumpeting, ears flapping like the sails of a man-of-war, and its trunk curled back over its head as it started towards the men. The bull was old with long, yellow, curving ivory tusks, and it stopped its charge just yards from where the men stood. Dropping its trunk and shaking its head, it started to back away from the men at the same time as they decided to flee the scene themselves.

Roly stood rooted, taken by surprise by the elephant's advance. The old bull, whose bad eyesight had worsened through age, caught a brief glimpse of the men darting away and his trunk filled with the hated scent of humans. This time, he charged to where he had seen the movement and where his nose told him it had come from. Without bluff this time, his ears stood straight out from his head, and his trunk was tucked

25

down between the spears of his tusks. Full seven tons of him rushed forward towards where Roly seemed to have lost the will to move, terrified as the huge mammal bore down on him. At about five yards, the elephant's fading eyes focussed upon Roly, standing stock still. Seeming to recognise Roly's raised rifle as a challenge, the elephant just stopped, an impossible manoeuvre, but it just dug its front legs in and came from a full charge to a total stop in two paces.

The elephant was now no more than six feet from the muzzle of Roly's rifle. Its trunk reached out, and its wet end brushed lightly against the flash eliminator of the rifle, taking in the odour of metal and rifle oil.

Grunting crossly, it shook its head, great tatty ears flapping, as it seemed to consider what to do next. The crashing of the herd and the squeals of their babies trying to keep up with their mothers were growing fainter. The old bull turned its head away and started to lumber after his herd. He had done his duty, and the threat had dissipated.

Slowly, Roly let the muzzle of his rifle droop. His legs were trembling, and his heart was thumping away like an express train. Nkala was the first of the soldiers to emerge from cover, and he walked over to Roly, shaking his head in disbelief.

"Ishe," he said, speaking in Matabele as a means of showing his respect. "You are surely a man, but ayaaah, that was dangerous."

Roly was coming out of his trance-like daze. As he looked at the big Sergeant, his eyes were caught by a newly laid, steaming pile of dung that the old bull had

26

released as it shambled off to join the herd. Roly pointed at it with his rifle.

"Is that his or mine?"

Lavatory humour does not come readily to the African. Their sense of fun is more practical, so Nkala was slightly taken aback by Roly's suggestion. But then he started to chuckle, which grew to a huge guffaw as he threw his head back, and unrestrained laughter ensued. Roly, still trembling, was laughing too, and as the rest of the men gathered around them, Sergeant Major Yangeni permitted himself a wry smile, seemingly a licence for all the men to participate in the joke. The new officer had passed the litmus test of acceptance as a leader far sooner than most were privileged to do.

The stampede of the elephant herd had eradicated any chance of picking up the spoor of the terrorist group that evening. Roly decided to base up for the night and, in the morning, McNair deployed them into an ambush area in case the terrorists doubled back without crossing the Portuguese road, where they stayed for the whole of the next day before the call came from McNair that the group had most probably evaded the stop line and crossed the river.

The criss-cross patrol routine returned. This time they headed south again. The new-found respect that Roly had acquired reinforced the physical efforts that Roly's men could clearly see that he had made. It manifested itself in Roly sharing the communal meal, squatting around the pot, and chatting about the day's events and what they were going to do next. It became a ritual which all enjoyed, remarkably informal, and Roly began to regain the ability to understand and even join in the easy banter of the Shona language. In the evening, he would repeat the meeting, a much more serious affair with just Yangeni and Nkala.

They were now in the southeast of the country, even crossing the Mozambique border from time to time. Roly and his weary men had started to wend their way back to a prearranged pick-up point when McNair called them again, indicating that a motorised patrol from the South African Police ('SAP') had got lost and that there was a chance that they were in a network of tracks to the east of Rapanguwana on the Sabi river, their return route, and across the border.

Roly was to keep his eyes open and not make a special deviation to look for them but had almost blundered into the South African camp within six hours of receiving the call.

Kiripo, one of Roly's trackers who was the butt of a great deal of cruel humour because of his huge, flat nose, had stopped the platoon and told Roly that he could smell cooking. There was a titter in the platoon until, thirty minutes later, Nkala claimed that he could hear voices as well.

With no villages in the vicinity, Roly went forward with Nkala to scout the source of the noise and told Yangeni to bring the platoon behind them in support.

Flitting from tree to tree and covering each other as they moved closer, with the voices getting ever louder, Roly and Nkala reached the top of a small, rocky knoll and looked down. The sight that met their eyes defied description. A motley collection of African and European troops, in an unfamiliar camouflage uniform, were lolling about a number of Bedford trucks. Two mobile field ovens were on the go, overseen by a large sweating European, and two of five soldiers, posted as so-called sentries, were chatting and smoking.

By Roly's calculation, these South Africans were about seventy miles into Mozambique from their own border in a hostile country effectively controlled by Frelimo guerrillas. Zanu terrorist groups, Roly's particular concern, also ran freely through the area. Roly turned to Nkala and whispered.

"Who are they?"

"Ma SAPees," said Nkala. "Excuse me, Ishe, but sometimes they are not very good with tactic."

Nkala tried not to snigger. This was clearly the group that Roly had been told to keep his eyes open for.

"Stay here, Sergeant," said Roly as he got up, handed his rifle to Nkala and walked straight towards the vehicles. One of the unsuspecting sentries nonchalantly strolled over.

"Oo the fuck are you?" he questioned, and Roly replied in his best English.

"Good Morning. Is your Commanding Officer here?"

The effect on the sentry was electric. This guy was a foreigner. He tried to bring his rifle up but had set his sling too long. The loop trapped around his pouches, and the safety catch was off. In the process of stumbling and recovering his balance, he snatched at the trigger, and there was a loud explosion as a round was fired. It hit the ground about six inches in front of Roly's foot.

Pandemonium broke out in the SAP laager, people running everywhere, and one of the ovens overturned.

"I'm Lieutenant Roly Flashman of the Rhodesian African Rifles. I've been asked to find you and point you in the right direction. I'd like to speak to your boss, please."

Roly had not been able to resist himself. The accent was pure British. At that moment, a large, florid-faced man erupted from behind one of the Bedfords. He had a big yellow star embossed on the epaulettes of his camouflage shirt, and Roly assumed him to be a Major. The angry expletives that he uttered in Afrikaans died on his lips. Repeating the sentry's question, he exclaimed in a way that indicated it was not his day for original conversation

"Jeez. Oo, the fuck are you." He glowered at Roly.

The man's jaw dropped as Roly replied. The thrusting, aggressive posture of his body slackened as Roly reminded him what he already knew – that he was lost – but to find that he had strayed so far into bandit country was all but loosening his bowels. His eyes widened, and he looked earnestly at Roly

"Bloedige hel. This place must be crawling with terrs." His eyes widened. "Did you come on your own?"

"Er no. I have one or two others. I'll just go and fetch them."

With a wry smile, Roly retraced his steps to his platoon. One look at Yangeni and Nkala told him that their sides were aching with suppressed laughter, Yangeni with his head between his knees and Nkala, teeth sunk into his forearm, shaking and with tears running down his face.

"Quiet," he hissed. "Quiet. Get a grip of yourselves." But Nkala looked up and caught his eye, and Roly bubbled over himself as a paroxysm of laughter engulfed him too. Eventually, they calmed down, and Roly led the platoon into the SAP camp. It was a mixed force of sixty European constables and their officers and one hundred and twenty African constables and their NCOs. They all watched in awestruck silence as Roly and his men filed into the circle of vehicles.

In later years, Roly would reflect on the impact that his platoon must have made. None of them had bathed or shaved for the better part of two months. They stunk to high heaven. Their uniforms were tattered and ripped, and many of them wore simple, ragged gym shoes.

Only their weapons gleamed, immaculately clean and lightly oiled, but it would have taken a seasoned observer to have noticed that. The awe gave way to an expression of mild contempt, particularly in the eyes of the European element. This was more in line with the image of kaffir armies.

The SAP were, however, in the Afrikaner tradition, totally hospitable. They had mobile, paraffin-powered refrigerators in the vehicles, and the Major had offered Roly a beer which Roly had declined in favour of a Coca-Cola. It was, without doubt, one of the most refreshing liquids he had ever drunk, and he gulped it down with unrestrained greed that had made the Major smile indulgently. The SAP were on fresh rations, and he insisted that they share their midday meal before they 'bugged out', as he put it.

Roly guided them back across the Mozambique border into Rhodesia, having suggested to the Major that his safest route back to South African territory would be via Rhodesian roads. If they turned south at Nvungu, from where McNair would arrange their own collection, he would welcome the lift for his own men to Nvungu, and they were dropped at a ruined store. The small cache of Rhodesian money that he carried with him was sufficient to buy three beers and thirty cokes from the SAP for his platoon.

As they were about to depart, the SAP Commandant took Roly to one side.

"Tell me, Jong," he said. "Are you really the only wit with these kaffirs for three months?"

When Roly assured him that that was, indeed, the case, he had shaken his head and asked quite seriously.

"Do you disarm them at night?"

This time, Roly could not restrain his laughter. The vision was so ridiculous he could not help himself, and the SAP officer had driven away, convinced that the Rhodesians were a lost and godless cause.

McNair, himself, turned up at Nvungu with the three Bedfords needed. The sight of Roly, filthy, sitting between two African NCOs, passing the last bottle of beer from mouth to mouth as they swapped memories of the patrol, made him think. Face covered with a rich, dark, bushy beard, a necessity borne of a daily decision between having a full canteen or the worry of finding a replenishment source, with his clothing hanging off him and his webbing belt pinched in at the waist caused him to wonder to himself.

"Roly Saves," he pondered.

The nickname had already stuck. He prodded Roly's hardened and much-reduced belly.

"Your mother wouldn't recognise you!"

Two days later, Lieutenant Roly Flashman and his men were back in Salisbury, and he was able to relax. Sitting in the bath, prior to dinner in the RAR mess that evening, Roly was surprised that, over the last three months, his thoughts had not dwelled on Kate. England seemed so far away; Belfast and the IRA, insurance claims in the City and the 11th Hussars, the Cherry Pickers. Could there be a military world further away from Lord Cardigan's bloodhounds and the modern mechanised infantry battalion that he had been with only six months previously in Belfast?

August 2018

Westridge: Residential and Care Home

Brigadier Roland Spermot Dinks Flashman MC, DFC lay in bed at the Westridge Residential Complex where he now lived. He dreamt a lot and slept well these days. Early morning was his favourite time of the day. Lost in last night's dream of the war in Rhodesia, he lay there, staring at the ceiling with a wry smile on his face as the near scrapes, amusements, and people from his twenties flashed through his mind and sent him back to sleep to dream some more.

So many experiences, so much fun, so many places. Memories of School, the City, the Army, Cricket, Investigative work, and then MI6. Did they all happen? Last night's dream of Rhodesia certainly had. At 68, Roly was still fit enough to enjoy most things that life had to offer in 2018. Possibly a little shorter than in his 6'3" prime, his jet-black hair had taken on an authoritarian shade of white at the temples, revealed, also, in his whiskers. Good-looking as he was, he retained the same sparkle in his eye and a ready smile that always helped others to feel at ease in his company.

Prospects for making the rank of Brigadier had seemed slender in 1973 when he had been awaiting court martial after events in Belfast. For it to happen twice was, to put it mildly, unusual, a fact which gave Flashman legendary status within his regiment. The British government had had a unique need for Roly's special set of skills and knowledge leading up to Zimbabwe's Independence Day in 1979, such that

Roly was able to determine the basis upon which he would return. A brief period in command of a squadron of Chieftain tanks in the 11th Hussars was followed, six months later, by double promotion and a posting to the Ministry of Defence in MI6, which meant that Roly had become the youngest, serving Brigadier in the Army.

The apartment in Westridge Court's Residential/Care Home that he had bought on a lifetime lease included a large drawing/living room plus a decent size bedroom with en-suite facilities of a shower room and loo off to the side. It included a spare bedroom and a small kitchen. If not cooking for himself, Flashman could use the central restaurant within the Residential Home, hardly a chore as the chef was well-considered, and large discounts were available to residents.

Westridge was a large independent home, purpose-built on land previously occupied by a 'stately', knocked down and now redeveloped. In addition to apartments lived in by the 10 Founding Investors (who had been looking to secure their own futures in a unique and clever investment scheme), it had 40 individually owned Maisonettes, apartments and flats accompanied by an 80-bed Care Home, fully staffed. Council approval of its construction was on the basis of 10% of care beds being available to the needy.

Flashman's apartment was not huge but very comfortable. He had furnished it himself with the mementoes and paintings that he had collated during the course of his fascinating career. Each told a vivid story of the many countries that he had visited and wonderful memories; pleasant moments but a lot of uncomfortable ones too! There was little to remind him of a number of close female relationships over the years, but he did keep a few photos in his desk.

The whole place was, in residential home terms, quite outstanding. It included a 4-star restaurant, a spa complex complete with a swimming pool, sauna, whirlpool and steam rooms, hairdressing/beauty treatment and an anteroom with bar, meeting rooms, snooker room and a Conference centre. Outside there was a croquet lawn, tennis courts and a 9-hole golf course where Roly played at least twice a week. Daily exercise classes were offered – Pilates, Yoga and Balance – in the gymnasium as well as the swimming pool, plus ad hoc diverse activities.

Westridge had been financed and built only five years before by a few prescient golf club members seeking to secure their own potential future retirement needs. Most of them simply didn't wish to be a burden to their own families. Their individual £800,000 investments had secured them a lifetime leasehold interest in either a Maisonette or a Flat and, in due course, the Care Home. It was a carefully structured and extremely tax-efficient scheme achieved via share ownership rather than as property owners. Investor residents had the comfort of knowing that they would never become a burden to their families whilst protecting the value of their capital from Inheritance Tax.

Flashman was not a founding investor but had bought some shares. He reckoned that these were a double whammy, both as an investment and as expulsion insurance. After all, at 68, he wasn't going to stop enjoying himself!

Recently, a late-night dash from London back to his apartment had resulted in a hefty fine and immediate loss of his driving license. His treasured BMW soft top was now sitting on bricks in a friend's barn. Luckily for him, Westridge laid on several minibuses into town during the week. The only downside was having to make polite conversation with a few of the deaf old bats also using the service.

What had been a struggling local Golf Club was now thriving. It had been marketed, hugely successfully, on the basis of "You will all need Westridge one day, so why not get to know the golf club first?" Most of the residents were pretty well-heeled, much to Flashman's liking, and a lot of them had known each other from the prior association at the Golf Club.

Flashman sighed at the thought of the previous day's confrontation with the Ladies Captain, who had reproached him for pushing his trolley onto the strip of grass between a greenside bunker and the green itself. He enjoyed his golf, although he was tired of the pettifogging rules, and lady golfers had always been a problem for him. They had found themselves behind a Ladies four that morning, and it had been a slow round.

Later, in the Bar, after words had been offered in the Clubhouse by one of the Ladies foursome ahead of Roly and his friends about the corded jeans that he had been wearing, Flashman had muttered, sotto voce, to Johnny Jeffries (a retired Wing Commander) beside him, "Struth Johnny. I don't think Deborah Pootling knows Byelaw 19 of her own club's constitution."

"What's that, Roly?" asked Johnny.

"That ladies should shave before playing."

Judging by the chortling from behind the bar, Kevin, the barman, had heard him as well.

"Now, now, Kevin," said Roly. "You clearly didn't hear that, OK?"

"Oh no, Sahib," replied Kevin, waggling his head. "It is being most definitely not for public consumption, and we are calling this hush hush."

Flashman smiled and reckoned he might have anything from 15 to 20 years to enjoy Westridge. He knew three of the Founding shareholders from old. In addition, Kevin seemed on-side, and some of the younger female staff had shown promise in him being able to match the experiences of his illustrious forebear – Major General Sir Harry Paget Flashman VC, KVCO – his grandfather – who had died in 1915 and whose reputation had been something that Roly had had to contend with ever since Mum, Anne, had sent him to Rugby School at the age of 13.

That morning, as last night's dream morphed into wakefulness, Roly pressed the bell beside his bed and switched on the TV for the morning news. He sighed at the false chumminess of the young BBC presenters. "They and the politicians deserve each other," he thought.

Flashman's own life had been a joy, and he had survived a number of dangerous scrapes, occasionally of his grandfather's proportions. As a child, his father had largely ignored him, but the consequent freedom had encouraged Flashman's self-confidence on the ranch in Kenya, where he was brought up. Flashman's closest friends had been the Kikuyu tribesmen and, later, after his parent's divorce, the Philippine locals of

Manila. He had been schooled overseas, adored by his mother Anne (his father's 3rd wife and whom his father had abandoned).

Roly had become an expert in the ways of the Kikuyu, catching snakes and tracking animals. Most misdemeanours had been overlooked by Mum. At school, he was disinterested in Maths and the Sciences, but a keen sense of hearing meant that he excelled in languages. By the age of 17, Flashman was already multilingual with eyesight that could spot something at twice the range of his contemporaries. He had been an outstanding shot, and his athletic skills, more often than not, saw him escape the clutches of both wild animals and those seeking to do harm to his wellbeing.

Piercing blue eyes and olive skin that tanned readily had made him an insufferably handsome nuisance to the ambitions of rivals for the attention of ladies. Now 68, he still had a full head of hair. He should really get it cut more often, but the length made him feel younger, and he used a hair tonic to smooth it backwards. Surely a little vanity was no bad thing?

Westridge had its routines designed so that Residents could, as far as possible, maintain their independence as well as enjoy the central facilities that were offered. For those that wished, residents could take advantage of activity classes, theatre visits and trips to places of interest. The recipe was a great success, reflective of the very high occupancy and waiting lists that had been enjoyed since opening.

A couple of days previously, he had woken from a heavy sleep with the noise of a helicopter that had landed on the field behind the stable block at Westridge.

"Bloody antisocial at this time of the day," he had thought to himself at the time, and it must have stuck in his head as it was, probably, what prompted last night's dream about being in the Rhodesian bush during UDI.

There was a knock on his apartment door, and before he had a chance to reply, the knock came again. Instead of the normal, slightly built, young Philippine girl who cleaned his room, that officious bag Critchley waddled in. He had long given up on reminding her to wait prior to entry. She must have been about 50 with a short, masculine haircut and was immensely strong. She had already heard about his behaviour following a good evening in Westridge's bar the previous night.

Critchley was a Scot, an ex NHS Nurse whose talents were much admired by the management of Westridge. She came from the "old school" of nursing, where personal disciplines were valued alongside nursing qualifications. Critchley had found the NHS tiresome, top heavy and lacking leadership. Her first three years as a nurse had been spent as a QARANC in the Army, and she was as well qualified to handle a medical crisis as she was to manage the team who worked under her in the Care Home. She had been nervous about agreeing to be Flashman's health mentor when pushed by Westridge's management. Surprisingly, she had a soft spot for Flashman, although she would never let him know it. It must have been a bond formed by mutual experience in the services, and he was a change from the other residents of Westridge who rather quivered in her presence.

"I'll have to get them to widen that door for ye, Critchley," Flashman muttered quietly, forgetting that one day Critchley might just need to dispense her nursing skills upon him!

"Mr Flashman. The desk asked me to give this to ye," she re-joined in her sharp Scots accent as she reached into the pocket of her overtight nurse's uniform and handed Roly an envelope containing an admonishment and reminding him of the rules of residence.

"I think yer going to be reported to the Committee. Keeping the barman there until 1130 last night is against the rules and exceeds this place's license approval. Management has received several complaints about the noise, and all those breakages were nae clever."

The evening had been a laugh. They had played a hand of Bridge after supper. With every whisky that was consumed, the standard seemed to slip, but the evening got more fun. Johnny had partnered him against the Lesters – Reggie and Joanna– a couple who had spent their lives as District Commissioners in the South Pacific somewhere.

Reggie and Joanna were Founding Members at Westridge. They had overcome their initial concern of making such a large investment in a project that had yet to deliver a tangible asset. But the project management had a proven track record, the banks were up for the financing, and the owner of the development company had offered his personal guarantee for whatever that was worth.

Now, here they were, some 6 years later, with a lifetime lease, at no further cost, on their superb apartment with their investment value represented by

EIS shares rather than the property itself, tax efficient within an ISA and secure from Inheritance Tax.

And a first dividend had even recently been declared!

Reggie had been regaling anyone who would listen with improbable stories of his time on some South Sea island. Things started to get out of hand when he went to get his cocked hat, the plumage of which consisted of real chicken feathers.

At the sight of this, an energetic and rather stroppy little Jack Russell terrier called Nipper suddenly took objection and, yapping noisily, made a grab for it. Its owner, Lady Jane Ponsonby ("the Punce"), who was walking past, made absolutely no effort to disengage the dog's teeth from the hat. Reggie was too nice to say anything, but Johnny Jeffries had no problem holding back, "Madame, would you mind controlling your flaming dog?"

"Don't speak to me like that, you dreadful little man," came the reply, at which Flashman joined in.

"Lady Ponsonby. We are trying to play Bridge, and dogs are verboten in here. Reggie's hat means a lot to him. Give your dog a cushion to roger or something."

"Oh, you rude so and so. Don't talk to me about rules, Flashman. There's enough of us here who know that you are continuously flouting them."

Reggie had managed to disengage the dog's teeth from the hat's plumage, but Nipper then turned his attention to the turn-up on Flashman's trousers and was shaking this rigorously. Roly's instant reaction was to kick out, and to his amazement, the dog went soaring over the bar, taking some wine glasses with it onto the floor on the other side. Glass shards went everywhere. It was Jeff's, the younger barman's turn to manage the bar, but he didn't seem to mind. As far as he was concerned, Brigadier Flashman was one of the few who injected a bit of liveliness into Westridge.

Lady Ponsonby had flown into a rage, cast a stream of ineffective invective at Flashman and then stomped out with Nipper under her arm. Flashman had, until then, been enjoying the evening. Sharp comments, delivered with humour, were one thing, but Lady Ponsonby's diatribe in front of all those in the bar had been unnecessary. So he didn't have his heart in the two more hands of Bridge that they played before packing up for bed. There seemed to be something familiar about Jane Ponsonby, and he would be thinking about what he could do to level the scores.

On the other side of Flashman's bedroom, Critchley was opening the curtains and window. "I suggest you bill that old bag Ponsonby," said Flashman. "It was that ragbag mutt of hers that caused the problem, and while you're at it, tell the Punce that Cocked Hats don't come cheap either. What have we got on today then, sister?"

"Not much, Mr Flashman. Why don't ye play golf or something? There's a bus going into town tomorrow at 12 o'clock if ye want to go to the Cinema or anything. Time for yez to have a wee lunch here before the bus leaves perhaps, do some shopping and then the vicar has said ye can all attend the choir practice, if yer wants, afore the bus comes back at 4.30. I hope yer going, Mr Flashman. We could do with a bit of peace and quiet. But, listen, laddie, if yer want to go, ye might have to get out of bed quicker than today."

"'Brigadier' to you, sister. I think I'll put my name down for that. As it happens, I am playing golf this morning. Please ensure my rooms are cleaned whilst I'm out - but properly this time. Tell those Flippo staff what's good for them if they want a Christmas tip, will you? Off you go, sister. I'm still alive, and I'd say you were welcome to share my shower, but it's only big enough for two."

Critchley laughed at Flashman's jibe and left. Roly had been in this place for 9 months now. Heaven knows how he had been lucky enough to get the apartment, modern with largely agreeable fellow residents and well-maintained gardens with parkland. He still played tennis which at least justified his occasional lunchtime pint with the group of friends that he had made in the area. They called themselves "The Knackers".

Life was good, and he was comfortable, both physically and, for the first time in his life, living within his means. It was a Wednesday morning, late August 2018, nearly 41 years after his shocking experiences in Rhodesia, and he wondered if all this dreaming of late would soon be a thing of the past.

October 1966

Rugby School: Victoria Mason

At the age of 16, Flashman had arrived at Aiglon College, located at the western end of Lake Geneva in Switzerland, in October 1966. Almost the first person he met had been Gunther von Custer, later becoming known to Flashman as 'Krautie' but who, despite his name, was a second-generation Englishman. Attendance at Aiglon was part of Gunther's family's plan that he should be an internationalist in outlook but, particularly, come to terms with his German heritage.

Flashman was there for different reasons.

His mother, Anne, had endured the family reputation for a long time. She had decided to pay for Roly to go to Rugby School, helped by a bursary from the school who thought that the presence of another Flashman would enhance their recruitment efforts. On the other hand, Mum had been thinking that Roly might just confound the long-held and preconceived expectations of the family character, a consequence of Thomas Hughes' famous book – 'Tom Brown's Schooldays'. You would have thought that the actual or, rather, deemed achievements of his illustrious (notorious to those who knew) grandfather would have expelled any notions that resided, but the family name needed rehabilitation!

But Roly Flashman's character was more like his mother's. Roly was not an instigator of trouble. He just attracted it! Far from being the bully that his grandfather's reputation might have suggested, Roly actually despised those that evinced such tendencies and would often present himself as a bulwark to the person who was the bully. In fact, he sought to avoid confrontation, but there was always a limit to his patience. Something inexplicable would snap inside him, and he would overcome a residual fear and charge in, most often verbally but occasionally physically. He was certainly not a coward, and it was his penchant for fun and practical jokes that, more often than not, got him into trouble.

So it was that in September 1964, Roly arrived at Rugby School to join Field House.

He fancied himself as an actor. When a notice went up, towards the end of his first year at Rugby, for volunteers for the school's autumn production of Shakespeare's Twelfth Night, Flashman decided to put his name down. Two weeks later, there were auditions and Roly, whose voice had not yet broken, found himself short-listed for the role of Olivia in the production to be staged at the end of the following term.

The schoolmaster in charge of acting was Major Trench, an elderly bachelor who taught French. He was an ex-soldier, highly decorated, who had served most of his war in a cavalry regiment in North Africa and the advance up the spine of Italy. His assistant, responsible also for the wardrobe, was a second-year 6th former called Gavin Pelly. Trench and Pelly worked quite well together. Pelly had been in all the productions during his time at Rugby, and some had remarked that the chemistry between the pair was uncomfortably close. They were, clearly, both dedicated thespians, but the ease they evidenced in each other's company didn't seem right. What was more, Pelly was distinctly mean-spirited. No one really liked him. He enjoyed the discomfort of others, and members of the cast were, too frequently, the objects of his snide remarks. But, anyone wanting to act in the school play just had to endure Pelly.

Of course, the very nature of Twelfth Night explores gender identity and sexual attraction. With a cross-dressing heroine, the convention has long dictated that adolescent boys play the role of Viola, and it was for this reason that Trench loved this play. All had gone well with rehearsals until two weeks before the opening night. They had gathered to rehearse Act III Scene 1 in the Garden, where Viola declares her love for Osorio to Olivia, unaware that Osorio and Olivia are one and the same person.

"Alors, mes braves, il faut commencer. Olivia, you are looking especially ravaging this evening," said Trench to Flashman in front of the assembled company.

"Vraiment; il est mignon," added Pelly in a pointed, malicious way. He had this feeling that Trench was becoming more attentive to the charms of others than his own and didn't like the constant praise and encouragement aimed at this new boy.

"Vaffanculo," retorted Roly, squirming in a croaky voice, and in Italian, as he sought to make it abundantly clear to Pelly that he would not stand for his barbed jibes. Mum, Anne, had warned him about this. He was acutely aware of the predatory capabilities of ageing homosexuals and elder boys prevalent in the public school system. The obvious suggestion in everything that this pair said made him wince, but Roly also enjoyed their acerbic verbal exchanges, more often than not, in French. This time, by replying in Italian, Roly had hoped that he had made his point forcefully.

Roly had had this sore throat for a couple of weeks and was worried as it seemed to be lingering. The school production did not run to understudies, so he needed to be fully fit if he was going to deliver a half-decent performance as a principal female lead. It wasn't so much that his throat was sore but more that it changed tone the whole time. He better go and see the Matron in the Sanatorium.

Rehearsals went well that evening. There was the odd smile of amusement by Roly's fluctuating tones, but the order was upheld, and he went back to his house feeling comfortable that he would get the full acclaim of not just the audience of parents who would be attending the production but possible encouragement to go on to acting school when the time came to leave Rugby.

But all that was to change. As he stood in front of Matron in the Sanatorium the next morning, thinking that he had a sore throat, Matron smiled and told him not to be so silly. His voice was perfectly normal, and there was no infection.

"Your voice is breaking, my dear. That's all," she said kindly.

It was as if a thunderbolt had hit Roly. Of course, how could he have been so stupid? It was all his year group talked about, and now that it was happening to him, he hadn't even recognised it. Over the course of the next three days, Roly's voice developed with a deepish resonance.

Christ! Trench was not going to be pleased.

In the riotous disorder of the play, Flashman, as the female Viola, was about the only character who was not hiding their sexuality and here she was with a deep voice. Having got used to the relationship between the characters, there was the distinct possibility that confusion might reign amongst the cast with its love triangle theme between the Duke of Orsino, Olivia and Viola. Olivia, a female character who pretended at masculinity and Viola, a female character whose femininity was being challenged by a young actor whose voice had just broken.

Trench was unhappy, but there was little he could do about it. The first of the production's three nights started in just four days' time. Caterers were engaged. Parents had kept their diaries free, and even the balance of 600 boys at Rugby were looking forward to attending one of the three performances. There was no chance that a replacement Olivia could be found. The cast and production would just have to grin and bear it, a fact of life with adolescents which hardly needed explaining to Sir Arthur, the headmaster.

Unfortunately for Trench, there had to be a lot of grinning and bearing. Pelly was upset. Trench seemed to be less attentive towards him than before. Trench had seemed furtive, and his eyes had been evasive, almost unfriendly. Pelly could see that the relationship was ending, but he thought that Trench could, at least, have waited until he was due to leave Rugby – only 2 months hence. He thought that Trench might have had his eye on Flashman. Trench had snapped at him, and all that Pelly could now think about was how to get even. When Trench called in to say that he had flu and was happy that the cast could do the last two rehearsals without him, it gave Pelly his chance.

Like a lot of homosexuals, Pelly could turn on the charm at a whim. He now did this with the cast. In the space of the next 48 hours, he had them thinking that, just maybe, they had misjudged him before. Pelly smiled and had them smiling back. Pelly encouraged them, and they felt his praise. And Pelly lied to them and had them believing that Trench had embraced the change of tone in Flashman's voice. After all, Twelfth Night is a comedy. The remedy to the problem lay in Flashman hamming up the role of Viola and getting the audience to laugh at this alternate interpretation that its principal characters were all cross-dressing homosexuals.

For Pelly, the opening night went down as a triumph. Trench, however, was invited to leave Rugby. Sir Arthur, the headmaster, was mortified as one indignant parent after another came forward to express their disgust at the school's promotion of homosexuality. But no one could be 100% sure of the audience's reaction. It had been difficult to distinguish between what had seemed like the boys' howls of laughter or the parents' silence. No one knew which had had the greater impact.

Malvolio had minced onto the stage with one hand on his hip and kept it there for the whole production, raising his eyebrows and 'oohing' and 'aahing' at any hint of suggestiveness. The Duke of Orsino had effected a gay lisp and a breathy voice with every double entendre in the script, and the cross-dressing Olivia had revealed her suspenders as she bent provocatively towards the audience and patted her own backside like some tart in a Vaudeville theatre.

Roly entered into all this with the greatest gusto. As Viola, he blew kisses at Olivia, dressed as Osorio. He winks at Sir Toby Belch, nudges everyone and flicks V signs at the Duke as if his life depended on it, while Pelly encourages all this from the wings by madly waving arms and applauding silently. He didn't care. Trench was in charge, and the old bastard could pay.

Chaos and hilarity ruled on stage and off.

The production had become more of a pantomime than the Shakespearean comedy befitting of the school syllabus. The audience had sat there, fascinated, stunned and horrified by equal measure, but all that was to change on the following nights. Lightning-fast in his need to recover from a potentially disastrous set of circumstances, Sir Arthur sought to explain the production as a life lesson in keeping with the school's broad-minded principles.

Word spread fast amongst the parents, and the play now received a critical review, extraordinarily reaching The Times as an enlightened, new, exciting interpretation of Shakespeare's time-honoured masterpiece. Trench's apparent triumph, in a later production with professional actors, opened in London two years later.

Without Pelly!

Roly had loved it all.

Towards the end of the third year, he was 6'1" tall and still growing. Although he had the inability to manage his personal affairs and was not good at the Sciences, Roly showed above-average linguistic, artistic and sporting talents. Through sheer determination, he

51

looked to pass all his "O" levels, and he expected to enter the Sixth Form, in the autumn, with high hopes of gaining a University entrance pass in two years' time. The summer of 1965 had been an epic. Approaching full maturity and 6'3" tall, Roly was indistinguishable from boys in the Upper Sixth. He had been Captain of the Colts at cricket and, as a fast bowler capable of some extremely nasty bumpers, his developing brawn had brought him a record number of wickets. The Colts had won all their games and, notwithstanding a difficult relationship with Mr Mason, the master in charge of cricket, who happened to be his housemaster, looked set to leapfrog straight into the 1st X1 the following year.

But Roly had had to leave Rugby School early, and his family's reputation, borne of his grandfather's exploits, had lived on. Roly's cricketing exploits had caught the eye of Sir Arthur Fforde, the headmaster. Sir Arthur also thought that the boy had leadership potential. He mentioned as such to Roly's housemaster, who seemed strangely cussed at the idea. The reason was the Housemaster's wife.

Victoria Mason was a beautiful woman and the epitome of a supportive schoolmaster's wife. At 32, she was all of 12 years younger than her husband. She was 5'6" tall, with jet black, silky, shoulder-length hair and the figure of someone who was keen on daily exercise and sport. When you passed Victoria, it was impossible not to look back over your shoulder and admire her figure. She tripped lightly along on her toes, and her arms swung freely at her sides. She had a ready smile, had time for everyone, without favour, and was a head-turner!

No one knew why she had no children of her own as she was a marvellous "shoulder" and confidante for all the boys in her husband's house. If a boy needed something from town, Victoria would get it for them. She had a first-class degree from Dublin, and if a student needed help with a Maths problem, Victoria was always there. If their socks needed darning, Victoria would do this willingly. In short, she was far more popular than her husband and the glue that made the house run well.

Her husband found this difficult. He realised the asset that she represented to his career but was simultaneously resentful of the influence that she had over the boys. Gone were the days in the Masons' personal lives when something would be done on a whim. The routine of school and its responsibilities seemed to be all that interested him. They didn't chat much. Their marriage had become humdrum. There was little social activity with others, and his desire for sex had diminished.

So it was that one evening during Prep that Victoria came across Roly in his Common Room, elbows on the desk and the palms of each of his hands on his temples. His muscled torso, height, square chin and chiselled features had always made it difficult for Victoria not to notice Roly. He was staring at the paper in front of him.

"Is everything all right, Roly?" enquired Victoria silkily.

"I don't think I can do this," replied Roly softly and in a flat voice. It was an equilateral equation of the kind that he was likely to encounter in the Maths "O" level exam that he was about to take.

"Here, let me see," whispered Victoria. No talking was permitted during Prep. She leant over Roly in his "horsebox", the enclosure that served as all boy's personal space when working. She looked at the paper and then said to Roly, "OK. I think I can help. Would you like that?" as she reached for the pencil on Roly's desk, touching, in the process, Roly's arm with her breast.

"Oops! Sorry! Budge over a bit." said Victoria as she sat down beside him and began to explain the steps for solving these equations. As she explained, Roly became aware of her delicate aroma. When she had leant over, he had felt the firmness of her breast, and her voice was soothing. He felt quite intoxicated. He was becoming confused. It was all he could do to concentrate on what she was saying.

Any form of work in the Junior Common Room appeared to have stopped, and the other boys were watching in envy. Roly could feel her warmth and started to sweat.

Something similar seemed to be happening to Victoria. "I don't think we can do this here. It's disturbing all the other boys. Why don't we go down to my husband's study?"

The words had slipped out. Oh God, she shouldn't have said them, but it was too late. She couldn't retract them and risk the normality of trying, simply, to help Flashman with his work, so she left promptly with Flashman tripping in her wake, down to the bottom of the corridor and through the door that connected the school house to the flat she shared with her husband.

Mr Mason was at Choir practice and, afterwards, was attending the Housemasters' regular weekly meeting with the Head. He wouldn't be back until 10:30 pm after the boys had gone to bed, 3 hours hence.

They sat down, side by side, at the table in her husband's study and recommenced the problem. He didn't need to sense her proximity. His confusion was complete. Three equations later, Flashman was not getting the hang of it. Victoria's mouth felt dry. She said she could do with a drink and went to get herself a glass of wine.

Losing his shyness, Flashman thought he would chance his arm, "I don't suppose you've got another one of those, have you?"

"Certainly not, Roly. I'll be had up. On the other hand, if I didn't spot you drinking from my own glass behind my back, then that would be a different matter," replied Victoria.

Well, things moved very fast after that. Victoria's glass was filled, he took a sip, and the wine was instantly intoxicating to him. When Victoria put a hand on Roly's shoulder, he stood up, turned around, lifted her up and embraced her, sinking into her large breasts and kissing her all the while. She was very agitated and started to cry.

But it was a losing battle. Her husband's strictures had long pent up the desire. Instead of pushing him away, she lay down on the table and pulled him down to her.

"Come on, Roly," she said, "Don't worry and slow down. I'll show you how."

Summer Term ended three weeks later. Roly's desire for this newly experienced, ultimate sensation of sex with Victoria had consumed his every waking minute. Whenever possible, they had met in the local town, and Victoria had driven them somewhere for a bit of "flagrante delicto" in the open air. For the first time in his life, Flashman had spent the whole of his summer holiday wanting to get back to school. He couldn't call her, and he daren't write. He was in love. He wanted to protect her. He needed to see her urgently. Chancing his arm with his mother, Roly told her that new sixth formers were required back a day early and took the train up to Rugby.

Flashman gave Mr Mason a plausible explanation for his early return, who said that he better have supper with Victoria and himself that evening, but she needed warning, so he was to go and find her in the apartment and let her know. Victoria was lovelier than ever. That afternoon, in the warm autumn Sun, they were able to rekindle their acquaintance.

The affair was wonderful, but they would have to be careful. For the next two weeks, Victoria would put a packet of OMO washing powder in the kitchen window, visible as you approached the house from the school. It made Flashman smile every time. Victoria had said that OMO stood for "Old Man's Out"!! It was an ingenious plan and meant that her husband was not expected at home that afternoon. Sometimes they would agree to make their separate way to the wood across the playing fields.

Flashman hungered for a daily meeting. Victoria became his muse. She taught him a girl's needs and how to satisfy them. Flashman tempered his desperation for haste. He learnt to savour the wonderful softness of her body and to bring her to the heights of pleasure before releasing the pair of them, together, to places that only two people in love can reach.

But he had become besotted and, dangerously, considered himself to be her protector.

Three weeks after the start of the autumn term, he heard noises at the end of the corridor. The Masons were having an argument. Perhaps Mr Mason was confronting Victoria about her infidelity? He couldn't hear what was happening. Nor could he find out because Victoria had not made it to their normal rendezvous the next day. Something was amiss because Fuller, the deputy housemaster, told Flashman that he better stay in his study for the rest of the afternoon.

Flashman never made it to the evening meal. He was ordered to put his things together. A taxi arrived, his trunk and tuck box were loaded, and Flashman was delivered to the station with a one-way ticket to London, where he was met by Mum, who told him that he and Victoria had been discovered. The school had sat on the problem all of twenty-four hrs before deciding on their course of action. Both Flashman and the Masons had to go.

Three days later, he was in Aiglon in Switzerland, a school that had been founded on a distinctive ethos: the balanced development of mind, body, and spirit. Flashman missed Victoria badly but was never to see her again. The Masons had also been asked to leave the Rugby area, and he couldn't find out where they had gone. It had been a miserable time for him, but in Aiglon, he was soon to find that there were many new acquaintances for him to meet. The mixture of nationalities, the different outlooks and cultures, and the weekend skiing trips were so much to Flashman's liking. Above all, Aiglon was co-educational!

Autumn 2018

Westridge: Nipper's Demise

On Thursday, it was raining at Westridge, and even though it was 9 o'clock in the morning, daylight hardly seemed to have dawned. Roly rose, stretched, and put on his swimming trunks. He slipped into his dressing gown, had a quick bowl of Muesli and padded down the corridor to the lift, down to the basement, and made his way to the "Wellness Spa" for a swim prior to a planned visit to the cinema that afternoon on the bus that Westridge laid on for the residents.

"Wellness. Where the hell do they get these names from?" thought Flashman, just as he passed Reggie, towel round his neck and humming, coming the other way.

"Good morning Roly," said Reggie in his perpetually cheerful way. "Good game the other night, though. I don't suppose we've heard the last of it from that old bag Ponsonby."

"Don't worry, Reggie, I've got the measure of the Punce. Plan of action already in train. I expect you'll hear about it. Good swim? Anything doing in the pool?"

"No," said Reggie. "The Spa manager isn't on 'mornings' today." Flashman understood perfectly what he meant. That was a shame. She was a gorgeous fit blonde of about 33 called Kirsty. Flashman asked Reggie whether he and Joanna might like to join him for dinner that evening in the Restaurant at 1930 hrs.

Back in the apartment after 40 lengths of the 25-metre pool and a 15-minute Sauna, Flashman showered and shaved, slapped on the Eau Sauvage that his goddaughter Cordelia had given him last Christmas (good girl that) and got dressed, ready to go into town later on.

That business in the Bar, a few evenings ago, had needled him. Lady Ponsonby seemed to have it in for him. Her acerbic comments, from a mouth that looked as though she had just sucked a lemon, made it clear that she disapproved of Roly. It hadn't been him who started the rumpus and, surely, it was the Punce who should have been apologising to him for Nipper's behaviour.

So he tripped down to Westridge's Reception area 40 minutes early for the bus to the cinema. He had a plan. He went into the bar before slipping out through a pair of French windows to a gravelled area at the front of Westridge, an area with rose beds and benches where the residents often sat. He could still smell the lavender which had yet to be cut back to its winter levels. Flashman had noticed that, on sunny days, the Punce also had a habit of sitting out there with that little mutt of hers. The Westridge grounds were beautifully maintained and, even in winter, calming to sit in and enjoy any warmth that the weakening Sun still had to offer. He found what he wanted, so wandered back into the bar to enjoy a quick sandwich and chat with Kevin about his plans for the evening.

"I know nothing, Brigadier," said Kevin and winked. "Mum's the word." He was fond of Flashman and quietly enjoyed watching his antics, thinking to himself, what sort of a palaver he would land himself in this time.

Flashman had found what he had been expecting outside, a fresh dog turd that lay there, which he had put into a plastic bag. Better than anything, the 'pooh' was sizeable, from a largish dog long and very fresh. He concealed this under a bush for later before walking back into the building.

Having briefed Kevin on the plan of action and barely concealing his own mirth at the prospect, Flashman made his way to the entrance hall to await the bus into town with three others, one of whom was Johnny Jeffries. He was still chuckling as they arrived in Marlborough, where the bus deposited them outside the cinema.

"Come on, Roly," said Jeffries. "Do share the joke, old man."

"Nothing doing, Johnny, though you might want to be at dinner tonight. I think there will be some fun. 1930 hrs, OK?"

The film in town ended. For some reason, he felt nervous, so Flashman reckoned he could do without attending that day's Choir practice. Anyway, he still had plans for that evening, so after 30 mins walking round the local shops, he caught the bus back to Westridge and had a nap before walking down to the bar for a whisky prior to dinner in the Restaurant at 7:30 pm.

Westridge ran an external Membership scheme, and the bar was full with locals as well as residents, most of them planning to eat in the popular restaurant. Together with the spa and golf course, it contributed to Westridge's commercial success and meant the place was a bit livelier than it might otherwise have been and free of any of the less desirable sorts to be found in pubs in the local area.

Flashman's meal routine was generally a light breakfast and snack at lunchtime in the apartment or in the Bar. When he wasn't a guest at one of his fellow inmates' apartments, Flashman often took dinner in the Restaurant. The dining room produced very decent food, and there was always a smattering of outsiders, either spa members, those that had just had 9 holes of golf or people visiting relatives at Westridge. Tonight was no exception, with probably 30 or so enjoying a drink before dinner, including Lady Ponsonby with that rotten little dog of hers, emitting a low rumbling growl at anyone who passed too close.

The Punce was sitting and talking with a large, loud lady with huge breasts and short dark hair whom Roly had seen before somewhere, visibly assertive in her opinions and sharing these at the same time with anyone, in addition to Lady Ponsonby, who she thought might be listening. Her husband was something in the City, he thought, and Flashman was unsurprised that the chap liked to stay up there during the week.

"I would if I was him," thought Flashman. He was glad to see that Lady Ponsonby was distracted. "Like owner, like dog," he muttered as he sauntered past the sitting pair of ladies en route to the bar, carrying a plastic bag containing some whiffy dog-treat things that he had got in town that afternoon.

"Gin and Tonic please, Kevin," said Roly and dropped a couple of the treats on the floor at his feet.

Lady Ponsonby's Terrier had its beady eye on Flashman and knew what he was holding. It had smelt them as he had passed, and you could see it doing an appreciation of the relative risks of going near Flashman with the reward of sating any dog's natural greed. It only took 3 minutes, and Nipper edged in nervously to gobble the little bits of flavoured biscuit which comprised the treat. Luckily, Lady Ponsonby had not seemed unduly moved by this behaviour and when Flashman said good evening to her, "Good evening, I better make friends. What's your chap's name?"

"Nipper," she replied proudly. "He's not such a bad dog, you know." Lady Ponsonby's friend looked irritated at having her conversation interrupted.

"Have you met Lady Barlow?" enquired the Punce.

"Hello. I'm Bella. How do you do?" Roly was impressed how Lady Barlow managed to smile and yet give a withering stare at the same time as she re-engaged Lady Ponsonby in conversation. So Roly stepped back to the bar and gently dropped another one of the treats onto the carpet below him. The terrier trotted over and ate it up without attracting the Punce's notice.

Johnny walked into the bar and joined Flashman. The intelligent little dog had quickly learnt the routine and was now doing all sorts of tricks, sit up and beg routines, rolling over on its back when told to do so, seeking out the hidden treat when instructed etc. The bar had been filling up with residents, and all seemed to be enjoying the show, including Lady Ponsonby and her friend, who both seemed rather proud of the little dog's antics, nodding knowingly and accepting the enthusiastic remarks of other residents as if they were praising their own children.

"Excuse me, Wing Commander," whispered Flashman. "Just got to go the loo. Perhaps you'd like to carry on," and handed the treats to Johnny to continue the action.

Roly left the room unnoticed and quickly whipped outside to fetch his pre-hidden treasure, the 4" dog turd, still fresh and much larger than the little Nipper's capabilities, but that was half the fun. He furtively returned to the Bar and quietly slipped behind Lady Ponsonby's friend and, whilst pretending to do up an errant shoelace, emptied the bag's contents under Lady Barlow's chair. The kerfuffle that Johnny and the dog were creating on the other side of the room meant that he was not seen by anyone, so Flashman left the room again, walked down the corridor and re-entered by another door, this time remarking loudly as he entered so that everyone could see where he was coming from.

One of the other residents remarked. "Oh goodness, Lady Ponsonby, that dog of yours is so intelligent. You must have put a lot of your time into training him. I wish other dogs that came to this place were as well-behaved."

Lady Ponsonby beamed with pride. Maybe Flashman was not such a bad sort, after all, she thought, as her Amazonian friend's nose beside her began to twitch.

"Thank you, Flashman. I'll show you another trick. Here Nipper. Come on. Come and sit beside mother. Now watch this, everyone," as she did a rolling motion with her hands, and Nipper did a 360-degree backward somersault and everyone applauded!

But the smell of the dog turd was now beginning to permeate the room, and everyone's noses were twitching. Suddenly, one of the residents spotted the offending item and, with a loud remark, warned Lady Ponsonby that her dog had perhaps got a little too excited for its own good. Had she seen what was under her friend's chair?

Flashman couldn't help himself. His schoolboy humour got the better of him and looking directly at the Punce's friend. He raised his eyebrows questioningly.

"Are you sure it's the dog's?"

Lady Barlow, the Amazonian friend, was used to such smells from her own dog. She stood up with concern. At Flashman's insinuation, eyes had flickered her way and her decorum deserted. The dog had actually done it under her very own chair and whilst she had been sitting there. They were all staring at her as if she had done it herself. How ghastly! How humiliating! In anguish, she remarked that she had forgotten about having to pick her husband up at the station, so she was sorry she couldn't join Lady Ponsonby for supper after all and nearly ran out of the room.

Lady Ponsonby was now on her own. The dog was on her lap. The residents were leaving the Bar for the Dining Room, and Flashman was walking out with them with a look of disgust on his face, glancing at the other residents as he did so and thereby encouraging them to do the same. It was a masterpiece of auto-suggestion. No one could bear to look at Lady Ponsonby. It was all too embarrassing, and all the while, Flashman could barely conceal a grin.

The next morning, Roly thought that he had better go to Lady Ponsonby's rescue. Critchley had popped into his apartment and suggested that some sort of gesture might be politic. She remarked that Lady Ponsonby had told her that she had complained to the management. What Critchley didn't say was that word had come back to her, independently, from the representative with responsibility at Newclere Council that it might be an opportunity to put the skids under Roly's tenure at Westridge. The chap had suggested that Lady Ponsonby should be encouraged to lodge an official complaint to the owners, saying that she had been bullied.

Critchley's demeanour seemed odd. She looked cagey and seemed worried.

"Why is she telling me this?" wondered Roly. She seemed to want to tell him more, but something held her back.

So Roly walked down to the main office at Reception and had a word with the Manager. The previous evening, Kevin, the barman, had removed the item pretty promptly, but Flashman insisted that the ratio of dog size to turd size made her Terrier unlikely to be the culprit. The matter was resolved when Roly suggested to Lady Ponsonby that she might make a donation to her Water Aid charity. The decision to ban the dog from the public rooms of Westridge was reversed, and the matter forgotten.

Lady Ponsonby became butter in Roly's hands.

But Critchley's behaviour was strange and out of character. He thought that she had wanted to get something off her chest, and it seemed that if he had pressed her, she might start weeping. That wasn't like Critchley at all. It all seemed a bit odd.

October 1966

Switzerland: Aiglon College

Aiglon, in Chesières, Switzerland, seemed like a different world after the restrictions of an English public school. Students were from a wide range of nationalities, and a vast range of backgrounds, and Aiglon was co-educational. The sons and daughters of rich Americans, Muslim Royalty, Chinese Triad leaders and African despots mixed with the scions of noble European families and dodgy *nouveau riche* traders seeking respectability. At 16 years plus, most of them had yet to be infused with the worst traits and prejudices of their parents, and there was an unlikely camaraderie amongst the pupils, principles upon which the college had been founded.

Mum, Anne, had been able to get a job at The Palais des Nations, the building that had housed the European headquarters of the UN on the banks of Lake Geneva since the previous year. With help from the UN, she was able to scrape together the astronomical cost of attendance at Aiglon. Roly's own charm, sporting prowess and a bursary carried the rest of the day. He spent two summers in the Mediterranean on vessels that had to be seen to be believed, a holiday in Shemiran, Tehran, Iran, an amazing fortnight in Kentucky, USA and, all the while, his attendance at 'eagles' nests' in the Alps of various tycoons was keenly sought by fellow pupils who enjoyed his company.

Roly was always quick to assimilate himself into the etiquette of his hosts and learnt a huge amount about national traits, ambitions, grudges and behavioural protocols.

His closest friends seemed unlikely. They were Persian. Their names were Farukh Mehedi Parviz and Hassan Fereydoun. Parviz came from an upper-class family of Persian industrialists, and Hassan was the son of a politically active spice trader in Iran. Hassan's family were under the surveillance of SAVAK (Iran's pre-revolutionary intelligence agency). Hassan's friendship with Farukh was unlikely because they came from the opposite end of the social spectrum, but from having rather relied upon each other during the early weeks of their attendance at Aiglon, they came to realise that they had much in common. With Roly, the two Iranians had sensed someone else for whom Aiglon seemed elitist and who felt temporarily out of place with the backgrounds of the other students. Parviz had invited Roly to Tehran at the end of the first term, to the Sa'dabad Palace Complex, home to the court of Mohammad Reza Pahlavi, the Shah of Iran. The visit was ostensibly a week-long skiing trip to Shemsak, but Roly was there long enough to see how the other half lived and to have experienced some gross injustices to members of the palace staff. One particular experience had rattled him, and he felt that Iran's drift towards the west was not being true to its own identity. He even said as much to Parviz, who agreed. This being Hassan's point of view as well, it became the subject of frequent evening conversations between the three of them, but all three had distinctly different views as to how a change in Iran should be achieved.

Hassan was quite a religious guy. The nearest mosques were in Geneva and Zurich, each about 150 km away, but he always found time to pray five times per day. He didn't drink, but he still participated in College activities, as well as outward bound, and appeared emancipated and open-minded about world affairs. Roly found him engaging, and they would have long chats into the evening, and he would sometimes accompany Hassan to Geneva on weekend visits to see his mother.

On one such weekend, Roly had sensed that there was a Middle Eastern guy, who looked vaguely familiar, taking an interest in them from a neighbouring table in a café where they were eating their lunch. He was wearing dark glasses and obviously watching them over the top of his newspaper. When Roly and Hassan got up from their meal, Roly glanced over his shoulder and saw that the man was paying his own bill. Later on, he saw him again as they walked through Vielle Ville, the Old Town in the centre of Geneva.

He consulted his mother, who thought he was being melodramatic. It wasn't impossible, but who would be interested in the activities of a 17-year-old from Iran attending school in Switzerland? As far as Roly knew, Hassan's background hardly suggested that his family had influence.

So he forgot about the incident until three weeks later. Roly had joined a number of friends who had decided to go to the British Ski Club that evening in the centre of Chesières, up the hill from Aiglon College. They were attending a foreign affairs lecture, and Hassan was there too. The lecture was interesting and, at the end, they trooped out to cross the road and walk back down the hill to the College.

Roly had already crossed the road, and Hassan had yet to do so, but the growling sound of the 350cc motorbike with a black helmeted rider made Roly turn around to see what was going on. The rider was clearly taking liberties as he appeared to have no intention of slowing down as he rode up the hill towards them.

Roly knew what a Browning Hi Power 9mm pistol looked like. His father had had one, and he now saw the rider pull the familiar shape from his pocket and hold it so that it was pointing down, parallel with his right shin. He had his forefinger on the trigger. The students were all talking animatedly in that usual teenage way, and no one other than Roly had noticed.

It must have been his background in Kenya that made him see the danger. Pistols and black-clad motorbike riders who weren't going to stop, in remote Switzerland, were not a normal state of affairs. He was too far away to intercept the guy, and the rider was doing about 20 mph. He would be gone before he could be intercepted but Roly had his satchel with him. Someone was the target. But who? At that moment, Roly suddenly remembered the incident in Geneva and saw Hassan waiting at the crossing for the rider to pass through.

As the rider raised his right arm to take aim, there was no time for a warning. Roly waved the leather satchel above his head by the long straps and, in the same movement, swung it and released it at the rider. The stiff leather edges of the satchel caught the rider on the back of his gun hand catching him completely unawares and making him drop his gun, which fell to the ground whilst the rider's momentum carried him through the pedestrian crossing. The intention had been clear, and now, witnessed by many, there was no way the rider could retrieve the weapon. He twisted the grip of his throttle and sped away, up the hill and out of sight.

Amidst the horrified shrieks of the girls, Roly leaned down to pick up the weapon and retrieve his bag. Everyone was looking at him. No one, apart from Roly and Hassan, knew that Hassan had been the target. Hassan stood there as pale as a ghost, and Roly quickly took his arm, guided him back to the Ski Club and sat him down whilst the rest of the students ran back to the College.

Recovering his composure, Hassan looked at Roly and said, "I think I owe you my life, Roly. My father warned me, only the other day, about how tough things were for him back in Tehran. We never imagined that I might be a proxy target over here. It was clearly intended as a warning to my family and others of the consequences of their political activities in Tehran. I feel quite shocked. Shall we have a drink?"

Roly smiled. He knew that a drink was the last thing Hassan would turn to. He was as straight as they come, highly principled and, despite his immediate shock at the unexpected nature of this attack, as cool as a cucumber.

The next day, they were both interviewed by the Gendarmerie from that Canton. It was Hassan's wish that he should not be identified as the target, and both professed confusion as to what had happened. The police thanked Roly for his swift reaction. The gun was handed over, and Roly had made a friend for life.

Autumn 2018

Westridge: The Hot Tub

A Good night's sleep. Flashman awoke later than usual. He lay there laughing at the evening's fun that they had had with Nipper a couple of weeks before. It had been of the kind which you just couldn't invent. He and Johnny had cried with laughter at the Bar afterwards, and now, as Flashman padded down the Corridor towards the Wellness Spa for his swim, he tried to remember what was on today's schedule.

That was the trouble with age. He was physically good for a 68-year-old, and the memory still seemed to be there, but he had to be careful in the heat of the sun. He was on tablets for an enlarged prostate, but they didn't seem to do much good when he had excessed on the vino. Still, it could have been worse, he thought, as he pushed open the door to the Spa reception area.

Young Sharon was behind the desk, and it seemed that louder than normal sounds and splashes were coming from the swimming pool area.

"What's going on in here then, Sharon?" enquired Flashman.

"Oh, it's the locals. Mr Flashman. It's their regular Wednesday morning slot. Kirsty is putting them through their paces."

"Brigadier Flashman to you," thought Flashman as he went through to the male changing room and emerged poolside to find some eight middle-aged women doing Pool Yoga with Kirsty.

God, she was lovely in that swimming costume! It was thin enough to reveal the outlines of her nipples and lower treasures. The middle-aged group of friends weren't bad either, but he didn't have his lenses in, and the noise was hardly conducive to the quiet reflective few lengths that was Flashman's normal routine, so he went to sit in the whirlpool thing and observe the female form from afar!

None of the locals were really listening to Kirsty, talking over each other, expressing fake shock-horror at the latest gossip whilst simultaneously trying to outdo each other with their own stories.

Kirsty looked weary from her travails, and the session was nearly over, so she got out of the pool and came over to join Flashman in the Hot Tub.

"You know you can get the bubbles going in zones in that one, Mr Flashman, with matching vibrations to help whichever part of the body needs it, innit. It's really relaxing. It's normally full up, Mr Flashman. You're ever so lucky to have it to yourself," said Kirsty.

"Brigadier Flashman to you," thought Flashman again but never mind, this looked promising.

"No, I didn't know that," re-joined Flashers, sensing there was an opportunity here. She was a cheeky little thing and was always chatty, which made it difficult not to enjoy their near-daily exchanges. In fact, it was probably time she started to call him Roly.

"Show me how," said Flashman with only his head above the surface of the Hot Tub.

"Well, you have to sit in the bit that's shaped like a chair for a start. Over this side, Mr Flashman and I'll show you."

Flashman went to the other side to join Kirsty, who got in. Side by side in the Hot tub, Flashman felt a flush caused by more than the heat of the water. Kirsty had a tan, against which her teeth looked very white. Her eyes were sparkly, of the sort when the body is in good shape. Now she was so close, the shape of her full and firm breasts was even more obvious through her one-piece costume, more than he had noted on previous trips to the Spa, and she was speaking in a gushing fashion.

"Now press the button on your left, and it'll start to agitate." Flashman feigned misunderstanding and winked at her. Kirsty leant over him to press the button herself.

"Christ, don't do it, Flashman," he thought to himself. "Haven't had titillation like this for years since Samantha Fox in The Sun."

"When you've had 5 minutes of that, Mr Flashman, you'll be able to do some of the floor exercises that me and me boyfriend do in the mornings every day."

"And every night, I bet," said Flashman.

Kirsty giggled. "Oh, Mr Flashman. That's very naughty of you. I only meant... Well, you know what I meant."

Flashman was thinking that Kirsty probably didn't know what he meant when their conversation was interrupted. The ladies were getting out of the pool. It was time for lunch in the Restaurant. En route to the changing rooms, they were standing right above and behind Flashman, who, distracted by Kirsty, had forgotten all about the swimming exercise session that had been going on

One of them, slightly older than the rest, remarked, "Don't you think you're too old for that, Roly?"

It was Rosemary Fenwick, a sort of ringleader for the ladies. Kirsty was about the same age as her daughters, and Roly knew Rosemary's family well. He played golf with her husband sometimes. Silently, Flashman agreed with her, but not wishing to hurt Kirsty, he ignored Rosemary's pointed remark and replied, "Oh, hello, Rosemary. You're probably right. Kirsty was just showing me how this gizmo works. I don't understand it at all. I think I need to go on a course to appreciate what it can do. Do you mind turning it off for me? Just there," he said, pointing at the controls to the side.

Rosemary bent over to turn off the floor-mounted switch. As she did so, she slipped and reached out to grab something to hold onto. The only thing to grab, however, was one of her friend's swimsuits which ripped completely from the waist down. Her friend squealed in horror at her exposure. The same manoeuvre made them both lose their balance, and the two women fell towards the place with the softest landing and, with a great splash, into the hot tub.

No harm done, thankfully. But Flashers now found himself one of four in a hot tub made for six. He had had a real eyeful of the half-exposed lady's nether regions. He thought levity might be the antidote to her embarrassment.

"Glad to see you keep the front garden nicely trimmed," said Flashman to Rosemary's friend.

Shrieks of laughter went up from all the girls as they all now piled in. Nine women and Flashman. About the right ratio, really! It was difficult to move, and one of them was bottomless!

"Johnny won't believe this, but he will when he sees the tape from the security camera," thought Flashman and stayed there for the next half hour wondering, all the while, whether he dared get out himself.

Kirsty's image stayed with him all day! He couldn't get it out of his mind.

October 1969

Aldershot: Mons Officer Cadet School

He awoke with a start and lay there wondering if that night's vivid dream about Aiglon had been the cause. It might have been his prostate. It had been playing up recently and now he wanted a pee. His bedside clock said 3:45 am, and getting up in the night was starting to be tiresome. Padding uncertainly to the bathroom in the dark, he reckoned it was partly Johnny's fault. That afternoon, they had beaten a team from Swinley Forest in an annual fourball competition. Most of the opposition lived locally to Westridge and had stayed for a fun meal before tottering back to their homes in a minibus from the local taxi service. Johnny, mindful of Swinley's hospitality whenever the match was played at their course, had produced some very fine Palmer 18-year-old Tawny Port, which had gone down a treat with everyone. As usual, they had all forgotten that their recovery powers weren't what they used to be.

One of the opposition had been at Mons Officer Cadet School with him, and they had laughed as they reminisced together. As Roly's head relaxed back onto his pillow again, he remembered the circumstances when they first met.

It had been a cold Sunday afternoon that new Intake 42, Salerno Company, had been briefed to arrive on their first day. They had been told to be on parade at 2 pm, and it had seemed a long way from the warmth, the previous night, of Sophie Lanyard's bed. Having arrived at Mons that morning by taxi from Aldershot station, Roly was standing on the parade square in

78

freezing conditions with some 80 other young men who had been selected for 5 months of intensive Officer Training. Uniforms had not yet been issued, and Roly wore his suit, best tie, brogue shoes and Herbert Johnson Trilby as detailed on the joining instructions.

He had been nervous all week. After 9 months, firstly at the depot in Winchester with recruits for The Light Division regiments where he had been the butt of substantial invective for being a potential officer by the squaddies destined elsewhere and then with the Royal Green Jackets as a Rifleman, Flashman had spent the week in London, interspersing fun with friends, daily exercise in Battersea Park.... and Sophie!

He had thought about joining an Infantry Battalion, but the pull of his illustrious ancestor and his mum's expectations meant that there was never any real alternative to seeking a commission in the 11th Hussars.

Now, lined up on the drill square, a Coldstream Guards Colour Sergeant, Andrews, wearing his staff dress complete with his Colour Sergeant's red sash, warned them that they were at Mons, its expectations, that day's remaining routine and went through the roll call, "Adams," he cried.

There was no response.

"Adams," he cried again. "Where are you?" he asked with hardly disguised menace from between clenched teeth.

"I'm over here," came a quiet response.

"Right, Sirs," shouted Andrews. "When I call your name, you reply, 'Yes, sir'. When I speak to you, I will also call you 'Sir'. The only difference is that, whilst you are at Mons, you mean it. Now then, Mr Adams, sir, are you present?" he said, snarling at Adams whilst also casting his gaze up and down the ranks of assembled young men.

"Yes sir, present, sir."

"Good. Let's get on with it then."

The roll call progressed again.

"Anson, Amawa (from Uganda), Archer, Asquith, Astor, Atkinson, Auchinleck, Baker, Baring, Bathurst, Bell-Willoughby." They all replied, "Yes, sir," with alacrity, and Andrews looked up to see who owned the double-barrelled name. The names could have been a roll call from the good and great of British history, and Flashman could sense the relish with which Andrews was imagining the contretemps to come. When he came to a name he couldn't pronounce, he spat it out, "Broccoli!"

"That's pronounced 'Bruffly', sir, actually, 'Lord Broughleigh'," came the reply from someone with a laconic, rather bored drawl responding from the ranks.

This was music to Andrew's ears. There were a number of names that he could recognise from amongst, in particular, his own Guards' regiment, forebears with famous names, socialites from the gossip columns and so on, all names that comprised possible candidates for his cruel amusement over the next five months and here was a real live Lord!

"Lord Broccoli it is then," cried Andrews with relish and carried on with the roll call of names.

Andrews continued. "Cecil, Chichester, Coleridge, De Trafford. Shouldn't we be joining the French Army, Mr De Trafford, sir?" It was slow going… interspersed by barks from Andrews to stand still on parade and stop smiling.

"Eagles, Ecclestone, Edwards, Egerton, Eyre." Roly knew his turn was coming, and he responded with a quick, "Yes, sir!" But Andrews hesitated. Why did he know this name? And then it twigged that he had enjoyed stories about a Flashman from history, a preening Cavalry Officer who had a reputation as a Cad and womaniser.

"Planning to be a donkey walloper are we, Mr Flashman, sir, or will it be Rommel with his goggles?"

But he chose his target badly. He hadn't known that Roly had already done 9 months as a recruit at Winchester and in a battalion. Roly knew his jargon and knew that bullies had to be stood up to.

"Well, it was either that or the Wooden Tops, sir, and I wanted to be something other than a parade ground Wallah bulling my boots all day," he said, generating a ripple of laughter through the ranks.

Andrews didn't like this one bit. Roly was a marked man, and Andrews was the Platoon Sergeant of the platoon that he was in.

"…F…F…F…F… Fox," said Andrews with a mock stutter. Some of the new recruits knew what he meant. Fox was the family name of the Earls of Ilchester, and the old man had had a terrible stutter. What they didn't know was that Andrews had endured time as a Lance Corporal in this Fox's father's platoon in the Coldstream Guards. The outlook for the next 5 months did not look good for Fox, a rather weasely-looking individual who looked as though he missed the benefit of being dressed by his family nanny despite being in his twenties and already married, badly, according to the gossip columns to a lower middle-class wife with a reputation of being a harridan.

And so on.

The next six weeks went by in a whirl. The cadets were given no time to themselves other than Sunday afternoons after the compulsory Church Parade, and all were confined to camp. When they weren't marching, they were doubling everywhere. Kit inspections were held twice a day. It didn't matter how well your kit was presented. Something was always rejected and had to be redone, and Roly's Platoon Commander, Captain Blundell from the King's Own Scottish Borderers, became known as 'Dusty Blunder' for the habit of running his finger over any surface, coming up with imagined dust on his finger and turning to his accompanying Platoon Sergeant and saying dryly, "I think this needs cleaning." In Flashman's case, Colour Sergeant Andrews, with a smile, pulled the entire contents of Roly's locker onto the floor, followed by the locker itself and announced to Roly that he would be back after the evening meal and expected better.

But Andrews had a hard time getting to Roly. The earlier months at Winchester had prepared him well. Kit preparation, bulling your boots, Drill, Fieldcraft and Weapons training meant there was little opportunity for Andrews to berate him. Roly did, however, feel incarcerated. Even Winchester had given him some basic freedoms, such as evenings to yourself and weekends. There was nothing like that at Mons.

For a boy who, in February the previous year, was skiing weekly in Switzerland, who grew up with the freedoms of Africa and who, without real parental guidance, had been used to making his own decisions, this period was difficult. In addition, he had only met Sophie Lanyard two months before going to Mons, and a promising relationship was developing. They had had a fun week just before Roly had arrived at Mons. He knew Sophie was missing his charms just as much as he was missing their lively encounters, always marginally dangerous and very exciting. They hadn't seen each other for six weeks now, but Flashman had written to her with a crafty plan for a secret rendezvous that afternoon.

Sunday mornings were reserved for the Church Parade, and the whole company would be marched down to the Garrison Church. After lunch, back at camp, everyone was expected to study military manuals and do coursework for the following week.

That sixth weekend, the company was formed up and waiting to be marched off to church when three coaches turned up suddenly, and the officer cadets were ordered to embark. No one knew where they were going until it was announced by the Company Sergeant Major that, for their heathen benefits, they were being taken to the Army Chaplains' College at Bagshot, just for a change. Thirty minutes later, they arrived at Bagshot and were marched into the chapel. As they chose their pews, the Sergeant Major's voice rang out.

"Listen in! All Officer Cadets will sit on the right-hand side," he boomed.

Roly was on the left, so he stood up, crossed the aisle and went to sit down. He didn't quite understand what this was all about, but it was nice to escape Mons for a change, and he had the prospect of seeing Sophie that afternoon which he was looking forward to.

After sitting there for 10 minutes, there was a noise from the back and in trooped more people in uniform. As they got halfway down the aisle, the whole of Mons contingent turned their necks in awe with their mouths open. It was the girls from the WRAC College – all sixty of them – and they hadn't seen a man for six weeks either!

The girls sat down, and a hubbub arose. One or two on each side of the chapel actually knew each other. Furtive glances shot backwards and forwards as mute understandings to meet after the service were reached. And everyone wondered how long this service was going to be. The chords of sexual tension were as taut as they could get without snapping!

Three hymns, a sermon and a few prayers later, the blessing was delivered, and both sides of the church arose, eager with anticipation to meet once they were outside the chapel. The atmosphere could be cut with a knife.

The Mons Company Sergeant Major lifted his voice.

"Where are your manners, gentlemen? I'm sure you'll like to let the ladies leave first," he said. "I suggest that you all sit down until it's your turn, and we can all meet outside."

Without even speaking, the two sides understood each other perfectly. It only took a meeting of the eyes for each to know that they were making a commitment to meet outside the chapel, and as the last of the WRAC contingent filed out of the entrance into the porch, the Mons contingent stood up and started to leave.

"As you were," barked the CSM. "I haven't given the order yet, Gentlemen."

Well, after sexual tension comes sexual frustration, and if no one knows the definition, here it was in physical form. The Mons cadets were made to sit down and wait five minutes before filing out in expectation.

But the girls had gone!

The mood in the coach going back was dire. The amusement of the Directing Staff at what had obviously been planned only made things worse. Roly was hoping more than ever that his arrangement with Sophie that afternoon would come off. He didn't even know if she had received his letter.

Back at Camp, the coach parked beside the cookhouse, and they all trooped into lunch. Amawa, the Ugandan, was reproached by the RSM, who suggested that the process of putting your pudding of Spotted Dick and Custard on top of and on the same plate as one's main course of Roast Pork and all the trappings might be frowned upon in most British Army Officer Messes. If he wanted to pass out as an Officer these things were important.

Amawa was a huge, engaging man who had been a sergeant in the Ugandan police. One of his three wives was a commissioned officer in the Ugandan Army, close to Idi Amin.

"Sah, ma waff say to eat evrytin when I here."

"I hope that excludes us, Mr Amawa," responded the RSM.

"Oh yes, Sah, but I do what dis waff tell me as she a Captain. I salute her before I go baba even."

"I wonder what you salute her with, Mr Amawa. Someone tells me you've got three wives."

Amawa beamed with pride. He had been a full Ugandan football international and had been sent to Mons at Idi Amin's personal direction following a hat trick of goals against the Congo Team the previous year. Three wives would help him with his personal goal of creating his own football team of sons. There was something ominous about Amawa. He was engaging but quite simple, and Flashman was not surprised when, in late 1972, The Daily Telegraph carried a story and photo of Colonel Amawa, Ugandan Defence Force, in charge of the expulsion of Ugandan Asians, and known in Uganda as "The Crocodile". Ugandan soldiers, during this period, engaged in theft and physical and sexual violence against Asians with impunity. Many bodies had floated down the river. Flashman was sure that the Crocodile was closely involved, and he remembered thinking at the time that the Mons RSM had better watch his step!

Flashman didn't eat much. He had to get to the RV he had arranged with Sophie. He wasn't allowed to leave camp and so had suggested to Sophie that she blag her way into the camp by saying, "I've got an appointment to see Captain Blundell in the Officer's Mess," and add, if necessary, "If you know what I mean."

A wink to the gate guard would probably complete the trick.

And it did. There was Sophie parked in the staff quarters at the back of the Officer's Mess. It had seemed a good place, and Flashman could approach without being seen. How great was this? She had only had to wait thirty minutes. Roly jumped into the passenger seat of her Cortina. No words passed. They just grabbed each other and smothered each other with kisses. Soon hands began to wander. Sophie was up for it in the back seat, but Flashman couldn't afford to be discovered, so suggested that they leave Camp and head off to Hankley Common or somewhere.

"I'll get in the boot," he said, "and you can drive out."

Roly got out and climbed into Sophie's boot. Sophie closed the lid and drove back towards the Camp exit beside the guardroom. Slowing down to allow the sentry to open the barrier, she thought it a little odd to see Colour Sergeant Andrews standing there as well, smiling broadly, and it was he, rather than the sentry, who leant forward and indicated that he wanted to say something before the barrier was lifted.

Sophie stopped and wound down the window.

"You want to get your demister working, Ma'am. It looks a bit steamy in there," said Colour Sergeant Andrews. "Have you got a cloth? I'll get one for you."

"No, it's all right, Sergeant," replied Sophie, feeling uncomfortable. The windscreen seemed pretty clear to her! "It always clears just as soon as I put on a bit of speed. It's always the same with the colder weather."

"No, I insist," said Andrews. "I've got just the thing in the guardroom."

Just as he walked up the guardroom steps, the RSM came round the corner with the duty officer that day from the Cookhouse.

"Hello, madam. Any problem?" said the RSM, with a smile, ram rod straight and moustache curling.

Sophie glanced between him and the officer. She felt very uneasy. They were smiling.

"I heard you were visiting Alistair Blundell. I thought he was picking up Nelson, his dog, from his parents today," said the Duty Officer. "You know they're in Newcastle, don't you?"

"I know. Silly me!" said Sophie. "I should have remembered. He asked me to look after Nelson last week, and I couldn't. I think he even said that his parents were going to have him."

Andrews came back with a cloth.

"Just hop out, Ma'am, and I'll wipe the windscreen for you."

Sophie could but oblige. She was now as deep into the lie as she could be, and she had a horrible feeling in the pit of her tummy. Something was wrong. Why were all of these people here? Andrews took his time. He cleaned inside and out, chattering and making a noise all the while.

Inside the boot, Roly could tell that they had been rumbled. Sophie knew it, and Andrews, the RSM and the duty officer knew it because Roly had been seen as he got into the boot. All was confirmed because Blundell didn't have a dog and his parents, in fact, lived in Edinburgh. After two minutes, Andrews said, "Well, Ma'am. There we go. That should be better. I ought, however, to just look around your car. We've had a series of problems with intruders in the Camp lately, and young Smith here on sentry is just learning the ropes. Would you mind if I show him the key points and perhaps ask you to open the boot?"

There was no point in arguing the toss. Sophie opened the boot, and there was Roly, blinking as the bright light hit him.

"Oh, dear. What have we here? Not what we might call the Great Escape, sir," said Andrews.

"Come on, let the man have some fresh air. Is that too much too much to ask?" Roly said struggling to get out of the boot of the car.

"My, my, my. It's Mr Flashman. Impersonating a bit of baggage, I see or are we just tired and lying down? Out you get. Private Smith! Take him into the Guard Room, please. There's a much comfier bed in there. Stand to attention, Mr Flashman, sir. Ready. Quick March. Left, right, left, right, leeeft…"

Roly was marched off to the Guardroom in quick time, where he had his belt, tie and laces removed and was put in a cell. The door was locked firmly behind him and Sophie was advised that her presence was no longer needed. Not that she had to endure any consequences, and she'd been looking forward to a bit of flagrante delicto, but Sophie had enjoyed herself. With Roly, things were never predictable!

Otherwise, things had gone pretty well for Roly at Mons. He kept his nose clean, won the prize for the best shot, was Victor Ludorum in the Athletics meeting with the Sandhurst cadets and had succeeded in all his appointments bar one - a pretty minor thing which had happened at Battle Camp two weeks before the Passing-Out Parade.

The Mons School's Regimental Sergeant Major was a man who was upright, always immaculate and lived by a set of rules imparted by over thirty years in the Irish Guards. He had been at Dunkirk, in Korea and Malaysia and had seen good times and bad. He was impatient of excuses or complaints from anyone as there was no need for these if you lived by the same rules. In his opinion, there was no such thing as an officer making a mistake. Officers could never do this. They knew things that were beyond the ken of the rank and file, and his job was to ensure that there was orderliness in the ranks.

For him, family life was a distinct second priority, but it was a shock for him when his 17-year-old daughter became pregnant. He knew that it was one of the cadets from Roly's Company, but his daughter wouldn't tell him, and, in fact, she had laughed in his face at home and told him to take his pick. The cadets knew. One of them, in particular, was sure – Officer Cadet Sir Roger Canter, aka Knight Rider - and it was a standing joke which made things difficult for the RSM. How dare they laugh behind his back? How shameful at the end of a fine career for this to happen? The girl had come into their barrack block one evening, clearly drunk, and challenged a number of the cadets to have their way. Roly had been there and had turned his back, but the Knight Rider hadn't. Roly hated this sort of thing, and thank you very much, Sophie was his girl.

But, because of the incident when Roly had been found in the boot of his girlfriend's car, the RSM suspected Roly as one of the possible culprits and wanted to confront him, amongst others. The most obvious way, in his mind, to do this was to be close to each of the suspects, individually, whilst they performed a particular given task at the end-of-course Battle Camp at Sennybridge, Brecon, Wales. He could put them under pressure whilst he, as a member of the Directing Staff, helped assess the individual performance of the Officer Cadets as they performed the roles that they were given, whether as Radio Operator, Platoon Commander, Machine Gunner or whatever.

In Roly's case, he was, on this occasion, made Company Guide for a dawn attack. His job was to meet the Company at a pre-arranged Rendezvous and then lead them to a Forming Up point. From here they would advance towards the enemy at the instruction of and to the plan devised by the Company Commander (an appointment performed by one of Roly's fellow officer cadets). Simple, really, but it was teeming with rain (the main reason, as far as anyone can see, for the Army using this area of Wales as one of their pre-eminent Training Areas - because it always rains in Brecon), and the RV was scheduled for 3 am.

All went fine initially. Roly had left the Company HQ half an hour before the scheduled RV and walked back through the pitched blackness of the wood, downhill mostly. The rain seemed to have got worse, and his clothes were completely sodden, and his feet were really quite sore. He needed the clean pair of socks that he was not going to get after 10 days on this exercise. He was very tired, very cold, and constantly slipping on the muddy and rutted surface. He was aware that his fatigue meant that he was becoming delusional. But it should be OK as he had recce'd the route earlier. All he needed to do was put one foot in front of the other, and he would lead the Company to the selected location. He had a torch in case of need.

He RV'd, successfully, with the Company, and they shook themselves out, equally tired from their fortnight of exertions. Roly set off back through the woods, remembering all the time that he shouldn't deviate from the path. The Directing Staff, including the RSM, were liberally sprinkled amongst the line of cadets that he was leading.

Ten minutes after setting off back through the wood, always with a gentle incline upwards but stumbling in the slippery mud, Roly saw a light in front of him about thirty yards to the fore. Quite a relief!

The track was just taking them around a big bend, which Roly just about remembered from his recce, and it must be someone ahead of him going to the same location, so he headed towards it, thinking that this made life somewhat easier since he dare not use his own torch.

The light was still there as he got round the bend, and as he caught up, he could see that it was the RSM, so that was all right. He would follow him and the one or two other crew that appeared to be in front of the RSM. But after ten minutes, Roly was sure that they were crossing a small ditch that he had just crossed some 5 minutes before. Thinking that this was a symptom of his tiredness, he stuck to his guns and carried on behind the RSM, who, by this time, had looked back at Roly a couple of times.

But when they crossed the small ditch again, the RSM couldn't contain himself. He had doubted that Roly was the culprit so far as his daughter was concerned, and, anyway, it just wasn't in the boy's character. He said to Roly, "Might we be unsure where we're going, sir, Mr Flashman, sir?"

"Yes, sir. I can't go any faster because you lot are in the way," replied Roly wearily. "I'm a bit worried about making it to the Forming Up point in time, so if you wouldn't mind me overtaking, I'd be very grateful, and you could get onto the back of the line."

"But we are on the back of the line already, Mr Flashman." The RSM looked grim. "Might we be a little lost, sir?"

At which point Roly twigged. "You fool," he thought to himself. "For the last 15 minutes, I've been following the back of the line that I have been leading and have now gone round in two almighty circles."

The matter was resolved with some mirth from the Directing Staff, and it remained the only blot on Roly's military record whilst at Mons. The Sophie incident became folklore in the annals of military history as a potential new heading on a military 'charge sheet' as 'Conduct definitely becoming of an Officer but needing better planning'.

Roly obtained his commission at Mons and was posted to Germany, where the 11th Hussars were stationed. Before departing, he spent a wonderful final weekend in London with Sophie. They walked through the parks, resplendent in spring cherry blossom as London cast off its winter gloom, went to the theatre, dined and made love.

On Monday morning, Roly climbed into his white MGB and set off for Dover to catch the boat and then the long journey via Belgium, Holland and Germany to Hohne, where the 11th Hussars were stationed. He was sad to leave Sophie, knew that she would come over to Germany when she could but knew, also, that Sophie was one of those girls who was intent on enjoying life as much as himself. So there was an understanding that the other was unlikely to be a long-term partner and that there would be no regrets, no recriminations.

April 1972

Aldeburgh: A Hole in One

The 9-hole Westridge Golf course could not be described as championship material. Some of its members were a bit rough (as were some of the greens), but Roly enjoyed being able to get round in one hour and thirty-eight minutes (or so the notice told you as you came off the 9th). Weather and aching bones permitting, Roly and his friends participated in the regular Monday morning round-up.

"Washed your balls this morning?" Reggie enquired of Roly. To Roly's recollection, Reggie said this every time they played as if it was an original and the wittiest joke ever.

"No, I haven't," retorted Roly, "and I haven't washed yours either. But I expect you get Joanna to do that. She might think, in fact, that it's time you had new ones." This always made Reggie cackle with laughter.

Tom Budge, who was also a Westridge resident, was playing with them that morning. Tom and Roly had been life-long friends ever since meeting in the Alps in the early seventies. He remembered playing with Tom soon after meeting, some 45 years before, during a weekend at Tom's family cottage on the Suffolk coast. He had been in his early twenties and on R&R from a Northern Ireland tour in charge of a three Ferret scout car detachment attached to The Royal Green Jackets in the Falls district of Belfast.

Tom Budge had been a medical student at St Bart's Hospital in those days, a great sportsman, great company and generous with his invitations up to the family's weekend retreat in the heart of Aldeburgh.

The weekends were always active. Tom's family had a wide circle of local friends. They owned a little 15-foot clinker-built dinghy which was kept there, and on the flood, Tom fished for Bass on the river Alde over the muscle beds near the tower. One weekend, Roly remembered spending his brief escape from Northern Ireland with an uproarious Saturday night in the Cross Keys pub in the centre of town. The session had culminated in a two-hour stint in the local nick. It wasn't his fault, really, as the kind locals, on hearing of his current posting, had insisted on buying him pint after pint of the local Adnams beer.

8 pints of Adnams to the good and each able, only to wobble, the two of them had collapsed in hysterics on the Town Steps en route back to Tom's Cottage, where they lay on their backs and sang at the top of their voices. Unfortunately, the noise was too much for Mrs Phillimore, who lived opposite, and she complained to the town's policeman. Of her two daughters, Jane, the eldest at 24, was rather plain and definitely pleased with herself. She was revising for her university finals at the moment and couldn't sleep. Natasha, 19, was rather prettier and more fun. Mrs Phillimore, however, had ambitions for both her daughters that didn't involve the ruffian likes of Roly and Tom or lack of sleep! PC Biggins knew Tom's family. He came round in his Police Ford Escort and carted them both off.

Biggins read them the riot act and left them staring at the plain brick walls of the cell before releasing them to get back to their beds by 2:30 am.

"You ought to know better, Mr Flashman. Leader of men, are we? Lieutenant in Her Majesty's Armed Services?" he said as they signed for the return of their possessions. "As for you, Tom, your choice of friends could be improved. Bugger off and make sure you don't wake that old harridan's daughters again," he admonished as they departed.

Hardly sober from the night before, they arrived at the local golf course for a 1056 hrs T off slot. They were going over to The Maltings for Sunday lunch, later, at the Innes's house, friends of Tom's, and the son of the family, Richard Innes, had thought it would be fun to slip in 9 holes prior to the 'Roast Beef and Yorkshires' that beckoned. Roly had met Richard the last time he had been up in Suffolk and remembered Richard's hugely pretty sister, Annabella, whom he knew from parties in London, so the lunch looked promising.

Tom and Richard were members at Aldeburgh Golf Club and, despite the fact that they were 10 minutes late for the T-off time, managed to persuade the pro to let them slip onto the 9-hole River Course behind a Ladies Roll-up, which had recently finished teeing off.

They couldn't, in fact, see anyone ahead, so Tom, Richard and Roly imagined that they would have plenty of time to do the 9 holes and be back in time for lunch down the road at Richard's parents' house.

As is often the case, their relaxed state engendered some rather good golf. Both Tom and Roly had Par 4's

97

on the first, and the Par 3 second yielded a similar achievement. They talked about last night's fun, their mutual friends and the skiing which Roly had missed that year. Following in the footsteps of his father (a renowned Virologist who also obtained an MC and Bar for extraordinary action in 1942) and grandfather, Tom was aiming to become a GP and enter local practice.

The third hole went without incident, with Richard hanging on by dint of a superb bunker shot which saved his par. Teeing off at the Par 5 fourth, they could see that they were catching up with a pair of ladies playing in front of them. If they were part of the Ladies Roll-up that morning, then they seemed to be lagging as there was no one in front of them. By the time the chaps came to play their third shots to the green, the ladies were still on it, putting out, but no more than a temporary delay was experienced, and the chaps marched through the gap in the heather to the fifth Tee.

The two women were no more than 70 or so yards ahead on the side of the 5th fairway. One of them, who looked familiar to Tom, was clearly looking for her ball in the short grass just off the fairway, so they just had to wait to do their drives. But 6-7 minutes is longer than is reasonable and a long time when you are tight for lunch. These ladies didn't seem in a hurry!

As one of the women glanced back, she could clearly see the impatient stance adopted by Tom, leaning on the shaft of his driver, with the other arm, crooked at the elbow with the hand on his waist – teapot style - a time honoured way of suggesting to the pair in front that they might like to consider letting them through.

But there was no getting this message through to these two, one of whom had pointed at Tom from afar, in a rather accusatory way and, in the same movement, suggested something derogatory to her partner by waving her hand at them in a dismissive motion.

It didn't look good for the chaps. It took 20 minutes to complete the hole, and their frustration was mounting.

"The least they could do would be to let us play through," said Richard.

Tom had twigged that one of those in front was Mrs Phillimore from the previous evening. He hadn't said anything as he knew that Roly was easily wound up. She was, in fact, the Ladies Club Captain, and there didn't seem much future in forcing the pace, especially in view of last night's antics!

The only thing Richard knew about Mrs Phillimore was the fact that her younger daughter was a friend of his sister and a bit of a 'goer', but he certainly didn't associate that fact with the old bat ahead whom he had never met anyway. He was T'eed up and ready to drive off. In his mind, this pair ahead were clearly obstructing their progress, and Richard was becoming impatient.

Up ahead, Mrs Phillimore would have agreed that she was being obstructive! This was the course she had played on for some 30 years now, and she was certainly not going to be dictated to by ghastly young men with no manners. She and her husband had lived opposite Professor Budge since they had bought their own cottage some ten years earlier, and she felt that the

Budges had never been over-friendly to them as 'new' arrivals.

"They can bloody well wait and learn some manners," mused Mrs Phillimore, emboldened by her status as Ladies Captain.

The ladies were some 200 yards away now, addressing their second shots to the green. The chaps could see that their pace was not going to heat up, and Richard reckoned since they were being studiously ignored, that a warning shot might not go amiss. It wouldn't be what you might term a sharp reminder. They were too far away. He never usually drove over 200 yards, and his accuracy was normally wanting; perhaps a 3-wood, to be sure?

Well, it was a gorgeous morning, it hadn't rained for a couple of weeks, and the surface was bone hard! As Richard hit a perfectly struck shot off the T, he knew it was a good one. That feeling when you know you have hit a good shot; a blend of timing, balance and the noise of a perfect connection of club head and ball. The ball sailed away into the yonder, it rose and rose, and its trajectory then flattened before it made its descent, worryingly in line with Mrs Phillimore, who was now some 20 yards from the green.

Mrs Phillimore was replacing a divot from her latest fluffed shot. She bent over to pick up the sod that she had just created and, suddenly, felt a sharp whack in the middle of her backside. Actually, the ball couldn't have been more perfectly central. It bulls-eyed the folds of flesh dividing her gluteus maximus!

And it hurt! She pitched forward onto her head and then rolled over before getting up, hopping about and rubbing her backside vigorously, an activity assisted by her partner.

"Unless I'm badly mistaken, Richard, that looks awfully like a hole-in-one," remarked Roly, still half-drunk from the previous night. "What you might call an absolute cracker!" There was something inordinately funny about Mrs Phillimore's predicament, and he and Tom just cried with laughter, laughter that hurt so much that they held their tummies and cried out loud.

"Now she can perhaps justify being a pain in the arse," rejoined Tom, setting off a second peel of laughter between the pair.

Richard, sober as a judge, didn't quite share their amusement. "Bloody hell," he thought, "this is going to have consequences."

Up ahead, Mrs Phillimore and her partner looked back down the fairway. Bruised but otherwise unhurt, she could see two figures lying on the ground, and she could just hear the distant screams of laughter.

"How dare they laugh at me?" she murmured menacingly to her partner, who replied.

"We can't allow this, Sarah. That is just disgraceful, and they aren't even coming up to apologise. In fact, I can now see them slinking off to the clubhouse. You should have their guts for gaiters."

Arriving back at the Clubhouse, Sarah Phillimore enquired to discover that the three chaps had already departed for lunch. They had seen little to be gained by hanging around.

The boys had given a brief description of their predicament to the Pro and received his agreement that, knowing this Ladies Captain, there was no apology that would be accepted, at this juncture, by waiting around for Mrs Phillimore's return.

"Send her some flowers next week or something, Tom. She'll have a bee in her bonnet today. I'll enjoy taking the flak in your absence. Remember me in your wills, please!"

They all drove over to Richard's house in Tom's car for lunch. Richard made no mention to his parents of the morning's charade.

Richard's mother's Sunday lunches were legendary. If you were invited, you dropped everything else. They were always noisy affairs, the wine Premier Cru and they often lasted until the early evenings. Apart from the Inneses (Mum, Dad, Richard, and his sister, Annabella) and Tom and Roly, the party had been joined by the Greenlocks and the Blakely's, local long-term friends of the Inneses and a fund of risqué stories and good patter.

Richard Innes made the introductions as he heard the crunch of a car coming up the drive with the last couple. He hadn't checked with his mother who it was, but he knew it would be another couple of girls to keep Roly and Tom amused.

Richard went through the hall and opened the front door to greet them on the drive, and his jaw dropped. It nearly hit the floor! Clambering out of the Mini that they were driving in were Jane Phillimore and her sister, Natasha. They hadn't seen Richard for a while and offered him a smile and a peck on the cheek.

"Christ," thought Richard, "this must be a bad dream. It just ain't real." But the Phillimore girls showed no awkwardness, no hostility, and they were here. If they knew about this morning's escapade, they would surely have made their excuses.

"Come in, come in," beckoned Richard.

The significance of these two turning up was lost on Roly.

Jane Phillimore was a rather stern girl, difficult to force a smile from, lips like they had just been stung by a bee, and no great conversationalist. Natasha Phillimore, on the other hand, was something else. Slim and tall, vivacious and engaging, beautiful hair and smiling eyes.

Natasha and Roly sat next to each other at lunch. It was pretty poor form, really, since they had eyes and ears for no one else right the way through lunch. For two hours, they talked solidly, barely did justice to the food, and were the last to get up when everyone went through to the Innes's Drawing Room for coffee.

In fact, they went into the garden. It was cold, and Roly gave Natasha his scarf. As they passed the large, modern Greenhouse, Roly feigned interest in the huge leaves that were growing there. The Inneses were cultivating all sorts of tropical plants, and the greenhouse was kept at a constant temperature all year round.

Natasha could tell that Roly couldn't care less about tropical plants. She had a haunted and worried look on her face. She knew what was going to happen, but her heart was pounding, and she felt helpless. It took all of 5 seconds, and as Roly put his arm around her waist, Natasha whipped round and buried herself in his body. Natasha was shivering with lust and desire. As she wrapped her arms around his shoulders, he lifted her from the floor, and new meaning was given to the table, which was used for 'potting' plants.

Later that week, Tom and Richard had their Club membership withdrawn for 12 months.

September 1972

Mosel Valley: The Harvest

The cork that Kevin was pulling from a bottle of Mosel Riesling came out with a distinct pop and caught Roly's attention as he entered the Westridge Bar that evening. Johnny Jeffries had selected one of his favourites as an accompaniment to the fish that was on the menu.

"Care to join me, Roly, old chap? Good little number this one. Developed a fondness for Riesling and the Liebfraumilch when I was in Germany flying Phantoms, though Blue Nun put paid to any reputation that Liebfraumilch used to have! I don't suppose that your grand lot touched either of them!"

Johnny's remarks pricked contrary memories of an embarrassing event in Germany when, back from an attachment to the Royal Green Jackets in Belfast, he had taken a detachment of men to the Mosel Valley.

The 11th Hussars (Prince Albert's Own) had a long association with royalty. In Victorian times, the 11th had been home to Prince Albert of Saxe-Coburg, subsequently husband to Queen Victoria and whom Roly's grandfather had known, and, more recently, Prince Michael of Kent, serving in the 1970s and the Earl of Ulster. Other than two rather inconvenient wars, the Regiment's long association with Germany and its own aristocracy had served the regiment well. When Roly passed out of Mons in 1970 and arrived in

Germany, he was soon joined by another connection with his illustrious grandfather's past.

Gunther von Custer, the grandson of a former German noble, arrived from Sandhurst some 3 months after Roly had settled in. There had been a long tradition of association between the British and German armies, and Gunther, despite the fact that he was now second-generation English and had attended a British public school, was reflective of this. His commission into the 11th Hussars seemed almost inevitable.

In fact, von Custer's father had a proud war record. He had served as a regimental commander with the 1st Panzer Division during the Battle of France in 1940 and then had survived the Eastern Front from June 1942, where his division was destroyed during the Battle of Stalingrad.

In December 1943, he was assigned command of the 79th Static Infantry Division based in Normandy, France, and was there when the invasion took place, and thus fought in the early days of the Battle of Normandy, quickly becoming trapped as remnants of the Division fell back on Caen.

Von Custer surrendered to the Commander of the U.S. 9th Infantry Division and was important enough to have been held at Trent Park Interrogation Centre in Cockfosters before he was transferred to Island Farm in South Wales and then released in October 1947. Little did he know that his son Gunther would serve in the same unit that he had confronted at both Caen as well as their withdrawal to Dunkirk in 1940! Indeed, weirder than that, Von Custer's ancestor and

Flashman's grandfather had even once been on the same side when, immediately following the great victory at the Battle of Waterloo, on 19th June 1815, the 11th Hussars had been attached to Blucher's German forces in the pursuit of the defeated French army towards Paris.

All the younger members of the 11th's Officers Mess were quietly in awe of Flashman. Immensely impressed that they might have been of Roly's grandfather's connection to the Regiment and quietly proud of his dubious exploits, they were still fearful that his worse traits and character might be repeated in his grandson. They would not wish to be the victim of this modern-day officer's antics.

Despite their trepidation, they were soon to think otherwise. Roly's upbringing had taught him to be the opposite. He poked fun at pomposity, questioned the sometimes pedantic formality of the Regiment, promoted professionalism among his colleagues, and was a reliable companion.

Although some of the stuffier staff officers in the 11th rather resented this, it was difficult for Roly's colleagues not to go along with the example (or otherwise) that Roly set, and any high jinks were simply in keeping with a long tradition.

The best cure for a hangover is being fit, and outside of the cricket season, Roly's regime included Squash, Riding, and Running. It was needed due to the near-nightly parties in the Officer's Mess Keller ('Cellar') bar attended by not only the QARANC nurses and

Army teachers but also a growing number of German civilians from the nearby town of Hanover.

Gunther (or Krautie as he was now known by his colleagues) was a draw for these young local ladies whose presence also attracted a number of the Regiment's staff officers, with or without their wives!

Roly and Krautie were firm friends. Krautie's weekends involved activities generally unavailable to the young British officers. There were house parties in Bavaria at the family ski lodge, invitations to attend the Olympics in Munich, riding out with the local hunts, and attendance at dinners held by local aristocrats, always much more formal affairs than anything Roly had experienced with the British well-to-do. The two had also been back to London together – for a weekend – twice in four months.

It made a change from the rather seedy trips to Hamburg, the local strip joint, or gambling excesses in the Mess that was the normal outlet for British Army Officers at that time. What's more, Krautie was very generous.

That late summer, Roly had been wondering about his future.

He had just returned from an attachment to The Royal Green Jackets in Belfast as commander of three Ferrets, armoured vehicles pretty useless in those circumstances for anything other than an apparent deterrent to the thicker Irish who weren't to know. Although he loved Regimental life, the prospect of a career spent on the north German plains in the uncomfortable Chieftain tank defending West

Germany against possible Warsaw Pact incursions during the Cold War and a diminishing prospect of interesting postings as Britain's international influence dwindled was unappealing. There seemed to be two alternatives. The first to leave the Army altogether and head for either London or Africa. The second option had been sold by a fellow officer, just returned from a three-year flying tour with the Army Air Corps. It sounded tremendous, so Roly thought he might just as well attend a two-day Flying Aptitude Test at Biggin Hill and see if this option remained. As with most things in his life, Roly passed the interview with flying colours and was offered the chance to start at Middle Wallop in Hampshire the following July.

Meantime, things settled into the well-worn routines of a tank regiment training for deployment against the Eastern bloc; maintaining readiness, live firing exercises, speedy deployment, sport, and adventure training. Roly had the idea that the men of 'B' Squadron might like to participate in the vendage in the Mosel valley and, after consultation with his squadron commander and the CO's blessing, he tested the feasibility of this on Krautie, who thought it to be an excellent idea. He would ring around his contacts and see what he could do. And so it was that, in late September, some 40 men, including NCOs and two other officers, came to be billeted in the old cow sheds within the keep of a medieval fortress, Hoffenberg Castle, with the Roth family. The Roths had been making wine, for over 500 years, from the steepest and best vineyards in the Bernkastel area, producing internationally renowned Rieslings, best known for their apple and fruit tree notes and sugary undertones.

Old man Roth was close to retirement, and the wine-making side of this family business was effectively being run by Willi Roth, Krautie's friend, and his beautiful wife, Helga.

The awesome castle, complete with crenulations and turrets, seemed to rise high above the Mosel valley, eerie in its grandeur and daunting in its presence. For all that, once inside its imposing walls, it has a very friendly atmosphere for the visitor and is also home to a number of the winery's employees in cottages around the castle's inner courtyard contributing to the close-knit community atmosphere.

External labour was always extensively used at harvest time by the vineyard owners. The men of the 11th would get free wine but would otherwise self-cater, and, for this reason, compo rations had been taken, and one of the regimental chefs had gone with them to set up a field kitchen. Although the accommodation was basic, there was the incentive of as much wine as you could drink at the end of the day! It would be good physical exercise and a chance to foster relations with the locals.

In many ways, the grape harvest in the Mosel is no different than in all winemaking regions. Teams are buzzing with conversation. Tractors are constantly on the move. There is shouting, laughter, and singing. And yet the Mosel has its own very specific rituals and factors that make this a unique experience. Fog, for one. Not only does the river "smoke", but the whole region is also then embraced under a mantle of fog. But then, suddenly, seemingly out of nowhere, the Sun cuts through the fog, and the harvest can start!

It boils down to manual slave labour, really. The slopes of the Mosel are very steep. Some vehicular access is possible, but the back-breaking work of carrying baskets full of grapes to a central collection point still has to be undertaken.

After the first 24 hours, the men, who had endured a cold and damp misty morning, only for it to turn into a blisteringly hot afternoon, had been savouring the idea of all the booze that they could drink, were completely knackered. Still, nothing ever stopped the determined squaddie, and enough wine was downed, under Roly's careful gaze, before an early check-in and kip.

That is except for Trooper Brakspear. When Brakspear wasn't performing the role of Loader in Roly's Chieftain Battle tank, representing one of the four under Roly's command, he was Roly's Batman. Brakspear could be surly and was a shirker, which is why Roly elected to have him in his own tank so that he could keep an eye on him. Batmen still existed but not in the historical sense as an officer's servant. Although a Batman's duties extended to the preparation of his officer's ceremonial dress, this was due to the need for officers to do their jobs rather than spend all day polishing. Consider a batman to be a military PA rather than a servant. If good, they were quite often promoted or deliberately kept the job long term, as they liked it so much.

Neither was the case with Brakspear, a London East Ender, intelligent but frustrated by his own shortcomings and character failings. As far as Brakspear was concerned, he saw no reason why the frigging officers couldn't run their own errands, bull

111

their own kit, and prepare their own food. He didn't like the ribbing he got from his squaddie peer group about being the officer's lapdog, and when either Roly or his Troop Sergeant, Smith, had him up for a task done badly or unfulfilled, which was a regular occurrence, he got the hump and never seemed to learn from his mistakes.

B Squadron had returned from their second day's picking as knackered as anyone could be. All day they had picked grapes and then plodded either uphill or downhill to a central collection point. The day wasn't over until 7 o'clock, and they got back to a prepared meal of Chicken Supreme and Rice, eaten outdoors on hay bales around a big brazier that had been lit, and some very cool beers, courtesy of Roly's generosity.

Roly could tell they were tired as none of them were quite savouring the thought of wine with their meal, but a couple of fresh beers just hit the spot before they turned in for a good night's sleep. That is all except Brakspear and the two Chefs.

Having claimed to be feeling sick at reveille, Brakspear had managed to bunk out of any work that day, remained at the castle to help the chefs, and had been drinking wine pretty much all day. By the time Roly's men returned from the slopes, he was already well-oiled from the free supply provided by the castle. It was only 9:20 pm, the Sun hadn't even gone down, and everyone had disappeared to their bashers, bar Brakspear, and the Chefs. What was the point of looking a gift horse in the face?

And so, as they sat around the flaming brazier, the first cork of another bottle was pulled. The conversation had its usual measure of grousing about their circumstances, about fresh-faced young officers who didn't know what they were doing and whether any of the others had seen that tall leggy blonde with the pigtail and big breasts who seemed to cross the courtyard several times a day?

"I wouldn't mind giving her one," opined Brakspear with a knowing grin.

"Two's up," replied one of the chefs. "She might like some British sausage for a change."

They had just finished their fifth bottle of wine, and it was 11 o'clock when Brakspear, ignoring the next day's workload, started to sing a raucous and self-congratulatory rendition of "Three German officers crossed the line," delivered hesitantly and then repeated when they had remembered all the words.

As the final carousal ended with the words "Inky binky parlez-vous," it seemed that Brakspear and his mates hadn't disturbed anyone. Nothing moved outside other than the flicker of the flames so, seeing as there was no reaction from any of the Germans that he knew lived around the courtyard that they were in, Brakspear thought he would try his luck with another...

"Hitler has only got one ball..."

He got no further. A window in the courtyard opened, and a man leant out.

"Bleib Ruhig Englander. Sie sind hier ein Gast" and the window shut again.

"Who the hell was that?" said Brakspear. "Who does he think he is, bloody Squarehead?" before launching into the British National Anthem. "God save our Gracious Queen...happy and glorious... God save our Queen."

A German and his wife came out of one of the houses. Sergeant Smith came out of the barn.

"How dare you insult us like that? You come here as guests of the Roths, and this is how you repay them."

Sergeant Smith, who was Roly's troop sergeant, was equally furious.

"Get out of here, Brakspear, you ridiculous worm. And I want you up at 5 am, shaved and washed in your working dress." He apologised to the Germans and despatched the chefs in a similar manner.

Roly had been dining with the Roths. He, too, was tired, but he and his two fellow officers had had a very enjoyable evening in good company and with generous hosts. He knew nothing of the incident until being briefed the following morning by Sergeant Smith at 0730 hrs rollcall. The decision was taken to send Brakspear back to the Regiment but not before Sergeant Smith had personally supervised his apology to the Roths. Roly would deal with Brakspear and the chefs on return to barracks the following week.

Unfortunately, word got back to the CO, so it was hardly surprising that when the Light Infantry battalion, part of the same Armoured Brigade of which the 11th were members, requested a detachment of a Troop of Hussars and an Officer to augment their numbers for their forthcoming Northern Ireland tour, the CO thought fit to send Roly. Maybe the mess could get back to a sense of normality without his perpetually high spirits.

Roly's earlier trip that year to Belfast had been in charge of a troop of Ferret Scout cars attached to the Royal Green Jackets. This time, it would be different as his troop of 10 men would be out-and-out infanteers, on their feet, as one section complementing 6 Platoon of B company of which Roly was to be the Platoon Commander.

Brakspear was to come too. Four months later, and after going through training with The Light Infantry, Roly found himself in Belfast.

January 1973

Belfast: Prelude

Roly had been watching the news on his TV in his apartment in Westridge. It was full of the tantalising question of whether revised terms would be agreed upon with the EU for the UK's relationship with the EU on trade.

The Prime Minister, David Cameron, had resigned in June 2016, the day after the vote became known, and six months later, the new Prime Minister formally triggered the process and began the two-year countdown to the UK formally leaving the EU (commonly known as 'Brexit'). Negotiation on the terms of departure, in particular a trade agreement, had been difficult, and it looked, in December 2018, that the UK would crash out of the EU without any agreement. In some part this was due to the fact that terms could not be agreed on how to treat the Irish border, the sole land border with the EU. However, at the last minute, a protocol was agreed upon whereby certain goods entering Northern Ireland from the UK would be checked at Northern Irish ports by EU officials. Northern Ireland would otherwise continue to follow EU rules on product standards (known as the single market) to prevent checks along the border.

"That won't last," thought Roly to himself.

Unionists in Northern Ireland were strongly opposed to the checks because they didn't want Northern

Ireland to be treated differently to the rest of the UK, and the news was reporting demonstrations and protests as well as "sinister" threats being made to some border staff checking goods.

Roly went to bed, deeply depressed, recalling the same grey, leaden sky that the pictures on the News had been showing and hanging over Belfast like a shroud when he had been there. As he morphed into a deep sleep, it all came back so vividly. Every so often, as if in sympathy with the tortured province that it covered, the clouds would weep a shower of cold, sleety moisture, and the huddled pedestrians would scurry for sanctuary. Some, seemingly inured and insensitive, simply plodded on, their grey faces matching the grey buildings that reflected the morose clouds.

Somewhere to the west of the city, on the road out to Aldergrove Airport, the suburb of Ardoyne squats on the western fringes of Belfast. The old part of the Ardoyne is sited on the northern side of the Crumlin Road before you climb the hill to Ligoniel that commands a view across Belfast city. Most of the terraced houses there were built because of the patronage of the wealthy flax mill owner, a mill which had fallen into disuse and was now the base for the army battalion to which Roly was now deployed.

In time, the church of Holy Cross was completed in the early 20th Century, a feature that dominates the Ardoyne, like the Catholic community that it serves.

Protestant Shankill Road lay to the south of the Ardoyne. The shipyards that its' predominantly loyalist occupants served were some distance away.

Rather than try to breathe new life into the reeking slums there, the city fathers of the time had decided to build new houses elsewhere for skilled workers who wanted the newest and the best and sought to enhance the lot of those that remained by funding a municipal transport system, designed to be the pride of Europe. How were they to know that, in six short years in the early 70s, a future generation of buses would be turned into mobile bonfires, hijacked at will every time some Protestant bigot or Republican hell raiser decided it was time to turn mobs onto the streets?

Ligoniel had suffered little, comparatively, since 'The Troubles' had started in '68. The few Catholics who occupied the old tenements beside the mill and the even fewer who had managed to be allocated one of the properties on the new estate had been hounded out early in 1970/71 when the conflict had really escalated. Some had been threatened and had their windows broken.

Others had left to be with their own community, and the last, dauntless three families had decided that the brutal beating and tar and feathering of a young Catholic boy from Turf Lodge, engaged to a Protestant girl on the Estate, was the last straw and moved out.

So, because it was so comparatively peaceful, one of the ever-rotating commanders of 39 Brigade of her Majesty's Land Forces, based in Lisburn but responsible for Belfast, had decided that Ligoniel would be home-from-home for the quick reaction reserve company for Belfast district. As a result, the 120 men of B Company, 4th Battalion The Light Infantry, commanded by Major Simon Davenport, found themselves sharing the squalid, hastily prepared accommodation with 14 drivers from The Royal Corps of Transport, responsible for driving and maintaining the Saracens armoured cars and aging Humber 1 ton 'Pigs' that would deliver them to wherever they were needed.

Roly had been there before, attached and providing support to the Royal Green Jackets, with three ancient Ferret scout cars and a Saladin heavy armoured car. Roly remembered how totally pointless these had seemed. It was common knowledge, both to the soldiers and the whole Northern Irish community, that the cavalrymen were totally forbidden to use the .3-inch Browning machine gun armament on the Ferrets unless they were under attack by a heavy tank regiment and the only allowable circumstance for using the 75mm canon on the Saladin was the imminent arrival of Armageddon. Still, they looked impressive! This time, however, Roly would be on his feet and, together with the men from his troop in the 11th Hussars, supplementing B Company's numbers with his troop and in charge of 6 Platoon thereof.

Finally, just to ensure that no cranny went unused, the two floors of the mill also housed six cooks from the Army Catering Corps (speciality - bacon and egg butties 24 hours per day), plus personnel from the Royal Signals, the Royal and Electrical Mechanical Engineers, the Royal Army Medical Corps and a Sergeant and two Privates from the Ordnance Corps (bomb disposal, otherwise known as 'Felix Minor').

It also had a dog. Not a recognisable dog, but a truly ghastly mutt called Bomber.

119

Bomber was handed over from company to company as they rotated through the province. Several Company Commanders, appalled by this hideous apparition lurking by the Cookhouse door, waiting for scraps, had tried to ban him. To the soldiers, however, there was something special about Bomber. He was their mascot, their lucky rabbit's foot, so they hid him, fed him, never washed him, and protected him from mongrel-hating, Labrador-loving officers who were all bastards anyway, as every right-thinking squaddie knows.

Rumours abounded about Bomber. About how he got his name alerting a sentry when the IRA placed a bomb at the Sanger guarding the mill. About how he barked a warning when the IRA tried to shoot up the mill with a bazooka – probably all untrue but, to the soldiers, they made the legend.

The dog liked everyone and would sashay up to any pompous and distinguished, pedigree-Retriever-owning, Sandhurst trained, batman polished, mutt-hating Staff Officer, happily wagging his tail and peeing on the officer's immaculate boots and then look hurt when he was kicked and abused. The only person he did not like was Sergeant Frederikson, RAOC ('Felix Minor' as the bomb disposal personnel were known). Perhaps it was because he was named after a Cat, and Bomber did not like cats. This dislike was clearly getting on Frederikson's nerves. Frederikson performed one of the most dangerous jobs in the Province, trying to defuse the lethal concoctions of explosives and booby traps that the IRA littered around the city. He and his team were called out daily, often supported by one of B Company's platoons, and he would return from these nerve-wracking forays to be met by ankle-snapping yelps and snarls from Bomber.

Although it amused the soldiers immensely, it was getting him down because Sgt Frederikson actually loved dogs.

For some of the men of B Company 4LI, this was their fourth visit to the province in three years. This one was a four-month tour, the previous being a two-month deployment in July of the previous year for Operation Motorman, when the IRA-controlled, Catholic no-go areas had been opened up by the simple expedient of deploying a huge number of soldiers for a short time. The IRA had known they were coming for weeks beforehand and had moved out, lock, stock, and all the barrels of what they hidden under their floorboards, so all the military had had to endure was a bit of malevolent stone-throwing. In the year that followed, however, the shooting and bombing had increased as the IRA, confident of political support from America and armed to the teeth by a mad Libyan, Colonel Muammar Gaddafi, increased the tempo to try and break the resolve of the British Government to continue to uphold the peace and retain the sovereignty of the six counties of Ulster.

They seemed to be getting there too. Political pressures from abroad had forced the Government to abandon internment and release some of the most dangerous men in the IRA back to the streets. Restrictions had been placed on interrogation techniques, and the mass intimidation of juries was reducing the judicial system to shambles. The commitment of the Labour Government started to be called into doubt.

For the men of 4LI, the fun had gone out of the game. In the good old days, they had discos and had been able to go down to the boozers in the City centre for the odd half day off. Now there was no fraternising at all, a policy that Roly thought probably made sense, but it was as if none of them spoke the same language.

Roly's circumstances were not helped by his Company Commander, Simon Davenport. Davenport was a cold and reserved man who had spent an unusually long time away from the regiment. It is generally accepted that one of the great strengths of the British Army is the intensely close, family attitude of the regimental system, particularly in the infantry and cavalry regiments.

There is nothing artificial in this. A quick comparison of almost any modern regiment's roll call list will see the same names cropping up time over time, and Davenport's was one of these. Thus for a regimental officer to have spent in excess of ten years away from the Regiment was not only unusual but led to him losing touch with the soldiers that formed its core.

That little purple and green ribbon on the left breast of Roly's barrathea service dress, obtained from his previous tour as commander of a troop of ferret scout cars, had told his colleagues that Roly was not a novice and it was one more medal than Simon Davenport had. He had also struck lucky with Sergeant Smith coming with him from the 11th Hussars. Smith had been appointed as his new Platoon Sergeant, was a veteran from previous tours, and one that Roly knew would have done his homework.

At the end of pre-tour training, Smith had invited Roly back to the Sergeant's Mess for a beer one evening.

They already understood and trusted each other well, and after the 2 months of training leading up to this tour, Smith had quickly established that a combination of Davenport's chilly-eyed hauteur and not knowing his arse from his elbow was going to be bad news. Smith liked Roly, and he and his wife, Patti, had frequently had the young officer around for dinner. Patti seemed to adore Roly and was forever working out how to get him married. All that had achieved was Roly getting his leg over three of her best friends and being on the receiving end of a full-blown haymaker from Patti when she discovered about one of them. Smith and Roly never stood on ceremony when they were together, although it was the only time in his 15-year career that Smith had addressed an officer by his Christian name. Somehow with Roly, it didn't seem to matter. Now he tried to help.

"These LI guys are different, Roly. We've got a new Company Commander who doesn't know which end is up. A new CSM and he is a bastard, believe me."

"You've got 20 new guys under your command who don't really know you yet, and the other platoon commanders don't have your experience. If you are going to get through the next two months before we get to Ireland, you are going to have to go by the book a bit more. By the way, you need to watch out for that bugger Tregus too, and I'm not sure it was wise to put Brakspear in his section."

Corporal Tregus was one of the Platoon Corporals, a section commander, and an ebullient Cornishman who had been promoted and demoted so often that they had lost count. He had made it to Sergeant once. It was always the same with Tregus, first the drink and then the women. On his last tour, he had been busted after being discovered by his Platoon Commander humping a girl against the side of his Saracen down an alley in Andersonstown. The officer lacked a sense of humour and didn't appreciate Tregus' suggestion that the girl should give the officer a blow job, and they could then, perhaps, forget all about it. He was cunning and cynical and needed a firm hand.

"I know, Smithy," he replied. "Davenport's riding my case already. Did you see what he wanted us to do in training the other day?"

Roly's voice rose incredulously, "Platoons will advance in a box formation with long shields in the front rank. I asked him if he had indented for coffins for the whole Company as well, and he slapped me with a week's extra Orderly Officers."

Smith sighed, "That's what I mean, Roly. You've done it so often that its second nature to you, but Davenport has never had any sort of command in an operational zone. Also, you're a donkey walloper, and you've got a big mouth. If you want to change the way he does things, you'll have to do it by gentle persuasion."

"Ach, he's such an arrogant, pompous, and dried-out prick you couldn't change his mind with a sledgehammer. I don't know how his wife puts up with it."

124

Sergeant Smith didn't say anything to that. Davenport's wife was a very, very attractive, vivacious, dark-haired woman in her early thirties with a dangerous look in her eye. She had come into the Company office the other day, and there had been a bit of flirting with Roly while Davenport was out of the room. Smith just prayed that Roly had enough sense not to cap his career by screwing another officer's wife.

They'd finished their beers and gone their separate ways. Smithy's advice had proved out. The build-up to the tour had been uncomfortable, with Roly constantly at loggerheads over Davenport's ponderous thought process. There had been an ugly scene with the CSM, too, when the Warrant Officer tried to read the riot act about the casual way that he let the corporals call him 'Boss' rather than 'Sir'. A few days later, the CO had praised Roly for his professionalism which had seemed an excuse for Davenport to move on to the issue of discipline and the relationship between Roly and his platoon.

Davenport was a menace. He had an offensively cold manner and hated it when junior officers used his Christian name. He was a very good administrator and seemed almost happy that the company lacked a second-in-command, giving him the opportunity to ensure that the company's books were spic and span. It also gave him a chance to hand some of the administrative chores to Roly, the senior of the three platoon commanders. He was visibly upset to find that he could not fault Roly's paperwork.

125

But it was Davenport's soldier skills that really caught in Roly's craw. He couldn't get the simplest thing right and he stuck, desperately, to outdated formulas that even the CO found worrying. He was terribly slow and needed the CSM to gently prod him in more or less the right direction. Roly's attempt to treat him in a similar way was only met with distant contempt. On the last day of training before block leave, Roly took Sergeant Smith to one side.

"You've been quiet for the last couple of weeks, Smithy. If you've got some points, why don't we go over them now?"

"Actually, sir," Smithy replied, "I think you've got it pretty well taped, and the lads are sharp and confident. The Corporals seem pretty good though I'm not sure about Tregus. Still, can't give the dog a name yet, and I'll keep an eye on him." He paused. "You're the problem, sir, with respect."

He waited, not knowing how this tall young man was going to take it, but Roly merely raised his eyebrows, indicating that he should continue.

"There's no doubt that the OC and CSM have got it in for you, sir. I've had eight Troop or Platoon Commanders since I joined the Army, and for what it's worth, I'd say you were head and shoulders the best that I've served under. But you're too aggressive, sir, and you are a threat to them, and you need to calm down."

Roly considered the grave face of Smith, ten years his senior but a closer friend than most of his fellow officers, and his parting remarks over their last beer.

126

"Thanks," he said. "I'd appreciate you repeating that advice when you see it happening. Don't be shy about it, even if I'm looking pissed off." Smith laughed aloud.

"I can't remember the last time I was called shy."

They had had a party in the 4LI mess two days before they left for Belfast and Roly screwed Elizabeth Davenport. More accurately, she screwed him.

Davenport was above in the Ante Room, talking earnestly to anyone who would listen, and she and Roly had been dancing in the impromptu disco that the officers had constructed in the cellar bar below. It had been heaving with dancing couples, the tune was 'Bad Moon Rising' by Credence Clearwater Revival, and she had leaned across and, in a voice that he was sure the entire room heard, she said, "When are you going to take me to bed?" and laughed at the look of shock that crossed his face.

Later, in his room on the second floor of the Mess, they rested briefly, and he poured Champagne into a couple of toothmugs. She lay on her stomach, watching him with mocking cat's eyes.

"Why?" he asked. Her eyes brightened, and the mockery was reflected in her voice.

"Why have I chosen to honour you with the prize of my virtue?" The question tripped lightly off her tongue, but the sarcasm was brittle behind the apparently flip question.

127

"No, why Davenport? You're like chalk and cheese. What on earth holds you together?"

She made an irritated gesture, and her mouth formed a pouting distaste as she reached into her bag for a cigarette.

"Oh, Simon. He wasn't always like this, you know." Her voice became dreamy, as if she was looking into a trance. "He was quite dashing when we met and a brilliant dancer. Why is it that marriage makes men dull?" She cocked her head and looked at Roly quizzically. "Don't get married, Roly darling. Not for a long time – it wouldn't suit you. But, as for poor Simon – well, he is the father of my children – one of them for certain anyway; and he is going to be fabulously wealthy!"

He looked at her. She had rolled over and laid stretched out, languid, and despite having had a child, her breasts were round and firm, tipped by dark nipples with small areolae. She had long, firm legs, rising to a slender waist, curiously unblemished by stretch marks. He felt the need rising in him again.

"And this?" he asked, waving at their nakedness and the dishevelled bed. She laughed out loud.

"You mean, am I going to sacrifice all, leave Simon, and bind myself to you in sexual bliss forever, having tasted a moment of blind passion?"

"No. I mean, does Simon get treated to you indulging yourself like this on a regular basis, or does he still get a dip at the goodies now and then too?" Her mockery had irritated him, and his reply was sharper than either

128

of them had expected, prompted partly by his own feeling of guilt.

She slapped his face hard, wanting to hurt him. He had gripped her wrist, and they wrestled briefly before making love again.

In one of their brief pauses, he had been dripping champagne onto her breasts and gently sucking the frothing liquid off her erect nipples. She had been stroking his hair as she murmured, "He hates you, you know. He hates your size, your strength, your confidence, your bond with your men, and your sheer colonial bumptiousness." And she rolled over and pushed him onto his back, and looked intently into his eyes.

"You must be careful, my dear. He wants to see you hurt."

And she had lowered her head, kissing his neck and his chest and his hard, flat stomach, and she kissed the tip of his hard member again, grinning impishly and saying, "And if he knew what you had been doing with the big feller here, he would probably shoot you himself!" she smiled.

Autumn 2018

Westridge: Cordelia

Weekends at Westridge were always enjoyable. Cordelia Flashman was coming for lunch before the Autumn International against New Zealand. Watching rugby together had almost become a tradition. Cordelia was Flashman's 25-year-old niece. After his parents' divorce, Flashman's father remarried. His half-brother Boris was the outcome, and Cordelia was Boris's daughter. Despite the 12-year age difference, Flashman had become very fond of Boris, and they frequently spent time together in London, so when Boris was tragically killed in a road accident in Kenya, Cordelia looked to Uncle Roly for advice and company in difficult moments. In his memory, they both laughed a lot, referring to him as BF, she in accusatory terms for leaving her and Flashman because he had lost a good mate.

Despite an invitation to lunch at 1230 hrs, Cordelia had arrived at Westridge at 11 o'clock. When she came, she always liked to have a swim in the spa's heated swimming pool, and she was now sitting in the bar waiting for Flashman, duly refreshed. Kirsty came in, and they chatted for five minutes before Flashman joined them.

"Hello, Uncle Roly. How lovely to see you," said Cordelia as she stood up, hugged Flashman, and kissed him on both cheeks. "Hello, darling," responded Roly. "You're looking as gorgeous as ever, I see." Roly stood back. Cordelia was exceptionally pretty. She had inherited Boris's flaxen blonde hair, had naturally tanned skin the colour of honey, and kept her beautifully proportioned body in perfect trim without being skinny. Roly was glad to see Kirsty, the spa manager, there as well.

Roly perceived an opening. "Might you join us for lunch, Kirsty? My two favourite girls at once? It would make an old man especially happy, and you two seem to know each other!"

"I suppose you've come to see that lucky boyfriend of yours whom I never seem to meet. When are you going to introduce me, darling? I was hoping to walk you down the aisle one day. Don't forget to drop in on Granny Anne. She always loves to see you and hear your news."

"I know, Roly," said Cordelia, appearing embarrassed and looking down at her feet. "Trouble is my current boyfriend is always working on Saturday mornings, but we'll get there one day. He's certainly looking forward to meeting you! How is your mum?"

"Brilliant, really. Always suggesting that there is a conspiracy amongst the staff to get hold of her jewellery and likes to think she keeps a bottle of brandy hidden in her cupboard for a secret tipple every evening. There is a great Matron called Critchley who seems especially concerned about her welfare, really, and I pop in a couple of times a week."

Kirsty was pleased to join them, and Roly wondered how much better a Saturday could get. The anticipation of a game was sometimes better than the reality. In the past, pints of "Big Match Atmosphere" with mates at the Barmy Arms beside the river in Twickenham had been the norm, joyously followed, more often than not, by more pints of "Disaster Relief" after the game, food at a restaurant in Fulham Road, unimagined hilarity somewhere and, then, barking at the ants in the gutter at 1 a.m.

Before lunch in the Dining Room, they went for a little stroll around the grounds and had a beer at the Golf Club. The most extraordinary thing then happened on the way back. Roly spotted someone who looked like the spitting image of his former batman in the 11th Hussars, Brakspear, getting out of a Mercedes at the side entrance to Westridge. He was carrying a briefcase and dressed in a suit, somewhat worn and without a tie. He walked with a limp, had the other hand in his pocket, and, frankly, looked pretty unhealthy. He had aged badly and appeared overweight and balding, but there was no mistaking him. Excusing himself to Kirsty and Cordelia by saying that he would meet them in the Dining Room in ten minutes or so, Roly walked over to see if he was mistaken.

Roly was on the wrong side of Brakspear to notice the vivid scar on Brakspear's face.

"Well, well, well. Brakspear! It is you! Thought my eyes were deceiving me just then, but there will only ever be one Brakspear, eh? Still don't know how to brush your shoes, I see."

It must have been some 30 years since their last encounter. The uproar, at the time, caused by Roly being discovered in the MOD in London, in flagrante delicto with not only the Junior Minister for Defence but also her 20-year-old work experience assistant, Oxford UOTC student Vanessa Richards, and the gleeful press coverage that ensued, left the Army and Flashman's regiment, in this current day and age, red-faced and with little option but to have him court-martialled, all but for a second time, for conduct unbecoming of an officer.

Winking at the Army Legal Service female judge conducting the Court Martial looked likely to have sealed his fate. But the media presence and the enormous crowd that had gathered outside, on Northumberland Avenue, on the news of his predicament, had cheered him up and caused someone in the Government to intervene on the grounds of the nation's security.

"Good old Flashers," the crowd had cried, "Just like his grandfather." The outcome had been predictable, so Roly had felt in reasonable spirits and hoped that the future would hold no real obstacles. No-one knew how he had kept his pension rights, but the suspicion was there that he knew more than just the size of the Junior Minister's bra.

If romping with two women at once was "conduct unbecoming", then it was just as well that the press hadn't delved into the full details of Flashman's past relationships. Anyway, public pressure and some strange influence within the government had intervened, concerned at any further revelations that might emerge at Flashman's hand, and although the charges were withdrawn, Roly was informed that if he did not immediately hand in his resignation, his Brigadier's pension would be seriously imperilled.

One week later, he had driven down to Tidworth on the edge of Salisbury Plain, a place that, with its many chimneys, Flashman thought bore the unique distinction in Hampshire of looking like a depressed mining town with everyone waiting for the next pit disaster.

Roly knew Tidworth well as he had often played Polo and Cricket there for the Army. Currently, it housed the Officer's Mess of the King's Royal Hussars who were dining him out. The evening had descended into the usual havoc. The subalterns had egged him on, sustained by some Remy Martin XO and the legendary Kummel.

Autumn had come early to the Colonel's wife's flower arrangements, and Flashman had demonstrated how golf balls could be driven through the Bar's frontage.

"Top shot Flashers," cried his fellow officers. Most of the chandeliers had gone. The mirror behind the bar had been blown out, and Flashman had woken up the next morning in bed, unable to move. He didn't know how he had made it there after knocking himself out in the ante-room Steeplechase (a horse had been brought in to jump the G-Plan 'tables occasional') all under the gaze of his illustrious forebear – his grandfather whose actions at the infamous Khyber Pass defeat in 1842 were depicted by a famous painting by James Rattray. It had been a notorious example of how the ineptitude and indecision of one senior officer could compromise the morale and effectiveness of a whole army, and

Flashman's grandfather was one of the few personnel to emerge both alive and with credit.

"Surprised they've still got the old bugger up," Flashman had mused, not above the fireplace (that was reserved for the Colonel in Chief, Princess Alice, Duchess of Gloucester) but at the other end of the anteroom and alongside that fool Cardigan in a wonderful painting depicting the Charge of the Light Brigade.

But the fondness that the regiment retained for his grandfather, their notorious bad boy, and the unique publicity forged by the publication of what had become known as the Flashman Papers had outweighed the damage that his grandfather had on occasions done to the Regiment's reputation. Far from it, it seemed that the King's Royal Hussars, as they were now known, had become the Regiment of Choice for a lot of aspiring young cavalry officers these days. The Royal Hussars, and its antecedents, the 11th Hussars, were no more. They had been done for by the same sweeping budgetary cuts visited upon the whole military.

So, after a momentous evening, Flashman had woken up in Tidworth and wondered where he was. He had thought that his legs were paralysed and started to panic. However, Brakspear, his grudging former batman who was still serving with the regiment, had helped him to bed and, vengefully, as a final act of insubordination and wishing to leave his mark on the retiring Brigadier, had stuffed both of Roly's legs down only one leg of the pyjamas that he was wearing.

That terrible momentary nightmare had stayed with him ever since. He would rather have forgotten about Brakspear. Unknown to Roly, and the reason for now bumping into him at Westridge, Brakspear, no doubt through some deviousness, had done well in the Civil Service career that he had carved for himself after the army. Somehow he had become Director of Social Services at the local Newclere Council. Although Residential Care Homes lay outside the normal remit of his job description, this seemed to give him leverage in taking an interest in the daily affairs at Westridge.

Brakspear had become aware of Flashman's impending arrival at Westridge and had tried but failed to succeed in putting a block on Roly's residence. Then, he had done his level best to at least ensure that he got the smallest apartment, as if there was anything other than a superbly appointed apartment throughout the complex. Brakspear ensured, however, behind the scenes, that Sister Critchley, the matron in overall charge, was allocated as his staff "point of contact" – a system where all residents were allocated a member of the Care Home nursing staff for any well-being issues.

But Flashman had frustrated Brakspear's best efforts by arriving at the same time that a previous flat occupant was being carried out feet first. As a friend of the owner of Westridge's Management Company and courtesy of a quick arrangement with Westridge Court's head porter cum head barman, Rajiv Singh ('Kevin'), Roly had secured himself a very comfortable apartment This was downstairs with access through large patio doors to a beautiful rose

136

garden and Roly had been unaware of the efforts that had been made to thwart his residence there. Brakspear had been furious, but Flashman had put down his anchor, and the vendors' estate was very pleased with such a quick sale of their leasehold interest.

"So it really is you, Brakspear!"

Brakspear looked up and considered his reply. He resented what Flashman knew about him, his own worst traits, and the difference in what he saw as the inherited privileges and disadvantages that they mutually represented. But twenty years in local government had given him confidence in his own rights as well as a seniority which gave him the forced respect of his colleagues. Here was Flashman, without so much as any regard for his achievements, even if he had known them, addressing him as if he was still on a parade ground somewhere in Germany.

"I'd probably be better off not seeing you, actually. I'm in a hurry and don't have time to dawdle. What do you want?" said Brakspear as he shuffled awkwardly towards the entrance.

"Whoops, this looks tricky. I better get straight to the point," thought Roly as he fell into a slow pace beside him.

"Well. I just wondered how you were. Someone said you had gone into local government. How come you are here, though?"

"I am the local Director for Social Services actually, Flashman, and it might pain you to know that I have a say in how this place is run," responded Brakspear, relishing the opportunity to drop the 'Mr' bit in return.

"I don't need to account for my actions to the likes of you," he said dismissively and limped on.

Roly stood there watching him go.

"Christ," he thought, "that was unpleasant. How does a prat like Brakspear get to such a position?"

Anyway, he quickly parked the encounter to the back of his mind. He and the girls enjoyed lunch together and, fortified by a delicious bottle of Malbec, went back to Roly's apartment and settled down to watch the rugby. As the two girls sat down on Roly's sofa and curled their legs up in anticipation, Roly couldn't help thinking how nice it was that they got on so well and felt so comfortable in his presence.

"Stop it, Roly," he said, mentally, to himself. It wasn't that he found Kirsty, alone, so attractive. He was now looking at them together, imagining them as a pair, attending to his needs, naked in bed... "Stop it, Flashers. Think of the combustion engine or something!" He was only 68 years old, after all, trim as anything and still able to attract the ladies' eyes, albeit not quite as young as Cordelia. The circumstances weren't quite the "screwing on the job" occasion at the MOD in 1988, giving proper meaning to the shag pile carpet in the Minister's office.

"God Flashers, don't you ever learn?! She is your niece, you know. You can't think like that," he mused to himself.

"But wouldn't that be delightful? Ah, stop it, nasty Flashers! Not again," he continued, fighting with his thoughts.

"Come on, Roly. Come and sit here," interrupted Cordelia. The big chintz-covered sofa was able to take the three easily, so he sat down between the pair to watch the match play out.

"Hope Critchley doesn't come now," he remarked to Kirsty, "she might get the wrong idea."

"Ahem, why's that, Mr Flashman?" Kirsty replied. She had partially unzipped her tracksuit top, and Flashers could see her breasts quite easily above the low-cut vest that she was wearing underneath, stretched by their fullness, the nipples clearly hard. She quite obviously knew the point of Flashman's remark. All three of them, fortified by another bottle that Flashman had opened, had sung a rousing National Anthem, watched the Haka, got to their feet when England scored, and acted out "Swing Low, Sweet Chariot".

It was an epic match. England 15-16 New Zealand. The All Blacks had fought back and then hung on to win a thriller by a single point after Sam Underhill's late try was controversially ruled out. Roly hadn't enjoyed himself so much for a long time. "Just the best antidote to a grey, cold afternoon," he thought. The girls had enjoyed it too. Cordelia was down again three weeks later when England were due to host the Fijians, so everyone made a note in their diaries for a repeat.

"Oh, Uncle Roly. You're so kind. Thanks for lunch, but we, I mean "I" must go. I won't forget about

139

popping in to see Granny Anne," said Cordelia, to which Kirsty added her thanks. Cordelia gave Roly a big hug and a kiss on both cheeks. Kirsty also gave him a kiss and squeeze on the arm.

"I didn't think I was supposed to have a relationship with the staff, Kirsty," said Roly.

"Well, I'm only fooling around. Duh!" with a naughty wink, Kristy also left.

January 1973

Belfast: Anatomy of a Riot

January 1973 proved to be a turning point in Roly's life. The tour had started fairly calmly. B Company had settled into the 2nd Floor of Ligoniel Mill, trying to find some shred of comfort and privacy. When the accommodation had been hastily erected in the huge floors of the Mill, the engineers had tacked together a series of cubicles out of two-by-four planks and hessian. The idea had been to attempt some sort of segregation for those on rotational duties through a 24-hour cycle. It had never been intended that the cubicles be permanent. Four years later, they still stood, tatty, greying with the smell of old socks and cooked cabbage seemingly ingrained in the rotting fibres.

The soldiers seemed housed in accommodation that could have been used as a film set for one of the Gulags. And there was no privacy.

Roly had allocated Brakspear to Tregus's section. It seemed the best place for him. Brakspear's habits and cunning would be no match for Tregus's experience, who had seen it all before.

Officers and Sergeants shared a mess. It was just a boarded-up area next to the Ops Room, but they could relax after a fashion, and they could not be overheard. It had a dining table at one end and a television set at the other, surrounded by a motley collection of old armchairs and a couple of sofas.

141

When they arrived, Davenport had gravely produced a couple of bottles of Hungarian 'Bulls Blood' wine and solemnly toasted to the success of their tour. Roly winked at the long-serving platoon sergeants who had difficulty in not laughing at the preposterous nature of Davenport's behaviour.

For the first few days, there had been little to occupy the men. The ready platoon was called out regularly to provide protection for Felix. Otherwise, there was just some routine patrolling, the odd roadblock, and the daily exercise in keeping school children of opposite faiths separated on their journeys home from school along the Crumlin Road, which, unsupervised, had had a historic tendency to develop into full-blown riots between the two communities.

The first excitement came in the middle of the second week. Roly's platoon was 'at the ready' when the call came through that there was serious rioting in the Unity Flats area, a Catholic enclave at the bottom of the Shankill Road quite close to the city centre.

Roly was ordered to take his platoon down to Leopold Street police station and wait for orders.

The Saracens had already been loaded with their rifles as well as the riot shields, baton guns, and the visor-equipped steel helmets that they would need. The men lounged around the open doors of the big, six-wheeled armoured personnel carriers, smoking, and chatting. With their green berets moulded to their heads and the heavy padding of their flak jackets giving them bulk, Roly thought that they looked like a competent crew, but he wished that Brakspear would man up a bit.

142

When the word to move came, they piled into the vehicles, and Roly's lead carrier was rolling out of the Mill gates within seconds.

The Saracen engine had a very distinctive whine - one of the most distinctive noises in Ulster. They raced down the Crumlin Road, veering left at the junction with the upper Shankill, by the Holy Cross Catholic Church, with the mean, hate-filled streets of the Ardoyne to the left and the steaming slums of the Shankill to their right, and sped onto Leopold Street. There were few passers-by to watch them, even if they had been interested. Most streets looking out onto the Crumlin Road had been blocked off with ten-foot-high barriers of corrugated iron. Festooned with graffiti, they were little more than banners of hate. This was the so-called 'Peace Line' between the Protestant Shankill and the heartland of Catholic Republicanism, the ultimate home turf of the Belfast Brigade of the IRA, the Ardoyne.

When they got to the heavily fortified barracks at Leopold Street, Roly was told to move out without delay and report to the Colonel of the famous Scottish Regiment, whose two companies were taking the brunt of rioting at Unity Flats.

The Colonel was a short, aggressive man. He barely acknowledged Roly's salute before spreading out a fablon-covered map of Belfast on the bonnet of the Saracen. The map had been coloured in purple and yellow to depict the tribal loyalties of the populations of the various parts of Belfast.

"All right, young man," he said, nodding in return to Sergeant Smith's salute as he joined them. "This is where the aggro is at the moment," pointing to a cluster of small streets at the edge of the flats. "Usual story. All the 'prods' on their way home from the match and half a dozen, pissed as newts, decide they are going to finish the Fenian problem, once and for all – result – two sets of bloody-minded bog trotters enjoying a traditional Saturday in Belfast. Can't have done more than half a million quid's worth of damage yet."

The returning supporters from the football match were usually quite well-shepherded, so Roly asked, "How did they get through?"

"There's more trouble down the Falls, so the Fusiliers are short-handed. They had the street covered by a Land-Rover mobile, but the Prods just ran over it, and then the shit hit the fan."

"Your Company Commander and another platoon are on their way down here, but I don't think I can wait for them. I want you to position yourself here, fast," he said, pointing to a crossroads just below the area affected by the rioting. "I'm putting in one of my companies to clear any Prods out of the flats. When my Jocks go in, they will be holding these three streets, so I want you to move up to this same location in their lieu. Fast and hard. Use the three Saracens in line abreast across the road."

He looked closely at Roly, sensing his youth and seeing his non-infantry cap badge " Have you done this before?" he asked, and his gaze passed to Smith behind

Roly's shoulder as though seeking the older man's opinion.

As a wry smile crossed over Sergeant Smith's face, the CO knew the answer at once. Here was a young officer whose professionalism would match his height and square jaw, and he relaxed visibly at the way Roly assimilated his instructions.

"Don't worry, sir. I know this patch. I was here last year for Op Motorman."

"Well, you know the form then. Your Colonel..." he paused and seemed to change his mind. "Do you know who I mean by Liam Deggan?" he asked. He was referring to one of the more notorious IRA suspects. Deggan was a well-known marksman and was reputed to be responsible for the deaths of several soldiers in the previous six months. His trademark was to fire one round from an Armalite, making him very difficult to trace – one round, always lethal, always a headshot.

"Well, we think he's in the Flats, so make sure your boys are on the lookout. Not that that'll help much with Deggan." The Scotsman looked grim and became brisk. "Cut along then. You've got four minutes to be in position. Report when you get there, and we'll be going in virtually at once."

Roly and Sergeant Smith clambered into the command Saracen, and Roly called for his three section corporals to join him. He briefed them while Smith led the small convoy down to the crossroads. Roly called that they were in position as the three corporals ran back to join their own sections. They had barely had time to close the doors when the Scot's Colonel's voice came over the command net.

"Two Three, this is Niner. Move now. Go, Go, Go." Switching to the platoon net, Roly called out, "All units Two Three, move now. Two Three Bravo and Two Three Charlie; one of you on either side of me, and make sure you cover the pavement gaps. Two Three Alpha, I want you behind in the hollow we create. Sunray wants a few arrests."

Two three Bravo was Corporal Tregus' section, and his Saracen moved up alongside Roly as they made a left turn into the street leading to the main thoroughfare, completely blocking the street. Roly could see the milling crowd of youths through the periscope of his vehicle as they mocked the young Scots soldiers beyond them. Shouting, taunting, hurling stones, and every so often, throwing a petrol bomb.

As he watched, the crowd seemed to stagger and pause, and even though the mount of the Saracen was closed, Roly could faintly hear the volley of baton rounds fired by the Scots company as they advanced down the road. The youths in the crowd were starting to turn and run back up the road, away from the advancing Scots, when Roly's four Saracens came rocketing out of the side road into the middle of the crowd, completely undetected until that moment.

Sgt Smith had done two short tours in the province in the early days of "The Troubles" when minimum force meant exactly that, and the little public disorder that there was had been handled with tact or tear gas. Gas was now banned. So he was totally unprepared for what happened next. It bore no relation to the rather sanitary preparation exercises that they had just gone through in Germany.

Roly's four twenty-ton armoured cars drove straight into the crowd facing them. How no-one was run over, he would never be able to explain. They stopped in a tight arrowhead, protruding halfway into the main road and completely blocking the side street from which they had emerged. This had the effect of creating an impassable obstacle against which the panicking crowd of erstwhile rioters, trying to escape the charging Scots, built up like the rolling waves of the sea bursting on a long pier. This was definitely not in the training manual, which said that you should always give rioters a clear exit.

Then Roly's men poured out of the vehicles, and Smith watched spellbound as they tore into the crowd with vicious and determined aggression that was outside his experience. The long, Macrolon bullet-resistant shields, much loved by Major Davenport, were nowhere to be seen. Smith watched as Tregus' eight men spewed out into the road. The first of them was Private Clark, a rather docile young man from County Durham who had joined the army in order to stay out of the pits. As his feet hit the ground, he lifted the one-and-a-half-inch calibre Greener gun to his shoulder and fired the six-inch long black rubber bullet directly into the groin of a gaping youth who had turned to look at them about five feet away. The boy screamed and doubled over in agony.

147

This was really not in the book. The instructions were very clear that rubber bullets were not, repeat not, to be fired directly at human targets but were to be fired into the ground in front of them, relying on the ricochet effect to disperse the velocity and merely incapacitate the target. Glancing quickly around, Smith saw that all four of Tregus' Greener operators were ignoring standing orders and firing directly at their targets from very close range, relishing their roles, although Brakspear, who was assigned as cover for the section, had a worried look on his face, sweating profusely and obviously shaking. The young soldiers were loading and firing as fast as the cumbersome and soon-to-be-obsolete single-shot weapons would allow. From the other side of the road, there were more reports as the Fusiliers blocking the side roads to the north fired into the passing crowd as the Scots charged down the street.

All around him, Smith's own corporals and their men, directed by the young Lieutenant, were darting in and out of the heaving throng in pairs, snatching anyone who had been knocked down by a baton round without being over careful themselves with the use of their truncheons. In the hollow area behind the Saracens, there was a growing group of groaning, cursing, and vomiting prisoners, their arms secured behind their backs with disposable plasticuffs and a demeaning label attesting their names and who had arrested them.

It was the familiar clatter of the cocking action of the L1 A1 Self-Loading Rifle that made Smith whirl and look behind him. Two of the soldiers from C Section, concealed in doorways some 20 yards down the street they had just driven out of, had been looking back the way they had just come, their weapons trained on the threatening high roofs behind the platoon. Both men were marksmen, and their weapons were fitted with the RARDE optical sight, a kind of miniscope giving the firer a 3x definition of his target. The target acquisition arrow in the sight had a tiny phosphorescent tip for night firing.

"Watch out, Sarge," cried one of the soldiers. "There's a guy with a rifle, looks like a hunting rifle, on the balcony of the right-hand flat, one down from the top."

At that moment, the street was lit by the headlights of a Landover turning up from the crossroads. "OC coming, Sarge," said the soldier, whose name was Fendall. Smith's heart dropped. The inexperienced Davenport was the last thing he needed right now.

"You," Smith called out to Fendall, and the other soldier in the adjacent doorway looked up at him. "Load. Quickly!" The soldier snapped back the cocking handle of his rifle and then released the action to feed one of the deadly 7.62mm copper-jacketed bullets into the chamber. "Keep your eyes peeled, both of you. If you identify a target, call me! Do not open fire unless he has or you think he is about to." Smith realised he had just taken the dangerous step of following Roly Flashman down the slippery slope of putting common sense before the Holy Grail of Standing Orders.

The rules of engagement were very precise about what constituted grounds for shooting someone. The mere fact that a man was carrying a rifle in a riot was insufficient. Everyone in the Army knew that the little

Yellow book containing these rules was the serviceman's passport to suicide. It was the politician's shield and a General's passage to a pension. Smith had just given a young soldier an order that directly contravened the guidelines in the Yellow book.

Frankly, he didn't care after what the Scots Colonel had recently warned as he darted back to warn Flashman about the arrival of Major Davenport. He got to the lead Saracen just as there was a roar from the crowd, who were now effectively pinned between the advancing Scots and Roly's Saracens. As he peered across the bonnet, looking for Roly, he realised that the behaviour of his own men was nothing compared to the carnage that the Scots were wreaking.

Showing complete contempt for the Irish rabble they were facing, the Jocks had scorned their own steel helmets for their fore and aft Glengarries with the bright red and white check and big silver cap badges. The officer in charge had grouped all his baton guns, about twenty of them, in at the centre of an advancing phalanx, marching up the street and firing in volleys. Smith thought it looked like a scene from the film 'Zulu'. On the flanks, the Jocks were using their truncheons like some sort of flail.

Looking around, Smith now saw Roly at the rear of the vehicles with all three of their sections. He was talking quickly into the radio attached to his flak vest. Almost simultaneously, every single baton gun in the advancing company of Jocks was fired, and the Jocks then went forward as one into the panic-stricken crowd and chasing them the full length of the street.

Smith's heart sank as he sensed Davenport standing a few yards behind, mouth wide open in horror. Davenport had seen the last throes of Roly's men in action prior to leaving it all to the Jocks, and even now, they were holding several young and scruffy Irishmen in arm locks as they fitted their plasticuffs.

"Flashman! Come here at once."

Clearly caught off guard by the presence of the OC, Roly looked up and over to Smith, who merely shrugged.

"In a moment, Simon," he replied, struggling to force a young Irishman's arm up behind his back to put the plasticuffs on.

"Now!" the senior officer screamed. Roly shoved the youth towards Tregus and walked over to Davenport.

"What the hell do you think you were doing?" The Major hardly bothered to lower his voice, and some of the young rioters, recently arrested, looked up with quickening interest. Roly, the adrenalin coursing through his system cooling quickly, was keenly aware of their presence.

"Not here, Simon," he cautioned.

He looked up and saw that the OC's Macrolon-protected Landover was parked behind one of the Saracens. The CSM had walked over to talk to Sgt Smith, but the driver, radio operator, and one of two riflemen who formed the crew were lolling against the vehicle, lighting up cigarettes. The other rifleman was poking out of the hatch at the back of the vehicle, entranced by the sight of the manacled football fans. He noticed Brakspear being sick beside the vehicle's wheels.

"I think you should get your crew undercover, Simon," he said. "The Jocks think Deggan is in the flats, and this is just his sort of scene."

The warning seemed to be the final straw for Davenport. He grabbed Roly by the arm and strode with him across to the Command vehicle. His voice was lower but filled with fury as he hissed.

"I know all about Deggan, and he has nothing to do with the case. I will not have the men of this company scrabbling about in doorways. You know full well that the Colonel and I have laid down strict rules against behaviour which merely serves to distress the civilian population. I want an explanation for your men's' disgraceful behaviour just now." He paused. "I have never witnessed such a shameful and barbaric display of naked aggression by British troops in my life in total disregard for orders. It's time you went back to your Cavalry Regiment, Flashman."

"But perfectly in line with the orders I issued when this young man was deployed under my command," The Scots CO had just come round the corner, and his voice held a silky menace. His eyes challenged Davenport to contradict him. Neither of them had seen his approach, and the rubber soles of his issue DMS boots had made him virtually silent. "That was a first-class performance there," he said, turning to Roly. "I shall make sure that both your CO and the Brigade Commander are informed that you carried out my orders to the letter and with considerable courage and skill."

Davenport had been about to reply when the high-pitched crack of an ultra-high velocity bullet passing overhead made everybody dive for cover.

Manacled rioters, all too readily recognising the distinctive sound of a live round, scrambled to get under the Saracens, and the soldiers of Roly's platoon either took cover or dived into the back of their APCs to retrieve their weapons.

The high-pitched crack of the incoming round was almost immediately drowned by the blast of a British Army SLR as Private Fendall returned fire.

"Enemy rifleman on the balcony, sir, second flat down, left end of the building," he shouted. Then, more quietly, "He's moved now, sir."

The Scots CO was talking urgently to his radio operator and his adjutant who had accompanied him. Davenport, who had not moved at the sound of the incoming round, stood with his feet rooted to the ground, looking around, his face dark in the subdued light of the infrequent street lamps, and his eyes seemed to bulge from their sockets. He turned again to Roly.

"That....that....that man," he squeezed the words out, pointing at Fendall, "must have had a live round in his chamber. How dare you allow such a gross violation of orders? I have no doubt that you are responsible. It

153

is totally typical of your cowboy approach in all that you do...."

"Major!" The Scots CO's voice cracked like a whip. "One of your men is dead." He nodded to where the second rifleman in Davenport's protection group was slumped in the hatch at the rear of the Landover. From where they stood, Roly could see that most of the back of his head was missing. "It is just possible that if you had listened to this officer's advice on getting your men into the cover instead of bleating, he would still be alive." He had made no attempt to hide his contempt or to shield Davenport from his censure in front of the many junior ranks watching.

The soldier, a twenty-year-old from Birmingham called Covell, was extricated from the Landover and driven away in one of the Saracens. But the danger had not yet receded, and Roly's platoon was patched into a hasty cordon around the block of flats where the shooting was thought to have come from, and the building was searched. No bodies were found, but it was thought that Fendall had been effective – heavy bloodstains were found on the balcony where he had been seen, and the occupants were arrested.

Covell's death threw a pall of depression over the Company and seemed to make Davenport even more morose and introverted. Two days after the incident, Roly received a letter from the Scots Colonel. It was a copy of the letter he had written to his own CO and the Brigade Commander, commending his actions that day.

At the bottom of the letter, the Scotsman had penned a P.S. "Watch your back and, next time, don't stick your APCs so far out into the road!"

Roly had been summoned down to Flax Street Mill for an interview with the new Colonel, which Davenport sat in on. The Colonel was in something of a cleft stick. On the one hand, he had received a highly complementary report from a fellow Battalion Commanding Officer about Roly's performance, which had been copied to the Brigadier of the 39 Brigade. On the other hand, he had received a scathing and bitter denunciation from Davenport. He had little doubt that Davenport's report better mirrored his own attitude. Against that, the Scots Colonel, on the phone, had laid the blame for Cowell's death squarely at Davenport's door and had been unflattering in the extreme about Davenport's troop handling through the rest of the deployment. So Roly received a milder reproach than he had expected, although there had been an explicit warning about violence by his troops and the excessive use of baton guns, plus a blanket ban on authorising his men to load live ammunition outside the Yellow Card guidelines.

The next four weeks had passed slowly. Davenport hardly spoke to any of the Company's officers and virtually never to Roly. He passed orders and schedules down via the CSM and retreated into a world of his own. Occasionally he would join a small patrol around the area, but even that ceased after a while.

He invariably ate on his own, having a small tray sent to his room.

Roly's platoon was sent twice more to crowd control situations, and on the second occasion, Roly again received an admonishment for excessive use of baton rounds. The whole platoon, indeed the whole company, realised by now that Roly was the target of a vendetta and tried to protect him by ensuring that their own discipline could not be criticised. The other two platoon commanders, newly arrived in the Battalion, stood off as if from fear of being tainted. Sergeant Smith was friendly but wary and knew that Roly was going to have to watch his step.

The depression that everyone felt came to a head on a grey morning. The one weak link in the platoon had always been Tregus. Roly had been impressed in the early stages with the way that he got on with the job and the way that he held the confidence of the soldiers in his section. Even Brakspear was towing the line, or "was it that they were two peas from the same pod?" wondered Roly. Recently there had been signs of old habits re-emerging on two occasions when he had come back from local patrols. Tregus had clearly been drinking and explained it away by saying that it was necessary if he was to chat up the local Ulster Defence Force protestant paramilitaries. Sergeant Smith had dealt with Brakspear privately about his drinking, and Roly never wanted to ask.

This, in itself, was not unusual. B Company frequently placed a roadblock on the main road leading to the airport, particularly when there had been an incident in the centre of Belfast. The roadblock nearly always went in at the same place, a road junction where three roads from the city converged and where there was a popular local Pub.

Over the years, the locals had built up a rapport with the squaddies and some of the men of B Company, 4LI, were familiar faces. It was not unusual for the locals to offer the ubiquitous Guinness. The other two platoon commanders, mindful of Davenport's ire, always refused. Roly, however, who had met most of the locals and was popular with them, could see little harm and, therefore, strictly only when the block or VCP (Vehicle Check Point) was being lifted, sometimes accepted a pint, discretely drunk in the back of a Pig or Saracen.

Tregus, typically, had extended the privilege to his own, local patrols, and it was pretty obvious that a lot more than one pint was being sunk. There was a hard and fast rule throughout the army in Ulster, limiting consumption to two pints per day. Roly and Sgt Smith had taken him out of the Mill and read him the riot act. He had wheedled and tried to excuse his behaviour but backed down when asked if he would like to be paraded in front of the Company Commander that afternoon. The drinking appeared to have stopped after that until the previous evening.

The 'Ready' platoon had been called out, and Roly's platoon's status had been lifted from 'resting' to 'reserve'. It was always the 'resting' platoon that carried out the local patrols. Tregus' section had been out on patrol, and Roly had tried to raise them on the radio in the Ops Room. The last message from Tregus had come from the new estate in Ligoniel, just below the Mill, which, in certain conditions and at night, could make radio communications difficult. From the front of the Landrover in which he and Sergeant Smith were now sitting, Roly called Tregus on the radio.

He thumbed the Pressel switch and called, "Hello, Two Three Bravo, this is Two Three, over."

There had been a long pause, and he was about to repeat the call when the handset squawked.

"Sunray, this is Two Three Bravo; reading you. Over."

This meant that, on a scale of one to five, Tregus was getting a signal that was relatively poor. This was surprising to Roly since Tregus' message had sounded rather strong. He pressed his Pressel again.

"Roger Two Three Bravo. Send locstats, over."

"Two Three. This is Two Three Bravo. I'm by the fish shop and moving shortly to Kilo four."

Roly, acutely aware that this conversation was taking place on the Company net rather than the Platoon net, replied.

"Two three Bravo. Stay where you are. Do not move to Kilo Four. I will meet you at your location in two minutes. Out."

Roly had a tight feeling in his chest. Something was wrong. Tregus was unlikely to be in difficulty in this area, and he had sounded composed, but when Roly arrived at the chippie, Tregus wasn't there.

"I knew that bastard was up to something," the Sergeant growled. "I heard a rumour that he's got a bird on the estate. If he's been tomcatting again, I'll rip his nuts off."

Three minutes later, a lone "Pig" careered around the corner, far too fast for safety, and pulled up beside the Landrover. Tregus looked at Roly's face and his scowling Sergeant and knew that he was in trouble. Roly strode over to the vehicle and looked in. Apart from a rather worried-looking Brakspear, who was silent but clearly pissed, and the driver, the vehicle was empty. Roly looked at Tregus and, with studied calm, said, "And the rest of your section is where?"

"Well, Sur, we sees these kids lurking behind the flats…"

"Don't bother Tregus. Get in the Rover," Roly said sharply.

"Do you know where the rest of your patrol is?" he asked the driver.

"Y…Y…Yes, sir," the man answered.

"Sarn't Smith. Take the 'Pig' and round up the Section. Get hold of Lance Corporal Collier and get the full story. I'll meet you at the base. Brakspear, go and present yourself to the Company Sergeant Major and tell him what you've been up to."

"Sir," pleaded Tregus as Roly climbed into the front of the Landrover.

"Not a word Tregus, not another fucking word, or I'll probably do something I'll regret." Tregus subsided, and they made their way the short distance back to the Mill.

When they got back to the base, Roly had ordered Tregus to go and sit in one of the other sections 'Pigs' and told another of his NCOs to keep an eye on him and the men away from him. He then reported into the Ops Room, had a quick word with the Company Sergeant Major about Brakspear, and told them the news that the section was on its way in and the Platoon had reverted to 'Reserve' status. He did not mention Tregus or give the impression that anything was amiss. He picked up a thermos of coffee and a couple of sandwiches and marched outside, calling for Tregus to join him.

Sitting down in the back of the empty 'Pig' with Tregus, he looked at the worried Tregus and handed him a paper cup of coffee and one of the sandwiches.

"Are you going to tell me, or are we going to have to wait for Sergeant Smith to beat it out of one of your chaps?" he asked quietly.

Tregus seemed to ponder, and then a look of resignation passed over his face, and he replied, with his Cornish accent, always strong but, now, noticeably thicker.

"Don't you'm trouble the Sergeant, Zur." He sighed. "It'll be moi lot this 'un, not just moi bloody stroipes."

The story came out. Tregus had run into a woman he knew from a previous tour. In those less sensitive days, the soldiers had run discos in their makeshift barracks, and all sorts had gone on. A lot of the soldiers had married Belfast girls and for many girls, getting on with a soldier was a passport out of the drudgery and hopelessness of the Belfast slums to the relative luxury

160

of married quarters and the financial security of army life. You could always tell where a military unit had served because of the nationality of the wives, but fully fifty percent of these marriages broke up within a couple of years.

Tregus had met the woman at the disco. She was married to a Harland & Wolfe foreman working on a lucrative contract in the Middle East, and she was bored and looking for some fun. Tregus had provided some entertainment, and they had managed to sneak a few assignations as well as the shenanigans they would get up to at the disco. She had a biggish house on the Estate and did not need money, so she had joined him on his four-day Rest & Recuperation period in the Isle of Man. He had not contacted her after the tour, and she would not have wished it.

When he had been posted into Ligoniel, he called her, and they had met a few times. A couple of the other men in Tregus' section knew some of the Ligoniel girls too. It had not taken Tregus long to organise a system that, when they knew they had a night patrol in the local area, a party would be organised at one of the girls' houses. Tregus would drop the section off at the girl's house and then drive round to see his paramour. He would park the Pig in the big shed behind the house and roger away for the four hours or so that the patrol would last. The new lightweight VHF radios that the army had recently been issued with allowed him to bounce away merrily while sending bogus situation reports and apocryphal locstats to the woman's huge amusement.

161

For Roly, it was about the worst situation he could have thought of. This was precisely the kind of disciplinary balls up that the CO and Davenport had hoped would allow them to have his guts for garters. Roly wondered if he could try to ride this one out, but it was too serious to ignore. The whole company would know about it by morning. The likes of Brakspear would make sure of that.

The fact was that, realistically, there had been no physical threat to the members of the patrol, and there had been no terrorist-inspired incident in Ligoniel in two years since those three poor boys from the Royal Highland Fusiliers had been murdered and dumped on a local lane in 1971. But Roly could hardly ignore behaviour which, were it to happen to another platoon, he would roundly condemn. He, himself, had effectively allowed this to happen.

He should have been more aware, and it was his responsibility.

The draconian rhetoric that he knew he was about to be exposed to from the Colonel, calling up doomsday scenarios of soldiers seduced and mutilated, would not even be hot air. What was also at stake was the reputation for Roly's relationship with his NCOs.

Smithy joined them shortly after Tregus started pulling himself together, pulling at his lower lip and looking more and more worried. He shook his head as if to divorce himself from the situation and looked at the Sergeant and Roly. His fine sense of survival and cunning, bred of long service, told him that Roly would crawl on broken glass rather than expose

162

himself as linked to Tregus' tainted character and actions.

Tregus raised his head and looked at Roly directly for the first time since he had started to spill the beans. He had nothing against Roly, but it was his skin too, and he had given up feeling sorry for officers a long time ago. He spoke low and softly.

"No harm done, Zur, just a bit of fun for the lads, loike. Don't charge oi, Zur, just bollock oi and fuck oi off."

He risked a glimpse at Sergeant Smith, who was looking at him as if he had just crawled out of a hole. He reckoned he could fix the Sergeant too, and all.

"It's too late for that, Tregus," said Roly. "You're under open arrest with immediate effect." His voice was harsher than either of the two NCOs had heard him speak before.

"You will carry on with your duties as normal until the OC can see you, but you know full well that this is a Commanding Officer's offence. You should be in the box at Flax Street, but for reasons I cannot imagine, I'm going to try to keep this low key."

"Jesus wept," groaned Roly as he swung himself out of the Pig. "You have to be the biggest bloody idiot I've ever met," wondering whether he was talking to Tregus or himself. "Keep an eye on him, Sergeant." With that, he walked off into the Mill towards the Ops Room.

The CSM was there, its walls festooned with large maps of the city. A radio operator sat at the desk, idly thumbing through a book.

"I need to see the OC," said Roly.

"He's in his room, sir," the Warrant Officer replied. "I think he's just checking the CQMS's requisitions for tomorrow. Anything I can do?" The question was largely rhetorical.

"Yes," replied Roly, much to the CSM's surprise. "Corporal Tregus is under open arrest. I shall need you to assist Sergeant Smith in preparing the charges, which look as though they could be quite serious. They will certainly warrant Commanding Officer's Orders. Sergeant Smith is taking statements at the moment."

A look of self-knowing satisfaction appeared to cross the Sergeant Major's face, but there was a dangerous glint in the young officer's eyes, so with unctuous politeness, he asked, "Was there a particular offence, sir?"

"Tregus and Brakspear appear to have been drinking," Roly replied, knowing that would disappoint the older man. Tregus had no less than eleven drink-related incidents on his charge sheet. "There could be no other way, though. Sergeant Smith will update you when we've got a clearer picture of the whole." Roly turned to go.

"Shouldn't they be in close arrest, under the circumstances, sir? He could try and do a runner. Also, you can hardly deploy him if he's bottled and you get called out."

Roly turned and looked at the CSM. There was no attempt by the Warrant Officer to hide his dislike, and to the fascinated signaller sitting there, it looked as though Roly might take a swing at him. The CSM evidently thought so too, for he took a quick pace away from the officer.

Instead, in a voice as cold as ice, Roly responded, "There'll be plenty of time for close arrest. In the meantime, he's had a drink. He's not completely bottled, and if you think that I'm going to leave that section in the hands of a 20-year-old Lance Corporal who has only recently got his stripe, then you can think again. Also, he might do something dumb from time to time, but he is not going to be so stupid as to do a runner." Remembering Tregus's face as he had left him, Roly was not so sure of that last statement.

He walked out and found Davenport in his room – the old Mill manager's office. He knocked and entered when Davenport called. The Major was looking tired and drawn. There were great bags under his eyes, and he was clearly not sleeping well. The fact was that Davenport was finding his command to be a serious strain. He was an ordered, tidy man and hated being rushed into decisions. When the Company was deployed, he would rather avoid ordering his men into action, and the death of young Covell had hit him hard. He was also intensely jealous of the easy speed with which Flashman would assess a situation and quickly and unerringly shake his men out to deal with it.

He held Flashman responsible for Covell's death and was determined to see him brought down. His early dislike had hardened into an irrational and fixed hatred, so there was no warmth in greeting when Flashman saluted.

"What is it?" he demanded brusquely.

"I'm sorry to disturb you, Simon," Roly offered, "but I felt that you needed to know at once that I have had to place Corporal Tregus under open arrest.

There is evidence that he has been drinking on duty, and there could be other, more serious charges as well. Sergeant Smith and I are assessing the full impact, and I will have a full report for you tomorrow when we have finished interviewing others involved."

Davenport looked at him coldly. "There is very little satisfaction in being proven right. I knew from the beginning that if there was to be an incident, it would come from your platoon. There is a Company Commanders' Conference at Flax Street tomorrow. Have a full report and charges ready for me when I get back tomorrow afternoon."

February 1973

Belfast: Trouble in the Ardoyne

The next day Roly was sitting glumly in the shared office at Ligoniel Mill as he began to prepare his report on Corporal Tregus. It was grey outside, and Bomber, the dog, had his head on his knee while Roly stroked him absent-mindedly behind the ears. It was as if Bomber understood Roly's despair. But the eternal devotion of one misbegotten mongrel was not really doing much for his state of mind. The charges against Tregus were indeed serious. He would probably face a Court Martial. His Second-in-command, the young Lance Corporal, was also being charged and would almost certainly lose his stripe.

Roly had been phoned by Arthur Black, the Adjutant, one of his few friends and supporters, and been told to prepare his own case carefully as Davenport was encouraging the Colonel to put him in front of the Brigade Commander.

Just then, there was increased chatter from the radios, and the Ops Officer popped his head round the door.

"Roly. Bring your boys up to 'Ready' will you? Pete Luce is already on his way down to Flax Street with 5 Platoon as there's been a bomb in The Ardoyne. I've got to go with him, so could you dig out Andy Davies to take over ops as well?"

"A bomb in the Ardoyne!" Roly exclaimed. "Sounds like coals to Newcastle to me. Couldn't happen to a nicer lot."

He went up to the Officers' accommodation and woke Andrew Davies, the next senior Platoon Commander who had been on the streets all of the previous night, and told him to bring his platoon up to one state of readiness and then take over the Ops Room. He could take his time as Roly said he would stand in at Ops until he was ready. He then roused Smithy, who was dozing on his pit with his boots on and his flak vest as an extra pillow. He told him to get the Platoon out to the Saracens and kitted up for crowd control. He then told a Chef to shake a leg and to fix the Platoon up for Tea and Sandwiches in case they were called out before their regular meal and went back to the Ops Room.

There were three radios in the Ops Room – one tuned to the Battalion net, one to the Company net, and the third could be tuned to a spare frequency in case of need. The sets were usually manned by two operators, one from the Company and one who was attached from the Royal Signals. On this occasion, Roly told both operatives to put both nets on the loudspeakers so that he could catch up on what was going on.

It appeared that a very large bomb had detonated beside one of the many illegal drinking clubs that had proliferated through the Ardoyne since "The Troubles" had begun. In Africa, Roly mused, they would have been called

Shebeens. These clubs had been allowed to spring up because the district was effectively unpoliced ever since Jim Callaghan, the Labour Government Home Secretary, had all but disbanded the Royal Ulster Constabulary in the early days of the Army being sent in. At the time, it had seemed like a good idea to take the biased, anti-Catholic, and almost wholly Protestant-recruited force out of the Catholic areas while the Army restored the calm. What happened, however, was the police were more or less barred from these Catholic enclaves for years afterwards.

The result was farcical. Heavily armed soldiers patrolled these enclaves, powerless to enforce any sort of law. The soldiers were not equipped with police powers. As a result, soldiers would stop a car driving at night with no lights, the driver drunk as a skunk, with no car tax and clearly no insurance, and could only hold the car on suspicion. Only if the car was stolen could the soldiers apprehend the driver acting as if they were 'In aid of the Civil Power'.

The powers to arrest were no more or less than any normal citizen's. As a result of this total breakdown of legal infrastructure, the drinking clubs started up, unlicensed and untaxed. They opened and closed when they wished and their profits, which were considerable, went straight to the IRA. In this case, it appeared that one of the clubs had been blown to pieces. It was sited just one hundred yards from the walls of the old Flax Street Mill, which was used as the principal barracks and headquarters of the Battalion charged with maintaining the peace in the Ardoyne and Northern Shankill – in this case, 4LI.

To Roly, it seemed as though there might be two alternatives. Either the IRA, constructing a bomb to use against the barracks, had caused a massive home goal by detonating it prematurely, blowing up the bomber as well, or Protestant paramilitaries had smuggled a device into the Ardoyne. The first option seemed the more probable. Nonetheless, barely seconds after the explosion, a Catholic mob had exploded onto the streets, baying for blood. The two resident companies in Flax Street were fully occupied in trying to bring the situation under control, and by the sound of it, the new CO's strictures about the restrained use of baton rounds were being largely ignored.

The Ardoyne was a triangular piece of Real Estate, with each side of the triangle about half a mile long. It is split into two distinguishable sections, the Old and the New. The Old, which forms a triangle within a triangle, consisted of mean and reeking slums built for the wretched workers who, in the late Victorian and early Edwardian days, toiled eighteen hours a day spinning raw flax into high-grade linen for a pittance, in the grim, prison-like edifice of Flax Street Mill.

The Mill towers over the filthy streets, and its long shadow keeps the morning Sun from the narrow lanes and back alleys until well into the day. Even in the early 1970s, most of the houses had primitive outdoor privvies. The conditions inside the terraced houses were appalling – rat infested and damp.

One of the most telling elements in the conflict in Ulster was the deafening silence by successive Westminster Governments and parties, of whatever persuasion, about the very real repression of the Catholic community in the period prior to 1969. The failure of the Municipal authorities to provide services and improvements was a manifestation of this repression in the Old Ardoyne. By contrast, the New Ardoyne was a different exercise in social engineering, a housing estate built in the early fifties and benefitting from a sizeable presence of Protestants with services that were at least regular.

As the intimidation of the Catholic minorities in the Protestant areas increased in 1968 and 1969, the Catholic communities, too, turned inwards and forced the Protestant groups out of their areas. A gradual transmogrification took place in which the displaced refugees of each community rehoused themselves in the vacated houses of the opposition.

By and large, for the Protestant communities, this was achieved without fuss. For the Catholic minority, however, the full majesty of the law was unleashed as they squatted in the recently vacated houses. Or it would have been unleashed if the police and bailiffs had been allowed to enter and enforce the judgements handed down by the courts. The police were emasculated, and the Bailiffs, Protestant to a man, were not stupid either. They were not going near the place. The lamp posts were quite well enough decorated with Orange, White, and Green bunting to serve as a warning to any Ulster Bailiff stupid enough to attempt to serve an eviction order in the Ardoyne.

So the Ardoyne deteriorated swiftly. As the Council cut its services, the community, one in four out of work, withdrew into a stagnant attitude of dumb insolence, lawlessness, and an almost religious acceptance of the Irish Republican Army's creed of violence and unswerving loyalty to their community. The cycle of self-destruction was completed by the British Army. Almost by accident, Britain's colonial Army had achieved extraordinary success against the Sino/Malay insurgents in Malaya in the 1950s. The architect of that success had been General Sir Gerald Templar, and the keystone of the campaign had been the strategy of 'Hearts and Minds'.

It had not worked very well elsewhere, but his pupils were the commanders of the Army now in Ulster, and they still clung to it. So the Army was instructed to win their Hearts and Minds. Thus it was that the descendants of the soldiers that had sieged Drogheda in 1649, lifted the siege of Derry in 1689, and turned the Boyne crimson with their sabres in 1690, now sallied into the streets of the Ardoyne, clustered behind the six-foot plastic walls of their Macrolon shields, determined to show the citizens of that disadvantaged triangle the benefits of the British way of life. The new Colonel of 4LI insisted that this was the way.

The M1 A4 MkIII Browning .5-inch heavy machine gun is a complicated piece of equipment. The breech and barrel alone weigh some 42 lbs, and the tripod necessary to keep the mechanism firing in a straight line weighs a further 37 lbs. It was designed in 1912 and was still the preferred heavy machine gun of half the armies in NATO. It has a complicated gas blow-back action with a semi-rotating bolt mechanism that is an absolute bitch to strip and assemble, but it is lethal. When fired, it throws a huge 3.5-ounce, half-inch diameter bullet at speed five times the speed of sound to a range of two and a half miles. It will go further if you crank the barrel angle up more, and it can spit the rounds out at a rate of 650 per minute. The tungsten-headed ones will penetrate half an inch of high-tensile armour plate and still have lots of energy. A more usual rate is 3-5 rounds every 10 seconds because the recoil really does knock the tripod about, and it takes a bit of realigning. 3-5 rounds will knock down the wall of the average Council house. The IRA had two of them in the Ardoyne that day. Their fifty-round belts were loaded with one round of ball, one round of tracer, and three rounds of Armoured Piercing Tungsten, in that sequence.

From the back windows of the last houses of the new Ardoyne, you can just see the main gate of Flax Street Mill, opening out onto Flax Street and abutting Butler Street, the arterial road of the old Ardoyne. The angle is very tight, and the range, across a belt of waste ground, is about five hundred yards. In the roof cavity of one of these houses, just under the eaves, Jason Doherty, the commander of the Ardoyne battalion of the Belfast Brigade of the newly emerged Provisional IRA, had set up one of the big guns. A tile in the roof had been lifted to give barrel clearance, but to the soldier looking down from the Sanger on top of the mill, the missing tile would not have looked out of place.

The gun had been carefully laid on the gate, and Doherty had brought Liam Deggan in to supervise the adjustment. A different person would actually do the firing, and all that the young volunteer who did this

173

had to do, was press the trigger between the two hand grips, fire the five rounds, replace the tile, drop through the trap door out of the roof and walk casually out of the house. Doherty was certain that the diversion that he had laid on would be holding the attention of the troops in the Sanger, and the army would not be expecting an attack from a weapon of that calibre and at that range.

To an extent, he was right, but the diversion had gone badly. The bomb that had blown up the drinking club had been intended to explode under the walls of Flax Street Mill. It had been prepared in the boot of a car and weighed nearly five hundred pounds. Butler St ran down a slight hill, and the car had been parked at the top. The steering had been rigged to keep the car in a straight line, and the idea was for the handbrake to be gear-engaged and for the car to roll down Butler Street and crash into the wall of the mill. The shaped charge in the boot would focus most of the force of the explosion into the wall.

A volunteer had got into the car, put it into gear, laid a brick on the accelerator, and jumped out as the car began to roll. Something, however, had gone wrong with the detonator circuitry, which was electric rather than initiated. Three-quarters of the way down the street, the bomb had gone off with a huge explosion. Fortunately for the residents, the car was just passing the empty school at the time, and all that happened was for every window to be blown out. The drinking club on the other side, however, was blown apart, and the three young organisers, waiting for the crowd to come out and the barman, became another statistic in the grim rollcall of violent death in the province.

The IRA organisers had their youth mobs ready to spill out onto the streets and pour into the wreckage of the Mill. When the bomb went off, the mob duly came onto the street, but instead of finding a dazed and shocked soldiery, they ran headlong into the fully prepared 'Ready' platoons of the two Companies based at the Mill, sallying out to cordon off the source of the explosion, rapidly reinforced by the 'Reserve' Units. The crowd's frustration and their rage at the foiled plan prevented the 4LI Colonel from enacting his favourite 'Take the heat out of the situation and withdrawal plan'. There was a serious alarm that the crowd intended to storm the Mill. The screaming mob was pelting the soldiers with petrol bombs, bricks, and long steel angle picket stakes that they had ripped from the school's fences and hurled like javelins.

2nd Lieutenant Peter Luce, perched in the Commander's cupola of the leading Saracen, three months out of University and terribly nervous of making a mistake, followed the three ferrets of B Company's attached Cavalry Unit off the Crumlin Road and into Flax Street, turning right into the Mill yard when they reached the gate. This was the target that the young volunteer squatting in the eaves had been told to wait for. He gripped the wooden handles of the long-barrelled gun firmly, and his thumb quietly took up the first pressure on the trigger button as he peered along the barrel. He would have dearly loved to have taken one of the Ferrets, but his instructions were absolute. So he waited until the bonnet of the leading

Saracen nosed into the gate and pressed the trigger. The noise of the blast was enormous. The big gun bucked in his hands and the dingy attic filled with fumes. The blast from the muzzle, pumping the bullets out at 2,750 ft. per second, scattered the roof tiles like confetti and the heaving recoil of the barrel jerked the unweighted tripod up and sideways. The boy, petrified, let go of the handles, dropped through the trap door of the attic, and heedless of instructions, bolted out of the house and sprinted down the road. The big telephoto lens in the Sanger caught a vivid frame of a petrified face.

But he had done his work. The first round had struck the side of the Saracen with a clang. The sloped armour had diverted the bullet, which crashed harmlessly into one of the spotlights above the gate and whined away into the distance. The tracer of the second round lit, two hundred yards out from the muzzle, over the waste ground and tracked its course good and true, striking the big APC just behind the driver's position and, again, the sloping plate of half-inch armour deflected the bullet into the fat, inflated rubber of the middle of six wheels. The bullet tumbled, shredding the rubber, and embedded itself into the bucking springs of a shock absorber. The third bullet, with its hardened, Tungsten head, left the barrel just as the muzzle started to lift. Its slightly higher trajectory and milli-second delay impacted the round slightly further back and eight inches higher on the vehicle than the tracer. The whirling, heated point of Tungsten drilled through the armour as though it were paper and erupted in the vehicle.

It just missed the head of the young soldier with his back to the side, but the shock wave of the passing bullet caused his ears to bleed. Peter Luce was in the Commander's cupola with his head in the turret, and he peered through the periscope. The big bullet, its head flattened by the impact upon the armour, tore through the layered nylon of Luce's flak jacket and ripped through his abdomen, shattered his spine, and exited through the back of the flak vest. Its impetus was starting to drop off rapidly, but the tumbling bullet still had the velocity to ricochet off the far side of the vehicle and tear through the upper arm of the soldier sitting there, eviscerating his bicep. Plunging on, it bounced off the roof of the APC and finally buried itself in the thigh of another of the soldiers sitting there.

The other two rounds arced over the moving vehicle. One smashed into the wall above the gatehouse, and the other soared over the city and landed harmlessly in a playing field two and a half miles to the south. For the young Royal Corps of Transport driver of the Saracen, it appeared that mayhem had broken out. The clang of the first two rounds hitting the side of the vehicle startled him, and he did not know what they were. The screams from the wounded in the back caused him to look over his shoulder as he instinctively put his foot down on the accelerator. The APC shot through the gate, collided with one of the Ferrets, still proceeding slowly in front, and crashed over onto its side, hurling the occupants, wounded and whole, into a gasping, screaming pile, seriously concussing Sergeant Bertram, the platoon sergeant.

Simon Davenport had been standing in the yard of the Mill, waiting for his troops to arrive. He was impatient to be deployed but typically fearful of the possible results. When the first of the Ferrets had turned into the gate, he had turned to the CSM and told him to bring the cavalryman and Peter Luce to his command Landrover.

The crack and clatter of the incoming rounds caused him to whirl around and watch the tragedy of Peter Luce's command vehicle crashing through the gate. Ashen-faced, he stood, rooted to the spot while the guard troops frenziedly tried to extricate the injured and the remaining Saracens squeezed into the yard. It was fortunate for Davenport that the resident troops had practiced the drills for just such an emergency, and under the watchful eye of the Regimental Police Sergeant, 'Skull' McCormick, the wounded were carried off to await Casualty evacuation by ambulance. If Davenport had been called upon to react, he would have been unable to do so.

He watched, transfixed, as Peter Luce's body, virtually cut in half by the huge bullet, was carefully eased out, laid on a stretcher, and covered with a blanket. He only dimly heard the voice of the CSM asking for instructions and pushed past him into the Mill. Grimly, the CSM watched his retreating back. He turned to the shaken soldiers in the remaining Saracens and quickly got them busy.

Some were put to righting the overturned APC, others were sent scurrying for some scram (food), and the remainder were sent, under the command of the senior corporal, for a totally unnecessary patrol onto Crumlin

Road and back. "Keep them busy, and they would not brood," was his theory.

Five minutes later, Flashman and his reserve platoon swept into the courtyard and quickly assimilated Luce's leaderless section into their own tight organisation. The relief of Luce's Corporals was almost tangible. The CSM did not dislike Roly Flashman. As far as he was concerned, Flashman was simply persona non grata with his superiors, and therefore, an impediment to his own career. But what he could have freely admitted was that he would far rather go into action with Flashman in command than the shambling, pathetic figure who actually commanded the company.

For the CSM, the immediate crisis was resolved, but he was deeply worried about Davenport. The man had simply gone to pieces.

Flashman greeted the CSM with little warmth and was surprised by the urgency of the CSM's response.

"Sir! We're supposed to be out there supporting C and D Companies, but the OC and the boys from Two One have had a bad shock. The OC's inside, but we haven't had any orders from him."

Lt Peter Luce, mercifully, had died from loss of blood before the unconsciousness, induced by shock, had worn off. His platoon was, however, leaderless, and the situation outside the Mill was becoming desperate. Four platoons, numbering just under 140 men, were trying to hold several thousand enraged and totally hostile people from storming the Mill. The soldiers outside had not seen the results of the Browning shooting, but they had all heard it. They all knew that this was a weapon previously outside their experience. The depth of noise alone had sent most of them scuttling for the cover of doorways.

"OK CSM," Roly replied. "Hold onto the boys from Two One here. I've been talking to the Adjutant on the way down, and we're going to go in under Major Miller's command." Richard Miller was the OC of C Company. He had spent four years with the SAS and had a cool and unflappable nature. Roly called out, "Sarn't Smith! Get our lads together and get up to the Butler/Crumlin junction. Report to Major Miller. I'll join you shortly. You'd better take command of Two One. Hold yourself at the gate here but report in on the Battalion net with a ready report ASAP. If they deploy the platoon, you take them out. I'm going to check with the OC."

Roly's reading of the immediate necessity had been crisp and immediate. He had shown no hesitation in taking control of the situation and placed the Company's elements confidently in the hands of the two senior NCOs. How different, the CSM reflected ruefully, from the man who should have been there.

Roly tossed his SLR to Brakspear, who was beside him and strode into the Mill. He went straight to the Ops Room where the CO, Adjutant, Battalion 2 i/c, and the Intelligence Officer were taking reports and redirecting troop deployment. Roly saluted, and the CO looked up.

"What are you doing here? You're supposed to be supporting C Company," he demanded.

"Yes, sir," Roly replied. "My lads are up there with Sergeant Smith. I'm trying to find Simon though. With Peter Luce dead and his Sergeant casevaced, we've got a platoon adrift. I've told the CSM to take over for the moment, but I need to know what Simon wants done and where we're to send them. I thought that Simon would be in here."

The Colonel's face drained. "Peter! Dead?" he queried.

"Yes, sir." Roly was surprised that the Colonel did not know. Peter Luce was his wife's godson.

The adjutant cut in. "All we've had so far is a report from the gate of five casualties from gunfire. I've been calling Simon for details for the last ten minutes." He sounded cross.

"I'm sorry, sir. I thought you must have known," said Roly, sounding lame even to himself.

"Quite." said the CO. He wondered how he was going to break the news to his wife. Peter was her best friend's son. He had lost his own father in his early teens, and she had often accused the Colonel of bamboozling Peter into the army. "What exactly has happened?"

"It looks like the IRA opened up with a heavy just as the boys were entering our compound through the gate. They must have had armoured piercing rounds because three of our lads were hit. I'm afraid that Peter was killed instantly." The Colonel looked grim. "The driver panicked and raced the gate, hit one of the Ferrets, and rolled the Saracen. The driver and Sarn't

Bertram got hurt though it looks as though Sarn't Bertram isn't serious."

From outside, they could hear the sound of the rioting. The reports from the baton guns were almost continuous, and the Ops Room radios, monitoring both Company nets, chattered incessantly as the harassed Commanders tried to get the situation under control.

"Where the hell is Simon," the CO demanded.

"I've no idea, Colonel," replied the Adjutant. "He left when we broke up the meeting after the bomb went off, and I thought he was going straight down to meet B Company as they came in."

"RSM," the Colonel called to the other side of the Ops Room. "See if you can locate Major Davenport, will you?" He turned to the Intelligence Officer. "Since Roly's here, what do we know about this shooting?"

The Intelligence Officer, Johnny Higgins, was one of Roly's better friends in 4LI. He and Roly had been at Mons together. They hadn't seen each other since the tour had started.

Higgins nodded to Roly in an unspoken acknowledgement that he knew about the problems that Roly had been having with Davenport.

"We've located the firing point in Ardilee Street, sir. The trotters just pushed the tiles back, cut them loose, and then legged it. The OP reckons he got a good pic of one of them running away from the house. God only knows what kind of gun it is, though. It sounds a bit bigger than one of their Springfields."

He was referring to the US Army .300 calibre rifle that had recently been used by the IRA. It too could fire Tungsten strengthened bullets, but although it was effective against the thin armour of the Pigs, the bullets would have just bounced off the half-inch plate of the Saracens.

"The film is on its way down now, and we should have the face of the culprit within the hour."

Roly addressed the Colonel.

"I'm no ballistics expert, Colonel, but I saw one of the holes, and it's big. At least fifty Cal or more, I'd say. One of the armourers will probably be able to tell us. But if that's the case and they just did a runner, then either the gun will still be there, or the people in the house were involved. Enough to give us a lead anyway."

The four senior men looked at him, their attention fully held. "What are you suggesting?" the Colonel asked.

"If we're sharp, I could get my lads through the back and into Ardilee Street through the Triangle. We can check out the house while the rest of the Ardoyne is getting stuck outside here. If I take Tango Four (that was the Ligoniel Cavalry Unit of Ferrets), they can hold the Triangle around us while we go in."

The Triangle was a large open area where two of the perimeter roads of the Ardoyne formed an apex. There had been a garage and a supermarket there, but they had been burned down, leaving an open expanse of tar and concrete. There had been three recent occasions when the IRA had tried to ambush military or police

183

vehicles with RPG7 rocket launchers as they moved across the Triangle. Foot patrols hated it.

The Colonel stroked his chin pensively.

"You could be right, Roly! Get up to the Sanger with Johnny and think it through. Then get back here, and we can talk about it again. Arthur, get in touch with Richard Miller and see if he can give Two Two back to us. You'll be taking both platoons if you go. I don't need anyone snatched right now, but I do think it's a good idea to give the house the once over. Now," he grunted irritably, "Where's that bloody man Davenport?"

At that moment, the RSM walked in.

"We've found Davenport, sir," he said. "He was in the Officer's Mess. I understand he's on his way down."

Davenport entered almost as the RSM finished speaking. He looked flushed, and there was an odd glint in his eye that Roly had not seen before. He ignored Roly completely as he addressed the CO.

"Sorry about the delay, Colonel. I was just onto my CQMS to get poor young Luce's things together."

The Colonel eyed him oddly. It was a pretty silly story, and Davenport had been acting quite strangely recently. He decided to have a word with him later.

"Sit down, Simon," he said. "It's a tragic loss for all of us, but we just have to get on with it. I'm particularly concerned that the IRA appears to have managed to acquire such a high calibre weapon and been able to set it up under our very noses."

"We think we know where the firing point is, and Roly has come up with the idea that we could slip in quickly and check it over while the crowds are still occupied at the other end of the Ardoyne. There seems to be a faint chance that the gunmen might have run off and left the gun behind."

Davenport gave a downcast look as the CO continued.

"Johnny is on the roof with Roly now, working it out, and we've called for Roly's platoon to be sent back from C Company. As soon as they arrive, take two platoons around and search the place. Make it a very quick in and out job, and don't get involved with another crowd."

Johnny Higgins came into the room, puffing slightly from having run up and down two flights of stairs. As he came through the door, he blurted, "We've definitely got the firing point, sir. It looks as though the gun is still there too. I think they sited it too far back in the attic and didn't allow for the effect that the muzzle blast would have on the roof. I thought I could see the leg of a tripod through the hole, so it looks as if it got upended, and they panicked and left."

"Well, well. No time to lose then," said the Colonel. "Off you go, Simon. Take Johnny with you to check on the bits and pieces, and he can look after Peter Luce's boys as you go in." Davenport hesitated.

"Don't you think Peter's platoon might be a bit shaken for this sort of thing?" he enquired. "Won't Roly's platoon backed by Ferrets be sufficient?"

185

"Nonsense," replied the Colonel brusquely, "it's just the sort of thing they need to help them snap out of it. By the same token, I do not want them tearing in on some sort of revenge trip. Which is why you are also going in with them and, I repeat, avoid any crowd action."

The three officers left the room, and Davenport told Roly to go down and get the boys prepared. He had left his briefcase in the Mess and would join them in a minute. Meanwhile, Roly was to give the orders for what was to happen. He made it sound as though it were some form of largesse. Johnny's eyebrows rose almost to the brim of his beret. For a Company Commander to not control every stage of a prickly little operation like this, and especially, the deployment of the soldiers in the light of what else was going on in the Battalion area was unthinkable. He looked at Roly, who just shrugged.

In the yard, Sgt Smith had arrived with the platoon. They had had a hairy few minutes getting back to Flax Street, but Smith was grinning, and he had Tregus beside him, who seemed to be relishing everything.

With the young Cavalry officer there, as well as Johnny, Roly briefed them quickly about events and the plan. The Ferrets would follow Roly, who would lead them in a long loop around the back of the Mill and down a road that had a wall sheltering them from the Ardoyne. When they got to the Triangle, the Ferrets would overtake and take up a position where they could provide cover for the arrival of the Pigs and Roly's men. Johnny was to come with just one of his

186

Pigs, and the remainder would stay behind in case of need or provide a later diversion if needed.

Tregus's section was to follow the Ferrets, followed by one other section, and to stop outside the house, break the door down, and secure the outside of the house, providing cover with marksmen and baton guns. Johnny was to secure the rear of the house with the section from Luce's men and the remaining section from Roly's platoon while Roly, with Smithy, the radio operator, and Brakspear and three others would enter and forge their way upstairs to where they thought they would find the gun.

Roly briefed Johnny to also cover the alley at the back and be aware of anybody still in the house who might attempt to escape that way. Everyone was to be supremely conscious of the danger of booby traps, not just in the entrances and on the stairs but expressly if the gun was found.

The whole briefing took less than five minutes, and Davenport had still not joined them. As the men moved back to their vehicles, he came out of the Mill and almost tripped on the step. He came up to Roly, standing by the OC's Landrover, and seemed almost congenial.

"All set then? Fine, let's go!"

Roly, Johnny, and the CSM exchanged looks. Simon Davenport seemed drunk. He literally reeked of brandy. He got into the passenger seat of his Landrover as if he were just about to go for a drive in the country on a pleasant day. Roly, now seriously concerned, waved to Johnny and the young Cavalry Officer, and the nine-vehicle convoy set off.

On the Ardoyne side of the Mill wall, about halfway up Butler Street, Jason Doherty stood at the upstairs window of one of the mean little houses and seethed. Everything was going very wrong.

First, the bomb had been a catastrophe, and he had lost three of his trusted lieutenants in the drinking club. Secondly, the Army seemed to be coping with the rioters rather more efficiently than he had hoped. Nothing in the new 4LI Colonel's style had prepared him for such a robust response. He had already seen a couple of his Volunteers, acting as organisers, lifted by the Army's snatch squads, and he wasn't too sure about the loyalty of one of those snatched. Finally, it looked like the machine gun attack had not succeeded.

From where he was standing, he could just see the gate to Flax St Mill. When the firing had started, he had seen the tracer round strike, and he had seen the floodlight disintegrate, but the Saracen's momentum had taken it through the Mill's gates, and he didn't know about the final outcome. The dangling floodlight above the gate suggested that the target had been missed.

Now, Danny Keenan, one of his officers who had been left to watch the Volunteer who had fired the weapon did just that, reported that the terrified youth had bolted from the site, probably attracting the attention of the Sanger on the roof of the Mill.

Neither Doherty nor Keenan yet knew about the scattered roof tiles, and Doherty imagined that the

188

soldiers would not have traced the firing point yet. If he could just keep them tied up with the crowd, then he could use the cover of darkness to recover both the gun and its tripod. He could just imagine the Command Council's reaction if he lost the precious 'Heavy'. The mere fact that they had agreed to let him use it gave him huge stature in the movement. He was not going to take any chances, however.

"Danny," he called. "Have youse still got the Armalite at Riordan's?" He had a thick and ugly Belfast accent and a heavy drinker's guttural tone.

"Aye," the other man answered.

"Well, youse get down there (he pronounced it 'thar') and spot yourself so's if any of those fecking sojers get near to the Ardilee hoise, pop one. Unnerstan?"

Danny looked pleased. "Aye. I'll be away – how long youse want me to hang on?"

"Till the dark. We'll be down from Shankey's soon as the light's gone."

As Danny left, Doherty looked back at the Mill and watched the B Company convoy pull out of the back gate and, as he lost sight of them, wondered where they were off to. Probably taking the back way around to the Crumlin Rd, then up to the Bus Depot to try and get round the back of the crowd, he thought. So much the better. He had another mob standing by, ready up there too.

His thoughts turned to the young volunteer who had run from the gun. Doherty was anxious, very anxious, to make sure that the movement had tied him into its web. His name was Gerry Glove, and his uncle was Seamus Glove, a Belfast-based SDLP MP at Westminster. In the early days, Seamus had been one of the heroes of the Civil Rights movement, dedicated to the integration of the Six Counties into one Irish Republic. But in recent months, he had been making some very sharp attacks on the IRA and, particularly, on the Provisionals and their random bomb attacks on the civil population. The attacks were having an effect too, because Seamus was a highly respected man and donations to "The Cause" were badly down recently.

Gerry was the son that Seamus Glove never had and had been spotted by a Sinn Fein activist at Dublin University. There was no doubt about his political dedication. His physical condition needed some work though. He had been brought up soft and, to understand the Cause, Doherty considered you had to be brought up in the Ardoyne or The Falls or the Creggan or one of the other ghettoes to really get it. The University vacation had started, and young Glove had been persuaded to have a taste of the 'Front Line'. His enthusiasm meant that he had not baulked at being given the job of firing the heavy. Now he appeared to have messed it up.

Not that it really mattered, provided that they did not lose the gun. Doherty went cold at the thought. They had always intended to sell Gerry out to the RUC anyway. Seamus' nephew in the Maze prison might temper the oratory a bit, and if Gerry was not already dedicated to The Cause, then he soon would be after a

190

spell of internment or imprisonment. After firing the Browning,

Gerry had taken the stairs two at a time, gone out through the back into the reeking alley, and hadn't been seen since.

Leaving Doherty, Danny Keenan had gone from the Old to the New Ardoyne and, keeping a brisk pace, had reached the Riordan's house a few minutes later. He knocked sharply, and Sally Riordan's frightened face appeared when she opened the door a few inches against the chain.

'Her Dave' was in the Maze, and the Provos had always used her home at will. She was too frightened to stop them. Then one of her neighbours had reported that she had gone to one of the army discos, and they had pulled her in. She'd been taken to one of the clubs, stripped, and given a beating with a heavy electrical flex. Now, she just did what she was told. Her house was used as a weapons cache, and she was terrified of the day that the army would come.

As she opened the door and saw Danny, the fear came back like a physical lump in her stomach. It had been Danny who had administered her beating on Doherty's orders, and he had enjoyed it. Every time he looked at her, he remembered that naked flesh, writhing in pain, as the scything blows from the flex had rained down on her. Danny reckoned that he'd have her one of these days, whether she liked it or not. Dave Riordan wasn't going to see daylight for the next fifteen years, and it would be a shame to waste some tasty meat.

191

Sally knew what he had in mind, and she hated him. It made her flesh crawl. Whenever the Provos wanted to use her house, she and the baby were sent out while the men secreted whatever it was. She usually found her underwear strewn after such occasions, but right now, Danny was in a hurry. As she unlatched the door chain, he just cocked his thumb over his shoulder.

"Youse, out! Fast!" was all he said as he shouldered past her.

She ran to the kitchen and snatched up the baby girl who was playing on the floor. Grabbing a few warm clothes for the child and her own coat, she ran back to the narrow hall, pushed the child into a cheap pushchair, and as the child started to wail, fled through the front door.

Danny went straight to the unkempt living room. He pushed the ancient television set to one side and prised the skirting board away from the wall. In the excavated chamber behind the board, he reached for a long, plastic-wrapped shape that was taped to the damp rotting plasterwork. Almost devoutly, Danny lifted this out, unwrapped the plastic, and the ugly, black, Armalite rifle appeared, supplied courtesy of Noraid, the so-called American charity established to assist the underprivileged in Ireland but, in fact, providing funds and material directly to the IRA.

The weapon that Danny held had been used in two previous IRA attacks. As the covering was stripped away, two smaller plastic packages were revealed, taped to the butt. These contained magazines. Designed to hold thirty rounds each, they were only loaded with twenty in order to save wear on the springs.

Danny loaded one and shoved the other into the back pocket of his jeans. He carefully replaced the skirting board and pushed the television back, making sure that the table legs slotted exactly onto the marks that had been left before in the worn carpet. He then trotted up the stairs, into the back room, and peered out of the window at the house in Ardilee Street.

What he saw shocked him to the core.

Four Saracens and two Landrovers had pulled up outside the house in a tight box with Ferrets protecting them on the front and flanks. They appeared to have just arrived as the troops were disgorging from their rears, some darting to the rear, some taking up firing positions at the front behind any cover that was on offer, and others entering the house. They were all wearing helmets, and most had big plastic visors pushed to the back of their heads.

For the moment, he was frozen. He knew that he could not just open the window and start shooting. That would be suicide. The IRA would lose an officer and an arms cache, which would not be difficult to find in a sustained search. And he couldn't just unleash a sustained burst. There were at least four soldiers looking directly at him and another probably behind the trigger handles of the Browning in the turret of a Ferret.

Then he remembered the attic. The attic of Riordan's house was frequently used as a safe house for high-ranking members of the IRA passing through the

Ardoyne. There were no walls to the attic, and it allowed access to the next-door house on either side and so on down the terraced line so that a man had a chance of escape if soldiers arrived at the front door. A discarded old mattress and old eiderdowns were kept up there as a makeshift bed, and the attic skylight was always left open to allow air to circulate.

Crouching quickly back to the landing and using the butt of the Armalite to open the trap to the attic, he hoisted himself onto the bannister rail that circled the top of the stairs and was able to get his arms through the narrow opening and haul himself into the dingy space under the eaves.

The only light came from the grimy skylight, but there was a chink of brighter light from the edge, indicating that the skylight was still open. Danny was relying on two things to help him. Firstly that the noise of firing would bring a crowd, and they would be able to prevent the soldiers from getting away with the big gun, secondly, although the rifle would make a considerable bang, it was very difficult to trace the source of a bullet in a built-up area with all its echoes. The cartridge produced very little smoke, and there would be no visible muzzle flash.

He was hoping that he could get two three-round bursts off before scuttling along the length of the attics and coming out onto the street or in the alley behind about ten houses down. Once there, he could get to work on the gathering crowd. An aimed shot was, however, difficult. The gap around the skylight was tiny, enough for the barrel, but the Armalite's sights were mounted above the carrying handle over the breach and a good

194

three inches higher than the line of the barrel. After trying a couple of times, he eventually twisted the rifle over on its side and was able to bring a target into the aperture.

Roly had jumped out of the Saracen as it drew to a halt outside the small terraced house. Men from the other vehicles were spewing out, some following Johnny to the rear of the house and others taking up firing positions at the front in case of a sniper. Simon Davenport seemed strangely fixed to the front seat of his Landrover whilst the Ferrets took up positions to cover the party from all sides, hatches down.

The place had obviously not been occupied for some time. The front patch had not been tended, and the windows had been crudely boarded up. The worry now was that the house had been booby-trapped, but if this was going to be a quick operation, then there would be no time to take the usual precautions. For this reason, Roly had a long scaffolding pole with them with an old Landrover tyre which had been lashed to the end, which was in turn lashed to the Saracen and protruding from the back through the firing port in the door.

Even though the door was open, Roly wasn't taking chances. His Saracen driver reversed into the door, which fell to the floor, its glass shattering on the floor of the hall. Sergeant Smith then rolled another tyre down the hall in case of trip wires and then followed Roly and three others, who advanced carefully up the stairs.

The house seemed empty, and the attic trapdoor yawned open above them. Roly could clearly see one of the tripod legs and the two wooden handles of the Browning above him.

"We've got it!" he shouted triumphantly. "Someone please radio that back to Zero and let them know we won't be dwelling here very long."

He allocated a man to the back windows to provide further cover and Private Revenham, a trained sniper, to the front windows to provide further protection from any IRA gunmen and then hoisted Corporal Collier onto his shoulders. The young Lance Corporal pulled himself up into the attic.

It was light up there from the gaping hole in the roof, and the big gun lay on its side where it had tilted off a ceiling joist by the fleeing Gerry Glove. Collier quickly made the gun safe, took the belt out of the receiver, and passed it and the scattered cartridges, which he placed in a plastic bag, down to Roly. He was just turning back to lift the gun off the pintle of the tripod when there was the sound of gunfire and a shout from the front bedroom with further gunfire.

Immediately upon entering the house, Private Revenham raced up to the front bedroom overlooking the street. He stood slightly back from the window and peered out into the street. There was a small group, mostly children, gathering down the road towards the Old Ardoyne. He could hear the popping of baton guns in the distance and felt thankful that the trouble a short way away was causing a diversion from their own activities.

As he watched Major Davenport getting out of his Landrover, his attention was caught by a flicker of movement from one of the houses opposite and just down the street.

Roly had chosen Revenham because he was far and away the best shot in the platoon, possibly the best in the Battalion. He was a calm young man of 24 who came from the Yorkshire dales. He was definite NCO material, but the guy shunned authority and had repeatedly turned down the opportunity. He was taciturn and had few friends apart from Wardle, who had been a tramp before he joined the Army. Roly had been told that the two of them were known to poach, on a fairly large scale, in the woods behind the barracks in Germany, but no one had ever caught them. Revenham's eyesight was extraordinary, and his reactions with a rifle were split second.

What he had seen was a shifting shadow behind a grimy skylight in one of the houses on the other side of the street, about seventy yards away. He lifted the rifle to his shoulder and peered through the RARDE sight. With the extra magnification, he was able to see that the skylight was open, just a crack, with something moving within the crack. He couldn't be sure and cocked the rifle.

He knew that Mr Flashman would support him if it came to being questioned as to why he had done this, and anyway, who would know if he never came to fire it?

Revenham was just wondering whether to warn the Lieutenant when it happened again and this time, he was sure. He shouted his warning and flicked the safety catch off just as the gunman opposite started to shoot.

"Gunman! Base of roof, 15 houses down to the left. Small skylight," followed by the double bellow of an SLR firing.

Danny Keenan, lying uncomfortably in the attic, could not see Revenham, and it would probably have made no difference if he had. Having worked out how to get a shot by twisting the rifle as well as his body, he now needed a suitable target, and as he squinted through the crack, he saw a man get out of the front of an armoured Landrover, possibly a relatively senior officer because he was carrying a pistol rather than a rifle.

He pushed the rifle through the crack. The man had to be mad; he was just standing out in the open. It registered on him that the other soldiers were alarmed as they were waving at him to take cover, so he snatched his first shot. It missed, but the officer had still not moved, and he fired again. As he pulled the trigger, he saw the officer being smothered as one of his men ran towards him to push him out of the way, into cover to the side of the Landrover. Taking aim for a third shot was the last thing that Danny Keenan ever knew.

Keenan could see that he had hit his target and was preparing to fire at a different target when his head blew off. The first two shots had been fired by the time Revenham had followed the barrel back and worked out where the sniper's head would be. He took the pressure up on his own trigger and fired twice. It was a practice known as a 'double tap' and increased the chances of a kill. In this case, the first shot was quite sufficient.

Close by, on that same street, that afternoon, Corporal Tregus was a worried man. The present operation had nothing to do with things. It was his own position that he was worried about because there was a chance, unlikely but still a chance, of being banged up in the military prison at Colchester for what he had done, especially when he was inevitably asked to account for some 7.62 ammunition that had gone missing, a box of 200 which had gone adrift to local Protestant paramilitaries.

Squatting behind the mudguard of his Saracen, he watched the OC climb out of his Landrover. It irritated him to the core of his being that it was going to be a wanker like Davenport, who was going to be the judge of what to do with him. Flashman was OK. You knew where you were with him, and if you fucked up, he was going to drill you. It was arrogant shitbags like Davenport who made a soldier's life miserable, and Tregus resented him.

He was brought back to earth by the first crack of a rifle and Revenham's shout. Tregus had an instinct in such circumstances. He snatched a quick look around at his section to ensure they were all covered. At the same time, his mind registered that the OC was just standing there in the middle of the street as though in shock. Without knowing why, he launched himself at the officer, smothering him and bringing him to the ground.

Danny Keenan's first shot had missed, but his second shot, which should have hit Davenport squarely in the middle of his chest, hit Tregus in the back, at an angle, just below the left shoulder.

The woven nylon of his flak jacket did its work well, and the velocity bled off the bullet as it ploughed its way through the concentrated mesh. The bullet, substantially deformed, had then pierced Tregus' back, scraped a groove across his shoulder blade, and come to a halt under his collar bone, cracking it. It was very painful but far from fatal.

Roly ran into the front room just as Revenham fired. He didn't even have to ask.

"Got him, sir, in t'attic; about ten houses down," Roly shouted up to Collier.

"Get that weapon down here ASAP," and was down the stairs in two bounds, tumbling out into the street.

"Billen," he roared. Roly's other Section Corporal looked around. "Rev got him. In the attic, ten houses down there," he pointed. "Get your lads over there quick and recover the gun and the casualty but watch out! He might not be stiff yet, and he might have a back-up. Move!"

As Billen and his men ran down to the house, Roly looked round for Tregus and became aware of the huddle of bodies beside the OC's Landrover. He ran over to where Sergeant Smith was bending over Tregus. All he could see was the bullet's entry hole in the back of the flak jacket and the spreading, dark patch of blood at the top of the shoulder. Tregus was wincing, breathing stentoriously, and lying on his side. One of his section was holding the platoon medical kit and fumbling for a morphine capsule. Davenport was sitting on the ground, pop-eyed and shocked, against the rear wheel of the Landrover.

He looked at Roly as Roly leaned over Tregus.

"You," he panted. "This was your idea. You'll get us all killed yet, but I'll see to you first."

There was pure hatred in his eyes. Roly ignored him and spoke to Smith. "How bad?"

"He should be OK, sir. It looks like the bullet went in at an angle, and the vest has soaked most of it up. Trouble is I don't want to take the vest off in case it's holding up damaged tissue." The Sergeant replied as he thrust the needle of the ampoule through the cloth of Tregus's combat jacket and then carefully injected the drug into his upper arm.

"Any way of telling where it has ended up?"

"Not really, sir," said Smith. "I've got a field dressing tucked between the vest and the entry wound, so the bleeding should slow, but the best thing would be to get him back to the RMO quickly."

"OK. We're getting the hell out any second. Get him into my vehicle and set off for the Mill at once. Reed, get onto Battalion and put the Casualty station on standby. Tell them it's an emergency."

"Yes, sir," replied the signaller.

Roly turned to the house down the road. He could see one of Billen's men tucked behind a wall where the section had broken in the front door. At the far end of the street, a crowd, attracted by the shooting, was rapidly gathering and moving threateningly down the street. Roly called his other section commander and told him to charge the crowd with his Saracen, fire a couple of rubber bullets, and then reverse back up the street to the house.

He looked over at Davenport. The man was still staring at him with hate-filled eyes. Roly had never felt such an overwhelming urge to kick something more in his life. Instead, as his own Saracen started to leave for the Mill, he said calmly.

"It's going to get a bit exposed around here shortly, Simon. You might be more comfortable in your Landrover." He went back into the house where Collier and Brakspear were manoeuvring the long Browning barrel down the stairs.

In the Sanger at the top of the Mill, the Colonel and Adjutant were watching the operation, accompanied by a couple of signallers tuned into Battalion and B Company nets. The Colonel watched approvingly as Roly locked his platoon vehicles into a tight protective formation around the house. Only the hardened front armour was presented to any possible ambush, and the box gave the troops good protection. The colonel assumed, naturally, that Davenport was controlling the deployment, and he wondered if he had been a bit harsh earlier. He watched the troops burst into the house and was amused by the Saracen's manoeuvre in breaking down the door. Clever move, and well

202

thought out. In his binoculars, he saw Davenport get out of the Landrover and stand in the road. Now that is very silly, he thought. It might be going well, but this is no time to forget basic drills. He watched the soldiers ducking, and Tregus' leap at the Major before the noise of the shooting carried to him.

Then his heart sank. He was able to recognise the distinctive difference between the crack of the Armalite and the deep note of the SLR. Bloody Flashman had all his men tooled up again. He followed Billen's section as they sprinted across the road and looked back to see Tregus being lifted into one of the Saracens, which promptly started up, and he heard the Battalion net crackling on the radio behind him. He watched as the clearly recognisable figure of Davenport pushed himself upright and staggered into the front seat of his Landrover, clearly shocked.

"Serve him right, the bloody fool, tarting around in the open like a Soho whore." He muttered under his breath. The Adjutant, watching as well, heard and smiled grimly to himself.

As the Saracen pulled away, a couple of soldiers staggered out of the house with the distinctive long barrelled machine gun between them, closely followed by another with the tripod. Gun and mounting were bundled into one of the remaining Saracens.

The Saracen that had charged the crowd, even the Colonel, had to admit that it had been a good ruse, reversed quickly to the main body of the platoon, and troops started to scramble aboard. Davenport's Landrover turned in the street and made off towards the Triangle and base. The Colonel turned to the Adjutant.

"What on earth is Simon playing at?" he demanded in bewilderment. "First of all, he's dancing around in the open like some tart on the catwalk, and now he's damned well leaving his troops in the middle of an operation – what does he think he's doing?" The Adjutant just shrugged. There was a time for comment and another for silence when senior officers were talking about each other. He turned his glasses back on the developing scene in Ardilee Street in time to see Corporal Billen and his men stumble out of Riordan's house carrying a body between them.

"I think they got the sniper, Colonel," the Adjutant said.

The Colonel snatched up his glasses and peered at the scene. In his binoculars, the men's images sprang closer, and he felt he could recognise their faces. Four of them were clutching an arm or a leg, each of what looked like a dead man.

Billen trotted behind them, holding an Armalite delicately by the barrel. The other three members of the section closed up behind them, their rifles sweeping the threatening windows and rooftops.

"Well, thank God for that," said the Colonel with a sigh of relief. "At least there's no question of hitting the wrong man."

As the afternoon wore on, the rioting outside the Mill gradually died down to sporadic bouts of stone-throwing at troops patrolling the area. The Colonel and the headquarters officers, joined by The Deputy Brigade Commander from Lisburn, along with two officers loosely identified as belonging to the Int Section and an Inspector from the RUC Special Branch, tried to analyse the day's events. Their consensus was that it had been a bad day for the Provisionals and a pretty poor one for the Army.

From the Regiment's point of view, it had been a morale-sapping day, despite the triumph of recovering the big machine gun and the fact that they had killed Danny Keenan, who was known to be number two in the Ardoyne. A British infantry battalion is a close-knit community incorporating some 650 men and, then, all their wives and dependants. The point is that virtually all of the men knew each other. Although there is always a limbo group of men who are just arriving, passing through, and coming back, at any one time, at least two-thirds of the men are on better than basic recognition terms with their fellows.

So to lose an officer killed, a Sergeant severely injured, a Corporal and three soldiers wounded and critical to terrorist gunfire in one day hits hard at that family-like community spirit. It also, as the Colonel knew, bred a dangerous desire for revenge amongst the men whose whole ethos is based on a controlled system of the exploitation of violence. The casualties that the battalion had suffered in the rioting had also been relatively severe due to its unusually aggressive nature. Notwithstanding casualties on the other side, including an unknown number at the hands of the premature bomb, from the squaddies' point of view, there was an imbalance that presented the CO with a major problem for keeping control of the streets that coming night. It was going to be vital that a policy of aggressive foot patrols would be necessary in the Ardoyne that night in order to prevent further gatherings of angry young Irishmen, their aggression rekindled by the anonymity of darkness and alcohol.

But there were no fresh troops. All over the city, as the Ardoyne rioters tried to penetrate the citadel of Flax Street, the Provisionals had called their young supporters onto the streets to tie up Army reinforcements. In the Protestant sectors, the paramilitaries, always nervous of mob violence in the Catholic enclaves, had prepared in force on the streets. Hooded with balaclavas or with bandanas on their faces, they threw up roadblocks across the main arterial roads through the suburbs. The mere threat of their presence drove the law-abiding off the streets and forced further strains on the army to clear these blocks without further disorder.

The Deputy Brigade Commander, a bibulous full Colonel, lately of the Staffordshire Regiment, had organised for two companies of the resident Londonderry battalion to be sent down to relieve the pressure, but it would be some hours before they arrived. In the meantime, the least physically exhausted men the Colonel had available were the three platoons of B Company, the unit that had suffered the most severe casualties and about whose commander he was starting to harbour the gravest reservations.

The Colonel had ordered the gate sentry to tell him when Davenport arrived, and he had stormed down to the courtyard, determined to get an explanation from the Major of his extraordinary behaviour and why he had left his men. He marched into the courtyard and saw that Davenport was still sitting in the front of his Landrover. He walked across to it and opened the passenger door, saying in a calm but recognisably displeased voice, "Simon, may I have a word with you in private?"

Davenport turned his head to face him, and the Colonel was shocked by his empty eyes and grey, drained face.

"The killing has to stop," said Davenport flatly. "How can this madness continue when we are the same people, the same race?" His voice rose a pitch, indignantly. "My God, they're not Chinese, you know." He subsided again, staring at the dashboard while the nonplussed Colonel tried to think what to say. "I need a drink," muttered Davenport, heaving himself out of the Landrover, shrugging his shoulders. Apart from an occasional glass of wine, the Colonel knew that Davenport never drank.

When the rest of the Company arrived 10 minutes later, the Colonel quickly debriefed Roly and told him to get the Company fed and rested. They were to stay on standby at Flax Street for the moment. The CO wanted to discuss the very obvious problem that Davenport presented with his Second in Command.

One of the problems was that B Company did not have a Second in Command of their own. He could not just send Davenport off for psychiatric assessment and leave Flashman, the senior Platoon Commander, in charge. Live wire that he was, and clearly with the respect of his men, the clear evidence that Flashman might be a liability had already presented itself, and besides, Flashman was hardly a trained Infanteer. He was a Cavalry Officer.

Back in the Ops Room, Arthur Black, the Adjutant, asked for a private word and the two men went into the Colonel's office. The Adjutant looked uncomfortable, and as he closed the door, the Colonel spoke.

"What's the problem, Art? If it's what I think it is and Simon Davenport is involved, then I'm not sure that I want to discuss it at the moment. I believe that he's had a bit of a shock, and I want the Doc to have a look at him."

The Adjutant, always upbeat with a ready smile, was completely the opposite. He looked extremely uncomfortable.

"I know, Colonel, but I think things are too serious not to mention them. Simon has just killed the best part of a bottle of brandy – he's completely legless, and he'd been at the bottle even before he went out. Roly Flashman ran the entire op, including giving the "O" Group before they went. Simon would be history were it not for Corporal Tregus pulling him down. Not only that, but when Tregus went down, he did nothing and just screamed at Roly right in front of the men. Then he just legged it. He's been drinking ever since."

The Colonel dropped his head in his hands. Black continued.

"I took the liberty of asking the RSM to have a little chat with B Company's CSM. CSM Reynolds is a very worried man. According to him, Davenport is wound up as tight as a spring. He can't make a decision, and the command function of the company is in, more or less, the hands of whichever Platoon Commander, or Reynolds himself, happens to be in their Ops Room whenever a call comes in. If Flashman hadn't turned up this morning when he did, Reynolds was on the verge of reporting in directly to you."

The Colonel looked up with a look of extreme weariness. He did not particularly like Davenport; he didn't like many people, but he had chosen him. They had worked together on the staff in Hong Kong, and he had impressed with his efficiency. When he had learned that he was to get the battalion, he had phoned Davenport and asked if he would like a regimental posting, knowing that he needed one for his career prospects. Davenport had accepted eagerly, and the Colonel had fixed it. But this was the end of the line.

"Alright, Arthur. Thanks for telling me. I'll switch Maurice Findlater to B Company, and I have asked for a Second in Command ASAP from Regimental headquarters. Get hold of Maurice for me, please and while you're out there, brief the doc about Simon when he's finished with the casualties. I don't want that bastard Baines knowing about all of this," he ended savagely. Baines was the Deputy Brigade Commander.

Halfway up Butler Street, not far from where the Colonel was talking, in a house overlooking the rubble-strewn street where most of the rioting had taken place, Jason Doherty was trying to sort out his problems. Compared to the Colonel's, they were fairly sharply defined. Coming to the end of your career in the Provisional IRA was a terminal business. Nor did you collect a pension. Right now, this was the prospect, and the hairs on the nape of his neck were tingling. He could almost feel the muzzle of the pistol that was going to exact the Council's price for the monstrous bungled events of that day.

The best he could hope for was to get some credit for damage limitation. The loss of the heavy calibre machine gun was a disaster, as was the loss of Keenan's Armalite. Weapons were always much harder to get hold of than volunteers. Keenan's loss was itself less of a problem. He had been becoming a liability anyway and throwing his weight around too much. Now he would give the British another PR victory as the funeral would be widely reported.

The priority now was to get the other weapons out of Riordan's before a search party was mounted. Jason had no doubt that the Ardoyne would be swamped with patrols throughout the night.

"Jesus," he thought to himself, "I've lost four of my best guys today." And went downstairs to give orders that the streets should be kept live with people until well beyond midnight. He knew that the patrols would minimise their 'stop and search' tactics. After their day's successes, they had little to gain now from stirring up the locals. So he told his two lieutenants in the room below that people should start stoning if they saw a search happening, and the women were told to bang their dustbin lids if they saw any soldiers sneaking down the alleys or wherever. He would have to offer half price beer in the Club to keep them at it.

One of the two men was told to get a couple of Active Service Volunteers and bring Gerry Glove in. He had stuffed up the operation, and now he was going to unstuff it. Doherty wanted him to go into Riordan's to recover the remaining weapons and Semtex, the Libyan-sourced plastic explosive that was hidden there.

In Flax Street Mill, the men of B Company 4LI had been fed and rested in the troops dining area, and they had taken advantage of the little NAAFI booth to stock up on cigarettes and chocolate. They had mingled with the exhausted men from the other Companies as they had passed through, swapping stories on what had happened that day, until all bar B Company had gone to their beds to rest, fully clothed and with their boots on in case those on duty needed backup.

As darkness started to fall at about 5 pm, the Company's Platoon Commanders were due to be briefed by Arthur Black. CSM Reynolds would continue to command Peter Luce's platoon, and Sergeant Smith took direct control of Tregus' section until a longer-term candidate could be found. Roly would organise the patrol pattern. The night was broken up into three, four-hour watches. Roly's plan was for 5 and 6 Platoons to be deployed for the first four-hour session, with 5 Platoon taking the Old Ardoyne and 6 Platoon taking The New Ardoyne. The CSM, with 4 Platoon, would provide the rapid reaction force but deploy for the last hour when the clubs were likely to be emptying. For the rest of the night, one section from each platoon, in rotation, would rove the streets for two hours at a time while the others rested. It was a punishing schedule for the men.

At the briefing itself, Arthur Black reminded all about the wanted men whom Intelligence suggested were now in the area and passed around photos of them all. One was Jason Doherty, a familiar face to them all. He was likely armed. The second was a man called Dillon, also a familiar face to the soldiers and who was thought likely to have taken over from Keenan now that he was dead, but unknown to the army and the police, he had been one of the three to have died in the bomb blast.

The third photo was a close-up of the terrified face of Gerry Glove, fleeing that morning's shooting location, but Alistair explained they did not yet have his name. If seen, he was to be brought in for questioning but not before a Saracen was on its way, as they didn't want any more rioting.

The patrols had moved out and begun their tortuous quartering of the enclave. The mean streets of the Old Ardoyne were filled with menace, and soldiers had to balance the instinct of sheltering in doorways against the need to appear in control with confidence. These patrols were always hostile, and the soldiers were always spat at and subjected to foul abuse. The area was poorly lit, and the dark, putrid alleys needed to be watched carefully. If the soldiers ventured down them, dustbin lids would begin to rattle out the tell-tale song of their whereabouts.

The New Ardoyne was easier but just as dangerous. The street lighting there was brighter. The back alleys were broader and relatively clear of obstacles, but the soldiers presented much clearer targets to the would-be sniper. The small front gardens offered little protection, and the low walls had mostly been knocked down at the IRA's instruction. Soldiers, darting from cover to cover, were the subject of much mockery.

The patrol programme had reached its third hour, and CSM Reynolds was rousing Luce's platoon for a cup of tea and a bacon butty before venturing out to reinforce their colleagues when an RUC Landrover had been ushered through the front gate of the Mill. An RUC Sergeant, in plain clothes, had got out and gone straight to the Ops Room where the CO, Colonel Baines, the Adjutant, the Battalion second in Command, the Int Officer, and an RUC Special Branch Inspector were finishing off their resume of the day's events.

The RUC Sergeant bade them all good evening and handed a blown-up photo and a sheaf of papers to the Inspector. He read the file and plucked at his eyebrow at the impact of what he read sank home.

"This is not necessarily good news, Gentlemen," he said, addressing the group gathered there. "We've identified the young man in the photo as Gerald Glove. He has no previous record, so we were not able to identify him sooner. He is Seamus Glove's nephew."

He let them all digest the news before carrying on.

"Friends of ours!" There was a chuckle around the table at the euphemism for MI6. "I have known for some time that he has been associated with radical Republicans in Dublin, where he is at University. I'd have been surprised if he hadn't, but this is more serious. We have not previously had any indication of a direct linkage between him and the Provos. He is, by all accounts, very close to Seamus."

He paused and leafed through the thin sheaf of papers in front of him.

"It raises two issues. Firstly, is Seamus involved, and is his recent denunciation of the Provisionals all humbug? And secondly, how do we play this young man if we catch him?"

The Inspector looked around the table.

"I've been watching Seamus for six years, and although he'll shoot his big gob off with the best of them, I do not believe that he has ever espoused the cause of political violence." He paused. "I also believe that Seamus has been hurting the Provos with his speeches of late."

He turned towards the Colonel.

"I know it goes against the grain, but I think you are going to have to tell your boys to stand off from pulling the laddie in until we know if we've got a case. I think this is going to be one of those 'softly, softly, catchee monkey' jobs. If Seamus Glove goes radical on us because we've come down on young Gerry, it could do a lot of harm."

The silence that followed was suddenly interrupted by the rattle of baton guns firing in the streets outside the Mill.

"Christ Almighty!" bellowed the CO, "Not again. It's like bloody D-Day down there." He stood up and turned to the Adjutant. "A pony says it's Flashman."

The battalion second-in-command had moved to the radio operators when the firing started. He turned to the CO and said, "You lose, Colonel. It's CSM Reynolds of all people."

"Well, I might as well get up to the roof. Great Augustus. Things must be bad. Thanks Inspector, and we'll get cracking on that, but with that lot going on outside, you might as well stay here for safety."

For a few minutes, the Ops Room was a scene of enhanced activity as sitreps flowed in and the hastily roused soldiers of the other companies got ready to deploy. Suddenly, above the clutter, the deep sound of a distant SLR opening fire brought silence to the room. They could all listen to Roly's report as he radioed in the news that another IRA gunman was down and that he would get back to them with further info in five minutes.

"I'm just praying that wasn't Gerry Glove, Colonel," said the Inspector. "If it was, we'd better hope he had a gun on him or that his dabs are on the Browning. If not, your boy is in danger of going to jail for a long time."

In the streets of the New Ardoyne, Roly had been trying to stretch the long patrol without creating a focal point for hostility by the residents. This had involved a complicated series of manoeuvres in which the platoon had split up into sections and tasked with specific jobs such as searching a specific back alley or stopping a car and its occupants. The key was to ensure that the patrols never wandered too far from the main body and that the tasks avoided, where possible, the ire of the locals.

There was a fairly continuous flow of pedestrians passing them, seemingly impervious to their presence but, more likely, not wishing to respond to the 'Evening mate' that soldiers would offer since talking to the soldiers would be seen as collaboration. It had all been fairly quiet so far. One man, who had stopped for a pee in the alley, was so startled when he was confronted by the face-blackened soldiers that he forgot to undo his fly with a wet consequence. About the only amusing thing that had happened all day for the soldiers.

Roly had placed his three sections to observe a major crossroads leading away from the New Ardoyne when CSM Reynolds called up on the radio to confirm the location of one of his sections, a natural safety precaution as they were on the boundary of the two Ardoyne's.

Flashman could hear the rattle of fire from baton guns being used by other members of Reynold's platoon and then a request for help as his two remaining sections had come under a hail of missiles from the school area. Roly could not help remembering the CSM's obstructive attitude when he had asked him for replacement rubber bullets to make up for those expended in previous riots!

There was a flurry of activity around them as some residents ran towards the action, intent on joining in, and others went the other way, convinced that there had been quite enough excitement for one day. Roly's earphones squawked as Corporal Carter came on the air, whispering into his handset.

"Two three, this is Alpha. Delta one seven (the code number for Gerry Glove) has just passed my position with a group of seven other locals. He is heading east towards you. Over."

Roly thumbed the Pressel switch of his handset.

"Roger Alpha, we'll move in a moment. Standby to cut him off if he tries to run back towards you. Out."

Roly realised he had a problem. His instructions were that no arrests should be made without transport support, in the form of a Saracen, immediately available. Yet if he did not act fast, then the man responsible for killing Luce and injuring others could well walk free. He decided to gamble by using the Ferrets to cover him instead of a Saracen. He knew that the Ferrets had been positioned, together with their Saladin, a heavy armoured car, in a roadblock at the Triangle, just a few moments' drive away, so he thumbed the Pressel switch and spoke, "Tango Four, Tango Four, this is Two Three, over."

The languid tones of the Honourable Henry Armitage, the young Cavalry Officer commanding the troop, replied, "Dear boy, how nice to hear from you. All this excitement, and we've been terribly bored. What is going on? Er, over."

Roly grinned at the cavalryman's laid-back reply but knew that it covered serious professionalism and that he would be there in an instant if needed.

"Tango Four. I'd love to gossip, but we're about to snatch a bandit, and I need the Big Momma to come in now, and carry him away. Can you help over?"

Armitage's answer was crisp and quick "Roger Two Three, where to? Over." Roly told him and then called up Sergeant Smith, in charge of Tregus' section.

"Bravo, this is Sunray. Can you see the subject? Over?" Round the corner of the alley, Roly saw that the group was now less than thirty yards from his position. He used the radio again.

"All units Two Three, move now and cut off his exit," as he moved with his own men towards the subject. Just then, a girl's voice screamed.

"Watch out, Gerry. Soldiers. Run." Roly and his men erupted into the road from where the alley exited, barely 10 yards from the small group who were scattering in all directions. Two were running back towards Sergeant Smith, and they had stopped stock still, fearing the worst, and were now covered by Corporal Carter's lot. Another two, however, had dodged past Carter and were sprinting away like demented whippets towards the next alley entrance about sixty yards away. In the street light, Roly recognised Gerry Glove, a mirror picture of the photo that had been taken. He also saw a glitter of light and a shape from the thing that Glove was carrying in his left hand. The man was armed.

Shaking off one of the girls who was clawing at him, Roly sprinted after the two but knew he would not catch them, unencumbered, like him, with equipment. They were both lithe and quick. Instead, he shouted, "Stop, or I shoot," He cocked the action on his SLR, knowing that they would have heard the clatter of the breach block being released to slide a deadly 7.62mm round into the breach.

Roly shouted again, "Stop, or I'll shoot!"

Glove, slightly ahead of his companion, was now not more than ten or fifteen yards from the alley's entrance and sprinting as fast as his legs would pump. Roly knew he had to follow the rules in his Yellow Card, which demanded that you warn three times before firing, so he stopped and dropped to one knee, bringing the rifle up to his shoulder and starting to aim at the fleeing youth. He called finally, "Stop! Now. Or I'll shoot."

The point of the arrow in his optical sight was centred on Glove's back as Roly let his right thumb slip down to flick the safety catch from 'Safe' to 'Fire' and his index finger took up the slack of the first trigger pressure.

Roly was a naturally good shot. Time as a boy in Africa had given him keen hand and eye coordination, and his uncle in Kisumu had often taken him and his cousins out hunting from an early age. It was he who insisted that you kill with the first shot and that you do not leave an animal wounded, that you never kill for pleasure, and how to offset for a moving target, so Roly did all these things by instinct.

219

But now he hesitated fractionally. The adrenaline was pumping around his body. He found it hard to breathe. For some reason, despite his training and despite his instinct, he did not want to do this. He took a deep breath and fired. In the heat of the moment, Roly snatched at the trigger.

The butt of the rifle bucked against his shoulder, padded by the flak jacket. He saw the boy in his sights stagger, obviously hit, but apparently able to continue. Roly realigned his aim. Glove was virtually in the safety of the alley now, although he seemed to be staggering badly, and Roly took aim again.

Taking a deep breath, he centred the arrow, aimed slightly low, and squeezed the trigger again. Glove spun round and fell. His companion had dropped flat at the first shot and lay, face down, raising his hands over his head.

Roly got slowly to his feet and walked over to the fallen figure of Gerry Glove. Blood was seeping out of the front of his jeans where Roly's first shot had delivered a non-lethal wound to the left-hand side of his lower back and, without hitting either bone or artery, had exited through his stomach wall. The shot would most likely have been enough, in time, and Roly was surprised that it had not brought Glove down in the first place. The second shot had hit him squarely in the centre of his back, between the shoulder blades, and although the body twitched as the nervous system shut down, Glove was clearly dead.

In his left hand, he clutched the six-inch-long, black casing of a hand-held two-way radio of the type often referred to as a "Walkie Talkie". It didn't look as though he was armed at all.

To Roly's eyes, he looked about fifteen. Now, the need for speed was vital. The sound of the shots and the girls' screams had brought people running onto the streets. Only in Ireland, Roly mused, would the sound of gunshots actually bring people out of their refuges.

Anywhere else in the world, they would be cowering for shelter indoors. The big Saladin armoured car, shadowed by Armitage's Ferret, pulled up next to him. Instead of taking the time to lower the inert body of the dead boy into the hatch, Roly and a couple of men slung his body onto the engine gratings behind the turret and secured it with plastic handcuffs. Roly jumped up onto Armitage's Ferret and told him to get the body back to Flax Street as quickly as possible. As Armitage disappeared around the corner, Roly mused that only four minutes had passed since the fatal shot had been fired.

The next five were spent picking up the second youth and reorganising 6 Platoon's sections so that they began the process of leapfrogging each other down the road towards the Triangle, alternately providing cover to the rear where a large crowd was now gathering to meet the prearranged Saracens.

Detaching one of his sections to go and assist 5 Platoon, under the CSM, who sounded as though they were continuing to struggle with the rioting, they arrived back at the Mill 15 minutes later, just as another two platoons were leaving to put a stop to what had become a major riot by flooding the area with soldiers.

In the little house over Butler Street, Jason Doherty had heard the news of Gerry's death from one of the girls. Beyond a certain sadness, he had also felt a small sense of triumph. He was prepared to place a fairly large bet that Seamus Glove would be singing a different song tomorrow. That feeling was quickly replaced by dread. He knew, full well, that the debacle of the day's events would never be forgiven and that his time as a senior Commander in the Provisionals was over.

One day, soon, his bullet-riddled body would be found in some country lane or backstreet alley. They would give him a hero's funeral, of course, and the IRA's efficient PR machine would ensure that his death would be blamed on the army or Protestant paramilitaries. But just as surely as he could remember his own finger curling around the trigger of the M16 that had blasted the life out of his predecessor, someone close to him today would be told to ensure that Jason Doherty was condemned to history.

Armed with that knowledge, he had no intention of being cast as a hostage to fortune. In the false bottom of the battered holdall that accompanied him everywhere, he had secreted a false passport, an open-air ticket to New York, and US$2,000 in cash. He had prepared his escape route months before, ensuring his liberty from whoever threatened him first.

He picked up the holdall, which apart from its secret cargo, contained little more than a change of clothes and a couple of books, and slipped out of the back door of the house into the alley. There was an old Ford parked in the New Ardoyne, and he made his way there, confident that, even if he was stopped by the Army, he would not be recognised. The flight to New York left Shannon at 0945 hrs. It was seldom full, and he fully intended to be on it.

February 1973

Belfast: Flashman v Establishment

He had barely had time to step out of the Saracen when the RSM told Roly that he was wanted, urgently, in the Ops Room. As he walked down the corridor, he was intercepted by a worried-looking Adjutant, Arthur Black, and ushered into the Commanding Officer's office in Flax Street Mill, which dominated the Ardoyne area of Belfast.

Around the table sat the CO, the Deputy Brigade Commander, and an RUC Inspector, all their faces grim.

Roly saluted. "I'm not going to beat around the bush, Roly. Was that young man armed when you shot him?" said the Colonel.

Roly reached into his pocket and produced the Walkie-Talkie, which he proffered to the Colonel.

"No, sir. But he had this in his hand as he ran past me, and young Gerry Glove is on the wanted list. I obviously couldn't see it clearly, and I thought it was a pistol. I called for him to stop three times. When he didn't, I shot him." The RUC Inspector snorted.

"That'll never hold up in court. A half-weaned Legal Aid Barrister would rip that apart, much less a Silk."

Roly looked puzzled. "Court?" he queried. "There is no question but that I acted according to the Rules of

Engagement, sir." He looked at the Colonel. "There'll just be a coroner's enquiry, won't there?"

The Deputy Brigade Commander heaved himself out of his chair and, resting his fists on the table in front of him, stared at the young officer.

"You have created a very serious incident, young man," he said. "Not only was your victim related to a very prominent community leader, but he was also a resident of the Republic. I think you can expect both the Irish Government and his relative to call on us for retribution for what may well be deemed to be a serious offence. An enquiry will judge."

He paused and then continued.

"I am informed by your Commanding Officer that he found it necessary to warn you against the excessive use of force before. It appears that you are quite incapable of controlling your hot-headed and intemperate actions that seriously damage the army's relationship with the local community."

His voice grew pompous.

"We are here to maintain the peace and uphold the rule of law. Irresponsible and reckless behaviour such as you have demonstrated serves only to thwart our efforts to win the hearts and minds of the local communities."

Roly's mind was reeling. It had been a long and emotional day. He was physically tired and nearing mental exhaustion. The sheer absurdity of this senior officer's last statement temporarily drowned the more sinister meaning of what he had been saying. That was the Ardoyne out there, and the notion that there remained any spark of affection for or sympathy with the British Army, or the policies of any British Government, was so absurd that it would have been funny if it had not been said so seriously. And it edged Roly to a dangerous level of anger.

"That's crap," he retorted, careless of the consequences. "What did you say?" said the Deputy Commander, his voice rising and his face reddening with anger.

"How dare you speak to me in that tone?!"

The full impact of what this man in front of him was saying started to penetrate the fog of fatigue that was clouding Roly's brain. He did not know who he had killed yet, but he knew what the dead man had done and he knew that he had, personally, acted by the book in his challenge and opening fire. Now it appeared that the dead man had some political clout which was going to create some fall-out, and the three men in this room had decided that Roly Flashman was going to be fed to the wolves to allay it. He realised with absolute clarity that they had found and bound their scapegoat and the anger rose in him like a tidal wave.

Roly stepped forward, thrusting his face into that of the angry, full Colonel, startling him to take a step backwards, not touching him but tripping him into the chair he had stood from and making him fall to the ground.

"You listen to me, you arrogant cunt." The anger was thick in Roly's throat, and his voice came out in a low growl. His eyes blazed hatred, and the deputy commander felt a genuine moment of fear as Roly loomed over him on the floor. "I've been out in those streets more often than you've had breakfast, and I know those people."

He gestured at the wall beyond which lay the Ardoyne.

"They hate us with a passion and depth that will never be eradicated. They look at these walls, and they see a prison erected by privilege, English privilege, your sort of privilege. To bind and enslave them for eternity. And there is no mercy, no mercy, no compassion, and no heart and certainly minds dulled only to hate all and anything English. You can suppress them. God knows that is what we are doing, but you will never woo them. Not while Saracens are delivering the search parties and baton rounds are beating away the relatives of the young men being dragged to jails."

The Deputy Brigade Commander got to his feet and sat down. Roly took a deep breath and continued more calmly.

"You have the gall to come in here and lecture me with your pompous drivel. You know nothing. You do nothing. You're beneath contempt, but it will be you, you pompous shit, that will feed me to the dogs and then seek a medal for services to the Queen."

For Roly, a free spirit throughout his life, a pragmatist who sought consideration in others, a fair man brought up in Kenya and the Philippines, schooled in Switzerland, it had all been too much. It was somehow the culmination of 4 years of succumbing to the British establishment. All those drill parades. All that sycophancy. Roly turned on his heel and walked towards the door.

"You can take your British Army and stick it up your arse."

The two Colonels stared at each other, thunderstruck. It was Roly's CO who recovered first, leapt to his feet and yelled at Roly's retreating back.

"Come back here, Flashman. Flashman, stop, damn you, and get back here at once."

Roly had reached the stairs leading up to the Officer's Mess and started up them. All along the corridor, heads were popping out of doors, startled by the CO's furious calls and curious to find the reason.

"Flashman," The CO called again. "Come back, damn you. You're under arrest." Roly's voice floated down the stairs.

"Fuck you too."

April 1973

London: Awaiting Court Martial

Arthur Black, the Adjutant, caught up with Roly in the mess as he poured his second, very stiff whisky down his throat. He took Roly to a room in Flax Street Mill, which was to be his own. Arthur explained that since Roly was under arrest, he would be accompanied by another officer at all times. He suggested that Roly might like to catch up on some sleep but, realising how unlikely that would be, he sent for a bottle of whisky and left him to his thoughts.

In the morning, Roly's kit, eagerly packed by Brakspear, taking joy in his discomfort but containing a good luck note signed by all his platoon, was ready. Escorted by a monosyllabic Military Policeman, he had been driven up to Aldergrove and flown back to Brize Norton on an RAF shuttle. There, an RMP Lance Corporal had handed him over to the escort of an officer of his own regiment, the 11th Hussars, who had driven to collect him from the Regiment's own depot and take him back up north.

One week later, the CO of the depot explained to Roly that he was to be released from arrest pending a review of his case by the Army Board and that he should attend a briefing session at Stanmore, where much of the army's wider administrative tasks were handled.

Upon arrival, he was ushered into the office of a large and ferocious-looking WRAC major, whose fierce exterior belied the kindness with which she now treated the anxious young officer. Whilst Roly did not regret his actions, he was concerned about its wider effects on either his civilian or military future, and it remained the case that he was looking forward to the start of his Army Air Corps helicopter course at Middle Wallop in July. The WRAC girl was attached to the Judge Advocate's department, and all sorts of cases crossed her desk. She had learned to recognise those cases where there was a genuinely serious breach of discipline and those that were being used 'pour encourager les autres'. Sometimes, there were unsavoury, political ones, as in this case. It looked as though Roly Flashman had been well and truly stitched up.

Advocates of military justice frequently and loudly claim that a court martial is the fairest system of justice on offer. What the WRAC Major knew was that the verdict and the sentence in nine out of ten Court Martials were determined before the first witness was called. As gently as she could, she explained to Flashman that he had placed himself in an invidious position. The Army Board would accept his resignation, immediately, or he could opt for a court martial.

She watched the emotions roll across Roly's face. Already hurt and disillusioned, she watched him battle with the decision to go for a court martial and make public his betrayal. She knew what was in store for him. She couldn't divulge this, but she could seek to protect him where possible.

She looked at him directly into his eyes.

"You haven't got a chance. If you opt for a court-martial, you will most likely end up in prison. Take the easy option," she said. "I really do advise you to resign."

Roly had driven back to the depot. The next morning, the CO of the depot had called for Roly to attend his office. It seemed a good moment to hand in his resignation, and he didn't expect any resistance. It was early May, and it would be a shame about the flying course that he was due to attend, but the green valleys and open spaces of Africa were always waiting for him.

There were two civilians sitting with the Colonel, and one of them stood up as Roly entered.

"Mr Roland Flashman?" he enquired as Roly walked further into the office.

"Yes," said Roly, puzzled by the man's question and by the Colonel's obvious discomfort.

"I am Sergeant Dixon of the Metropolitan Police," he said.

"I have a warrant for your arrest."

Simultaneously, Sergeant Dixon held out a folded piece of paper. "You are to be charged with the murder of Gerald Aloysius Glove." As the sergeant read out the familiar warning and caution, Roly's mind reeled. He felt sick, and it took all his efforts just to stay on his feet.

This was the final act of betrayal. He was to be charged as a civilian and stripped of the Army's protection and its resources as he tried to present his case that his action had been taken in the line of duty. Even if he managed to escape judgement, he would be a marked man, vulnerable and impotent, to defend himself from the most vicious killers in Europe at that time.

Flashman sat down. He only vaguely heard the Colonel tell the Adjutant to fetch some tea. When it arrived, he sipped it gratefully, for his mouth had gone dry. He was too dazed to reply, but he was able to nod in response to the policeman's enquiry if he was OK.

"This is just a formality," said Dixon. "We have to take you to London, and you will appear in front of a Magistrate. You will be given bail, which the army is putting up, but I'm afraid you will have to surrender your passport and report to us on a regular basis. You also need to understand that yours is one of seven cases involving members of the Security Forces shooting suspects in the line of duty."

The policeman looked closely at Flashman.

"Am I getting through to you?" he asked. Roly nodded. "The first case against an RUC Sergeant will be coming up shortly, and it is the test case for yours and the other five. If he is acquitted, it seems likely that all the others will be dropped. If he is found guilty of either murder or manslaughter, then all of your cases will be tried on their merits. What we can do for the moment, despite all the bleating from the boy's uncle, Seamus Glove, and the Irish Government, is to keep a lid on it."

The policeman slurped on his tea noisily.

"For the moment, there will be no public record of these cases and certainly no press. The RUC guy's case is already in the public domain, but we are determined that none of the others will be. OK?"

Dixon stooped to pick up his briefcase. "We had better get on with it then. The Judge Advocate has given me the name of a Solicitor you might like to contact so you might like to come down to London with me."

As the two policemen moved towards the door, Roly's boss looked up.

"I'd like to have a word with Flashman before he goes. Thank you, Sergeant Dixon. Do you mind? He can meet you at the entrance."

The policemen left and the Colonel looked across his desk.

"Roly, I am desperately sorry about all this. I had absolutely no idea that this was being cooked up. It is an absolute disgrace and a shabby business. If you have any problems on the legal side, you are to call me at once, OK? I suppose the Army is going to continue to pay you for the moment, but that is the end of their involvement in a civil case like this. The next couple of months are going to be tough. Have you given thought to remaining active? Have you got any money?"

Roly sat back in his chair, trying to sort out the chaos of emotions that were swamping him. "Christ, sir. No to both. You know I had hoped to go flying. I also like the idea of going to Uni in Africa, Cape Town or somewhere; perhaps Salisbury; do a B.Comm or something."

"Right," said the Colonel. "You haven't been found guilty yet, and flying remains an option. This thing might drag on a bit, even months, before they get to you. The Army has said nothing about restricting any moonlighting, so you might want to double up on your income whilst you are twiddling your thumbs. I'd like you to ring this chap. You might like to get some experience in the City. Who knows, it might turn into something permanent."

He scribbled something on a piece of paper.

"This is my brother, Jeremy's, telephone number. I phoned him earlier. He's a big cheese in one of those Lloyd's insurance firms and should be able to fix you up straight away. He has never told me much about it, but he knows all about your circumstances and has a certain sympathy. He was in the Regiment too for a short while but hated it and pushed off to be a millionaire instead."

"Colonel," said Roly, "I don't know how to thank…"

"Nonsense," the Colonel cut him off brusquely, "you are to come and stay with Susie and I next weekend and keep me informed about how things are getting on. Nobody, but nobody, is going to treat one of my officers like this. You'd better be off now, or we'll have Plod breaking the door down."

Roly had left the office and said goodbye to the Adjutant who gave him an address, his cousin's, who had a flat in Putney and was looking for someone to take the spare room. Dixon was waiting for him in the Lobby and drove him over to the Mess to pack sufficient kit for the week to come before Roly returned in 10 days' time to spend the weekend with the Colonel.

It took them some five hours to drive down to London as Dixon insisted on stopping at a pub and buying Roly a pint while he phoned the solicitor to have him waiting at the police station behind Victoria railway station where Roly was to be formally charged. With a bit of luck, he hoped that Roly could avoid being banged up for the night.

As good as his word, Dixon rushed through the procedure of formal charging, and an in-camera hearing with the Magistrates was arranged for when the normal court session ended. Roly's case was set for trial in the High Court at a time and date to be notified, and bail was set and presented by the Solicitor. There was no police objection to bail, and Roly handed over his passport. Three hours after entering the police station, Roly emerged with his suitcase with absolutely no idea what to do next.

The next few weeks sped by. Roly went to work for the Colonel's brother, Jeremy, in the City. The job as a junior claims broker in Caliph Security Services, which few, even in the industry, had heard of, seemed underwhelming, but the claims were out of the ordinary, and he spent a lot of time responding to questions and tasks from the firm's employees who were temporarily abroad. Jeremy took more interest in his work than seemed necessary. There were lunches, and he was introduced to Jeremy's senior colleagues.

Roly wondered when what seemed like a non-stop interview would end.

He had contacted the Adjutant's cousin, Harriet, a vivacious dark-haired girl who felt it would be safer to have a man about the house. She had warned him 'darkly' about 'no playing at home' and made it clear that he should have no thought, ever, about touching her. She had then gone on to prove, over the following weeks that she was in rigorous training for the 'nymphomaniac of the year' award, trailing a string of lovers through the house. It had ensured, however, that he had a ready-made social life, and it led to a couple of light liaisons for Roly.

Roly had gone up to see the Colonel and his wife, Susie, that first weekend. He had needed to fetch his car anyway, but he felt good in the feeling that here was a surrogate family. The weekend had proven to be a template for future weekends. There would normally be either some shooting or a bit of riding, traditional Sunday lunches, and an evening pint in the local pub. Although the Colonel asked for a progress report, they left the Army out of their conversation.

Jeremy, the Colonel's brother and Roly's boss, had come on one of these occasions. Jeremy had asked the Colonel to invite a colleague from Lloyds, who had a country cottage nearby, to dinner. He said that the man, Andrew DeLisle, was interested in the reports that Jeremy was giving about Flashman's demeanour at work, his work rate, and his relationship with others. Flashman was to be led to believe that DeLisle was simply a family friend, which wasn't exactly true, but they had, by chance, been at school together some 40 years earlier, so there was lots of common ground.

The dinner was over, and the men had stayed at the table with Susie's admonitions that they were not to hang around telling filthy stories for too long ringing in their ears. They had passed the port and the smokers had lit up. Roly found himself sitting next to DeLisle.

"Have you heard if your case is coming up?" asked DeLisle. He had kept his voice low so that none of the other guests heard. Roly looked startled, and DeLisle had smiled thinly. "It is my business to know about these things," he said. Roly, the evening suddenly ruined at the introduction of this axe that was hanging over him, shook his head. Weeks had now passed without any progress in the RUC Sergeant's case. Roly could see the chance of hitting the July deadline for his flying course at Middle Wallop in Hampshire declining very rapidly. He had begun to think that his fall-back plan of starting afresh in Africa was the only alternative. He could still pick up a Private Pilot's Licence there, he supposed.

Wholly indifferent to the grimace on Roly's face, DeLisle continued. "If you get a positive result, it might be appropriate for us to meet again. Lunch, perhaps. Just you, Roly, and me in a couple of weeks, eh?"

"Just what I had in mind, Andrew," replied Roly, though he was simply hedging his bets.

After the guests had all departed with the Colonel, Jeremy, and Roly finishing off the port that remained and turning to the Calvados, Roly had asked what DeLisle's function at Lloyds was.

"Well, it's a bit difficult, to be precise, really," he replied. "He tends to operate at the, er, more robust end of the market, so to speak. Fraud and that sort of thing."

"Didn't he spend quite a long time at Hereford?" queried the Colonel. "Yes, now you mention it. I rather believe that I had heard that somewhere." Jeremy answered vaguely.

Roly went to bed puzzling as to the precise meaning of his conversation with DeLisle, which had clearly been set up. DeLisle had seemed knowledgeable about his life to date and was able to bring up a recollection of his own time either in Switzerland, an acquaintance at Rugby School, or the Regiment. But the events of that night were quickly overshadowed in the early part of the following week by news that the trial of the RUC Sergeant had opened. The daily claims desk routine became trivia, and Roly actually felt ill when an almost immediate delay in proceedings was announced. Legal arguments had bogged it down for two days. Roly had called Sergeant Dixon for an update, and the two of them had met for a beer. Dixon was able to report that the trial was now set to restart properly for two days hence.

Roly needn't have bothered. It didn't last long. His solicitor had rung after he had gone to bed. The judge had thrown out the prosecution case. The RUC sergeant was free to go, and all the other cases were dropped.

238

Roly let out a whoop of joy, stark naked, had danced out of his room to grab a bottle of champagne from the fridge. Harriet, his landlady, had poked her head round the door to see what all the noise was about and had let out a squeal of joy and flung her arms around him when Roly told her the news. She was also stark naked and her latest lover, on the verge of exhaustion himself, looked very worried as he wondered what was going to happen next and whether he was to be involved.

The next morning, Roly had driven into the City. He had called Jeremy and asked him if he were free to join him for lunch, saying that it was important. Over lunch, a wonderful schoolboy meal at Simpson's Tavern washed down with a fine claret and finished off with their special toasted cheese, he passed on the news. He thanked Jeremy for giving him the job and asked him to waive his notice as his course at Middle Wallop was scheduled to start in the next few days.

"Well, Roly," he said, "I'm absolutely delighted for you. We all are, and I hope you will be able to put it behind you. I think you should take the time to speak with Andrew DeLisle, however. It could be very beneficial. Either for now or in the future. If you allow me, I will arrange that for tomorrow morning.

However, I think we can probably waive your notice period." He smiled. "With the way you seemed to have developed into your job, it was becoming increasingly difficult to justify your existence in Claims."

Roly was little the wiser for his meeting the next day. DeLisle simply proffered the advice that if he were ever at a loose end, then he should get in touch. He opined that there were not many people in this world with Roly's skill set – the languages, the commercial and military experience, and the eclectic group of international friends that he had met at Aiglon and the very evident talents and character traits that had been observed whilst under Jeremy's tutelage.

On Thursday that week, the sparkling Hampshire countryside whistled by as he sped down the M3, past Basingstoke towards Andover, in his MGB. He drove with the hood down. He felt free. This was good.

Roly reported to the Army Air Corps HQ at Middle Wallop, where he met his fellow course students for the next 9 months. There was no question other than, after his recent experiences, he was going to enjoy life to the full.

Chocks away!

Autumn 2018

Westridge: Brakspear Reappears

There was a notice on the Residents' Board beside Reception in the Hall at Westridge. It announced that the CQC (the Care and Quality Commission) would be visiting in a couple of weeks' time for Westridge's annual check-up. On visiting the office to find out who the CQC were, it was explained to residents that they were the supervisory body for England's Care Homes, particularly important as the care side was the main source of revenue for Westridge. For those residents who wanted to know more, they would be briefed in the Bar at 2 o'clock that afternoon by the Director of Social Services from the local Council. A clean Bill of Health from the CQC, the independent regulator of health and adult social care in England, was really vital to Westridge's reputation.

"Bloody hell," thought Roly. "That really was Brakspear, then."

Nothing ever happened on Wednesdays, and it was raining, so golf was "off" and Flashman thought he might as well pitch up and have some fun. Maybe he would go and watch the rugby at the local club that evening.

Chairs had been laid out, not in the Bar but in a side room, and there was a trestle table at the front intended for the Council rep. Roly sat down and chatted with one of the other residents. 10 minutes went by, and the

241

meeting was supposed to have started. Roly thought this typical of some of the sloppy management against whom he seemed to fight a lone battle but it wasn't their fault this time. They were waiting for Brakspear's arrival as he had personally asked to brief the residents.

After another 10 minutes of waiting and Roly was on his second cup of tea. He was about to go back to his apartment when there was a noise at the back, and 2 people in suits walked in, carrying briefcases and went to the front.

There he was, his old Batman in the 11th. Roly was shocked. A dark, vivid streak ran from Brakspear's left cheekbone down to the corner of his mouth, which seemed to give him an almost constant air of menace. One side of his mouth was raised as if he was smiling – but he wasn't.

Some sort of terrible dream! Who couldn't notice the scar that he still bore, inflicted upon him by Roly's fellow officers? Roly had not been involved when Brakspear got the injury. He hadn't even been there, but he had heard about it. It had happened well after Roly had left the Army. Brakspear had been promoted to Officer's Mess Corporal, and the incident had happened after dinner during a drunken Mess 'dining out' evening. He had been made to hold a Guidon whilst the Regiment's Officers, piggybacking each other, took it in turns to "gallop" at the Guidon and spear it with a lance.

Other than the fact that they were in a Hussar Regiment rather than the Lancers that they were trying to emulate, you wouldn't have thought that anything could have gone wrong, but someone slipped, the rider's lance went off track and sliced into Brakspear's cheek, causing permanent disfiguration. Luckily the Medical Officer had been present to save his life, but not his looks and Corporal Brakspear had sued the MOD for personal injury as well as loss of earnings potential and disfigurement.

Brakspear now just looked menacing. The crooked smile was ready-made to appear as permanent joy at the discomfort of others, and here he was, at Westridge, leering at Flashman and, despite Roly's own astonishment at this turn of events, unsurprised to see him sitting where he was.

"That incident must have been all of 20 years ago," thought Roly. He recalled that the MOD had been forced to pay Brakspear a large sum of money; enough to put down more than just a deposit for the purchase of a small, terraced house.

Roly had found out that Brakspear, only marginally younger than himself, had been the Director of Social Services at the local Labour-led Council for 9 or so years. Having taken his exams before leaving the army, his rise had been meteoric. His feet were well and truly under the table. His staff hated him, but he was apparently good at his job with the largest budget of all the Councillors. Despite Council funding difficulties, his operation was held up by Central Government as a paragon of efficiency, nationwide even, and a shining example of how these things should be run. In fact, it was not impossible that Brakspear had been nominated for a knighthood in the forthcoming New Year's Honours List. Quite why

Brakspear had decided to attend the meeting himself was a bit confusing for Westridge Management. A man in his position would not normally turn up for a CQC inspection, and Roly felt for sure that it was not in honour of him.

In fact, Brakspear should be thanking him. At the Enquiry following Brakspear's Guidon accident, Roly had agreed to be a witness, testifying as to his character without mentioning his worst traits, and his evidence was contributory in persuading the Judge to make the large award. Roly remembered thinking that, when describing Brakspear's future with the regiment as being always likely to be short-lived or, as he had put it, 'probably always a goodbye', the judge must have misheard this as a 'Good Buy'.

Still, of such things can empires be built, and that did not mean that Roly could not have a bit of fun now. He could ask some difficult questions.

Brakspear had prepared slides and now went through these. They were descriptive of the CQC's purpose and the issues that they focussed on when conducting Care Home Operational Reviews. Hygiene was always at the top of the list. Inevitably, where there was such a close relationship with a Residential facility, the overlap between the two came under the spotlight as well. The routine, therefore, included feedback from the Residents, and the CQC had already arranged to meet a couple in their apartment during the course of their 2-day visit. Roly asked a couple of questions which received non-committal answers from Brakspear that he would '....look into it' or '...see what could be done'.

"Two can play that game," thought Roly. "Before this job, I believe you were a corporal in the Army, Mr Brakspear. It must be gratifying, in your current role, to continue to serve other people, don't you think?" said Roly casually.

But Brakspear was not a high-ranking Councillor for nothing. "Yes, I was. Mr Flashman, isn't it?" he said, deliberately avoiding Roly's title as Brigadier.

"My time in the Services taught me all about the inequities of privilege and birth. To those who have never experienced the challenges of entering life at the bottom, I say that I shall always strive to deny their influence in controlling the lives of others and to eradicate their pomposity in thinking that they have a right to do so."

The meeting came to an end, and Roly felt stupid for having asked the question. It had been unnecessary. Brakspear's reply had been the perfect riposte to his attempt for cheap fun. One or two of the other residents who were there had rather chuckled at Roly's discomfort without appreciating the former relationship that existed between the two of them. Roly wasn't sure how to handle this, but he couldn't just let things pass. He'd show Brakspear somehow!

Brakspear walked towards the exit. He nearly got there, but Flashman caught him just in time.

"How are you, Brakspear? You seem to visit a lot. Nothing else to do?"

"Mr Flashman," he replied, "I am not in the Army anymore and would ask you to have the courtesy to call me Mr Brakspear. Everyone else in the meeting did so, and I imagine that they found you as aggressive as I did in your questioning."

Roly was not going to be deterred. "Oh, sorry Brakspear….Mr Brakspear, I mean. How are you anyway? Life seems to have been treating you well, judging by your waistline. You and Sister Critchley could have some fun together, if you know what I mean." Roly was not to know that Brakspear already knew Sister Critchley.

Brakspear then made a mistake. Out of long-standing habit, he said, "Please don't bring her into it, sir," wincing as he realised that he had just called Roly "SIR."

Wow, that was a hangover from years gone by! Furthermore, he looked strangely discomforted by the mention of Critchley's name, and Roly wondered what there was in it. Did he know her?

"Never mind, as if it mattered," said Roly and Brakspear commented that it would be as well if he made himself scarce for the CQC visit in a couple of weeks and moved on.

Waking up in bed a couple of days later, Roly never understood why his dreams seemed so vivid to him. He wasn't sure whether their frequency was a natural product of age or something deeper. He frequently experienced some unholy sweats whilst sleeping, ending up with his sheets and pyjamas absolutely soaking, and a visit to the doctor had suggested the possibility of PTSD (Post Traumatic Stress Disorder).

"Don't be so ruddy ridiculous," he mused to himself. "Nothing of the sort. Shouldn't have had that red wine last night." And, anyway, he was enjoying life. He certainly wasn't depressed, as was the case with some of those young men who were returning from their Afghanistan tours, having experienced the most intensive of conflicts for often up to six months at a time. For decades even centuries, PTSD had been a taboo subject, not talked about as if its symptoms were rather embarrassing. But real steps had now been made in identifying it and even giving it a name!

All the same, Roly was still feeling a little bit downcast at the memory of the previous night's dream about his time in Belfast, so he gave his usual routine of a visit to the spa a miss and stayed in his room that morning, thinking that he would shake himself out of his torpor a little later.

The dining room at Westridge was full as he walked towards it that Friday lunchtime in November 2018. It was cold outside, and the white tips of an early frost on the grass outside were finally dissipating in the weak autumn Sun.

As he turned to go into the Dining Room, he saw Brakspear again in the office at Reception. He'd almost forgotten that he had attended Brakspear's briefing a couple of days before.

"For God's sake, am I going crazy? Why is he here again? Brakspear shouldn't be here!" Roly mused.

Brakspear had an affluent air about him and a seriousness which belied his aura of earlier years. Despite being overweight, he was even half well dressed in a dark suit and white shirt, albeit no tie. Feeling that he had failed to conclude their brief conversation at the briefing earlier in that week, Roly couldn't let it pass without saying something, so he wandered over to the office and popped his head around the door. He thought he would ham it up a little.

"Hello, Private Brakspear and stand to attention when I speak to you!" he said cheerily and then, quite sincerely. "How nice to see you again. I forgot to ask how life has been treating you. Are you selling something?"

Brakspear wasn't going to allow Flashman to get away with this, so he replied. "Ah, Flashman. You again. I hear you're treating the place like an Officer's Mess of old? You'd better think again. My Council's policy is that all homes in the region be run without regard to gender, ethnicity or background and the need to apply an equal opportunities environment. The Council considers that this should apply to the residents as well. I'd watch your step if I were you!"

Brakspear had delivered his riposte in something other than quiet, measured tones. It had almost been a growl, perhaps a threat, and spoken in a defensive way. Could it be because Roly knew about Brakspear's background?

"No, come on old chap. Why are you here? What's your interest in this place?" prompted Roly.

Brakspear glowered at him. "Mr Flashman, I told you that I am the Director for Social Services in the local Council, and Westridge falls within my patch. I don't think I have to explain my actions to you."

248

There seemed to be a certain 'authority' about Brakspear, and Roly decided that it wasn't worth hanging around to argue the toss. He was sure that the contractual basis of his own existence at Westridge was sound, so no problem there, and he imagined that the Punce might have complained or something.

The decibels from the dining room were rising, so he raised a hand at Brakspear, gave him a cheerful, "See you around then!" and sauntered off.

There were no free tables in the Dining Room. Worse than that, the room was chocker, with women making the most God-awful noise as they strove to make their voices heard above each other.

"Bloody cheek. What is that lot up to? I pay to use this place," thought Roly to himself as he sauntered next door to the Bar, where he found his friends Reggie and Tom Budge sitting down in the leather wingback chairs close to the roaring fireplace. They were chuntering about the circumstances too. "What's this?" said Roly. "Women's Institute gathering? All on 'transmit' rather than 'receive' as usual. Bloody din - should be banned."

"Buggered if I know what's going on," replied Tom, "but the 'Punce' seems to be involved as she stood up a moment ago and said a few words about water shortages in Africa and the desperate need to do something about it."

The Punce was indeed involved. She was regional Chairman for Water Aid, a charity founded in 1981 to reach the millions of people living without clean water, decent toilets and good hygiene. Actually, Roly rather approved of this. He had been in too many places in Africa where he, himself, had been close to suffering the dreadful effects of contaminated water and drought, but why did they have to hold their annual lunch here?

Lunch for the ladies was ending, and a few of them were wandering out, looking around as if they owned the place. Roly was gathering a cup of coffee from the side table. He should have recognised her, of course, when he turned around as one of the ladies introduced herself from behind, "Hello, Roly. What a surprise. How are you?"

Without thinking, Flashman responded automatically. "Oh, dear. Memory ain't what it used to be. You'll have to forgive me, but where have we met?"

"Well. It was an awfully long time ago, Roly, in Suffolk. Jane Ponsonby is my sister! We met at a lovely lunch with the Inneses just after you managed to give my mother, an apoplectic fit on the golf course at Aldeburgh. Jane and I had not been aware at the time. You may recall that we sat next to each other at lunch. We had a lovely time. Jane had gone home on her own and… I don't suppose I should be ashamed… you might recall that we got to know each other rather well that afternoon before you dropped me off later on."

Roly smiled at the memory. It was one that had stuck in his mind for a long time after the event, and he had himself wondered what had happened to Natasha.

"Well, I had to face the music with my mother. It all makes me laugh now, but at the time, it wasn't funny.

Mummy had been furious about your antics on the golf course and the noise you had made the previous evening. When Jane, my sister, told me that life here at Westridge would be perfect were it not for the childish antics of those chaps from Suffolk, the whole story came out, and I have been looking forward to seeing you again so much."

"I have often thought about you, Roly! I never confided what we got up to that afternoon, but it has stayed with me for a long time. I tried to write, but they said you had gone overseas or something. No-one seemed to know where you were. It was as if you had disappeared off the face of the map."

It all suddenly came back to Roly, and he struggled for something to say. "Oh Gawd. I'm sorry, Natasha. How awful of me. I thought of you too, but I had to scarper to Rhodesia at short notice."

Over time, Roly had had time to construct a useful story in lieu of the real facts of his departure for Rhodesia.

Roly responded, "Er…I was bound by the terms of my contract. You weren't alone. There were a lot of friends and mates who I was unable to communicate with at the time. It was all too hush-hush, I'm afraid, and I've been apologising ever since."

Accompanying this with a wink usually did the trick, and Natasha explained that she had found a very nice man quite soon after, got married and had two lovely children, now both in their thirties. Sadly her husband had died a few years before, and she had come here today at her sister's behest, partly to size the place up for her own future needs.

"But you must remember Tom here then", said Roly. "Hey Tom, look who has turned up for the books after all these years."

Tom turned round, and there was a whoop from them both as they recognised each other, the first time in forty-six years, and stories were swapped, memories shared!

"So the Punce is your sister? Pull the other one!" said Reggie. "You don't look like it! Are you telling me that Tom here has been hiding info from us for the last few months? And what about the Punce? Surely she recognised one of these two?" pointing at Roly and Tom.

"Well, she did," said Natasha. "She just didn't want to admit it!"

They spent another thirty minutes exchanging their life stories, and Tom and Reggie sloped off for their afternoon kips.

Alone together, Roly and Natasha smiled at each other.

"Would you like a kip too, Natasha?" proffered Roly with a puzzled frown on his face. He wasn't sure how to put the question discretely, but there was something about this woman that the years hadn't diminished – an instant familiarity, the heart-melting, and a feeling of happiness and, help me God, a stirring from below!

"Thanks, Roly," replied Natasha with a smile. "You are kind but I promised to drive Jane into town.

Perhaps another time. Maybe you'd like to come over for a spot of sups. I don't live far away; twenty minutes or so in the car."

"Sorry, Natasha. I just didn't want to offend you by not asking! And, yes, I'd love to join you. Probably rather easier than here with your sister looking disapprovingly at me!"

He was going to have to try harder than that this time, she mused, but as she left, she kissed Roly on his cheek and pressed her contact details into the hand that she squeezed upon departure.

It had been an interesting afternoon. First, Brakspear and then Natasha. He knew which one he preferred!

Overnight, Roly developed his plan. Four CQC reps were due to arrive at 0900 hrs the following week for their two-day visit. The office would naturally be their first port of call, and Roly had thought of a pretty harmless way of disrupting their visit. He knew he was being childish. He was 68 years old, for goodness sake, but it still amused him to anticipate the bemused distaste on the faces of the CQC reps when they discovered what he had in store. For that matter, the reaction of the residents would be funny as well. His plan was to trivialise the CQC inspection and obtain some sort of harmless negative comment which would irritate Brakspear. Roly needed some idea of their schedule.

He couldn't go into the office for fear of being seen as showing too much interest, but he needed a rough idea of their itinerary so that he could plan his campaign. He didn't have to. Just then, Reggie came round the corner bearing a piece of paper showing the schedule for the whole visit. Reggie and Joanna's home had been chosen as the Residential Apartment that the CQC would visit on the second afternoon at 4 pm for a cup of tea and a discussion.

"I couldn't see why not," said Reggie. "They were offering a free lunch. Joanna enjoys these things, and she's got lots of issues to get off her chest. Here, look," said Reggie, holding out a piece of paper that showed the schedule.

- Staff Quarters
- The Care Home
- The Kitchen
- The Spa
- A Resident's Apartment
- Interviews with key staff
- Lunch on both days in the Restaurant

The CQC were really only interested in the Care Home Operation and Staff Accommodation, but the steady flow of positive media articles on the wider aspects of Westridge and its financial stability made them eager to see and understand how the residential side was operated and how this interacted with the care home.

Reggie and Roly said goodbye to each other, and Roly went for a swim to plan his campaign for the week to come. Afterwards, Kirsty did his toenails as a favour, and he asked if he could buy her lunch on her day off. She enjoyed Flashman's company, and she could see no reason why not. After all, they weren't hiding anything, and nothing in the rules said that you couldn't fraternise with guests/residents/patients. But they left it like that for another day, and Roly went back to his apartment to get dressed, ready for a trip to town to watch the local Rugby team who had a Cup match that evening against big opposition.

En route, he had time to call into the local Party Fancy Dress and Joke shop. The first half of the game was good. Roly's team had held their own, and he was enjoying a half-time pint in the Crush Bar when he heard Brakspear's name being mentioned. "Hello," he thought. "What's this?" and listened more intently to the conversation.

After eavesdropping for a couple of minutes, he couldn't help asking the two guys whether it was the same Brakspear that they were talking about and throwing in, on a speculative basis, that the bloke was at Westridge that day. He couldn't see why the Director of Social Services had had to attend a routine visit by the CQC.

By chance, Flashman's fellow rugby supporters worked for the Council and were themselves not fond of Brakspear. He was abrupt with staff and seemed to be out of the office a lot which Brakspear always put down to external conferences but the staff reckoned were overseas holidays. And it was rare that he missed days at the local Newbury Racecourse.

It had been a great game for the Town. The second half was very tense. The Town had pipped it with a great dropped goal by the fly half with 30 seconds to spare, overcoming much greater odds than expected, and the Bar was buzzing afterwards.

The two Council employees had reappeared, elated by Rugby's success. Roly bought them drinks and prompted them for more gen. It was fascinating stuff, and he could barely believe what he was hearing.

Vowing to look out for each other at the next game, Roly returned to Westridge and mused over what he had discovered. It seemed that Brakspear made frequent visits to other care homes within the Council's area as well as Westridge. It sounded as though Brakspear had a deeper interest in what went on.

May 1974

Flying: By the Seat of his Pants?

It must have been the helicopter that had landed outside on Westridge's front lawn earlier in the week that had twigged the latest dream. In 1974, after three years with the 11th Hussars, a messy tour in Belfast with The Light Infantry, and 10 months training at Middle Wallop to become a helicopter pilot, Roly had been posted to 666 Squadron Army Air Corps at Topcliffe in Yorkshire's North Riding, just outside Thirsk. Topcliffe gave young Flashman full reign for his talents. If you couldn't have a horse, then a helicopter was the next best thing, and the 'Sioux' that he was now qualified to fly allowed astonishing freedom to one so young. As far as Flashman was concerned, it might have been the best job in the world.

Amazing as it seemed to him, Roly was awarded the Military Cross. Two weeks after his court martial case had been dismissed, he learnt that he had been recommended for the award and that Tregus, whose injury had resulted in the Shankill incident being forgotten, was to get the Military Medal. The recommendation had hardly come from the CO of the Light Infantry Battalion he had been with but instead from the CO of the Scots Regiment that he had supported during the dangerous events at Unity Flats. The Scots CO had observed Roly's actions that afternoon and deemed them to be heroic, fearlessly done in order to save the day. On the day of his medal presentation, he went up to Buckingham Palace and had the thing pinned to his chest by Her Majesty. Roly knew he deserved a pat on the back as it was a great honour to be presented with the medal by the queen herself. Whatever the system and the cronies that surrounded her, what a supreme example of dedicated duty, beauty, and inspiration she was, and Roly felt proud that he was a member of Her Majesty's forces. He could see Princess Anne staring at him, and Flashman was at a bit of a loss how the establishment could turn him from zero to hero in the space of a few months, but it was worth it and quite a "bird puller." He might enjoy the attention and benefits that came with his newfound status. For Roly, the best part of the day was his mum's attendance, the pride on her face, and the lovely day they spent together afterwards. For Corporal Tregus, despite his shortcomings, it had been a huge day. He was a born soldier, and Roly was very pleased that his bravery had been properly rewarded.

The ten months that followed at Middle Wallop in Hampshire, learning to fly, had been better than any holiday. Teaming up with his fellow students, all bachelors and a couple with whom he had shared the Mons experience, any pressures that the course had to offer were, frankly, non-apparent. The ground school subjects covering navigation, meteorology, the principles of flight and mechanics seemed as natural to Roly as the flying training itself.

"To travel is to live," wrote Hans Christian Andersen and flying gave Roly a new dimension to this adage which he adopted as his own. Roly and his course colleagues at Wallop fully intended to live up to this ethos with parties in the mess, madcap mid-week dashes to London and weekends at each other's homes with shooting or fishing usually on the agenda and always in the hope that his colleagues might have sisters! Indeed, it seemed that the whole establishment at Wallop was bent upon the pursuit of flying joy, even the gnarled instructors, ex-Battle of Britain veterans, who knew the meaning of living life for the moment.

These guys, most of them in their mid-fifties, would take time out of a student's scheduled flying training to meet up in the air, usually over Chilbolton Observatory, and re-enact their battles with the Hun. For the student in the front seat, it was not a flying experience to be forgotten. Aerobatics, precision and flying suspension all at once as the instructor would attempt to get "the drop" on their colleague whilst the student in the front seat was often violently sick into the brown paper bag that was carried in all aircraft!

Two weeks into training, Roly was scheduled to go solo. When the day that Roly's first solo flight became due, he was prepared. His instructor, Piotr Jarovski, an ex-WW11 Pole who had flown his whole family out of Poland in the first days of the war by purloining one of Herman Goering's Messerschmitts, had a unique method of encouraging recalcitrant students, nervous of taking control of the small Chipmunk fixed-wing aircraft used for initial flying training.

Seated behind the student and when confident of the student's prowess, Piotr would, famously, in his guttural Eastern European accent, unclip his control column and hand it to the student in front whilst adding the words "You haf control." It was a supreme act of confidence, some would say completely foolhardy, but his actions were designed to help the student concentrate his mind and boost confidence that going solo was well within the chap's capabilities.

Someone had forewarned Roly that this was likely to happen, and Roly had, himself, managed to get hold of a spare control column which he secreted into the aircraft during his pre-flight check.

When Piotr, thirty minutes after take-off, unclipped his control column from its base and handed it forward to Roly, saying, with his guttural east European accent:

"You haf control," Roly was ready.

Accepting the proffered joy stick with mock worry and fake words of concern, Roly flew the aircraft, flying solo for five minutes, demonstrating his capabilities, then reached beneath his seat for the spare control column. Whilst, in fact, retaining control of the aircraft, Roly calmly handed two control columns back to Piotr and replied,

"Here you are, Piotr. I hope I'm doing this right. Control back to you!"

It might not have been the best move by Roly in his life. Piotr might have had a heart attack! But Piotr was big enough to accept that he had been out-thought, despite the fact that he himself had a spare control column in the back cockpit. Piotr was ribbed incessantly by his fellow instructors, and Roly's reputation duly rose amongst his flying colleagues.

****

At the end of the course, having gained his 'wings', the squadron that Roly joined in Yorkshire was diverse and fun, and he quickly came to love the area – proper countryside and people who spoke their minds. The Dales to the west and the Moors to the east, quite apart from a beautiful coastline, the dry stone walls, old-fashioned pubs, market towns and the myriad of race courses meant for the perfect posting. He quickly discovered that taking illicit aerial photos ("training!") of local mansions and fine estates acquired easy popularity amongst the local gentry, as well as invites to parties where he met their daughters.

The Brigadier who commanded Topcliffe Garrison was not pleased as he frequently found himself a guest at the same party held by the local Yorkshire landowners as Flashman and couldn't work out how Flashman was getting himself invited. Yorkies were such a notoriously insular lot and never particularly disposed towards Southerners. Moreover, Flashman was hardly in the "Yorkshire" mould.

The Brigadier considered Flashman to be batting higher in the order than his rank, a lieutenant, should predicate. He didn't know that, for Flashman, the dinner party invitations were usually the host's way of saying thank you to him for the photos he had taken of their properties. If he had known that, he would also have had the answer to how the grouse and partridge that regularly appeared on the Topcliffe Officer's Mess dining table had got there. No-one would normally have bought them. He was also irritated by the affected Cavalry Officer's drawl that Flashman could put on when it suited him. He wasn't sure whether Flashman did this on purpose, knowing how grating this was, or whether it was a genuine affectation.

The Brigadier had harboured his doubts about Flashman for a while. Two months earlier, he had witnessed him playing cricket in a 40 overs a side game.

Roly was occasionally a member of the Thorne Barrow village cricket team, ostensibly a village team in the Dales League but really the private amusement of the Von Custer family who owned the estate there (and most of the village too), the same Von Custers as his friend, Gunther ('Krautie'). Roly had met his sister Priscilla once and vaguely wondered if she would be around that day.

The cricket pitch was below their famous columned house and separated from the house by a manmade lake within landscaped gardens – real Capability Brown stuff. The Brigadier and his wife had been house guests, and after Sunday lunch that weekend, Manfred Von Custer took his guests down to the pitch to support the team as if they were his private property.

Sadly, Krautie wasn't there.

The opposition had something of a reputation as they had a young 22-year-old batsman in their team who played League Cricket but still occasionally turned out for the team that had nurtured his nascent all-round talents. The young chap was notorious for his temper, which had got him into trouble in the past.

Roly was no mean fast bowler himself. When available, he played for the Army and had been bowling at his vicious best on a warm but overcast day that had everyone sweating. The ball was swinging, and the pitch was wanting, with the result that Roly had inflicted a few bruises on opposition bodies.

With the opposition reeling on 27 for 3, all at Flashman's hand, the omens had been good for Thorne Barrow in this limited 40 overs a side game. But the opposition had batted bravely, and by tea, had reached 130 for 3 with six overs remaining. They were now in sight of the target that Thorne Barrow had posted of 178 all out. Their number 4 batsman, the aforesaid 22-year-old semi-professional, tall at 6' 1", ruddy-faced, broad Yorkshire and ginger whiskers everywhere, had got his eye in and was 18 short of a notable century.

He was a cocky chap, too noisy for his own team, really, and liked nothing better than a chance to get up the noses of anyone with privilege. At Thorne Barrow, he was in the right place for that!

The first over after tea had been bowled, and Roly was brought back on. With the house guests looking on, Ryan Sissons, for that was the name of the aggressive opposition batsman, hit Roly for two consecutive sixes off the first two balls, and it began to look as though the opposition might actually make their target. He accompanied the second six with a snide:

"Thou's looking vexed nah, toffee nose," he said, and on seeing the Von Custer family on the boundary, "Gizzyer gaffer on boundary yonder wor regards."

263

Roly had a knack for languages and was already versed in the local vernacular. He had picked up a few words in the preceding months, and he replied:

"Shut chuffin gob, yer wanker. Ecky thump thi-sen down pit on Monday," wondering if he had, in fact, got that right.

Clearly, he had, as this provoked a snorting laugh from Sissons, and the comment had driven home. Sissons, with an almighty heave, played and missed the next ball and then followed this with an irritating and fortunate, top-edged four to the boundary.

16 runs off 4 balls left Flashers seeking revenge. With Sissons needing only two for his century, Roly conjured up an 80mph bouncer that Sissons missed. The ball thumped into his chest and then sped by 2nd slip to 3rd Man, giving the batsman an easy bye. There was some satisfaction to be had as Roly could see that it had hurt Sissons, who having got to the other end, had dropped his bat and was wandering around the crease looking skywards, massaging his chest. 147 for 3.

"Friggin' Tyke Wazzock. Snowflake more like," Roly muttered, making sure that Sissons could hear but out of the umpire's range.

The sixth ball was a beauty, a fast outswinger on a perfect length, and Roly had the other batsman's off stump cartwheeling backwards.

147 for 4.

The next over played out with two runs scored, one of them to Sissons, and it was Roly's turn to bowl again with Sissons, the non-facing batsman, now on 99, not out.

The new batsman took his guard and played the ball straight back. Sissons gave Roly the evil eye, rather uncomfortably for Roly, who enjoyed confrontation but only when it was on his terms. Still, out of the umpire's view, he flicked Sissons with his middle finger and mouthed, "Fuck you, Ginger," as he walked back to his mark and waited for the next batsman to get ready.

Roly knew that he had probably wound Sissons up too much, so he needed to be careful. Sissons could sense that Roly wasn't enjoying the exchange and decided to exploit this by wandering to the bowler's side of the crease to delay Flashman's run-up for the next ball.

An intense examination of the pitch further delayed matters until the umpire stepped in and warned Sissons about his behaviour.

Turning at his mark, Roly started his run up with Sissons still trying to put him off by anticipating the chance of a run by advancing down the pitch at the point of release. Roly pulled up and remonstrated with the umpire that Sissons should 'stay behind the effing crease,' or he would have no hesitation in knocking off the bails next time.

"Me thinks thee southern fairies lack backbone," whispered Sissons in a quiet and mock conspiratorial way.

A further false start, down to another Sissons' belated pitch inspection, produced a final umpire's finger-wagging for Sissons.

Sadly, for Sissons, disaster then struck.

All Sissons had achieved was to distract himself, and he hadn't noticed the stray bootlace over which, at Roly's next attempt to bowl, he now tripped and went sprawling onto the pitch. Flashman, cross at his third attempt at a run-up and at the point of releasing the ball, saw this and had the bails off the wicket in a trice. He knew he should probably have given Sissons another warning about leaving his crease early, but it wasn't his fault that he had tripped, and this was a limited-overs match. The batsman should know better.

"Howzzaaaaaat," howled Roly, even as his colleagues in the Thorne Barrow team looked doubtful at the wisdom of this.

The umpire had no choice. After a 10-second delay to allow Roly a chance to redeem his appeal, he put up his forefinger to indicate dismissal.

"On yer bike, mutt face. Thah might get century one day but not at my expense," goaded Roly triumphantly.

For Sissons, on 99 and one short of the century, it was all too much. Roly saw him coming, supercharged with fury, ready to take a swing and was off, haring to the boundary chased by Sissons. He couldn't head for the pavilion, with the opposition there in force, so he ran towards his colleagues at the wicketkeeper's end, the same end as the Von Custer lunch party had gathered.

Roly, laughing hysterically, was quickly shepherded by his colleagues, and Sissons had to be wrestled to the ground and restrained whilst his teammates came and got him. The lunch party, and the Brigadier, witnessed it all while Sissons was calmed down. That later turned out to be the second time that Flashman set eyes on the beautiful 18-year-old Priscilla Von Custer, later known for a good reason as PVC, but the Brigadier saw everything that happened, including what he considered to be Flashman's bad sportsmanship.

****

The same summer that he had been playing cricket for the Yorkshire village of Thorne Barrow, Roly had had another cricketing incident. Sophie Miller, who Roly had been going out with just as he had been going to Mons some six years earlier, was, in fact, the daughter of the school doctor at Ampleforth College, a preeminent Roman Catholic Public School based in the village of the same name. She had always been great fun and seemed a good prospect for a bit of slap and tickle again. She was now a reporter in London and quite well known for her investigative journalism. When Roly asked to take Sophie Miller out the following evening, she chanced to remark that the recent spate of good weather that they were enjoying would give her the excuse to seek to improve her tan in her parents' garden that afternoon.

"See you at 7 pm. There's a good restaurant in Helmsley that I haven't tried yet," she said. She would look forward to seeing him.

267

As it happened, Roly was tasked at short notice the next day to help a police search party for a missing prisoner from Holme House prison who had been spotted just south of Rievaulx Abbey. He took off with an Observer from Topcliffe and flew east at 500 feet towards Rievaulx, passing just north of Ampleforth. Radio contact, with the Cleveland Police conducting the search, was established, and a search pattern was instigated with Roly flying above a wide cordon that was pressing in on an ever smaller radius upon itself. Roly and his observer located the prisoner on the ground fairly quickly, and Roly spent the next half hour giving directions as the man tried to flee the chasing officers.

With the prisoner recaptured, Roly landed on the chance that any accompanying press might like to get his photo for the local rag, liaise with the Cleveland Police Sergeant coordinating it all and then left to return to Topcliffe.

Passing Ampleforth, he thought about Sophie in her garden. If she was there, a bit of showing off in the chopper before dinner that evening would not go amiss, even though most of his female acquaintances needed no extra encouragement to go wobbly at the knees in his presence. After a marginal detour, there she was in the garden of the Ampleforth College house allocated to the doctor, soaking up the rays in her bikini and sunglasses. It took about a minute for Roly to get her attention before she twigged, and she stood up and waved with both arms. God knows why he thought he had to impress the young aircrewman sitting beside him just as much as Sophie on the ground but what should have been a 60-second waggle of the rotor blades and encirclement of the house turned into a 20-minute flying display, torque turns, low swoops, auto rotation and all, sometimes descending to as low as 100 feet.

Satisfied and knowing that the fuel gauge would soon limit him, Roly then returned back to Topcliffe airfield, performed his 'after flight' checks and went into the crew room to sign in. He was looking forward to dinner now. The evening had promise. Sophie had briefly removed her bikini top and waved it at him whilst simultaneously putting the other arm across her chest, unsuccessful in concealing her very, very large nipples.

Roly couldn't wait to get down on the ground to be with her.

As he sat back and sipped the coffee that he had just made, Roly's flight commander, Hamish McCuskey, stuck his head round the crew room door and enquired how the task had gone.

"Damn successful, actually. The guy wouldn't have been rounded up so quickly without us. Good liaison stuff with the police, I thought, and we might get a few other interesting tasks in the future. Let's hope anyway, and there might be a few cuttings from the local rag next week."

"Well done," said McCuskey, "and, by the way, I've just had Brigade HQ on the line asking to see you. Can you pop over and report to the Brigade Major as quickly as possible, please? I guess he wants to say that the police rang to say thanks for your efforts."

Roly strode cheerily up the road to Brigade HQ and walked into the Brigade Major's office.

"Stand there," said the Brigade Major rather formally. "The brigadier wants to see you. I'll just let him know you are here."

The Brigade Major re-emerged from the Brigadier's office after a couple of minutes, and his mood had clearly changed. Instead of being told simply that the Brigadier would see him now, Roly was invited to stand to attention, remove his beret and then quick march on the spot whilst the BM called out "Left, Right, Left, Right...." in quick time. All of this, in Roly's experience, was pretty unprecedented for an officer, and he worried whether he was the butt of some sort of joke or otherwise. But, true enough, he was marched into the Brigadier's office, marked time at his desk and called to attention in front of a clearly unamused Brigadier.

"What have you been up to, Roly?" demanded the Brigadier. "I don't know what you mean sir," replied Roly.

"Yes, you do. You've been overhead Ampleforth, haven't you?"

"Well, I passed it on the way back from a successful op on the Moors, sir, and may have lingered. Actually, I think the Cleveland Police were quite pleased, sir."

"I'm sure they were, Roly, but I'm told that you did more than linger over Ampleforth and well under the height limit. In fact, you were there for 20 minutes, and

I have just been rung by the Abbott himself, who is furious. What have you been up to?"

Roly told him about Sophie though he missed out on the sunbathing bit and denied flying just above the rooftops.

"For your information, Roly, the College's First XI were playing the MCC this afternoon. Whilst you were demonstrating your flaming Baron Richthoven antics, they lost their opening 5 wickets and, consequently, the game whilst achieving the remarkable record of the lowest score by a First XI side in the school's history."

"Oh shit," thought Roly, "this is not good," and it wasn't. Roly was gated and given 30 days as Orderly Officer. That put paid to any thoughts of Sophie that evening, and he had to write to the Abbott and apologise. He was going to miss Sophie. She was due back in London in four days' time, sounded upset with him and made only a vague commitment to contact Flashman when she was next back.

Roly was Orderly Officer that night, but that was the only extra duty he did. He had called Sophie again to commiserate. It turned into a long conversation, at the end of which Sophie said she would call him back in the morning.

The next morning, the local press had rung the Squadron to interview the pilot who had facilitated the police search. They wanted to have a few more photos and interview Roly about what he had been doing after the chase. One of the police drivers returning home had seen him above Ampleforth. Permission was required for any contact with the press, so the Squadron

Commander rang the Brigade Major. After a brief chat with his Squadron Commander, Roly was sent over to the BM's office.

"No, of course not, Flashman. You can't be interviewed while you are Orderly Officer, and I'm almost certain that the Brigadier doesn't want to get involved in our secondary role in supporting civilian authorities at the moment. There is a defence review going on about this whole topic, and he definitely wouldn't want to be seen entering the debate with muddy episodes like the one you've got yourself into. So, just bugger off!" responded the BM.

"That's a shame, sir. The press seemed to think that my flying display over Ampleforth College was at the actual request of Ampleforth and for the benefit of their Open Day. I suppose that it would be worse if they realised that I was, in fact, there for my girlfriend.

The fact that the MCC were playing is just grist to the mill for the local labour politicians, and it seems a perfect occasion for them to have one of their periodical moans at a divisive education system. They feel that it's a disgrace that military assets might be so easily available to the upper-class elite for free when their own budgets are so tightly controlled. They seem to think that it was about time that military resources were used more often in support of the civilian powers and my actions yesterday were a perfect example.

They also hinted awareness that the Abbott, Basil Hume, and the Brigadier were long-standing friends from school days, sir, and suggested that it might not go down well with the public when they find out that

that the pilot, the grandson of the Hero of Cawnpore (sorry to mention that, sir) and the supporter of their own local police force a couple of days ago ended up by being punished for his efforts."

The Brigade Major was no match for Roly on these occasions. The previous week he had had to concede that it was not just Roly who had wilfully broken a fair bit of Officer's Mess crockery and, if he was to punish Roly, then he would have to punish a number of senior visiting officers who had participated in Flashman's game.

"Bloody hell, Flashman, why is it always you when something like this happens? I'm going to have to speak with the Brigadier," and the BM goes into the Brigadier's office. 10 minutes later, he is out again to fetch Flashman.

The Brigadier looked less than pleased. He knew that Roly had even understated his personal relationship with the Abbott. Someone must know that he attended Catholic Mass there more than once a week.

"Have you a suggestion on how we can get out of this almighty mess of yours, Roly, or do I dispose of you in some fashion?" the Brigadier remarked icily.

"The Squadron Commander thinks we can turn this whole thing round if we react positively and quickly, sir. It doesn't look favourable from the outside, but I feel that it needs me to rebut their concerns and turn the whole thing to our advantage."

Roly explained that all it required was an assertion that it was Flying Familiarity Training for the College

Cadet Force (it had been a Wednesday afternoon, after all) and hinted that he didn't need to be anything other than be truthful about the other circumstances. Of course, it was probably not a good idea to mention his own punishment or the Brigadier's friendship.

So that was it. The Brigadier was left with the impression that the Squadron Commander already knew about the whole episode. In fact, he didn't. He had simply taken a call from this female reporter called Sophie with a request to interview the pilot. The Brigade Major relayed the Brigadier's decision to revoke his punishment, a revocation always intended – of course!

Roly spent the night in Helmsley, where Sophie had booked a room at the Boar Hotel!

****

It was his last night in Yorkshire for five months. The Turks had invaded Cyprus, and three Sioux helicopters from 666 Squadron were to be deployed as part of the reinforcement needed there.

Operation Atilla was launched on the 20th of July 1974 and was the codename under which the Turks invaded Cyprus, supposedly invoking their right to protect the Turkish Cypriot civilian population. Having landed at Kyrenia and made early incursions, their plans fell into disarray when the Greeks managed to kill the Turkish general in command. It was a temporary lull. The British Prime Minister, Harold Wilson, later disclosed that the U.S. Secretary of State Henry Kissinger "vetoed" at least one British Military attempt to pre-empt the second Turkish landing in August but not before a British reinforcement had, by then, been sent to protect the two Sovereign Base areas.

Roly Flashman, complete with his new wings from Middle Wallop, had arrived to join his squadron in Topcliffe, Yorkshire, in May. Twelve weeks later, Roly and his colleagues were climbing out of the belly of the huge Belfast aircraft made by Shorts of Northern Ireland to reassemble their three Sioux liaison helicopters in immense heat at the hugely important NATO airbase at RAF Akrotiri.

Four hours after landing, the aircraft had been reassembled, and a flight test was undertaken on each. Roly and his small detachment landed at the sizzling, dusty barrack square at Episcopi, home to the resident Battalion, 1st Royal Scots.

It was somewhat of a phoney war at that stage, but the helicopters were important. Road movement throughout the island had been outlawed, and they were the only means of communication between the two Sovereign Base (British territory) areas – Akrotiri in the west and Dhekelia in the east.

The British Army is often lauded for being one of the best in the world, and during uncertain or difficult times, they seem to only get better. Whilst training intensifies, life is lived to the full, as who knows what tomorrow will bring. When not on duty, parties were thrown in the Mess, barbeques were held on the beach, and ENSA, an organisation which was set up to entertain the troops after WW11, came out to strut their stuff. Frankie Howerd, himself a soldier during WW11 and who took part in D-Day, was there to amuse the troops in his own indomitable style with Julie Ege, a Page 3 model, to titillate them at the Greek amphitheatre at Kourian!

These two handled the jeering, drunken Jocks perfectly. Frankie's perfect 'put-downs' of loud-mouthed comments from his audience, born of long experience of entertaining the troops, and Julie flashing her tits – well, almost – and the Jocks went back to barracks, having had their minds side-tracked from their normal routines.

Frankie and Julie were to become Roly's passengers the next day. They needed to be taken to Dhekelia for their concert there on the following night, entertaining the troops in the east of the island with the same routine.

With the three strapped into the Sioux helicopter, they needed a decent distance to gain translational lift and scraped over the roof of the Officers' Mess before rising to 2000' for their one-hour journey to the east. Frankie was no small man, and Julie found herself rather squashed in the middle seat, left thigh pressed firmly against Roly's right! It was hot, and Roly had elected to fly without the doors, greatly reducing the apparent size of the platform to those inside. Frankie kept his right hand firmly on the passenger handle while Julie, rather nervous, felt the urge to get close to Flashman.

By nature, Frankie was a nervous man, and Roly saw fit to soothe him by asking him about his acting career, suggesting that Cyprus would have been the perfect spot for filming "A Funny Thing Happened on the

Way to the Forum", and "Up Pompeii". Frankie was being very funny and, even in the casual talk between the three of them, feigned innocence about the obvious and risqué double entendres that he constantly inserted into the conversation.

"Titter ye not," said Frankie as Roly and Julie laughed at something he said. His droll sense of humour and memories were wonderful.

With the Troodos Mountains on the left to the north and the glittering azure blue of the Mediterranean Sea to the south, with its wealth of visible submerged Roman ruins, Roly was rather enjoying himself. Both passengers were quickly getting over their initial nerves and were soon enjoying the cool breeze occasioned by having no doors on the Sioux, so much so that Frankie was lulled to sleep.

Julie carried on chatting. She talked about growing up in Norway and her Norwegian life before coming to Britain and "making it" as a Page 3 pin-up girl.

Roly described how he, too, was essentially a foreigner in Britain, his early life abroad, his joy on joining the Army, and what could be better than being paid to fly like this, adding by-the-by "with the most gorgeous girl for company."

"I'm just sorry that I'm tasked with another passenger back to Episcopi this afternoon," he said.

"I'm sorry too," replied Julie, smiling and pouting at the same time.

Roly was just considering how he could change his planned itinerary when thoughts of a romp with Julie were suddenly challenged.

Roly had received his 'wings' just three months earlier in a small ceremony in one of the hangers at Middle Wallop. His course had included the future Director of the Army Air Corps, a senior officer from the Royal Tank Regiment, a bachelor who, to his great credit, had fully contributed to the high spirits on Roly's course and had himself harboured a monstrous hangover from the party the night before their Wings Parade. Roly had laughed a lot at the General's unsuccessful attempt to suppress the official course photograph, which fully showed the hangdog after-effects of the previous night's excesses. Because of his position, General 'Boy' Warner was compelled to say a few words, so he spoke to the aspiring pilots, encouraging them. He focussed upon the challenges, as pilots, that those passing out that day would face in their future pilot careers.

He was right because, at that moment, Roly detected a change in the rhythm of the single piston 260 hp Lycoming VO-435 engine that he was now flying, with important passengers, in Cyprus. Or so Roly thought. Roly checked the gauges. The engine oil temperature looked good. Was the cylinder head temperature slightly higher than normal? Had one of the fan belts gone?

Three months is a very short time to become an 'experienced' pilot. What should he do? Frankie was still asleep. He looked at Julie, who could see the look of concern on his face.

278

"What's wrong, Roly?" she asked.

"Well, I don't think there is a problem, but would you mind keeping an eye on the gauges? Here, this one, and this one." Roly thought that the answer to any concern that he had raised in Julie's mind would be to keep her busy and anyway:

"You don't get such chances every day to make an impression, Flashers! She'll think I saved her life!" Roly ruminated to himself.

And then it happened. An experience that, luckily, is taught to military pilots who fly low level in difficult terrain. Vertical wind shear is characterised by wind oscillations caused by mountainous terrain in windy conditions. But here they were at 2000 ft, well away from the 6,500 ft peak of the Troodos Mountains, and the 'rate of climb' indicator was suddenly showing an ascent of 2000 ft per minute.

Roly immediately lowered his collective lever to take the aircraft down. But to no effect. They were still climbing. Frankie had woken, stunned into silence, and Julie was making whimperish noises. This was not funny. In any other circumstance, Roly would have welcomed this beautiful girl next to him, clutching at his body. But not now. He needed all his faculties.

The altimeter was now showing 4,300 ft but with a rate of ascent slowing to 1700 ft per minute.

"Christ! We'll need oxygen soon," thought Roly, concerned. "This is serious. Should I put out a pan call or not?"

In the event, he decided on normal communication with RAF Akrotiri. "Akrotiri, this is Army Air 232, experiencing a spot of bother. 5 miles southwest of Stavrovouni Monastery. Over."

"Receiving you 232. What seems to be the problem?"

"232. It's 'wind shear', I think, but I'm climbing to levels that you might not suspect and don't want to bump into any of your jet jockey assets."

"Roger, 232," replied the calm Akrotiri Controller. "We're experiencing stronger winds than normal today. But you should come out of it soon. Keep me appraised, over."

"232. Roger out."

The aircraft had now reached 5,800 ft, but the rate of ascent was slowing. Roly had been higher, but his passengers certainly hadn't. Not in such a light aircraft, anyway, and without doors! Roly hoped that they had heard the calm radio exchange. He needed to reassure them.

"Sorry about this, you two. We'll get there. Alive. No need to worry. Pilot Roly is with you!" Despite the fact that flying in quite such challenging conditions was rather greater than previously experienced in Snowdonia, he said, "This is a pretty regular occurrence but not a comforting one for either of you, I quite understand. We should emerge from this weather feature quite soon, but I'd be grateful if you could just keep your eyes on the horizon since, up here, there are faster aircraft than us about!"

Roly thought that if they looked down now, they might focus on the apparent fragility of this, their very, very small platform! So he gave them a job that kept them busy with their eyes on the horizon.

30 seconds later, the Sioux emerged from the up-draught. They were at 6,400 ft, and Julie's nipples were standing out like organ stops in the colder air at that level, and Frankie's hair looked like it was standing on end rather more than normal!

Roly established a sensible rate of descent, and 15 minutes later, the Sioux landed smoothly at Alexander Barracks in Dhekelia. As the two were departing, Julie went to kiss Roly on the cheek but mistakenly ended up planting the kiss on his lips instead.

"I think you just saved my life. If you don't go back to Episcopi this afternoon, I'd love to see you after the show!"

With a smile, Roly turned away and said in a low voice, "Nice one, Roly!" and gave himself a pat on the back. Roly's return task to Episcopi was, mysteriously, delayed until the following day, and they were able to meet that night, a precursor for many fun evenings in London, later that year.

****

As Roly tossed and turned in his bed, endless images played in his mind like a film reel on repeat. He couldn't help but wonder if the drugs he was taking to relieve his all too frequent headaches were the cause of his vivid dreams. 24 hours after falling for Julie

Ege's charms in 1974, Roly had dreamt about the summer of 1976.

He had always thought of Canada as the Wild West "with manners". While the brash Yanks could get up your nose, Canada had a certain reserve, a helpful dual Anglo and Francophone heritage, and they could spell properly. With a landmass that is 40 times bigger than the UK and a population of about half, there were freedoms that the UK could not offer, and through a shared Head of State, as a Commonwealth country and as a NATO ally, Flashman had long wanted to visit.

So when the opportunity to go in support of The Gordon Highlanders ("the Gay Gordons") on Exercise Skilful Slasher at Wainwright in Alberta for six weeks arose, Roly jumped at the opportunity. The form was basically four weeks on exercise plus a couple of weeks after that for the boys to go and enjoy themselves for R & R. Eight weeks later, Roly found himself landing at Edmonton Air Force base in charge of two Sioux helicopters, a fellow pilot, Sergeant Richardson, three REME techies, two AAC observers, and two AAC ground handlers.

Many hours had been spent in the back of a C42 Hercules aircraft getting there. The Sioux blades had been removed for transportation, and they refuelled at RAF Gander in Newfoundland before landing at Edmonton, the capital city of Alberta, reassembling the aircraft, and then flying about one and a half hours East, South East to Wainwright.

The flight across had been uneventful. After Newfoundland, Air Trooper Spinks and his mates had skinned Roly for about £20, playing cards 'Chase the Lady' in the back of the aircraft for which Flashman vowed silent retribution in due course. Flying in the C42 was much preferable to the standard VC10. It was noisy and slower but it had legroom, you could walk about, and Flashman spent a lot of time in the cockpit regaling flying stories and swapping experiences with the RAF pilots.

One of the joys of the AAC was the high level of trust that could be placed in its personnel. The air troopers and mechanics weren't the average squaddies. The trouble with this detachment was that Flashman, who saw little reason to comply with outdated military convention, was in charge and that Richardson was a wild boy making up for early service drudgery in the Royal Corps of Transport. It also had Spinks!

The CO of the Gordons made it easy for Flashman to do what he wanted. He seemed to treat all those on attachment to his regiment with a leniency that contrasted with the severity of treatment of his own Battalion's officers. But the man was a legend within his own Regiment, and the Jocks loved him. The six weeks there, comprising two and a half weeks working up to a 10-day field exercise with the Canadians as 'enemy' followed by an adventure training period of 6 days, was as tough as they might have expected.

Flashman's detachment was not affected by the CO's demeanour. The exercise was useful stuff. Casevac and underslung load routines were revisited, mortar fire control was performed, recces and general liaison work, without the sort of flying constrictions which prevailed in the UK, meant for great flying for

283

Flashman and his men. The Alberta plains were a bit flat, but it meant that low-level flying was unrestricted.

The Canadian civilian flying community held weekly events called "Fly-In Breakfasts" to which Richardson was invited, subject to making some interesting contribution so the three of them would go along; Roly, Richardson, and Air Trooper Spinks, who was a qualified, free-fall parachutist. Roly smooth-talked the locals, Richardson did the flying, and Spinks would jump from about 3,000 ft. Wainwright was already 2000 ft above sea level, so the air got thin any higher than that, and it was too much for the underpowered Sioux to go any higher.

Richardson, a superb pilot, also had a couple of bird strikes but no damage, and when the exercise came to an end, the Canadians arranged a large BBQ for all the officers back at the Mess in camp. The Gordons did what the British Army does best in terms of male amusement; mess rugby, regimental songs, and such like, as well as some Scottish reeling, much to their guests' delight. It was madcap stuff. The CO was very pleased with Flashman's unit's contribution to the exercise, and the consequence of a challenge from one of the Canadians suggested that Flashman climb a water tower next to the mess, mainly borne of a desire to test his own officers' merits.

"Christ," thought Roly. He'd had far too much to drink already. "Why on earth would I want to do that?" But honour was at stake, and there was goading from the Gordons' officers.

"I'll go up if you lot do," said Roly and without waiting for a reply, was off. After all, the thought of looking upwards at the bare arses of kilt-wearing heathens would make Roly feel somewhat vulnerable! He needed a lift to reach the first rung and then was off up the ladder. Reaching the top, he looked round to see what he had just climbed and was greeted by the sight of some eight or nine of the Gordons, all pissed out of their minds, following him up the ladder.

A Gordon was heard to say, "I see yer goin proper Commando t'neet Wullie," as he waited for the officer above him to climb the next rung on the ladder. "Ach no" came the reply, "Ahm wearin me socks as regulation and ahm trustin yee to be too!"

In suggesting that they match his efforts, Roly had meant one man at a time, not the whole officers' mess! The CO looked anxious that a major incident was about to happen. Would the ladder hold them all? Would one of them slip and bring down the others? The CO was now bellowing at them all to come down but was being ignored, and Roly couldn't get down until they got up. It all ended rather inevitably as one of the Jocks stood on the fingers of another on the ladder below. A cry of pain and a swear word preceded the letting go of the ladder without a drunken thought for the consequences for the officers below, and 5 of the 8 officers below tumbled onto each other on the ground, unhurt but demonstrating that they, too, were true Scotsmen, all the while, laughing their socks off.

At the end of the exercise, Roly decided to take his detachment to Banff in the Rockies, an area of incredible beauty, for a bit of adventure training and for the two pilots to practice their mountain flying skills. They arrived at a likely campsite near Lake Louise, big enough for the single helicopter that they had brought, a deuce (two) and a half-tonne truck for fuel and other supplies necessary for a 4-day stay.

The journey from Wainwright would have taken 4 flying hours but for the land party it would be two days, so Roly pre-arranged overnight accommodation at the PPCLI (Princess Patricia Canadian Light Infantry) barracks in Calgary. The self-styled 'Greatest Outdoor Show on Earth', the Calgary Stampede, a tournament-style Rodeo, was in full flight with events including ladies barrel racing, bareback riding, tie-down roping, steer wrestling, saddle bronc, and bull riding in prospect.

Roly and Richardson were sitting in the crowd, beers in hand, watching the dangerous chuck wagon racing that was in progress when they observed a fight that had broken out some 10 yards away.

"Oh Christ," said Roly to Richardson. "That's Spinks, isn't it?"

"I'll sort him out," said Richardson and went over to where the scuff was going on, grabbed Spinks by the collar, and hauled him away from some pretty cross Canadians. Spinks had enquired where they came from and when they told him that they were from Banff, Spinks had asked if they knew Lake Minnewanka or maybe, in their case, thinking he was funny and not realising the near spiritual nature of the name to the indigenous Canadians, "Majorwanka more like?" Adding a remark about gay Cowboys had sealed his fate; a bulbous nose and a shiner had been the outcome. It was an easy decision for Roly. He had been looking for a candidate to maintain security at the campsite in the Rockies that they were about to reach. So Spinks missed out, until the very last day, on the wonderful landscape and magnificent aerial views that were to be had there.

Time in Banff was spent on mountain flying for the pilots, adventure training and site seeing for those not flying. Confined to camp, Spinks had not had much fun, so Roly's kindness in including him as his observer on the last day's flying came as a relief to him. When they had arrived four days earlier, they had reported to the local park ranger, who warned them that a woman had been killed the week before by a Grizzly bear two miles up the road. Roly and Richardson had seen a few, albeit of the Brown Bear variety, and a lot of them were in the habit of hanging around some of the tourist camps, looking for scraps; more of a nuisance than a threat, but a Grizzly was something different.

Their last night in the Camp had been fun. They had gazed at traces of the Aurora Borealis streaking through the night sky, many beers had been sunk, and generous steaks were eaten with relish. Satisfied with their lot and with the flames of their large campfire dying down, Roly and his men had crawled into their bashers for a good night's sleep prior to the following day's flight back to Edmonton and their return trip to the UK.

Two hours later, Roly was woken by a sound coming from the direction of the deuce and a half-tonne truck on the far side of the camp clearing. It sounded like a muffled scream, pleading for help. It wasn't surprising. As he opened the flap to his bivouac, Roly could see the menacing eyes of a bear as it worked its way through the contents of the rubbish sack that they had used for storing all their waste.

The bear had somehow managed to get into the back of the truck and had dragged the bag of rubbish over to the fire pit, whose embers were still glowing. The bear was then able to find and demolish the tastier elements of rubbish.

Roly turned on his torch in an attempt to frighten the bear away, but it was unsuccessful. The bear wasn't going to be dissuaded. It just looked back and growled in defence of its recently acquired meal. The muffled scream had been Spinks'. Spinks' bivouac was a mere 4 metres from the fire, next to the truck and the bear was between him and the truck. After drinking too much and finally going to his 'basher', Spinks had removed all his clothes, collapsed onto his sleeping bag, and left the flap of his bivouac open. It didn't matter that the bear wasn't a Grizzly. Spinks had had too much beer to be able to discern the difference, and they had all been talking about the death down the road the previous week.

"If you can get out of there, then I think you should," said Flashman to Spinks, almost under his breath and shouting quietly between gritted teeth. "Crawl out, under the other end and jump up into the cab of the deuce and a half. I'll create a diversion" he hissed.

Spinks had just enough time to put his shoes on when Roly, feeling that the bear was now looking at him threateningly, turned off his torch. For some reason, this had the effect that he had wanted, and the bear scarpered.

The only trouble for Spinks was that the bear headed for the wood behind the truck. For a brief ten seconds, as Spinks was slithering under the back flap of his bivouac, he was also naked in front of the bear, a mere two feet away, before the bear ran on into the woods.

Speculation reigned for the next few weeks as to whether Spinks or the bear had been the more frightened!

Canada had fulfilled all of Roly's expectations, and he vowed to return there one day. Seven months later, he was sent back to Middle Wallop to train on the Scout AH1 helicopter, an aircraft that had been introduced in the early sixties and unreliable enough to bear the nickname of "Flying Brick" due to the habit of its Nimbus engine to fail or fuel lines to get blocked. Four to six flying hours per engine had even once been the norm, and a competition was allegedly held, in those days, with a prize for the first unit that could achieve an engine life of 25 flying hours! In those days, the main armament was two forward-firing General Purpose Machine Guns, electrically operated, being fired by the pilot and aimed using a rudimentary system of drawing a small cross on the windscreen with a chinagraph pencil! In dusty conditions, these weapons could jam, which necessitated one of the free crew leaning out of the cockpit door and 'booting' the offending weapon in the hope of clearing it, a procedure not strictly in accordance with the flight reference cards.

****

It wasn't long before Roly's squadron was back in Ireland for another 4-month flying tour. The Scouts had become much more reliable by the mid-Seventies and low scudding clouds and squalls met Roly on a Wednesday morning as he took off from RAF Aldergrove with a second Scout beside him. They were tasked with picking up two sticks of four infantry soldiers from the army base that had been built on the old RAF St Angelo airfield at Enniskillen on the edge of Lower Lough Erne in County Fermanagh. These were called Tandem Eagle patrols, the practice of landing beside a road to perform spot vehicle checks when deemed necessary whilst the other Scout waited expectantly in the sky to react in case anything developed.

Whilst one runway at St Angelo was used as an accommodation barracks for British Army regiments during The Troubles, the other, though in bad repair, was used by the Enniskillen Flying Club on Tuesday and Thursday afternoons. For that purpose, someone from the Club would man a radio as quasi Aircraft Traffic Control during times when the Club was flying. It was always the same guy on the radio. Roly hadn't met him, but he was always objectionable, slow to respond and definitely considered the needs of the military to be secondary to those of the Club.

The previous week he had kept Roly waiting for some 10 minutes on the airfield perimeter before giving permission to land, permission which the Army did not strictly require in the first place and permission which Roly was not in future going to seek, so Roly had hatched up a plan with his fellow Scout Commander to teach the guy a lesson.

Built for wartime operations, the airfield would not pass muster today. The disused Air Traffic Control Office (not a tower and more of a prefab shed) was itself a mere 25m to the side of the only operational runway, a runway that was just about fine for Cessna and any other light aircraft but not for any commercial aviation.

The disagreeable controller now operated from what could not be called anything other than a good garden shed, situated between the runway and the old Control Tower.

When Roly, with a false American accent, called up on the St Angelo frequency to inform that he was a PANAM 747, Flight No. 595, that had been diverted from Aldergrove due to weather conditions and requesting "Joining Instructions" and dispersal facilities for the 270 pax on board, he was met with silence.

Roly repeated his request, and there was silence again, but after a few seconds, he heard a low response:

"No, no, no. Yer carn't land 'ere" came the stifled, quietly disbelieving reply. "Yer pullin' me leg."

"St Angelo. Panama 595. We are long finals. Estimating your location one zero minutes, I repeat, one zero. Request Joining Instructions. Over," repeated Roly in a smooth Texan drawl.

Roly's fellow pilot, in the other Scout, came on the air urgently, simulating Aldergrove, the main Northern Ireland commercial airfield.

"Hello, St Angelo, this is Aldergrove. We confirm this is a no-duff transmission. PanAm 595 has been diverted to us from Manchester, and Aldergrove has zero-tenths visibility. Desist any current flying operations as you are the closest airfield with runway length to allow this aircraft to land. Acknowledge, over."

"No, no, no. Yer makin' a mistake," cried the controller, somewhat more loudly this time, seeing his own life in imminent jeopardy. "Yer carn't fecking well land 'ere. The runway's too short, and there's no sufficient clearance to the sides for a 747."

Roly then delivered the coup de grace. "St Angelo. PANAM 595. We have you visual. Long finals. Urgently request Joining Instructions. I say again. Request Joining Instructions."

A strangled scream muffled the Controller's final response. "Oi sez yer carn't fecking well land here," accompanied by a clunk as he threw the microphone to the floor and made a run for the exit and across the grass to the airfield perimeter.

As he reached the edge of the airfield, the two Scouts appeared over the hedge beside him, two pilots and their observers waving and laughing at him. He never lived it down!!

****

The next week, Roly was on duty in Londonderry as a standby pilot at the so-called Fort George. Situated on the west bank of the River Foyle, Fort George was the home for a company-sized detachment which, at the time, was a well-known Household Cavalry unit. Generally, not much happened, so Roly had taken his book along to read in the Ops Room whilst completing his duty roster. Suddenly the radio burst to life.

"Hello, Charlie Zero, this is Birdcage, over." Birdcage was the nickname for the Brigade Headquarters.

"Charlie Zero reading you, over," replied the smooth 27-year-old Ops Officer manning his Regiment's Ops Room that day. The Regiment was known for its laconic style, perhaps more used to ceremonial duties rather than the exigencies of Northern Irish internal security problems.

"Birdcage. Reports of two bombs in adjacent shops in Great James Street in the Shantallow district. Get your men out pronto and cordon off the area. Felix (the codename for the Bomb Disposal Officer) is on his way. Over."

Not much had happened in Derry since the Regiment had arrived nine weeks earlier, but the duty officer, who was both cool and languid but razor-sharp, quickly buzzed the message through to the duty squadron on his bleeper machine. One of his fellow officers, nicknamed Bunty, was on the other end.

"Bunty, old chap," he said and repeated the direction from Brigade HQ. "Chop, chop," he added.

A small pause ensued, followed by Bunty's response, the voice of blue-blooded aristocracy representing three hundred years of privilege and authority.

"No. I shan't."

"No, no, Bunty. You can't do that. No duff call from Brigade. Get the boys out quickly," and he gave the name of the two shops in question.

A considered pause ensued from Bunty, only ten seconds but sufficient to seem that life and limb were about to be lost.

"You can't have heard me, old chap. No, I shan't," repeated Bunty.

Little known to the Ops Officer, Bunty had, in fact, already set the train in motion by nodding to one of his troop commanders sitting beside him, and the young officer and his men were already climbing into their armoured Saracens to tear off towards St. James Street, but that didn't matter to the Ops Officer. He was unaware of this and saw both his job on the line and the potential loss of life in the Shantallow.

"Stop fucking about, Bunty!" he now screamed, "Why on earth not?"

"Because you haven't said 'Please'," came the haughty reply.

Flashman, sitting there and listening to this conversation, had just heard exactly what the Ops Officer had heard. But suddenly, as his jaw was hitting the floor, what he thought was unbelievable, a discredit to the ethos of every soldier serving in Northern

294

Ireland, was drowned out by the screaming engines of six armoured personnel carriers racing towards their destination in the centre of Londonderry.

As the realisation that Bunty had conned him sank in, the Ops Officer put his head in his hands and began muttering to himself.

"Bloody…. I'll get the bastard for that one. "

All proved to be okay in the Shantallow. The situation was well confined by Bunty's men, and Felix had been along to negate the threat. Far from effete, Roly was to discover that Bunty was, in fact, a daredevil. He was Captain of the Army Cresta Run team and the current British number one. The man was a legend, and Roly would come across him later in his career.

****

The Odeon in Marlborough was always popular on Thursday afternoons because it was OAP Day. Tickets were only £3, and you could even get a cup of tea for a discounted price. It was always fun to meet some of the locals from Marlborough to find out what was going on.

The low-budget production that was inspired by an incident in Belize brought back vivid memories for him of his time in the Army Air Corps. The Guatemalans had been eyeing the Belizean oil reserves for some time, and the incident in question had occurred during that period.

The film wasn't an accurate portrayal of events, but Flashman enjoyed it because he had been there when

295

it had happened. He was attached to a Gurkha Battalion at the time and remembered the men talking about the incident. They were a wonderful lot, very professional, and Flashman, on a six-month flying tour, had really enjoyed their company and the challenging flying experiences in hot conditions in support of their jungle operations.

Based at Airport Camp outside Belize City, the Gurkhas had cleaned up just about every challenge that the Guatemalans had presented.

It had been a great 6 months for Flashman, as close as he had ever come really to consider himself as part of a professional fighting force in the British Army. He was grateful that he didn't have to do any fighting himself – that was the job of the Gurkhas. After the fiasco in Belfast, he could do without insects or rashes in the jungle, bashers in a tropical rainforest or compo rations! The aircraft needed servicing on a daily basis, and you could only do that back at camp. The pilots needed their sleep, and some of the officers' wives needed company. If bullets flew and, on the ground, they did so with notable numbers of insurgents captured and killed, then he was sublimely unaware of those that sped silently, but in deadly fashion, past his helicopter.

Roly hadn't experienced the extent of personal freedom that he found in Belize. As long as you did your job well and stayed within acceptable bounds, no-one questioned what you were doing in your free time.

In between operational commitments, Roly had a great time at the Belle Vue Club in Belize City ('best rice and beans') and Cross Country dancing on Monday nights in the penthouse above Barclays Bank Dominion and Colonial Overseas. Roly would often fly out to the Cays with female companions to spend an afternoon sunbathing and snorkelling. He was particularly attracted to one girl – the Commander's daughter – for her sweet-natured beauty and sense of humour. Roly respected her stance. She didn't want to put her father in a compromising position, and Roly found himself curiously frustrated by having the company of others instead of this girl on such occasions.

There was also the occasional weekend's R&R (Rest and Recuperation) in Florida, Mexico, Tegucigalpa or El Salvador, often culminating in one officer or another's attendance in front of the Commanding Officer on Monday mornings. But the CO was usually forgiving as he was from the work hard, play hard school himself.

On one such occasion, it had been Roly who was up in front of the CO when he had failed to make it back in time for the first parade. He had gone off to San Salvador with his friend George Fricker ("Flicker") to have some fun. Flicker was easily led astray, and after 6 hours spent drinking at the Napoléon Duarte Hotel, they were unceremoniously turfed out and quickly found themselves on the main street of an ill-reputed part of town.

Flashman had wanted to experience one of the "hallowed traditions" bestowed upon the area by visiting American sailors – the ritualistic "Dance of the Flaming Arseholes" on top of the roof of some infamous toilets. More often than not, it was the matelots who would perform their act whilst their colleagues in the street below would chant the "Haul 'em down you Zulu Warrior" song, which subsequently became a staple song of many an all-male military binge!

The possibility of some other sort of "action" hadn't actually crossed Flashman's mind!

Flicker was first. He'd only walked 20 yards down the street and was regaled by a beautiful Central American girl offering him the full works. Too drunk to think of the consequences, Flicker was ushered without protest into a nearby doorway. Flashman, just as drunk as his friend, had a current 'squeeze' back in Belize and thought it might be a little unfair to pass on the dose of Syphilis or whatever else this place almost certainly offered. But, at the offer of refreshment from the Madame, he did go in and followed the Madame down what seemed like a small corridor, dimly lit with doors to three booths in quick succession every 2 yards or so. Flicker had disappeared, but there was a pretty wild noise coming from the middle booth, and Flashman assumed that Flicker was getting his money's worth.

Madame was a lady of some experience. They entered a parlour room at the bottom of the corridor occupied by two of the most beautiful local girls that Flashman had ever seen. Madame could see that Flashman couldn't take his eyes off them, sat him down and started to flatter him, walking round him as she did so, touching his shoulder, and Roly could feel his defences falling. One of the girls came over, and when he heard the immortal words, "Sir, wanna good time…..aah. Sir have oil applied....velly gentle," his defences nearly fell.

"So what the heck," thought Flashman, "I can't catch anything that way," but he couldn't bring himself to follow the girl into one of the booths.

It turned out that Flicker was unlucky. What had seemed to be an incredibly beautiful San Salvadorian girl proved to be a queen in full regalia? But Flicker still had his enjoyment and dozed off for 30 seconds, feeling intensely complete but regretful at what he had done.

"Shit, what if I get the clap?" was Flicker's instant first thought as he woke 10 minutes later and then wondered whether Flashman might have waited for him. Hearing creaking and laughter in the neighbouring cubicle, Flicker stood up on the bed to peer over the partition. It wasn't Roly but another customer, naked on the bed with his member being held by the girl from the parlour.

That was the end of Flicker's weekend in San Salvador.

He jerked his head back in an uncontrolled whoop of laughter and woke up in A&E at the Hospital de Diagnostico. In peering over the partition, Flicker had forgotten about the overhead fan and was instantly knocked out. There was blood everywhere.

Flashman, hearing Flicker's demise from the parlour where he was sitting, later recalled that Flicker's fellow officers reckoned it had been the worst value for money that anyone had ever received – about

Belize $1 per stroke. But it was even worse for Flicker, who had lost his wallet with his ID card inside.

Flicker was kept on one of Diagnostico's wards until Monday morning. The British embassy sorted Flicker out whilst Roly had tried to inform the Adjutant in Belize, but he knew it was a lost cause. They were both absent on Monday morning, and they were stuck with all the usual consequences: being confined to camp and doing a long spell of extra orderly officer duties.

****

Belize was the place where Flashman had won his Distinguished Flying Cross.

At Westridge, Johnny Jeffries, an Air Transport Command pilot who had flown Dakotas (DC3S) in the late 50s, had long been intrigued by how Flashman had won his DFC, an award more typically given to RAF officers. But he felt it would be impolite to ask. So he asked a friend's son who worked at The MOD if he could get the citation for him.

"For outstanding gallantry on active operations against the enemy from the air, Lieutenant Flashman single-handedly flushed out a large unit of enemy terrorists. He refused to leave the area of conflict for his own safety. Without his prompt actions, and alone in the face of considerable danger, other active British operations in the area would have been at risk. For this and outstanding flying skills, the award of a DFC is recommended."

Flashman was in the middle of resupplying the Gurkhas in the jungle near the Guatemalan border in the south of the country when his Hostile Fire Indicator, a small device attached to the underside of his Sioux helicopter, started going off.

"Bee, bee, beep," it went urgently and noisily in his flying helmet as all quadrants on the console display lit up and flashed, supposedly indicating the direction from which fire was coming.

This device worked on the basis of sensing the pressure wave in front of a bullet as it passed, although it wasn't very reliable and was often triggered when flying through heavy rain.

"Bee, bee, and beep," it went again, frantically. Having established the direction from which the hostile fire was coming, the pilot was supposed to fly away from the threat.

Resupply wasn't the only reason for the mission that day. He also had a senior officer on board. The Gurkhas, who had been posted here for six months, were part of 2 Division and Lieutenant General Sir Frank Trims-Parker, their divisional commander, had wanted to visit them.

Prior to his staff appointment, FTP, as he was known because of a symmetry with the same letters pasted on most walls of Protestant Belfast, had been a brother officer of Flashers in the 11th Hussars. He had been the CO just before Flashman had joined them in Germany five years before. He was a bit of a dandy but a very professional officer. He was also good company, and on this occasion, nervous about what lay below them and not keen on flying. He loved his old Cavalry Regiment. To find a fellow officer in Belize was unusual, so the banter had been good on the 50-minute journey from Belize Airport down to Punta Gorda, and Flashman caught up on the regimental gossip, helping the General forget his unease.

Roly was able to deploy a branded mixture of fake deference and charm, so it was easy to calm the General's nervousness in case of any contact with the enemy.

They were at about 700 ft above the ground and approaching the Gurkha base near the border, Flashman pointing out the ridge line on the starboard side of the aircraft (the side of the aircraft that the General sat) and remarking to the General that it was those hills where the Guatemalan infiltrators were suspected of having their base when it had happened.

"Bee, bee, beep," shrilled the Hostile Fire Indicator again while FTP was looking into the distance away from Flashman.

Its urgent, insistent beeping had immediately changed the mood of comparative serenity that the two had been enjoying. FTP forgot about the horizon and jerked his head, and gazed anxiously across at Flashman. As far as he was concerned, his life was now in Flashman's hands. Roly had to react fast.

The standard drill was to reduce height in order to reduce your profile to anyone on the ground whilst putting out a contact call on the radio.

"Hello, Zero. This is Alpha One One. Contact. Wait out," screamed Flashman as he put the aircraft into full autorotation. They immediately descended at 2,000 feet per minute, zigzagging all the while down to the very top of the jungle canopy whilst Flashman got his bearings.

"Hold on, General!" said Flashman and forty seconds later, they were skimming the top of the trees. "This could be a tough one."

They flew southwest at a low level, avoiding all varieties of startled birds before Roly was able to get back on the radio again to the Gurkha Company base. They were only five minutes flying from where they had made contact, but it might have felt like an eternity as Roly tried to get out of range of the enemy's weapons.

As he reset the Hostile Fire Indicator, he said, "Hello Zero. This is Alpha One One. Contact. Up to 15 Charlie Tangos. Grid 48992400. Landing your location imminently. Over".

They reached the jungle clearing that comprised the Gurkha HQ, and Roly lowered the collective lever to descend. Flaring at the bottom, he levelled the Sioux as they neared the ground and performed what might have been the perfect "engine off" landing.

"Christ," he said to Trims-Parker, wiping his brow, "Did you see them, sir?"

As the blades came to a halt, Trims-Parker, who had nearly wet himself, opened his mouth, but nothing came out for a moment.

"See who, Flashman?" he said, irritated by the shock to his own safety.

"About 15 of them, sir. I thought we were goners at that range. I'm just going to inform the Gurkha Company Commander of their location," as he unclipped his seatbelt, removed his helmet and ran off with a Gurkha Sergeant who was waiting to take him to a group standing a short way off in armed readiness.

60 seconds later, he was back again. The General was gathered up by the Gurkha Company Commander whilst Flashman wound up the engine, engaged the blades and took off again with a Gurkha observer, all within the space of four minutes from landing. He was going to attempt to flush the Guatemalans out into the open again while a Gurkha ground party, already departed, homed in on them.

It appeared that the Guatemalans looked like getting away, but after a two-hour search, the Gurkhas reported finding human trails. A more comprehensive plan with the aid of other Battalion elements would need to be put into place, so nothing more was likely to happen until the next day.

Three hours later, the General satisfied himself that he had sufficiently shown his face, discussed the plan of action with the Gurkha major, and then it was time to get back to HQ Belize City. Whilst, in reality, Trims-Parker had no jungle experience, he decided that it would be good for his reputation if he was seen to be taking some sort of overall active command of the follow-up. He contacted Battalion HQ on the radio and arranged to meet the CO immediately upon return to the Battalion HQ Ops Room.

The follow-up occurred the next day. It was a major success for the Gurkhas, with four insurgents captured and seven killed and widely reported with Trims-Parker's name prominent amongst those who were given credit. Whilst causing somewhat of a diplomatic stir, it was also a great statement to the Guatemalans of Britain's commitment to the Belizean Government. It did his reputation no harm at all, and he was grateful to Flashman, who he cited for a DFC as well as recommending promotion to Captain – all in all, a good day's work, thought Roly later on.

In truth, they had been flying along quite routinely. Nothing much happened on these liaison flights, and Flashman reckoned that a prank played on a fellow officer might go down quite well with the Regiment when related on the next Regimental dinner night.

He had distracted the General to look away from the console and out the other way. In the act of the General doing so, Flashman had furtively pressed the Hostile Fire Indicator's test button, and the whole thing had lit up.

The rest was pure fiction. Flashman had seen no Guatemalans on the ground. He had made the whole thing up. For the Gurkha patrol to then find the trail of insurgents was a stroke of luck.

A lot of celebratory and congratulatory drinks later and back in England the next year, waiting at Buckingham Palace to have the medal bestowed by Her Majesty, the Queen, it was barely all Captain RHA Flashman MC, DFC could do to contain himself; a Distinguished Flying Cross for playing a practical joke on the

General but he could now never share the joke with anyone. Not even Princess Anne, who was looking at him again!

Flashman's citation and justification for the medal reflected its purpose *"for acts of valour, courage and devotion to duty whilst flying on active operations against the enemy."*

"That'll do nicely," thought Flashman.

The arrival of a Harrier detachment meant that things started to quieten down in the south of the country, and flying duties became more routine. Pilots from Europe came out to receive "hot and high" training. The "do's and don'ts" of flying over the jungle were taught, and navigational training and light liaison duties meant that Flashman enjoyed the near-perfect life.

When things were quiet, Flashman would arrange to meet the Commander's daughter at a pre-ordained RV, and they would fly out to one of the Cays, where they would sunbathe, snorkel and barbecue a fish.

With all his regular duties well fulfilled, Roly was given pretty much free rein to do what he liked with his detachment for further "training". He would go shooting the blue-winged teal on the American-owned rice farms there, with the duck being beaten towards the line of guns in which he was standing at the far end of the paddy, and on other occasions, after pre-agreement with local Mayans, they would often shoot the iguana that lived in trees above the rivers into the hands of villagers who waited, hungrily and gratefully, in canoes in the river below.

No-one knew that he always wore his swimming trunks below his flying suit, and he loved his quasi-alternate role as a travel guide, especially to a friend called Nina, landing with her on top of the majestic beauty of Altun Ha, a Mayan ceremonial temple. Here, only ten years before, a nine-pound jade carving of the Sun God, Kinich Ahau, had been found. Viewing the rare Manatees, the hammerhead sharks and the graceful Manta rays along Belize's coast had been a rare privilege.

Not much had changed in Belize since the days of Admiral Nelson. Back then, it was known as British Honduras, and it was a den for privateers and pirates, gaining the soubriquet of The Mosquito Coast.

Roly enjoyed himself to the full. Six months of bliss and the DFC had sealed his reputation.

But he just couldn't get the Commander's daughter out of his mind!

November 2018

Westridge: The Knackers

"COUNCIL REJECTS PLANNING APPLICATION"

… ran the headline on Page 4 of The Hungerford Herald together with a photo of Sally and Hector Cummings outside their pub, 'The Pound of Flesh'.

"Despite a recommendation from the Town Planning Committee, the owners of The Pound of Flesh pub are up in arms that their pub has had its application for an extension declined. Disruption to the use of the towpath by walkers was cited as the reason, as it would be deemed to have an effect on tourism to the area during construction. The probable noise from a variety of events to be held in the extension was also considered to be unacceptable. Sally and Hector Cummings, the owners, had made pre-application enquiries of the Council, had the full blessing of the Parish Council and local residents, had themselves proposed restricted hours of operation for events and had twice modified the plans to accommodate Council pre-application comments."

Hector Cummings said he was 'at a loss'.

"That is why we want to build it," said Sally Cummings. "So many of our clients in the summer are spilling onto the towpath that it occasionally gets blocked, and our proposal seeks to alleviate the problem. We also wanted to create an event venue which we haven't got in our town. We are well out of earshot of residents. This is just politically motivated by that labour lot."

They certainly had the support of the Knackers, a group of older residents who met once a month on Friday lunchtimes at a predetermined local pub. Flashman, on arrival at Westridge, had quickly acquainted himself with a bunch of local roués. They self-styled as, collectively, "The Knackers", partly because of their age but mainly because they spoke utter bollocks. The form was usually a pint or two, pie from the menu accompanied by too much red wine and back home for a kip and a snore.

Most of them had achieved a certain level of respectability in their careers, yet here they were behaving like sixth formers again – exchanging bawdy jokes, faux rudeness, and discussing the prospects for England's Rugby team in the forthcoming Home Internationals and where they were going on holiday in the spring. They didn't seem to mind too much about any offence they caused to other fellow pub guests because it was never intended. They always looked forward to their sessions, and the banter was mockingly aggressive, which made for half the fun. Their wives sanctioned it all on the basis that they had a good three hours or more peace and quiet, in their absence, at home.

Now approaching 70, Flashman actually lowered the average age, but these lunches were enjoyable.

Two weeks before the headline in the local rag, the Knackers had lunch at The Pound of Flesh, the local pub on the canal that had been cited in the local newspaper. They hadn't been there for nearly a year, since the previous owner had banned them for a loose comment made by one of their group to a member of his staff.

"Morning Flashers, you're late," said the retired judge who now drove elderly care patients to the hospital most mornings. Flashman smiled back and cast his gaze around who was there. A couple of the regulars were away, cruising somewhere sunny overseas, but the insurance broker was there, the underwriter, two ex-bankers, another ex-Army officer (a logistics regiment) and a couple who had never worked in their lives.

"Yah, well…. I got detained in the spa. At least I don't have to do the hoovering like you lot. Or was the price for being here hanging out washing or mowing the lawn? Such wonderful lives you all have."

It was towards the end of lunch, and everyone had been feeling jolly. Each wanted to hold court, and the result was raised decibels which didn't seem to be causing too much irritation to the other pub clients who were there that day. A pair of late arrivals ('Ladies who Lunch') had just sat down, and Flashers nodded politely as he recognised the big-breasted foghorn, Lady Barlow, who had been sitting with Lady Ponsonby in the bar at Westridge a couple of weeks before.

As the waitress came over, there was a lull in the sound of conversation in the pub. It was the Foghorn's companion who was first to order and said she thought the Roast Pork sounded good, at which one of the knackers, an Australian, who had overheard and was seeking to impress his friends with his wit, had commented, rather too loudly:

"I wouldn't have the pork, lady. I think I've just had the arsehole!"

Attempts by the Knackers to suppress their amusement didn't work. Half of the other regulars in the pub had also heard the remark and were chuckling as the Foghorn feigned shock and her friend looked embarrassed. The Foghorn had spotted Flashman when entering the pub, and she hadn't forgotten the sleight delivered by Roly in the Westridge bar and here was a chance to get even. Quite calmly, she said to the waitress:

"I'd be grateful if you could fetch the manager, please."

"We're in trouble now," said the Australian to Roly. Silence reigned as Hector Cummings came in. He knew that the Knackers had been banned by the previous owner but wanted to give them a chance and had dropped the ban as he recognised that a number of them came to his pub independently with their families and acquaintances anyway. The Knackers were in luck. Hector was one of those who thought that any publicity was good publicity. He saw the Knackers as young at heart. It was just that they were slightly older in other places.

The Foghorn complained how unsufferingly awful their behaviour was. She asked Hector if he knew who her husband was because this sort of behaviour would not be good publicity for the pub. As she banged on for a good two minutes, Flashman's friends, for whom this was just the sort of sport that made these lunches such fun, started to yawn and spread their hands with their palms upwards, shoulders hunched and eyes rolling in looks of mock disbelief.

The Knackers were quite clearly enjoying themselves, and their suppressed mirth needled the Foghorn to spectacular effect.

"I am not going to put up with this," she screamed to Hector, "and I'll have this pub closed if you don't watch it."

The pub became silent in astonishment at her outburst. The Foghorn realised that she was the focus of everyone's amazement and couldn't take it. She got up, accidentally knocking her cutlery to the floor, and stormed out, leaving her friend still sitting at the table.

Flashman, sitting there, had seen it all before. Just as he had won Lady Ponsonby over, he now went to the Foghorn's friend, still sitting there and asked her to join the Knackers at their table, supported charmingly by his fellow Knackers. She rather enjoyed herself, and forty-five minutes later, after her own lunch, which the Knackers insisted on paying, even said as much before leaving.

"You know who that was we offended. Don't you, Roly?" said one of Flashman's friends afterwards.

"Yes, but go on, tell me then. I think it might be the second time that we've offended her in two weeks. Who is she?" responded Flashman.

"That was Bella Barlow, the wife of one of the local Councillors. Her husband is a banker and the local Tory party Chairman, Sir Ken Barlow."

Flashman's friends sniggered. One of them got up and said to Hector that he was sorry for the uproar. No-one could understand. It was obviously some chance remark that Lady Barlow had completely misunderstood.

Hector was good friends with the editor of the local newspaper and saw an opportunity when Lady Barlow made her preposterous threat. He knew that the Tories, under Sir Ken Barlow, would not want to be seen supporting the Labour Council's prejudice against the pub's plans, so he reckoned that this would help the Tories recapture the Council.

Life must be fun in the Barlow household!

December 2018

Westridge: An Unholy Stink

The 68-year-old Flashman waited in the lounge with a cup of coffee for the arrival of the Care Quality Commission, his jacket pocket containing a packet of small phials of Ching's Stink Bombs, bought a few days before from the joke shop in town. When their car pulled up outside at 9 o'clock, Flashman was quickly up and heading for the porch and entrance hall.

He planned to introduce the CQC to his plans for the day early on. Chuckling to himself, he dropped two phials and then used the heel of his shoe to crush them on the top step of Westridge's main entrance. He didn't wait around for the horrible odour to permeate before going back to the lounge to fill up his coffee cup and watch the fun begin.

The four reps, three women and one man with briefcases in hand walked towards the entrance. As they headed to the reception desk, Flashman heard one of the women:

"Gosh, that was pretty pongy. What on earth was it?" was her furtive comment, attempting to banish any suggestion that she was the cause.

They all wrinkled their noses, but no one was going to do anything about it. Flashman smiled and watched them go into the small office beside reception which they were using as a base for their visit. From behind the paper that he was pretending to read, Roly could see that they were talking about the smell as the manager, Mr Fletcher, was in there with them, and they were pointing towards the front door.

The morning went well for Westridge. The staff accommodation had been visited and checked. The staff, who operated a three-shift system, had seemed an exceptionally happy lot; a mixture of ex-NHS nurses, both male and female, and qualified Asians and East Europeans. All spoke good English. Those that didn't live locally were accommodated full-time at Westridge, with shared facilities. Above them sat Critchley as Matron in charge with three Deputy Matrons, all ex-QARANC and three senior nurses who comprised the nursing team. They had broken for lunch halfway through the day.

One of the two local GPs, Dr Huggins, who administered to Westridge, was also attending the afternoon's session with the CQC. The CQC seemed very happy with what they saw. Westridge was a modern and professionally run facility. Its customers were as happy as they were ever going to be, and they could only see positive comments in the visitors' book, made mainly by visiting relatives.

Care home management can be difficult as elderly patients can be uncooperative; some may suffer from dementia, and many have little to say. Their medication needs to be given precisely and on time. Most of them are unable to wash themselves. Almost all of them have impaired hearing or vision. Their rooms need to be cleaned, they need to be fed, and they nearly all have demanding relatives keen to ensure that their aged mother or uncle receives the best palliative care in a sympathetic and caring environment.

It can be very challenging for the staff. Without the discipline and leadership of someone like Critchley, standards can fall easily in such an environment, and the CQC could tell that she was doing a fine job.

Lunch had been weird because that same old smell was back, and it permeated the dining room. Westridge management was trying to figure out where it was coming from, but they didn't have any luck. It certainly ruined everyone's appetite. Some of the residents even complained about it. Johnny, with whom Flashman was sitting, commented:

"What's going on, Roly? Smells like a back alley in Delhi in here."

"Probably that little dog of Ponsonby's again," replied Flashman, and they both smiled conspiratorially.

For Johnny, Flashman's company was a godsend. They often shared their experiences of various military theatres over the previous 50 years at the bar. Johnny had been a fast jet pilot, and the pair maintained a mock disdain for each other's speciality and service arm.

"Chocks away, eh, Johnny? Let's eat. Crab cocktail on the menu?" Flashman asked.

"No, Roly. I think it's Compo, so you'll be alright. Any more squaddies in here tonight?"

Johnny knew that Flashman was proud of having made Brigadier, and a reference to squaddies usually got under his skin. Flashman and Johnny had never actually met whilst serving, but with a mutual love of flying, they shared many flying reminiscences and often had others listening, rapt, to their experiences and usually chuckling.

Back to thinking about the CQC visit, Flashman hoped that his lunchtime plan would come together. At 12 o'clock, he had snuck into the boiler room and broke another phial so that it could permeate the air conditioning system. The first place people had gathered that day was the restaurant, and by now, the foul smell had permeated all the main rooms. Some grumpy-looking faces were to be seen. One or two couldn't stand the stink and returned to their rooms, asking that their meals be brought to them there. But that didn't do any good for those with apartments in the main block since they were affected by the smell too.

Flashman could see that the awful odour was now making a lasting impression on the CQC. Later, after it had dissipated in the main rooms, there it was again, the same strange smell that had greeted them in the morning and at lunch, back in the entrance hall and porch as they bade farewell at 4 pm, only worse than when they had arrived.

That evening, in the bar, with deep satisfaction, Flashman reckoned that he had had a good strike rate - three definite 'hits', out of three! It was all anyone could talk about as they gathered for their evening meal, and Flashman had a wonderful time in his best 'wind up' mode.

"Who was that Brakspear chap from the Council the other day who seemed interested that we were all kept abreast of this CQC visit? I bet he's got something to do with it!" he said.

Someone chipped in with a complaint about pensions not keeping pace with inflation and Westridge's recent loss of council subsidy being a misguided 'tilt at the rich', and it was quickly concluded that the smell was all Brakspear's fault!

The next day, the CQC were back again. It seemed that the problem in the porch had been fixed as they smelt nothing as they entered the building and headed for the office.

Flashman had kept one bomb reserved for the corridor outside Reggie and Joanna's apartment for when they met the CQC at 4 pm and had plotted another for the Spa changing rooms when they visited there later that morning. He thought about getting something into the kitchen area again but reckoned that the kitchen staff probably didn't deserve the comments that would definitely flow this time. And he didn't want to be spotted!

He showered and felt clean after an hour in the Spa, and then he went to the bar for a lunchtime snifter. He had almost forgotten about anything else and just wanted to enjoy the rest of the day. The morning had been great.

The CQC visit to the Spa had been timed to coincide with the Water Pilates lesson that was held on Thursdays. At 10:45 am, Flashman had already had his swim and was sitting on an exercise bicycle in the fitness room when those attending the lesson arrived for their hour-long session. He could observe what was going on as there was a big plate glass window which looked out into the pool. One by one, those attending the class emerged from their respective changing rooms and lowered themselves into the water. It always amused him to spot the bubbles on the surface where the older residents swam, and he thought that today's smell would have them all, definitely considering their diets. Kirsty, who was taking the lesson, clapped her hands to get their attention, and the lesson began.

Flashman had wanted to get the CQC to be the architects of the smell on this occasion, and the thought had occurred to him when he had been chatting with Kirsty about their visit. Kirsty had asked him what he thought she might do for them when they arrived. Flashman suggested she put out some chairs and a table beside the pool so that they could have a cup of coffee while they watched Kirsty doing her Water Pilates routine in the pool. So coffee had been ordered for 11:15 am to coincide with the CQC's arrival.

Flashman reckoned he might have about twenty minutes to carefully affix two phials to the underside of two chairs before the Pilates lesson started. The idea was that when the CQC sat down for their coffee, the phials would be crushed, and the smell would be released. With all the water on the floor, they would be well-nigh invisible.

It worked like clockwork. Peddling his legs leisurely at the bicycle exercise machine, Flashman couldn't help but laugh helplessly at the sequential looks of

319

disdain, distaste and consternation, in that order, on the faces of the CQC as they watched Kirsty give her class. To begin with, their noses twitched as the smell registered, and they glanced furtively at each other in an accusatory manner. Their glances turned to agitation as they realised that it was the same smell that they had experienced the previous day. Finally, they stood up and called Kirsty over to ask her what this all meant.

Kirsty was totally clueless about the smell or problem. It was the first time she was aware of any issue. She agreed that it was awful, called an end to her class, and went off to phone Mr Fletcher to explain what was happening. Flashman was nearly aching with laughter at the situation. When he nearly fell off his bike from laughter, he quickly got down and went to the changing room to eavesdrop, gloriously, on the scandalised conversation of the swimmers. It seemed that the general opinion was that the smell had only started to happen when the CQC arrived, so they must be responsible. They all hoped that CQC visits wouldn't become too frequent.

The pre-lunch gin and tonic in the bar with Johnny was hitting all the right places, and he was about to have a second when Nipper came in without his owner, the 'Punce', and went to lie in his usual spot beside the chair that she invariably used. The sun was coming in through the window, casting a warm glow on everything.

Flashman chuckled to himself as the thought of giving an uncomfortable afternoon to Lady Ponsonby went through his mind. There could at least be a sound reason, for once, for the smell under her nose! No, he couldn't do that again! Anyway, he was feeling peckish and wanted to enjoy his lunch today. As he sat down, he could see the CQC arriving at their own table over on the other side of the room, together with Fletcher, who looked rather more flustered than usual. Flashman assumed Fletcher must have been giving them lunch in an attempt to take the sting out of developments.

Flashman finished his meal and wandered back to the bar for coffee. Passing the CQC's table, he hesitated and said to the manager: "What's up with the smells we've been getting for the last two days, Fletcher? Does Brakspear know? He didn't tell us about the smell when he briefed us about these chaps' visit on Tuesday" and walked on.

Flashman could have dropped a bomb. CQC inspections were supposed to be unscheduled, surprise events. He knew that the CQC were neither aware that any pre-meeting had taken place nor of Brakspear's personal involvement. In addition, it was highly unusual for the Director of Social Services to be involved in any of their visits other than in receipt of their final report. Fletcher was at a loss to their prompting for reasons, and he insisted that it was not his place to deny any request from the local Council – especially one that could potentially involve good and safe practice. After all, it was imperative to stay on the Council's good side.

At 4 pm, after a good kip in front of the racing on Channel 4, Flashman wandered upstairs to where Reggie and Joanna lived. He walked down the corridor and could hear the tones of conversation, so he presumed that the CQC were in there, interviewing the genial couple. There were even sounds of laughter coming from within. Reaching the end of the corridor, Flashman turned and sauntered back. As he passed their rooms again, Flashman dropped a phial and stood on it. A small crunch and the die was cast for Flashman's last childish act of the day. Or was it? There was one phial left.

Flashman got it out of the packet and crushed that too!

December 2018

Westridge: Brakspear's Downfall

Roly woke up and yawned. He picked up the iPad on his bedside table and downloaded that day's edition of The Times. There was some scandal about a Saudi guy being murdered within his own consulate in Istanbul and then sawn up into bits. The Saudis denied it. The Turkish president said that he had proof and President Trump of the USA wasn't concerned because the guy wasn't a US citizen when, really, everyone knew that he was more concerned about US arms sales to the Saudis.

Roly sighed. The Middle East was going to hell in a basket. Was religion the reason for it all? Roly didn't think so. More like the naked ambition of many a despot, mobilising the power of Muslims, Christians or Hindus in the name of Allah, Jesus or Shiva. Thank God he was playing golf that morning.

"T off at 1000 hrs," Reggie Lester had said. "We've got those 'Henrys' from the Berkshire Downs coming over for a Stapleford tomorrow, individual and team. It'd be good to level the score after what they did to us last time."

Normally, the outcome of these games against the rival clubs didn't bother him, but the Berkshire Downs Club was different. They needled Roly and his chums. It was the same when they played them at Bridge. If he made a bad shot or played a wrong card, they let him know about it.

Most of them were pretty loaded, either through inherited means or the product of a ruthless competitive streak which had seen them succeed at work, and some had a membership of at least two golf clubs.

An over-ambition for their offspring and a desire to tell everyone how much they had enjoyed their recent holiday overseas was usually accompanied by a comment about how much they did for a local charity. If these charitable traits were true, they hardly manifested themselves in the way they played their sport.

Roly and Reggie's four-ball/better-ball opposition that morning were both city types, one of them a man called Sir Ken Barlow. Roly remembered Barlow from their previous match. He was self-assured and obviously competent. He seemed to know a lot about Westridge, and Barlow mentioned that his wife had been sizing up locations for their own retirement.

Roly gulped and flushed.

"Christ," he thought. "This must be the Foghorn's husband. Steady as she goes, old boy," he muttered to himself.

Barlow's golf partner that day, Eric Cooper, knew even more about Westridge. He was his bank's Regional General Manager. He had been instrumental in funding Westridge's construction and continued to be involved in providing a line of credit for everyday purposes. His bank had been concerned for a while that a previously fluctuating credit facility seemed, over the course of the last year, to have turned into a hard-core borrowing which frequently breached its limits. The matter had recently been referred to the bank's credit committee and put on the 'watch' list. Cooper thought this would be a good opportunity to probe Roly about daily life there, and Barlow was interested in whether a potential investment for himself would be safe. So, the conversation was both informed and personal, with Reggie adding his own take on being a founding investor.

"The best decision I ever made," said Reggie. "Can't fault the place. We keep busy, healthy and socially active. What more could you want?"

"There does seem to be a waiting list to get into Westridge," Barlow offered to Roly. "How did you get in?"

"Bit of a fluke, really," responded Roly. "I knew the man behind its conception, and he swung it, thank god, or I don't know what I would have done. I know others who seem to have waited longer. They're almost top of the list, and then someone like me leapfrogs them! Seriously though, there seems to be a history of being pipped at the post by someone else. On average, about four or five of the apartments become available each year. The same seems to be true of the care side. It's a great facility and highly thought of, it seems."

Reggie nodded in agreement. "I'm not sure you should worry about its stability, Ken," he said "the apartments are only available on lifetime leases, and the cash flow isn't going away. It's almost a virtuous circle when you consider the equity release offers that Westridge makes to its residents!"

"And what about the care side of things?" asked Cooper. "It's been worrying us lately. They have been carrying some rather higher costs of late, and the budget has been exceeded for each of the last three years. Profit seems to be being swallowed by increased introductory fees and growing drug and staff costs."

Cooper turned to Reggie. "And you should worry about your dividend Reggie."

"Hmmm…" thought Reggie.

"Well, I wouldn't know about any of that," interjected Roly. "I'm on a different deal to Reggie, I know. The Care and Quality Commission have just finished their annual inspection. Why don't you ask them? Have you looked at their report? They look into the financial side as well. Or you could try that chap Brakspear at the Council. He seems to be around quite a lot and may know something."

"Brakspear!?" exclaimed Sir Ken. "What has he got to do with it? Westridge is a privately run operation. It's not under Council control."

"Buggered if I know," responded Roly. "He was my former batman when I was in the Army. Wouldn't trust him as far as I could throw a shovel, personally. He always had a dark side to him and a chip on his shoulder the size of Mount Everest, but I suppose there is a native cunning which has got him somewhere in life. Must have learnt it all from me! He seems to be here every week at the moment. Didn't use to be like that, or I'd have noticed."

"Are you sure, Flashman? Dean Brakspear has just been nominated for a knighthood," said Sir Ken, and then added, jokingly, "We can't have any old riff-raff wearing ermine, you know. But, seriously, this seems out of order. I think we better look into this, Eric."

Roly felt himself reeling from the shock of hearing this. Brakspear to be knighted? No, no, no. This was just not possible, but he had just heard it all with his own ears. Bloody hell. What is the world coming to? I can't let this happen, he thought, and then, he sensed some fun. "Why not?" he muttered, controlling his smile.

"Sorry? Did you say something?" said Sir Ken.

"Yeah, I'm saying I can probably help you there," he said. "I've spent a lifetime in fraud investigation and insurance recoveries, including some of the darker arts. Would you like me to get in touch with my former colleagues? You might have to pay them for their review, but then you might prefer that an investigation doesn't see the light of day - if nothing comes of it?"

Barlow and Cooper looked at each other. They could afford it, and as they drove their balls up the Par 5, 9th fairway, with the match all square, they decided that they would take their chances about the reimbursement if nothing was proven.

As they came off the 9th Green, things had been settled, and they decided to catch up in ten days' time with another round at Westridge to see if anything had been discovered. The two bankers had been preoccupied and hadn't noticed that Reggie had stood on their ball after their second shot. The sodden turf closed over the top of the ball, and the bankers were forced to take a penalty stroke. It was enough for Roly and Reggie to win the match.

Reggie looked at Roly and said, "Mum's the word, eh!"

On their website, Harlech DeLisle Associates "HDA" describe themselves as a specialist risk consultancy "committed to helping their clients to become secure, compliant and resilient in an age of ever-changing risk and connectivity." The truth was much more than the headlines. Crisis management, hostage recovery, kidnapping and ransom, travel security, online extortion and anti-corruption were their real bread and butter. HDA's success record had led to an unprecedented level of client trust, which has allowed them to cross-sell more standard insurance products as well. This included mass lines like cars and household products.

Their biggest client was the UK Government, but little was known about this to the outside world.

Consequently, their success resulted in their acquisition by a much larger insurance broker, which sought to secure and expand this more standard revenue by acquiring the HDA name.

Flashman had worked for a small subsidiary of HDA called Caliph Security Services for long periods in the eighties and nineties, extending right up to 2010. It had been the major source of his life's income, even though he had usually burnt the benefit within a shorter timescale than most. Andrew DeLisle had liked Roly from the start. Roly's mixture of discretion, bravery, reading of situations, savvy and trustworthiness meant that he was frequently one of the first names in the black book that DeLisle would reach for when there was a crisis to be sorted out. DeLisle had spotted Roly's capabilities following all those problems in Belfast back in the seventies. Although Roly had gone off the radar on flying duties, a job had been waiting for him at Caliph when he had subsequently left the army in 1977. Luckily, DeLisle had seen sufficient of Roly to ensure that, after another hiccough which saw his swift departure for Rhodesia, Roly had again returned a few years later with considerable experience under his belt, and the relationship had never looked back.

DeLisle had long since retired, but Roly still kept in contact, and the circumstances that needed investigation at Westridge were amongst the more routine of HDA's activities. He now called DeLisle. It was preferable and more discrete than going to HDA direct, and Roly knew that Andrew would take him for his word. Roly promised to provide Andrew with a small dossier of characters, Westridge's operations and the current situation. In return, Andrew agreed to get back to Roly within a week of receiving the information with an initial report.

Roly was familiar with how these types of investigations were carried out. They typically involved a mixture of disgruntled employees, extensive investigation of the target's accounts, further analysis of the target's relationships with third parties, analysis of CCTV footage, listening bugs, and observation of unusual behaviours. Roly had all the necessary contacts to conduct such an investigation.

In Westridge, Brakspear's true intentions were revealed to the public much quicker than anyone had anticipated. For three and a half years, Brakspear had been illegally taking money from the Council. If he hadn't been caught, judging by the sums that had gone missing, he would have been a very wealthy man. Because he had quite a few disgruntled employees at the Council, many already suspected him of his wrongdoing. They expressed their grievances and voiced their suspicions by pointing out the latest Mercedes CLS Coupe that he drove, the luxurious holidays that he took and his new house in a gated estate. Executive councillors were paid a lot these days, but these trappings were more than could be expected for the sort of lifestyle that Brakspear was enjoying.

A careful investigation of Westridge's accounts and analysis of its suppliers' circumstances revealed the high price that Westridge had been paying for its Care Home consumables. One particular supplier was investigated, and it was almost instantly discovered that the ownership of this supplier was legally the property of an offshore entity in the Isle of Man. The directors of this company represented a trust company, and the beneficial owner was Dean Brakspear.

Brakspear had been foolish and presumptuous enough to name the company "Cherry Products", a nod to the Cherry Pickers, the nickname of the 11th Hussars.

They had been given this name when one of its squadrons was forced to take cover in a cherry orchard during the Peninsula Campaign early on in the 19th Century. It was an easy mistake to make!

Roly didn't have to think twice. People like Brakspear always made mistakes and Brakspear's vanity in using the 'Cherry' name was a complete give-away.

"At least Brakspear maybe had a pride in something," thought Roly. The discovery gave Roly much satisfaction. The 20% mark-up on the regular price of the goods that Cherry Products had been supplying could not have been achieved without internal Westridge collusion. The assistant manager in the office was confronted in his home, confessed and then revealed another surprising angle to what had been going on involving Sister Critchley, of all people!

Any vulnerable elderly person in the Care Home with no known next of kin had been approached to write their wills. This typically is to make sure that the final wishes of the elderly are carried out and that they are well taken care of in the way they want to be. It had been a simple case of two witnesses and, depending on the size of the estate, allocation of up to 30% of the Will's residual value to a charity, with the explanation that if the testator left 10% or more of their taxable estate to charity, they could reduce their tax bill upon death. No solicitor was needed but having it approved by online experts gave credence to its authenticity. Brakspear's carefully crafted system only applied to those who entered the Care Home without any previous Will, and if the Will was contested, it was never, ever disputed.

Anyone who could afford a private Care Home was generally well off. The charity, bona fide in its support of worthy causes, raised tens of thousands of pounds annually. Dean Brakspear was the non-Executive Chairman and received a very, very handsome annual fee for his services, on top of his six-figure Council salary and the nefarious activities of Cherry Products.

Critchley's role was less obvious. Three years earlier, Brakspear had confronted Critchley when, extraordinarily, he had bumped into her whilst on an unauthorised summer holiday in Menorca. Critchley's escort that day was another woman. They were arm in arm, walking down the quayside in Mahon harbour. Brakspear had taken photos and then confronted Critchley, accusing her of taking a holiday in company time. Critchley had, in fact, been on holiday with her sister when she received a call from Brakspear. He led her to believe that if she didn't agree to advise him whenever she thought a likely candidate for pension advice had come within her care, then her job might be on the line. Innocently, Critchley felt browbeaten, and she agreed to his request.

That was it. Otherwise, she didn't know anything other than it being normal to use Cherry Products for the Care Home's supplies as part of Westridge's standard operating procedures. Although she had had her suspicions of a rather uncompetitive system, she had never received any form of financial inducement. It may have explained the sometimes agitated behaviour that Flashman had experienced when she came to see him as if she wanted to tell him something and the strange sensation that she was on the verge of tears. To anyone who knew Critchley, like Flashman, that had seemed unthinkable.

HDA's report was delivered to Roly and discussed with Sir Ken and Eric Cooper. Inevitably, Sir Ken wanted publicity for the report since it would be good for the local Tories, politically, to see a Labour Councillor take a tumble. Eric Cooper was pleased that he could play his part in guiding a significant bank client out of trouble, and Roly thought how happy he would be to no longer have Brakspear in his life. Brakspear's confrontation and arrest needed to be high profile in order to make an impact.

Fletcher, the Westridge Manager, was primed to ensure that Brakspear arrived at Westridge at an appointed hour and that his assistant would be there at the same time. The local police were to make the arrests, and the local newspaper would cover it all with regional TV on hand as well.

To Critchley, it was as if a weight had been lifted off her shoulders. The pressure she had been under for the last few years had taken a toll on her mental health, and she had felt ready to come clean about what she had been going through for some time, but the shame she felt always held her back.

Flashman was looking forward to seeing Brakspear get what he deserved – he could imagine the effect that Brakspear's disfigured face, with that crooked, evil, permanent smile, disguising the hate and fury that Brakspear would feel, would have on the public at large. They would be thinking that a twelve-year jail sentence would be little recompense for a man who took advantage of the elderly and stole from charities.

But Brakspear didn't turn up for his court case. He had done a runner!

November 1978

Seychelles: Sanctions Busting

Just three months after, he had been casevaced out of the bush. Captain Roly Flashman of the Rhodesian African Rifles swung the Rover 3500 through the gates of the Rhodesian Army headquarters and stopped at the chequered barrier in front of the guardroom, the V8 engine burbling quietly. When he saw the ID card and the pips on the shoulders of Roly's shirt, the African soldier saluted him. He entered Roly's details and car number into his book and opened the gate to let him through.

The road was lined with neatly trimmed hedges of Christ thorn, the vicious spines of the thorns disguised by pretty red flowers. Every so often, the green and crimson abundance of a bougainvillea towered like a sentry over the small thorn hedge. There were green, manicured lawns of Kikuyu grass leading down to where the undistinguished pink brick single-storey buildings sprawled across the barracks area, screened by a spread of tall eucalyptus trees. Roly turned the car into a parking area and walked across to the double doors of the main entrance to the headquarters.

Roly was a tall man, standing at 6'3". His shoulders were broad, and his waist was narrow with long, powerfully muscled legs. He had an open and cheerful face, which was shaded by the broad brim of the regulation green slouch hat that he wore as part of his uniform for the Rhodesian African Rifles. He showed his ID card to the European corporal sitting behind the glass screen at reception.

"Major Stockley is expecting you, sir. You know where to go, don't you?"

"Yes, thanks," said Roly and walked down the corridor. As he walked down the corridor, he was greeted by loud hails from a number of other officers working in the headquarters, and several said that they would meet him in the mess at lunchtime. Eventually, he got to the office that he was seeking and knocked on the open door.

The blond-haired major looked up from behind the desk and grinned at Roly standing in the doorway.

"Hey, Roly," he said, "How the devil are you? You're looking fit enough! Come on in."

Roly entered and saluted in front of the desk. Smiling, he replied: "Well enough, thanks, sir. I am pretty fit again, and how are things with you?"

Major Peter Stockley beckoned the younger officer to take a seat. He was paralyzed from the waist down and remained seated in his wheelchair. Early on in his career, during bush operations, he was shot through the spine while leading a charge against a terrorist base camp. The bullet had shattered a vertebra at the base of his spine and had left him paralysed. It said much for the way the Army looked after its own that he was now there, in a job he loved and promoted in line with his career schedule, albeit permanently assigned to administrative duties. Although he always had good humour and was willing and efficient, it was frustrating for him that his role was restricted at a time when the nation needed experienced officers.

He looked across at Roly. The crow's feet around Roly's eyes already spoke of long days squinting into the African sun and of humour. There was an early hint of white hair at the young officer's left temple. The set of his mouth, steady gaze and firm chin gave a clear indication of a determined and resolute character. And Stockley knew that Roly had only just escaped the jaws of death which had nearly left him in a state similar to his own. Three months earlier, Roly's parachute had failed to open properly, and the impact of his hastened descent had been cushioned by the branches of some young Mopane trees.

But he had still ended up with a cracked vertebra, cracked pelvis, and a bullet wound through his thigh that had only just missed the femoral artery when the terrorist gang, running from the encircling paratroopers, had paused briefly to shoot at the helpless officer dangling by his harness from the branches. He had been lucky and today was his first day reporting back for duty.

"So, how are you feeling, Roly? I've read your medical report, and they seem to think that you are almost there again. How do you feel, though?"

"It feels fine now, sir. The thigh still hurts a bit, but nothing that light-ish duties won't cure. I had my first jog the other day, and after about a couple of minutes, it didn't seem like a good idea. But I've been doing it every day, and I'm getting over the pain slowly."

"Yeah. But don't overdo it. We've been giving a bit of thought about how we should deploy you in the coming months. Only a few of us would appear to have a real future here, but that doesn't mean to say we should give up on pursuing the interests of the place, and I've got a rather specialised project that I'd like to try on you. I've got it on your record that you speak fluent French. Is that right?"

Slightly surprised, Roly responded.

"Yes, a bit rusty, perhaps. Shona and Ndebele seem to have taken over of late, but it shouldn't take too long to get it back again. I went to school in Switzerland for a couple of years, and there is nothing like learning a language 'on the pillow'."

Both men laughed, followed by silence whilst Roly could clearly sense that Stockley was thinking about what to say next.

"Okay, then," he said. "I don't know much about this op. It's all very hush hush. You need to go down to the Prime Minister's office after lunch, and they'll let you know there. It sounds like a six-week detachment. After that, I'll be sending you over to join B Company of the 2nd Battalion as 2 i/c. How does that suit you?"

Roly and Stockley chatted and then left for lunch in the mess. The Rhodesian Regular Army was a relatively small one, and all the officers knew of each other. Everyone had known of Roly's injuries, and he was given a warm greeting. During the pre-lunch drinks, the Commander of the Army came over to Roly and, leading him to one side, said quietly:

"How are you feeling, Roly? It's nice to see you back on your feet."

"Pretty good, thanks, sir, all things being considered," replied Roly.

"Good," said the General. "Peter Stockley has discussed your next job with you, hasn't he?"

"Hardly," said Roly.

"Well, you don't need to know anything for the moment. I expect we'll meet again in a couple of weeks or so to go into the thing in more detail. What you need to know now, and what I can't emphasise too strongly, is the absolute requirement that you talk to nobody about it. Understood?" Roly nodded. "By the way," the General said, raising his voice, "your Captaincy has been gazetted, so congratulations. Mine's a gin and tonic!"

There were ironic cheers from all of the officers, and after lunch, Roly made his way down to the Prime Minister's office on Union Street. He was well aware of how much beer he had consumed and didn't want to make a scene.

After parking his car at an available spot, he showed his ID to security and walked into the eerily dark courtyard of the bright white building. The Prime Minister's offices were sited just off the main parliament building and housed his immediate staff as well as a whole army of civil servants reporting directly to him, including the Prime Minister's own security detail, headed up by Roly's godfather, David. It was David who had reassured Roly five years earlier that if he was unable to go flying on account of his experiences in Northern Ireland, then a job would always be available in Rhodesia for a man with Roly's talents.

As he was ushered into David's office, Roly wondered just exactly what it was that David did. He was not alone in this. Very few of the people that knew David, even his closest friends, were aware precisely what the scope of his duties was.

He was a slim man in his late fifties. His dark curly hair, laid back with hair oil, showed little sign of grey. He chain-smoked and, as Roly knew well, was also partial to a drink as well. Socially, he was extremely entertaining, charming, garrulous and, when the company allowed, seemed to have an enormous and inexhaustible fund of very blue jokes. He was Roly's father's closest friend and, he too, had served in Kenya during the Mau Mau. When Roly's father had died, David had kept a watchful eye on Roly's development and had been a frequent visitor to Roly when in hospital.

"So, how are you feeling, youngster?" he smiled, and not waiting for a reply, he gestured to one of the easy chairs in front of him.

"Have a seat. I expect this has come as a bit of a surprise to you." "You can say that again," exclaimed Roly, "What the hell is going on?"

David had sat down opposite him and lit a cigarette. He looked at his young protégé for a moment and then started to explain.

"I'll be quite frank with you, Roly," he said. "I've laid myself on the line a bit with this one, and an awful lot of people are looking at me with big eyes at the moment. We've got a problem here in Rhodesia with obtaining new weapons systems. As you are aware, we've been supplied pretty easily by the Slopes (Chinese) up until now but, with them trying to open up a dialogue with our bordering states in order to release American financial assistance, it's getting harder. They're shutting the gate on us quite badly at the moment."

"Right now we're trying to put a deal together, and, frankly, you don't need to know the details. However, the intermediaries on this one only speak French, and we need someone who speaks the lingo fluently and who knows his way, sufficiently well, around weapons systems to help with the negotiations." He looked at his godson. "I recommended you."

"It won't come as any surprise to you that quite a few people baulked at the idea. Your problems in the past with the British hierarchy are quite well known and, because of that, the idea of you getting involved in clandestine activity is something that a few people aren't too keen on. How do you feel about it?"

"Yeah, ecstatic! I'm not sure where this is going at the moment, but the idea that I might be less dedicated to winning this war than anyone else is hardly encouraging. You know that I'll do anything I can to help. I have hardly spat out any state secrets or anything. I mean, why me? There must be other French-speaking people in Rhodesia who can help."

"Surprisingly few, Roly, and even fewer who speak it as fluently as you to carry on discussions about weapon systems. More importantly, we're looking at heavy infantry gear here." David replied.

"It's hardly been a heavy weapon war so far," said Roly.

"No," David replied. "But, so far, we haven't had Frelimo opposition armed with T54 tanks and Katyushin rocket systems. It is not improbable, on the basis of information that we are getting, that we could find ourselves facing ZANU and ZAPU tank units coming across restricted border zones."

There was a light tap at the door, which David's secretary opened to usher in a small, dapper man wearing horn-rimmed spectacles and an expression of permanent worry.

"Roly," David introduced the pair to each other. "This is Mr Naylor of the Reserve Bank. You'll be working with him for the next few weeks."

Roly left the Prime Minister's offices feeling overwhelmed by the implications of what he had just been told. He had been cast as a central figure in a sanctions-busting operation that was unlike anything he had previously experienced. The importance of secrecy had been emphasised repeatedly, and he had been made to sign a document similar to the Official Secrets Act.

Roly got back into his car and drove the short distance to the Highlands suburb of Salisbury. Turning off the main road that eventually led to the border town of

Umtali, he drove up a narrow suburban road whose sides were bordered by the manicured lawns and flowerbeds of well-to-do Rhodesians. Eventually, the road led to the white railings of the Borrowdale racecourse, and he turned the car into the driveway of a modern, red-brick bungalow. The building had been designed by an architect, and the semi-circular wall that faced the road had no windows, only a series of slits like those given to archers in medieval castles. Roly drove his car into the garage and locked it, for theft and burglary were rife in this part of town. He entered the house through the kitchen door and, ignoring the cheerful sound of splashing from the swimming pool next door, went straight through to the bedroom and plumped himself down on the large double bed, easing the pain that was starting to throb from his wounded thigh. Gradually, as his racing thoughts calmed down, he drifted into a light sleep.

He was woken by the sound of the bedroom door opening, and his eyes flew open. A girl, wearing the distinctive purple and blue uniform of an Air Rhodesia air hostess, stood framed in the door.

She was tall with long tapering dancer's legs. Her slender waist and full, round breasts were barely disguised by the uniform, and her long, ash blonde hair was pulled back tightly into a ponytail. Her heart-shaped face was dominated by huge sapphire eyes that tended to draw attention away from her warm, sensuous mouth and firm, pointed chin. She looked down at Roly's prostrate figure on the bed, and her face took on the expression of mock severity.

"Sleeping in the middle of the afternoon, eh?" she tut-tutted. "So much for action man," and a warm smile lit her face.

"How was the first day back, darling?"

She sat down on the bed, kissing Roly lightly on the mouth. His arms reached out, pulling her closer. As his hands started to explore, she laughingly pulled out of Roly's embrace.

"Remember doctor's orders, don't be naughty," she teased. "Broken pelvis, a bullet through the thigh, take it easy, no hanky-panky!"

She looked down at him fondly and then wrinkled her nose. "I smell horrid. I'm going to have a bath. You could fix us a couple of drinks." Roly grinned. "Room in the bath for two? I promise I'll behave."

She threw Roly a saucy look and stepped into the bathroom. While tugging at the zip on the back of her dress, she looked back teasingly at Roly and then slowly closed the door going in. Roly ignored the pains in his body and rose swiftly, heading for the sideboard in the sitting room. He mixed her a gin and tonic and grabbed a cold Castle lager for himself.

They had been an item for over a year now, but, up until the time that he was wounded, he could almost have counted the number of times they had been together on the fingers of his hands. The active service stints in the bush had seemed to get longer and longer, and the "R and R" periods shorter and shorter. At least he wasn't straight back to the Regiment this time, and he would now have a chance to see a bit more of Caroline.

Her genuine concern for his well-being had touched him deeply, and she had spent every spare minute when she was not flying with him either in the hospital or convalescing here at the house.

As Roly stepped into the bathtub, he slowly sat down while thinking about the grip this girl had on him. They sat there in silence for five minutes, just soaking and looking at each other in disbelief at how close they were. Soon enough, her eyes started to give him an unspoken suggestion, which led to Roly's toes exploring her body.

Caroline sat up with a start and began to get out of the bath. "Where are you going? Don't go…" cried Roly.

"Enemy submarine on the prowl. And I'm sure I spotted its periscope!" she squealed as Roly got out, too, and chased her back to the bedroom.

The next three weeks passed in something of a blur for Roly. He spent the days either sitting with Mr Naylor in his duty office in the Reserve Bank building in Stanley Street or at the university, polishing up his conversational French with an ebullient Belgian who ran the languages facility at Salisbury University. The Belgian had been fed a cover story that Roly was about to be invalided out of the army and was planning to go to Europe to do an adult education course in Business Studies, concentrating on the oil sector.

The oil industry connection was a puzzle for Roly. All that he had been told was that he would be involved in discussing firearms. Even in that small community, Roly never learned Naylor's Christian name, and Naylor was not going to enlighten him about the need for oil industry familiarity. Naylor was not an archetypical banker. He had no sense of humour, apparent little conversation outside the mechanics of his own profession and was not impressed by Flashman's repeated greeting 'Hi Nails' whenever they met! He spoke in the precise terms of English Suburbia and the years he had spent in Africa appeared to have left little impression upon him. He was clearly very clever and equally an important component in Rhodesia's sanction-busting machinery.

Roly took care to spend a part of each day exercising, ensuring that his recently healed shoulder and hip were fully exercised. The great gouge of muscle tissue that had been ripped out of his thigh by the 7.62mm bullet from the Kalashnikov assault rifle would never be replaced but could, at least, be compensated for. As the days went by and the throbbing reduced, mobility started to return.

Roly also spent two hours every day on a very different type of training.

In the afternoons, he reported to the Headquarters of 'C' squadron Rhodesian SAS where, under the tutelage of a gnarled colour sergeant who had served extensively in Aden and Northern Ireland with the British SAS, he was trained in the techniques of body-guarding and personal protection. These included instruction in unarmed combat, but the emphasis was on managing teams rather than receiving detailed instruction on how to be a bodyguard himself.

One evening, towards the end of the third week of this routine, Roly received a call from his godfather, David, and was told to report to his offices at the Prime Minister's department at 2 pm the next day. It wouldn't be a social visit, and he was warned against enjoying his lunch too much. Roly was there the next day, as appointed, wearing his olive green operational gear with, unusually, the formal green slouch hat of the Rhodesian African Rifles and found David in conversation with Naylor and another man whom he did not introduce.

"Ah, Roly," David greeted. "Glad you made it on time." He looked at the other two. "I think they are ready for us. Shall we go in?"

The four men left the office and walked down a corridor. They stopped in front of a polished wooden door, and David knocked before opening it and ushering the other three in. A group of men were seated around a heavy mahogany boardroom table, and Roly was taken back by the seniority of the group that confronted him. The Commander of the Army sat flanked by the Chief of Staff. Seated next to him, Roly clearly recognised the pale patrician's face of the Minister of Defence. But it was the man sitting next to him that fully caught Roly's attention. The narrow head, slightly curly, grey hair, clear pale eyes, thin mouth, drooping to one side where it had been affected by a mild stroke some years before, of the Prime Minister of Rhodesia were features that were all too familiar to Roly.

Roly, wearing his hat, saluted, took his hat off and sat down in the chair that was indicated. He found himself facing the Prime Minister whose chilly grey eyes flicked across him and then as if he was of no importance to the conversation that was about to take place, swivelled to concentrate on David. David coughed to clear his throat, took a packet of cigarettes out of his pocket and then thought the better of it as he folded back the top of the small notepad that he had in front of him.

"Sir," he addressed the Prime Minister, "Gentlemen. It would seem that we are ready to move on Operation Collector's Item."

Roly had never heard the expression before, but he presumed that Collector's Item was the codename for what was about to be unveiled. David continued.

"Parviz and Van der Veden will be in Victoria at the end of next week. We've had our assets assessed, and even at the discounted rate that we have to offer, we think that our team will be able to secure the right price for all the commodities that we are after. I think that we can also be reasonably confident about the quantities. Mr Naylor, as you all know, is fully familiar with all aspects of the operation. Captain Flashman," he gestured at Roly, "still requires to be brought up to speed. As far as the dealings with Van der Veden are concerned, Mr Naylor will be dealing with that, and Captain Flashman will be acting solely as a translator. Parviz's element is, however, more complicated. General," he looked at the Chief of Staff, "I understand that you have a detailed brief and codes organised for Captain Flashman?"

The Chief of Staff nodded.

"Sir," he addressed the Prime Minister, "all we need now is your sanction to go ahead."

The Prime Minister looked exhausted as he leaned back in his chair and closed his eyes for a moment, trying to block out the continuous debate going on around him. He pressed his hands tightly together to form a steeple with his fingers and, after opening his eyes, scanned the room. His voice, though familiar from all of the television and radio broadcasts, sounded thinner and softer than usual to Roly. The Prime Minister's words were spoken quickly and with precision.

"I had hoped that, even up to this last moment, our friends in South Africa might have assisted us through this difficult period," he said. "It appears, however, that they are unwilling to come to our aid again whilst the debate with Mr Kissinger continues. It is going to cost us dear, in both assets and reserves, but it seems inevitable that we no longer have any choice except to take this course on our own and unsupported."

He looked around the table again as though trying to read each face and judge each private reaction.

"Go ahead, gentlemen. And may god be with you, for the very survival of the nation depends upon your success."

He stood up and shook hands briefly with the Commander of the Army and then left the room, followed by the civilian that Roly had encountered in his godfather's office. As he left, another man in civilian clothes walked into the room, and Roly recognised him as Ken Flower, the head of Rhodesia's Intelligence Services. Flower nodded to the group and then came over to Roly, extending his hand.

"So you are Roly Flashman, eh? I am pleased to meet you. I'll tell you to your face because no-one else in this room will, that you are too young, too inexperienced, and in my view, too unreliable to have been given this job. But, apparently, we don't have anyone else," he said bitterly. He stared at Roly as though assessing his reaction. "Understand this, David's godson or otherwise, you are on trial during the course of this operation. Your loyalty is on trial, our intelligence is on trial, and your integrity is on trial. Any failure on your part in any of those areas will be the last mistake you will ever make."

Roly returned his gaze steadily enough. He realised, whether he liked it or not, that there could be no going back.

A fierce determination began to grow in his mind to ensure that the doubts harboured by the glowering figure of the Head of Intelligence, now sitting opposite him, were proved wrong and laid bare. He remained silent.

The Commander of the Army gazed at Roly with a mixture of approval and pity; the boy was lucky to be alive, as the Commander well knew. Now, instead of having to cope with the constant platoon action, he was being thrown into a boiling pot of international espionage.

Flower looked at the Chief of Staff.

"Okay, General," he said. "What can your boy tell us about the following weapons – G3, Milan, Saladin and M75?"

As Flower rattled off a list of further weapons, Roly jotted them down in the notepad beside him, and he now looked at them.

"Well, sir," he said, "the G3 is the standard issue rifle for the German Bundeswehr; 7.62 Nato; the same as our FNs. I believe it is manufactured under licence in a number of other countries, but I couldn't, off-hand, tell you which. It's a pretty cheap and cheerful piece of kit which presents a hard choice between itself and the FN in terms of muzzle velocity. Instead of a piston, it is operated on a blowback basis, and there is quite a lot of plastic in it – particularly in the butt, grip and foregrip. From a personal point of view, I find plastic to be the most negative feature of the weapon. The butt is delicate, far from soldier proof and tends to snap off if handled roughly. The foregrip, which has an aluminium sheet just inside the plastic, gets very hot, almost too hot to handle with sustained fire."

"I don't know that there is much more to say, sir. The German squaddies used to complain that it had a fairly high stoppage rate in the sandy conditions on Luneburg Heath but, that apart, I suspect it's a fairly standard, efficient piece of German engineering."

The General smiled at him and asked. "And is it a good piece of kit for African soldiers, in your opinion?"

"Off the top of my head, sir, I'd say not," Roly replied. "The two basic reasons are the brittle butt and, if it's true, that they have a tendency to stop in dusty or dirty conditions. That's the one thing that you really don't want to have with African troops who tend to go to pieces if the kit seizes up on them. Which is probably why they do so well with the AK47."

"Are you saying that African soldiers are incompetent to handle sophisticated weaponry?" Flower asked sharply.

"No, I am very definitely not saying that," replied Roly firmly. "RAR troops who have been properly trained and have some experience under their belts have proven time and again that their weapon handling skills are more than just competent. They are damn good and certainly better than most of the European TA troops serving with us."

The Chief of Staff, himself a former RAR officer, who had commanded the Battalion before moving permanently to staff duties, nodded his approval.

"What I am saying," Roly continued, "is that over the last year or so, and, from what I can see for the future, there has been a terrible drain on experienced troops in the RAR. On top of starting a Second Battalion at Victoria Falls and the cream of our crop going to the Selous Scouts, I had heard that a third battalion is under consideration. We are filling the companies with an awful lot of raw material at the moment, and they do get flustered when they find themselves with kit that doesn't work properly."

Roly felt the tension at the table rise as he made allusions, and in particular, his reference to the Selous Scouts.

But the Commander of the Army nodded his agreement. "You can't take issue with that, Ken," he said as the Intelligence Officer shook his head.

For the next hour, Roly went through the list of weapons that had been given to him. His favourite subject had always been guns and ballistics ever since he received his first gun at the age of eight on the family ranch in Kenya. He was left to his own devices there, under the tutelage of the Kikuyu. He had also had a passing experience with most of these weapons as a result of his time with the 11th Hussars and others in the British Army. As his confidence grew, it seemed clear that Roly probably had more intimacy and experience with these weapons than his interviewers were expecting. The conversation even became collegiate.

As was his style, Ken Flower finally interjected. "Alright," he said grudgingly, "you have obviously got reasonable knowledge, Captain Flashman. Your principal job is going to be to ensure that Mr Naylor here doesn't get bamboozled into accepting weaponry that would be inappropriate for us. It won't be as difficult as it sounds since you will be consulting back with us, here, on a daily basis. However, we won't be able to have an open discussion as we don't have access to a secure transmission system, and we might need you to use your judgement while making decisions."

Flower peered at Roly intensely. "Do you think you can handle that?"

Roly met his look squarely. He was not going to be the first to drop his eyes in this exchange!

"If you are asking me if I can sort out the weaponry and its evaluation testing for a Light Infantry Battalion to tackle a close-quarter armoured battle, then the answer is no problem."

Delivered with a faint smile, Roly then added, "Sir."

Flower gave a bark of laughter. "Cocky little bastard, aren't you?" Standing up, Flower prepared to leave the room, turning only to the Commander of the Army and the Chief of Staff.

"They move in forty-eight hours," he said, "I hope that you will be able to complete your briefing and get your codes organised in time. Well done, Flashman, and good luck." He made for the door.

"Ken!" The Commander of the Army stopped him. "Just a moment. There is one other thing that we might usefully add to this expedition." He turned to Roly. "Are you still shacked up with that Air Rhodesia dolly?"

Roly was taken aback by the sudden interest in his personal life, so he flushed and muttered that he was. The Commander nodded and looked at the Intelligence Officer. "I think Roly should take his bird along with him. We are very anxious that our team should look like ordinary tourists and, frankly, Nails is always going to stick out like a dog's bollocks which could end up being a problem. Having someone who can blend in and not draw too much attention to themselves would be ideal."

Flower looked down at Roly and chewed his thumb pensively.

"I thought you'd just had a little holiday," he said drily. "Have you been told where you will be going for this 'exercise' as your Commander chooses to call it?"

Roly shook his head. "No, sir."

Flower gave another harsh bark of laughter.

"What the Rhodesian taxpayer doesn't know about, the Rhodesian taxpayer can't complain about," he said sourly. "You and your girlfriend will be taking a little holiday in the Seychelles, courtesy of the Rhodesian Treasury." He raised his eyebrows. "Ever been there?"

Again, Roly shook his head. "No, sir."

"Oh, you'll like them," said the Intelligence Officer. "You'll definitely like them. They call the Seychelles the 'Islands of Love', five fish for a shilling and a woman for a fish." He seemed to be angry and turned on his heel towards the door. "You'll probably get charged corkage and serve you bloody well, right." He strode out of the room.

"You look like a stunned mullet, Flashman," said the Chief of Staff as he looked at the other officers and the Minister of Defence. "Anything else for Roly?" No-one said anything, so he continued. "You better get over to Army Headquarters and report to Sandy Walker. He'll start briefing you on what we want, and then you've got an appointment at Cranbourne Barracks for a final thrash with the 'Supremes' tomorrow, and I want to see you in my office at eleven sharp. Any questions?"

Roly had a thousand questions, but didn't know which one to ask first, so he, dumbly, shook his head. The Chief of Staff nodded at his dismissal, and Roly stood up, put on his hat, saluted, and left the room, followed by David and Mr Naylor.

In the corridor, he turned to his godfather. "So tell me, David, just what the hell is going on?" he demanded sharply.

David looked at Naylor, who nodded, and he ushered his godson into his own office. The trio sat down at the small meeting table in the window alcove of the office.

"Okay, Roly. There's no going back now, so I'll spell it out briefly, and you'll get the full briefing from the Chief of Staff tomorrow morning. However, you are going to be accompanying Nails here to the Seychelles in forty-eight hours' time and staying in a small hotel outside Victoria, the capital. You'll be meeting up with an Iranian and a German, Herr Botner, who has been doing business with us for a few years. You've got three jobs. First," he ticked off his fingers, "you make sure that Mr Naylor here gets a very clear idea of the material that is being offered by the Iranian. If you have any questions, you'll be given codes by the army, and you'll refer them back to us here."

"Second, you will, for one reason or another, have to be involved in the discussions that Mr Naylor will have with the financier and the oil broker. That's why you had to go through all the schlep at the University."

"Third. You make sure that nobody interferes with Nails here." He sat back in his chair and smiled at his godson. "Are you starting to get the idea now?"

"Where does Caroline come into this?" responded Roly. "Does she have a choice, and how are you going to get her out of the airline? She's had all her holidays and needs the money. I can't just ask her to tolerate all this with me."

"As the General said," David replied, "your cover will be that you're simply out on vacation. You'll go with Caroline, and explain to her that you have got a small amount of work to do, so she might have to spend some time on the beach on her own for a while. Although you and Nails will be staying in the same hotel, you must not be seen together. The meetings you'll be attending will be taking place on a different part of the island. I don't want to get bogged down in detail right now, but suffice it to say that I just want it to look as natural as possible. You can be sure that there will be no problem with the airline."

He stood up and patted Roly on the shoulder as he walked past to open the door. "Don't worry about it mate. You'll get the full SP at Army Headquarters."

Forty-eight hours after his briefing in Salisbury, Roly found himself peering past Caroline, sitting in the window seat of the Air Malawi VC10 as it made its final approach to Victoria Airport on Mahé, the main island of the Seychelles.

357

Descending gently over the deep, clear blue azure sea, Roly felt a sense of wonder as he gazed down on the long, almost unbroken, golden beach and watched the lush green tropical rainforest rip past. He couldn't help but question what he had gotten himself into.

To start with, trying to explain things to Caroline had not been easy. She was nobody's fool, and Roly found it hard to debunk her suggestion that she was being touted as eye candy. Roly had made a hash of answering her questions, leaving him no option other than a full explanation. Roly explained that he would have to leave Caroline for large parts of the day and that they were likely to have to socialise with others of whom he knew nothing. Thinking of Nails, he expected them to be extremely boring.

Caroline's emotions shuttled between incredulity that Roly had been chosen for the task and pleasure that the Rhodesian government should see fit to pay for her holiday, fear of the unknown and slightly menacing nature of the trip and finally, into a sense of deep belonging. This was the man she loved and together, they were embarking on a new adventure into the unknown. That night, after they had made love, there was a new tenderness and depth of feeling between them.

During the flight, Roly had recalled his time working in London some five years earlier, awaiting the outcome of whether he was to be court-martialled or not. Whilst nominally a junior claims broker with a small insurance broker, Roly had spent a lot of time fielding and responding to requests from company employees abroad. He didn't realize until shortly

358

before he left that these employees were actually in the personal security business, closely allied to the Kidnap & Ransom insurance that was part of the company's repertoire. So he was now feeling more and more like one of those overseas employees.

As they got off the plane and into the baking, humid heat of a late afternoon in the Seychelles, they passed quickly through Customs and Immigration. The airport seemed to ooze a cheerful insouciance and a laid-back torpor that defied the seriousness of world events and the chance of penetrating its happy veneer.

Roly kept his eye on Naylor, ahead of him in the Immigration queue, scuttling out of the arrivals lounge and loading his bag into a taxi as he made off. They were both going to the Beauvallon Beach Hotel, whose cheerful driver now swept them and eight of the other passengers on the plane, with a wide grin of welcome, towards the hotel minibus and set off in Naylor's footsteps.

Roly felt his lungs fill with fresh air as the road rose and they passed through swaying coconut palm trees and lush vegetation – the sleepy capital of Victoria was just starting to stir from the heat of the afternoon. He saw a few businessmen in safari suits shuffling towards the bars and the market vendors starting to pack up their stalls. As they rose higher towards the island's central ridge, they passed odd little huts, thrown together from planks and corrugated iron, and children of every hue and colour who bounced along beside the van and shrieked a cheerful greeting.

Five minutes after cresting the ridge, they arrived at a long cove of white coral sand where their hotel lay by the side of the Indian Ocean, lapping at the shore. The hotel had been built in a semi-circle around a large swimming pool and facing out over a long lawn that led down to the sea itself. By the look on Caroline's face, Roly could see that the tourist brochure that they had looked at back in Salisbury would never have been able to do it justice.

Having checked in, a grinning, dark-skin Tamil bell boy picked up their bags and showed them to the plainly decorated double room on the ground floor. It had its own bathroom and veranda and looked out directly onto the swimming pool, patio dining area and lawn.

Sitting down on the bed, Caroline said, "Well, that's it. I'm never going anywhere else ever again, ever. I'm staying here!"

"Just wait until you taste the food," replied Roly. "I bet you won't like it. All fish and chicken. You'll end up talking funny. I'll be watching," said Roly with a playful laugh.

At that precise moment, an envelope slid under the door. Roly strode over and picked it up, then opened the door to look out to see who had delivered it. The corridor was deserted. He opened the envelope to find a note from Naylor telling him which room number he was in and that he would be dining at the outside bar area at seven o'clock that evening if they would both like to be there at the same time, please. He would then have an early night and leave the young couple to their own devices. Roly glanced up at Caroline and smiled fleetingly.

"Just to remind you that we are here to work," the note added.

Roly and Caroline had placed themselves strategically at two bar stools around the outside bar where they could survey the whole bar and patio area when Naylor appeared shortly after 7 o'clock. "Oh boy, look at his transformation," Roly said to Caroline. Naylor had changed out of the stiff blazer and flannel trousers that he had arrived in into a startling and somewhat improbable Hawaiian shirt and white duck jeans, and blue bay liners. Initially stunned by the apparition, Roly didn't know which of the two Naylors he liked best, starchy or outrageous.

They had both ordered a long cocktail and sat chatting in a desultory fashion with a South African couple who had come in on the same flight. Roly's attention was caught by a florid, rather overweight man, also sitting at his own table, wearing a blue and white lightly striped jacket. The man looked normal enough, except for the loneliness in his eyes. He kept glancing suspiciously at Naylor and when Naylor rose to go and sit on the patio for dinner, the man followed shortly after and sat down diagonally opposite him.

Roly and Caroline, joined by the South African couple, strolled out shortly afterwards, and Roly seated himself where he could keep a good view of Naylor and a floor show that was scheduled for later. It seemed absurd. There they were on a balmy evening, sitting in a tropical paradise, chatting inconsequentially with two perfectly ordinary mortals whilst Roly conjured up, in the back of his mind, a wildly improbable James Bond scenario, albeit without a casino and jet-set audience.

Eventually, his meal over, Naylor rose and walked from the patio into the lobby of the hotel. The man in the stripy jacket, leaving his dessert half eaten, hurried after him and made straight for a bank of telephones besides the reception. He then came back, paid his bill and left the hotel. Roly, making his excuses, went to the same telephone and called Naylor in his room.

"I don't want to alarm you, Nails," he said, "but I think we've got company. There was a chap sitting on the patio while you were eating who has been watching you all evening."

"I know," said Naylor, "we were expecting to see him. He works for the British, and he'll be telling them that I am here. Don't let him twig you, please. I may want to keep an eye on him later. I also need to know if he ever has company."

There was a pause at the other end. "Have you settled in alright?"

Roly grunted in an affirmative. "Right. First thing in the morning I want you to hire a car. I'll be leaving the hotel at eleven by bus for the Mahé Beach Hotel on the other side of the island at Grande Anse. Follow the bus, but not too closely. You might like to take Caroline. It's the best beach in Mahé. When I get there, I shall be going straight up to the fourth floor, Room 408. I want you to check for any sign of a tail and then come straight up after me. Got that?"

362

"Yeah, no problem," replied Roly, "but seeing as this is the first day, I might leave Caroline behind."

Roly put the phone down and went back to his companions. They stayed for a couple of hours watching the floor show as well as trying to copy the movements of the 'Sago' dancing of the islanders. It's hyperactive African dance movements were interspersed by a slower, graceful pace reminding Roly of nothing so much as the nodding heads of coconut palms in the evening breeze, and their exertions eventually saw them seek the justice of a good night's sleep, replete in each other's arms.

They woke early the next morning, and Roly went through the carefully devised callisthenic routine that had been prepared for him by his SAS PT instructors.

He picked up a towel, and together they went out and splashed into the warm, welcoming Indian Ocean. Roly was a good swimmer, but so was Caroline, and the two struck out in a good-humoured race that would take them the five hundred yards or so to the reef. Roly quickly found that he was having to put every ounce of effort into just keeping up with Caroline, whose lithe, graceful body seemed to slide through the water with the effortless ease of a barracuda. The wound in his thigh quickly began to throb, and the tattered skin which peaked out from below the cut of his trunks tautened as though the pressure would split it again.

By the time they reached the reef, Roly was panting and was in considerable pain. They lay back, treading water, and Caroline looked at him with concern. She had seen how the pain had creased his brow, and his grunting breath clearly betrayed the effort that it had cost him to make the swim. They turned and headed back to the beach at a gentler pace, but the events of the night before, coupled with the fact that Roly was clearly unfit, were giving Caroline grounds for serious concern.

They had a leisurely breakfast, served on the balcony of their room, and Roly went down to the lobby and hired a Mini-Moke at the rent-a-car desk by the main door. It seemed that you could only hire Mini-Mokes.

"Odd," thought Roly, "because you can hardly see these anymore, anywhere else in the world." The thought made him smile. It seemed the epitome of this place.

He waited in the lobby, leafing through books in the small shop, and he picked up a copy of the previous day's Straits Times. Naylor came down and boarded the hotel bus, which was doing a circuit of the island. As he sat down internally, to the rear, a large black man climbed out of a car, parked in the hotel car park and stepped into the bus, seating himself a few rows in front of Naylor. Allowing the bus a couple of minutes to start, Roly jumped into his Mini-Moke and drove after it.

There was only one road that the bus could take, so he had no fear of losing his quarry. In fact, he struggled to drive any faster than the bus, and when they reached the northernmost tip of the island, he found himself overtaking as the bus stopped at a small post office. Cursing under his breath, he knew he had to complete the circuit and head for the rendezvous at the Mahé

Beach Hotel. Upon arrival, he took to browsing books again.

When the bus arrived, Naylor was the first off, walking into the lobby but stopping at the entrance, stock still, feigning a fumble for something in his briefcase. The black man, following a little way behind, had been forced to pass him, and as he walked over to the porter's desk, Roly turned sharply just as the door to one of the big bank of lifts started to close and squeezed through. The black man, looking rueful, bought a newspaper and sat down in the lobby. Roly, in turn, walked over to the cashier's desk and purchased some stamps for postcards. Then, he too, took a lift to the fourth floor.

Knocking on the door of Room 408, Roly was ushered in by a large man with a bulging waistline and a bright red, bald head and wearing gold-rimmed sunglasses. Naylor was there, seated in the alcove by the window and introduced the man.

"Ah, Flashman," said Naylor, "let me introduce you to Herr Botner."

Botner conspicuously failed to offer his hand, so the two just nodded at each other. Roly turned to Naylor.

"Someone is tailing you quite tightly," said Roly, "and they don't seem to be making an effort to disguise the fact."

"I know," said Naylor. "It was important that we let them establish that I am here. All the rest of the meetings will be taking place in Victoria, and that's one of the reasons I wanted you to have a vehicle. In

365

future, we'll be giving them the slip from the hotel. They'll really only need to see me in the mornings and evenings."

For the rest of the morning and the afternoon, Botner and Naylor haggled over figures and balance sheets which Botner produced. Shortly after one o'clock, Roly went downstairs to the lobby where he saw the black man still sitting, pretending to read a newspaper. Roly sat at the patio bar outside from where his peripheral vision could see the chap, and ordered a Seybrew beer and club sandwich. A few moments later, a tall Indian came over to the black man, and the two exchanged words before the black man left, his relief having arrived. Shortly, the replacement also came out to the patio and sat down to watch the elevators and the wider lobby.

The beer was delicious, light, and cool, and Roly ordered another, sipping it slowly as he watched some tourists on the beach struggling with a Hobie Cat yacht. The hotel, which was a huge brown pile of a place, had been built on a rocky promontory at the end of the great beach at Grande Anse, augmented by an artificial cove, complete with artificial sand and giving the tourists the air of the paradise that they sought. Eventually, Roly picked up his paper and went back up to the room, where the two men were still engrossed in their numbers.

"Okay," grunted Botner with his thick Germanic accent, "we are finished here. Tomorrow we meet the dealers, and you start to earn your money, my young friend."

Naylor told Roly that he was heading straight back to their hotel, where he would be taking room service for his evening meal. Roly was not to worry about the tail if the man were to follow him, but they would have to lose him first thing in the morning. He would meet Roly at 7 am at the gates of the neighbouring hotel, having slipped his trail, as he now proceeded to do with the Indian gentleman waiting on the patio.

Botner approached Roly from behind and tapped him on the shoulder. "I want a word with you," he said. "Come with me." The two men strolled out onto the grassy deck at the back of the hotel, looking out over the artificial bay. Botner turned to Roly and asked, "Are you armed?" Roly shook his head to the negative.

"That's a pity," the German grunted. He paused for a few moments. "Tomorrow is the first day that we have to be concerned. The Iranians are not a major problem. We will, however, be meeting another man later in the day. He is a Dutchman, an oil trader, and he is very dangerous." There was a grim note in his voice as he asked, "How fit are you?"

Roly shrugged. "As well as can be expected," he replied. "Running far and fast is improving, but I'm not there yet, and my injuries were only a few months ago." Roly didn't understand what the German was getting at. "Why do you ask?"

The German sighed, and clasping his hands behind his back, he strode towards the sea wall. He turned.

"The Dutchman has a bodyguard at all times. His guards are provided by a British outfit called Caliph Security Services. Have you heard of them?"

Roly tried not to blush. He thought back to the dinner party that his old British CO had given him at Catterick some four years earlier and the brief period he had spent with Caliph. He remembered the slender, impressive man with haughty features called De Lisle, who had vaguely tried to recruit him after the short period that he had spent supporting the small insurance broker's overseas activities from its London desk.

"Yes. I have heard of them," he replied non-committedly "by all accounts, they were a pretty ugly bunch, mostly ex-SAS men, and I heard that they consider the word 'ex' somewhat redundant."

"Ha, well" exclaimed Botner. "That's them. The problem is, young friend, that the British Government would be very happy if Mr Naylor and I discontinued our efforts to help your Prime Minister, Mr Ian Smith." He smiled sardonically. "We have had some evidence in the past that they are not too concerned about how this is achieved."

The two men started to stroll back towards the hotel.

"I have no evidence to support what I am about to say to you," said Botner, "but I believe that some of the men working for Caliph at the moment are specifically looking to do Mr Naylor and I some damage. Our problem is that anywhere the Dutchman goes, they go too. In himself, the Dutchman is extremely discreet. There is no reason for the guards to know precisely the manner of the meeting tomorrow, but there is no doubt at all that the British Government would stoop to most things if they could rupture the oil supply line to the

Rhodesian Government and bring it to its knees. Do you have any suggestions?"

"Where are we going to meet and when?" Roly asked. The German told him.

"I'll go and have a look at the place tonight," Roly said. "I haven't got much money, and I might need some to bribe the hotel servants."

Botner opened the little black bag that he carried and counted out a wad of notes which he gave to Roly. "I'll brief you first thing in the morning, possibly earlier."

"Ja, good," Botner grunted. "After that, you watch your back and your friend Naylor's. I shall be leaving the island now and will only join you again for the last day of negotiation. You must be very careful and very alert during the time that I am gone."

Roly strolled over to the Mini-Moke and started it up, thinking about the events of the day. His mind was racing. He had been told that the body-guarding would be a small part of this job, but nobody had told him that he would be taking on the SAS. Roly reached into the metal glove compartment and took out a map, glancing at it quickly before heading back to the hotel.

He decided it would be best to go and check out the rendezvous point immediately, rather than wait until evening and having to explain his actions to Caroline. He put the little Moke into gear, turned south out of the hotel instead of north, and after a short drive of barely a mile, turned left onto a twisting, concreted track that took him on a gut-wrenching detour over the spine of the mountain that ran down the centre of the island.

At that time of year, it was always said of the Seychelles that if it wasn't raining on one side of Mahé, it would be raining on the other, and the prognosis proved accurate in this instance. As the track wound up through thick tropical vegetation, the noise of the Moke disturbed whole squadrons of squawking, shrieking birds of every hue and colour. Roly could see the dark clouds scudding across the top of the mountain. No sooner had he passed the tiny col between the towering peaks than the rainstorm hit him. There was no roof to the jeep, and he was soaked to the skin in a moment. One moment he had been looking back at a sun-drenched view of a tropical paradise, the next, it was he who was drenched, with windscreen wipers flailing uselessly at the sheer weight of water hitting them.

Cursing steadily, Roly bounced the Moke down the track. The little car didn't have four-wheel drive, and it was slipping and skidding on the wet surface. In some places, the entire track would disappear under a pool of liquid, orange mud that was being washed off the mountainside by the torrential rain. Roly struggled to keep the vehicle under control. As suddenly as he had driven into the downpour, he drove out of it, and the scene of misery was replaced with paradise again as the great sweep of the tropical island and azure, blue ocean opened up before him.

Descending the mountain, shacks and little allotments began to appear with increasing regularity as, occasionally, some smiling Seychellois would wave at him and call a greeting, to which he happily responded. Eventually, he came to the main road that led either north to the capital or south below the big American radar station perched high up. He turned onto it and was soon driving through the relaxed streets of Victoria.

The day's commercial activity was coming to an end, but there were still plenty of people about as he turned past Government House, down the short main street, past the market and pulled up outside a garish hotel called The Pirate's Arms. If you had to think of an appropriate name for the transaction that was going to happen tomorrow, he thought to himself, you could hardly have chosen a better-named venue.

The hot sun and the wind streaming through the car as he drove had virtually dried Roly's wet clothing, but he still felt a bit of a wreck as he sat down on the patio looking out over the main street and ordered a Seybrew from the passing waiter. His position gave him a clear vantage point from which to study the front entrance to the hotel, and he realised, with a sinking heart, that if they were going to have to use the front access, their arrival could be detected from almost anywhere in the main street.

Finishing the beer, he sauntered into the lobby and went directly to the reception desk, where an attractive creole girl presided over the register. No fancy computers here.

"Good Evening," he smiled as she looked up at him. "I'm Mr McGregor. We have a room booked here for a conference tomorrow."

"Oh yes, sir," she beamed. "Would you like to look at it? It's our most comfortable suite."

371

Roly thanked her, and she picked a key off the board behind the desk and led him down a short hallway and up one flight of stairs. There she followed the hallway to the back of the building and opened a large pair of double doors that led into a sizeable suite. The double doors had opened into the main sitting room, which was furnished comfortably yet shabbily. The most notable features in the room were an enormous air conditioner in one corner, a large fridge (presumably stocked), and another set of double doors that led out onto a veranda.

Roly walked over to the French windows, opened them, and stepped out. The veranda overlooked a small tropical garden with a paved walkway meandering through it to a small door in the back wall that led to a lane used for services at the back of the building. Usefully, a steel-runged ladder, serving as a fire escape, was fixed to the wall beside the veranda.

Going back into the room, Roly asked the girl. "Is that door at the back of the garden locked?"

"Oh no, sir. We don' never lock noting in the Seychelles. Why yez ask?"

"Well," said Roly, smiling at her lilting Creole accent and putting a conspiratorial arm around her shoulders. "One of my friends is having a little bit of fun out here. He thinks his wife might have found out about it and has a private detective trailing him."

Her eyes widened, and her mouth made a little 'O' of surprise. "So when we've finished our business tomorrow, I want him to sneak out the back cos we think the fellow will be sitting in the bar. Will you help me?"

She giggled as Roly pressed a large denomination Seychelles money note into the palm of her hand.

"Great. Here's what we'll do then. When we have finished our business, I'll give you a call, and you can come up with a tray of beer, for which I will pay now in advance. If anybody asks you, you tell them that you think you have got some more people coming. Okay?"

Roly lifted his eyebrows, and said, "You're one smart woman," and she giggled, her cheeks red and blushing. The little Seychellois obviously thought that the whole thing was hugely funny but promised she would help as much as she could.

Roly went back to the Moke and made the short trip back to Beauvallon, stopping only to check the area around the entrance to the neighbouring hotel. He found Caroline lounging on a deck chair by the swimming pool, where she had spent virtually the whole day alternating between the pools and strolling into the waters of the Indian Ocean. That evening, taking Naylor at his word, Roly drove Caroline the short distance to a small restaurant that he had previously noticed. It was perched on a rocky outcrop looking down into a deep sheltered pool. The restaurant owner had trained a powerful searchlight into the water below so that the diners could see the brightly coloured exotic fish.

They dined on freshly caught lobster, washed down with a delicious cold South African Nederburg. They returned to their hotel, single-minded and smiling at each other about what was to come next. They made love slowly and tenderly.

Afterwards, they went down to the sea, and as he lay on his back staring at the stars with the sound of the gentle lapping of surf and the swishing sound of the palms in his ears, Roly held Caroline's hand. He tried to ignore the very niggling feeling of concern that was threatening to overtake the sense of unreality that was enveloping him. Perhaps it was the wine, but this was more ominous than anything he had faced in Belfast or Rhodesia, and he felt out of his comfort zone.

Rising early, he went for a gentle, short jog along the beach. The swimming seemed to have done him good, and there was very little of the stiffness that he had previously experienced from the wound on his leg. Passing the front lobby doors on return, he noticed a Seychellois in civilian clothes chatting to the receptionist at his desk and wondered if the guy was Naylor's latest shadow. Roly crept back to their room, trying to make as little noise as possible so as not to wake Caroline, who lay curled on the bed, her blonde hair sprawled across the pillow and a small smile on her lips.

He showered and shaved quickly and then dressed casually as a tourist might. Pausing only to kiss Caroline softly on her forehead, he slipped out of the room as quietly as he had entered and made his way around the side of the hotel and to the car park, taking time out as well to check for any sign of further watchers. A battered-looking black Austin 1100 with a radio in it looked as though it might belong to the man in the lobby. Otherwise, there seemed to be no sign of life apart from a few early risers and hotel staff reporting for the morning shift.

Roly climbed into the Moke and quickly drove around to the neighbouring hotel, parking the car as close to the main gates as possible. The early morning sun was already projecting considerable heat, giving promise of scorching temperatures in the day to come. He walked over to a Casuarina tree whose dense needles provided an oasis of shade and sat down on a bench pretending to read a copy of the Straits Times. He had placed himself in a position from where he could see Naylor approaching the gates and also check if anyone else was looking for him. Ten minutes later, he sighted Naylor striding along the beach. It didn't seem as if anyone was trailing him, so Roly jumped into the Moke and started it up, arriving at the gate at more or less the same time as Naylor.

The tyres spun on the dirt road surface as they drove off, quickly, in the direction of Victoria.

When they arrived at The Pirate's Arms, Roly instructed Naylor to go straight to the big suite around the block and parked the vehicle in the sanitary lane that he had recce'd the previous day. Then, entering the hotel via the garden gate, he found his little Creole friend, Josie, ensconced behind the reception desk, who gave him a broad smile and conspiratorial wink as she nodded towards the stairs that Naylor had already gone up. Roly did the same and knocked on the door. Botner, to his surprise, was already there, and it was he who opened the doors to let him in.

Roly quickly went through the plan to foil any watchers that might be arranged for their departure. He hadn't seen anything so far, but that didn't mean that a covert operation wasn't already underway. They ordered breakfast to be sent up to the room, and Naylor and Botner reviewed the papers that they would be going through with their visitor. They gave Roly a copy of everything and told him to concentrate on the annexes, detailing weaponry, delivery systems and a largish section detailing the Rhodesian government's requirement for heavy military transport. What was staggering to Roly were the financial costs involved, which seemed to be huge. Botner explained that there were, in fact, two transactions that would be completed that day. The first was with an Iranian who was expected shortly to reach an agreement on the items involved and what they would cost. That cost would then be converted into trade value of certain Rhodesian goods, mainly a complicated mix of food products, tobacco, chrome and gold. Once agreement had been reached, and only if the agreement had been reached on all the items concerned, Botner would make a call to the Dutchman who was staying at a private house on one of the islands. The Dutchman and his entourage would then fly in by helicopter, and Botner and the Iranian would work out a second deal under which the Dutchman would supply refined petroleum products to Rhodesia as part of the overall deal with the Iranians.

Roly, as a professional soldier, had spent most of the last twelve months deployed in the operational areas on Rhodesia's northern and eastern borders, where terrorist incursions were rapidly making some of the border areas ungovernable. The demise of the

Portuguese Government in Mozambique, replaced by Samora Michel's actively communist Frelimo movement, had opened a huge expanse of the Rhodesian frontier to the Guerrillas who were wasting no time capitalising upon it. His bush deployments had not left Roly with much time or opportunity to read the international news in the press.

He had, however, been able to catch up from time to time, even if only fleetingly, and one area that held his interest was the published figures for the Rhodesian budget. The numbers that he was looking at in the papers that Botner and Naylor had given him beggared belief, and it began to dawn upon him just how devious the central government was having to be, particularly in its declaration of a defence budget. The amounts of money being allocated for jet aviation fuel, alone, in the exchange being discussed here in the Seychelles, exceeded the entire declared defence budget by nearly two and a half times. It wasn't hard to see why the demand for secrecy had been hammered home to him so hard.

The telephone shrilled, and Roly picked it up. It was Josie in the Lobby, announcing that their visitor had arrived. A light tap on the door, moments later, announced his arrival, and Roly opened the door to him. He hadn't been quite sure what to expect when Naylor and Botner had talked about the Iranians. In his mind's eye, he conceded later, he had a vision of a greasy, little, hook-nosed Levantine rattling worry beads and rubbing his hands. The tall, slender, tanned man in an immaculate, lightweight suit and patterned Hermes silk tie who stood in front of him was not what he had been expecting. There was more to it than that, however, as Roly stood rooted to the ground in shock. This was Farukh Mehedi Parviz, his old friend from Aiglon College in Switzerland, whom he hadn't seen in 12 years.

Roly was still gathering his thoughts and was about to cry out a greeting when Parviz stepped smartly past him, almost rudely brushing Roly, as if ignoring him, and into the room, holding his hand out towards Naylor. The action had to be intentional. Neither would have forgotten the other, and Roly was clearly meant to keep his own counsel. Parviz, very intentionally, now had his back to Roly as he greeted Naylor in immaculate English.

"Ah, Mr Naylor, how nice to see you again," he said, shaking Naylor by the hand. "Herr Botner. Vairy good to see you again too. And who is this?" as he turned towards Roly, looking quizzical and vacant.

Roly knew that he could ill afford to blunder in front of his colleagues, so he responded.

"Je m'appele Roly Flashman, Monsieur. Je suis ici pour traduire ou c'est necessaire."

"Enchanté" responded Parviz "allors, commençons-nous?"

The Iranian sat down at the table, which had been cleared of the breakfast things and accepted a cup of coffee. He opened his sleek, Gucci briefcase and took out the sheets of papers – they were identical to the ones that Naylor and Botner had been examining previously but each paper had a neatly clipped Farsi translation attached to the back of it. For the next four hours, while the heat built up outside and the air conditioner thrummed to keep up, the men haggled back-and-forth, and Roly translated as necessary.

Although most of the spadework had been done by Botner and the Shah's representatives in Germany many months before, the Iranian was determined to wring a higher price for the vital products out of the Rhodesian representatives. He concentrated on the gold price element of the swap package. Ever since the Opec Oil Cartel had started to flex its muscles and pressure the west by forcing up the price of crude oil, the gold price had started to fluctuate wildly. Parviz was intent on ensuring that the swap package for the gold element of the deal was fixed at the lower end of recent international trades. Botner, however, was trying to insist upon a higher medium. It was Naylor who came up with a compromise that resolved the haggling, creating a linkage between the internationally traded price and the eventual price that Parviz was able to secure with the Dutchman later that afternoon.

At that point, Botner called for a break in the proceedings and asked Roly to have lunch sent up. Roly telephoned Josie, and in due course, a cold lunch with some wine, Seybrew beer and some soft drinks arrived. Roly was the only one who drank any of the alcohol, gratefully gulping down the cold Seybrew. Naylor and Botner had to excuse themselves and took their papers and calculators next door to the bedroom, where they could be heard muttering as they went through the figures, leaving Roly and Parviz together.

The elephant in the room needed to be released, and Parviz was quick and to the point. Roly knew well that Parviz spoke better English than he gave credence for, but they continued in French.

"Roly. We must continue in French for the moment. It's fantastic to see you again, and we can talk about all this, but we can't reveal our past friendship right now. I'm staying on Grande Anse, one of the other islands here, given to the Shah by the current President. I'm hoping that, at some time in the course of things here, I can get you over there where we can talk at length and catch up. Okay?"

"For the moment, all we can talk about is this. It is all a game for us but not for those two in there." He nodded at the door where the voices of the two bankers could be heard. "For them, it is deadly serious. But, for you and I, it is a game; and we are merely messengers."

"Why is the Shah prepared to break international sanctions to support Rhodesia in this fashion?" Roly asked, and Parviz chuckled.

"Ah. That, my friend, is where the game gets complicated. It could be that he has a soft spot for Southern Africa, which, by the way, is true. It might be that he has an emotional reason for doing this. On the other hand," a small smile played around the Iranian's mouth, "it might just be that because one very big and important nation doesn't want Rhodesia's chrome and gold to be used by another very important nation, they are prepared not to make a fuss if a smaller and slightly less important nation happens to acquire it and then, possibly, even sell it on to that very same important nation."

The two laughed together at the convoluted explanation.

"I think you're a soldier, yes?" the Iranian asked and then shook his head. "No, don't answer. You could be nothing else." He smiled at Roly. "Don't take offence. I will take the liberty of giving you some personal advice."

Roly looked at Parviz in an abashed way. "Was it so obvious?" he thought to himself.

"Go ahead, Parviz. I always valued your opinion."

"This material." He gestured towards the papers. "It is very important for your country, but I fear that it will not be enough. The world has decided that the form of government that you represent is an anachronism and must be destroyed. Whilst these weapons that we are discussing now might keep the nation going for a short time more, in war, it will never be enough."

His eyes, which were a clear, deep grey, held Roly's. "Don't think too hard for now but start thinking carefully about your own future when this game is played out."

Naylor and Botner re-entered the room at that moment, and the foursome sat back around the table to go through the papers one final time. The German reached for the telephone on the table and asked the hotel exchange to connect him to a number on the neighbouring island, Fregat. He had a brief conversation before he put the phone down.

"Van der Veden is on his way, gentlemen," he announced "he will be here in one hour. I take it that we are fully ready and agreed?"

There were nods of assent from around the table, and Roly stood up.

"I'll be on my way then, for now. If you need me, I think I'll make myself scarce in the main lobby area," he said.

Naylor nodded, and Roly said a brief au revoir to Parviz as he turned to the door.

"Roly" Parviz called "si tu as besoin d'assistance, donne moi un coup." As they shook hands, Roly felt the card discretely proffered within Parviz's hand, smiled his thanks and left the room.

He walked into the lobby and had a brief chat with Josie at the reception desk. She was thinking that the whole thing was immensely romantic and that the tall Rhodesian was very dashing and handsome. He said he had to wait for some friends, and she gave him a long provocative look from under her lashes as he turned and went out onto the patio bar, which looked over the main street. He sat down at a corner table, out of the sun, where he could see both the main street and the interior of the hotel, and ordered a coke.

Approximately half an hour later, the President's own Rolls Royce Cornice pulled up outside the hotel with the top up, followed closely on its tail by a Datsun taxi.

As the vehicles came to a halt, four men leapt out of the passenger seats. One man who had exited from the front seat of the Rolls stood beside the door and scanned the street up and down. The two men who had exited from the Datsun walked straight into the hotel lobby and then took the stairs up to the first floor. The third man from Datsun joined his colleagues at the Rolls Royce where, after a nod from one of the men who had entered the lobby, he leaned into the Rolls and pushed the passenger seat forward to usher out a slight, dark-haired man in a navy blue suit wearing dark glasses. The three men crossed the pavement quickly and disappeared into the hotel.

From his vantage point, Roly was able to observe them as they walked up the stairs. It was fascinating for him to watch the application of security methods they had been taught recently at Cranbourne Barracks in Rhodesia, but it was even better to see professionals carry out the manoeuvres in the flesh.

The scene would have been much lower-key had it not been for the Rolls. It all took place in less than thirty seconds, but it felt longer because Roly knew two of the bodyguards.

The man who had been controlling the team was blond-haired and of medium build. The last time that Roly had seen him, he had been wearing the uniform of the Scots Guards and had been sitting next to Roly in a group photograph taken outside of the Officers Mess at Harding Barracks, Warminster. Roly knew that he had then joined the SAS. His name was the Honourable Peter Chesney, and his father was an influential member of the Conservative Party. There

383

had been a rumour going around that Chesney himself had been involved in an ugly incident in Northern Ireland when four civilians had been killed. Now he appeared to be contracting for the civilian sector.

Roly couldn't remember the name of the other man that he had recognised. He recalled only that he was a secondee from the Metropolitan Police to the Royal Ulster Constabulary. Presumably, his name would be in his log book as a passenger on a reconnaissance flight down to Crossmaglen in South Armagh four years or so earlier.

Chesney paused at the top of the steps leading into the hotel lobby. Roly tried to look inconspicuous behind his newspaper, but it seemed to him that Chesney paused as his glance swept over him. Then he, too, turned on his heel and disappeared into the hotel lobby. A few minutes later, Roly caught a flicker of movement in the hotel bar out of the corner of his eye at the same time as the policeman's name came back to him suddenly.

"Bowen, that was it," he mused as, a moment later, a hand dropped on his shoulder, and a familiar voice said,

"Bowl me over! It's Roly Flashman. I thought I recognised you. Fancy meeting you here."

Roly swivelled in his seat and looked up as though taken by surprise. "Good heavens!" he exclaimed. "Peter. Well, you do run into the nicest people in paradise. Sit down and have a beer."

He gestured to the chair on the other side of his table. Chesney repositioned the chair to his own requirements and ordered a Coca-Cola from a passing waiter.

"I ran into Strawberry the other day," he said, mentioning the nickname of a mutual friend. "He told me about your shindig in the Ardoyne. I hear you ran fowl of your opprobrious CO."

Chesney's eyes had lifted questioningly. Roly just shrugged.

"You win a few, you lose a few. The LI were a great bunch, but that shit probably did me a favour in the long run. Despite his best efforts, the threat of the Court Martial was lifted, and I went flying."

Chesney smiled and nodded. "Hum," he said, "I had a bit of a problem like that myself. And what are you up to nowadays?"

The question had seemed innocent enough, but Roly detected an edge behind it.

"I did four years flying. Just the antidote to my recent experiences. I think I found my forté. Kept my nose clean, went to all sorts of places and just loved it, but I was never going back to Regimental life with the 11th Hussars in Germany after all that. I got my commercial licence just before leaving, and I'm thinking of doing something full-time now, but I initially had a short spell at Lloyds. Hideously boring, so I left, and I've been working as a courier since.

Which is why I'm out here. Holidays for the exotically wealthy, but I'm frankly not enjoying it that much. "

The lie seemed to have come quite naturally to Roly!

"I'm just waiting to have a chat with a bloke from Air Seychelles, but I'm not holding my breath that something will come of it. What about you?"

"Oh, I did the usual thing," replied Chesney easily. "Left the army and joined Securicor, that sort of thing." He smiled. "I'm here mixing a bit of business with pleasure, actually." The two men caught up on old times, chatting about common acquaintances, who was doing what and where.

Chesney had sat next to Roly, and from his position, he too could command a view of the hotel entrance lobby and bar. Roly didn't see the signal from Bowen that prompted Chesney to stand up, but he suddenly stood up, looking conspicuously at his watch.

"Gosh. Is that the time?" he asked. "I'm supposed to be meeting someone, must dash. Great to see you, Roly, and I hope we bump into each other again soon." He smiled, but there was no real warmth in the smile. "Who knows" replied Roly and walked into the bar from where Bowen had already disappeared.

About ten minutes later, a small group of men walked quickly out of the hotel, climbed into the waiting cars, and promptly drove off. The big blue Rolls, followed by the yellow Datsun taxi, turned left at the first junction they came to, and Roly, who was watching the departure closely, saw the brake lights of the Datsun flare briefly, just as it turned the corner but just long enough to hint that the taxi might be dropping one of its passengers.

Shortly afterwards, much as he had expected, he recognised one of the bodyguards come out of the junction, cross the road and take a seat at the small café virtually opposite the hotel.

Roly stood up, folded his paper, and left the hotel, walking in the opposite direction to that taken by the departing Rolls Royce. He turned right into a small street and broke into a gentle jog to get to the entrance to the sanitary lane in which the Mini-Moke was parked. He ducked into the lane and, flattening himself against the wall of the first house, he peered round into the road to see if he had been followed. Nobody appeared to be behind him, so he walked quickly up to the Moke and slipped through the garden entrance to the Pirate's Arms into the hotel's garden. He walked rapidly into the lobby and, winking at Josie, he took the stairs two at a time to the first floor and knocked on the door of the suite.

Nails opened the door, and Roly walked in. "How did it go?" he asked.

Botner, seated at the table with Parviz, made an impression of disgust, and Naylor just shrugged.

"He's a common little thief, that Van der Veden" said Parviz in French. His face lit with a smile of great charm "but I am an uncommon, big thief. I don't think he has done as well as he thought."

Botner and Naylor looked at Roly for a translation, but Parviz gave a little shake of the head. Roly wasn't quite sure why but he restricted his translation to the first sentence.

Parviz had gathered all his papers into his briefcase, and he stood up and shook hands with the two bankers. As Roly ushered him to the door, he repeated his earlier offer.

"As I said, if you need any help, don't hesitate to call me. We need each other in this."

He shook Roly's hand, patted him on the shoulder and then walked quickly down the corridor while Roly turned back into the room and telephoned down to Josie at reception, asking her to bring the bill. She appeared a few minutes later with a tray of Seybrew and the bill, which Botner paid for from a large sheaf of the Seychelles Rupees that he produced from his briefcase.

"When that man left, "said Josie, "another man came in from the street and asked what you was doing." She gave a shy smile at the two men at the table. "I tol' him you was waitin, for another gentleman. Did I done right?"

"Josie," said Roly, "you're an angel." He handed her another large denomination Rupee note. "We're going now. If he asks again, tell him you think we are still up here."

Josie giggled, said "As you say, handsome," and left the room with just a little extra twitch of her pert little bottom. She still thought it was all wildly romantic.

Roly went over to the French windows and opened them onto the balcony. He pulled down the ladder to the fire escape and motioned for Botner and Naylor to join him. Naylor looked slightly ill at the thought of climbing down the rickety ladder and handed his case to Roly, as did Botner. The two men scrambled down clumsily, and Roly followed them, simply sliding down the ladder with his feet locked to the steel outside the rungs. The three men hurried through the garden and gate, and clambered into the Moke. Roly started up and drove quickly down the alley but was concerned when he looked in the rearview mirror to see a face peeking around the edge of the alley, watching them depart.

They drove fast to the airport, well south of the capital and dropped Botner, who had had his cases sent forward from the Mahé Beach Hotel. They did not pause to see Botner depart, and Roly swung out of the airport entrance back down the coastal road. He carried on a few miles south to where The Reef, another of the large, modern hotels, had been built. He had told Caroline to meet him there, and as soon as the Moke had pulled into the hotel, Naylor jumped out and walked into reception while Roly, more slowly, took the Moke into the carpark and left it.

Naylor asked the receptionist to organise a taxi to take him back to Beauvallon whilst Roly, studiously ignoring him, went out to the swimming pool bar where Caroline was chatting to their South African acquaintances from the flight.

That evening, before they went down to dinner, Roly went up to the second floor and, taking care to ensure that nobody was observing, knocked lightly on Naylor's door. In their haste to get Botner onto his plane and then to drop Naylor back at the Reef Hotel, they had not had time to discuss their plans for the next day. Naylor gestured to the mini-bar, and Roly helped himself to a Seybrew and sat down.

"Well, now we wait," said Naylor. "Van der Veden is pressing for an outrageous price for the oil, and it could throw the rest of the commodities deal into reverse. Botner's gone back to Switzerland to see if he can skim something with the gold futures, and Parviz is in direct contact with the Shah. I don't know why but that man seems to be on our side. He seems to think he might be able to organise a higher level of credit for us rather than having to do the whole deal on a cash basis like we are at the moment." Naylor shook his head gloomily. "God knows what it might cost us in the long run, though."

"I've got to redo all the forecasts on the basis of the position that Parviz and Botner can deliver. It's going to take me a couple of days, and there's a courier coming through who'll take the message back to Salisbury for us on the evening flight the day after tomorrow. Until then," he gave one of his rare smiles to Roly, "you will ostentatiously be having a holiday, and I will be emulating Brer Rabbit by 'layin low and sayin nuttin'.'"

Roly told him about his recognition of Chesney and Bowen in the hotel and that he thought the watchers might have caught up with them as they left the alley in the Moke. Naylor nodded.

"Well, we've always known that Van der Veden was protected by heavies, but I hope it is no more than a coincidence that you know two of them. Do you think they are genuinely working in a private capacity?"

"Chesney, yes. I heard from somebody that he had been slung out of the army. Bowen, however, I can't answer for. I keep trying to remember what he was known for back in Northern Ireland. I think he was mostly down in bandit territory in Armagh, whereas I spent most of my time in Belfast, Derry and in-between in the north."

"Well," said Naylor. "Carry on keeping your eyes open, and if you see them again, let me know."

Later that evening, Roly and Caroline walked up the beach to Fisherman's Cove for dinner, where the Sago Troupe were performing again. Strolling back, hand in hand, they reached the edge of the hotel gardens and, dropping the few clothes that they were wearing, ran down the beach, laughing, into the lapping surf. They did what lovers do. Splashing water at each other, mock chasing each other in turns, and whooping, followed by a few short strokes and ending in an embrace. As they gazed intently into each other's eyes, Roly was feeling overwhelmed by love for this woman and wondered what Caroline saw in him. Maybe it was time to think about the future and build a life together.

After their short swim, they lay under the palms, letting the warm air dry them and just as their mutual thoughts were turning towards the bedroom, Caroline felt Roly's body suddenly go tense. Roly had seen the flickering shadow of a man moving through the trees, darting from one to the other, blending with their shadows and listening before moving on to the next. At first, Roly was inclined to believe that it might just have been a peeping tom, but then he realised that the man was moving with an explicit purpose and direction. There was something oddly familiar about the figure. Pressing his finger over Caroline's lips to hush her, he very gently eased himself back into his shorts, then put his dark shirt on to cover the whiteness of his torso.

His lips brushed her ear as he whispered very quietly, "Go back to the room and pack quickly. Move-in about five minutes."

Keeping his body very low to the ground, Roly began to stalk the unknown figure. He moved slowly and only when the other man moved himself. He was careful to approach from a converging angle, which would allow him to stay hidden until he was slightly ahead of his prey. He found cover for himself behind a large rhododendron bush, where his groping fingers soon found one of the large round stones that the hotel gardeners painted and used to ring the bushes. Picking it up, he continued his slow, stealthy pursuit.

About twenty yards from the hotel, the man stopped and leaned against the side of a tree, silhouetting himself clearly for the first time. Roly's suspicions were confirmed as he recognised the bearded outline of Bowen. He had also realised, early in his pursuit that the apex of the triangle on which he and Bowen had been moving had been the balcony of Naylor's room.

Roly now had an advantage. Every move that Bowen made was clearly silhouetted by the lights that were blazing in the hotel room, and his night vision would have been ruined if he had needed to look into the darkness behind him. Roly watched as Bowen knelt down and shrugged a small runner's knapsack off his back. He removed a long tubular object from it, and there was a sharp snap of metal on metal which Roly recognised as the sound of a magazine locking into its receiver. As Bowen stood up, Roly recognised the long tubular shape of an L34-A1 Sterling sub-machine gun, the standard sub-machine gun for the British Army, suggesting possible British involvement in this attempt on Naylor's life and the sort of weapon that, by itself, would have been hard to justify to customs officers inspecting the armoury of a legitimate bodyguarding unit.

Roly lowered himself onto his elbows and knees and inched himself, absolutely silently, towards where Bowen was standing with the vicious little weapon already lined up on Naylor's veranda. Naylor had the doors open, and although the light voile curtains were drawn, the gentle breeze was making them flap backwards and forwards. Every so often, they would open completely, and a shaft of light would appear. Twice, Roly saw Naylor stand up, dressed only in one of the hotel's complimentary bath robes. Suddenly he remembered then what it was that he had been trying to recall about Bowen. It was his nickname, 'Topper' acquired the day after an IRA sympathiser was found shot in mysterious circumstances.

393

The breeze from the sea was freshening, and it wouldn't be long, Roly knew, before Bowen would get a clear shot. Still, with infinite care, he crawled forward, assisted by the sound of the wind sighing through the palm trees. He could not afford to take any chances. The trunk of a palm tree now partially secured Bowen from his line of vision, and he crawled up behind it to a point where less than five yards separated the two.

Bowen was concentrating intently on the veranda whilst Roly used the tree trunk in front of him to lever himself up. He took two careful paces towards Bowen, but some sixth sense must have triggered an instinct, and Bowen was alerted. He started to duck and turn. Roly lifted the stone and leapt forward, covering the last couple of yards with the speed of a striking snake. He brought the stone down hard, behind Bowen's right ear, and the big man dropped with a grunt.

Roly checked under Bowen's left ear to ensure that there was still a pulse. It would really make life complicated if he had killed him. The artery pulsed weakly under his fingers, so he set to work to ensure that when Bowen woke up, there would be a delay before he could give the alarm.

He stripped off his belt and bound his hands together as tightly as he could. It would not hold him for long, but it could well be enough. He then untucked his shirt from the waistband of Bowen's trousers, pulled the buttoned front back over his head and forced it down over his elbows, making the struggle to release his hands that much harder. Bowen had been wearing sneakers and socks, so Roly took the sneakers off and threw them as far away as he could. He stuffed the socks into Bowen's mouth. He then unbuttoned the top of Bowen's trousers and pulled them down to the man's ankles. Picking up the jogger's bag, Roly made the Sterling safe and stuffed it back in the bag before trotting off to his room. He knocked sharply on the door, answering Caroline's enquiry before she let him in. She was pale-faced but calm, and a half-packed suitcase lay on the bed.

"Roly," she said, "I know I promised not to ask anything when you told me about this operation, but things do seem to be escalating rather. What's going on? I'm getting worried."

Roly nodded grimly and opened the rucksack, showing her the weapon inside. "A bit more out of hand than anyone thought, love," he replied. "We're getting out of here pretty quick as soon as the money boys have finished playing silly buggers."

He strode over to the phone and picked it up, dialling the number for Naylor's room. In a few brief moments, he had told Naylor what had happened, to pack his case and meet him within five minutes in the car park. Roly hurled his own few belongings in his bag, and, grabbing Caroline's suitcase, he walked out through the veranda doors. Moving steadily but carefully, they walked out to the carpark, hoping that they would not be detected. Roly tucked the suitcases onto the back seat, and they sat waiting for Naylor.

A few minutes later, he appeared. Not as Roly expected, from the side of the hotel but in the lobby. Roly could only stare in disbelief. The man had gone and paid his bill! As Naylor scurried across the car park, the big Negro 'minder', probably a policeman, who had been in the lobby all day, strode out a few paces behind. Almost at the same moment, 'Topper' appeared around the side of the hotel, hopping clumsily as he tried to get his trousers on, shouting to the minder to stop them.

Naylor, alerted by the cry and looking over his shoulder at the two men after him, broke into a shambling run, his knees bumping clumsily against his suitcase.

Roly swore and fired the engine. He popped the clutch, and the game little Mini-Moke shot forward with a squeal of tyres. He braked hard as he came abreast of Naylor and almost dragged the panting banker into the open vehicle. Ignoring the black man who had shouted at him to stop and was waving what looked like a badge, he accelerated hard, aiming the vehicle directly at Topper, catching him a glancing blow on the thigh as he went past. Mr Bowen was not going to be too pleased if they ever met again. Roly careered out into the main road whilst he heard, faintly, the sound of an engine being gunned behind him.

Only one headlight was working properly on the Moke, the other being on a permanent dipped beam, but there was plenty of moonlight, and Roly coaxed all the speed that he could get out of the car.

In the mirror, he could see two sets of headlights closing on him. It looked like Topper had an accomplice. There was no way that he could have driven a car after that crack on the head and the blow to his thigh. Roly raced the little car mercilessly along the road, now familiar from his morning's drive around the north of the island and towards Mahé beach. Behind him, the headlights were gaining remorselessly. One seemed to be faster than the other, and Roly reckoned that the leading car must be Topper and his accomplice in the yellow Datsun while the policeman, in a beaten-up old Morris, was struggling. The Moke was heavily overloaded, meaning it was very slow to recover from any reduction in speed necessitated by the many corners on the road. Roly's objective was the small track that he had taken over the top of the mountain when he had gone on his recce that morning.

The scudding clouds that occasionally obscured the moon indicated that it was probably raining or, at least, that there might be a low cloud mist on the other side of the island. Josie, the little receptionist at the Pirate's Arms, had let slip the information that her father ran a guest house called The Cottages, high up on the mountain slopes. Roly had seen the sign to the guesthouse when he had made the wild drive for the recce that morning. He was gambling on Josie's sense of romance and the very fat bribe that he had given her because he needed her help far more now than ever.

It was becoming obvious now that they weren't going to make the turning before the yellow Datsun caught up with them, so Roly was in a quandary. He didn't know the level of collusion that might exist between the British agent and the local Seychellois police. The fact that Van der Veden had been offered the use of the Presidential limousine during the afternoon did not necessarily mean that he, or the President, were involved with the British Secret Service plans to dispose of the Rhodesian financier. The inference, in fact, was the opposite. It was against Van der Veden's interest that any harm should come to Naylor.

Roly, therefore, decided on a fairly desperate course of action; to slow down the pursuit. Praying that the lead vehicle behind them was not the Seychelles policeman, he shouted at Caroline to grab the Sterling sub-machine gun and its magazine out of the bag. Caroline was in the passenger seat with her long flowing blonde hair streaming in the wind behind her. Nails, it appeared, had drifted into a world of his own. He sat on the back bench seat, hunched over his briefcase, as if in a bewildered daze. He looked irritated, as though he had just missed a comfortable bus, and the Moke had been the only other, but uncomfortable, transport available.

Caroline took the Sterling and held it on her lap with the magazine ready. Roly was aware that there was a sharp hairpin coming up, and this would probably be the best place for what he had in mind. The Datsun was now less than half a mile behind. Roly swerved the Moke through the bend, cursing the understeer on the underpowered front-wheel drive. As he came through the second part of the corner, he slewed the vehicle to a stop across the road.

Shouting at Caroline and Nails to lie down, Roly took the Sterling from Caroline, whacked the thirty-four round magazine into the receiver, and cocked the bolt as he jumped out of the car. In order to steady his aim, he flicked out the folding stock, and ignoring the telescopic sight that Topper had fitted, he aligned the silenced weapon to the centre of his chest. The pursuing Datsun skidded round the corner, and Roly opened fire.

The weapon made virtually no sound at all. The only noise that Roly could hear was the clatter of the breach block opening and closing and the pinging of spent cartridge cases hitting the road. As the pursuing car raced around the corner, Roly loosed off three short, three to four-round bursts.

The headlights of the oncoming Datsun were dazzling, but not so much that its driver could not see the stuttering flash from Sterling's muzzle. Roly raked the front of the oncoming vehicle and one of the headlights shattered. The car started to swerve wildly, and as the driver over-braked to avoid the spitting machine gun, the car slewed into a complete 360-degree turn and slid off the road ending with its rear wheels in the ditch and its one remaining headlight glaring uselessly at the sky. Roly jumped back into the Moke and set off again down the narrow road.

He recognised the small store which marked the turn-off onto the track and switched off his headlights as he swung the car off-road. Relying solely on the fitful light of the moon, Roly started to negotiate the winding and bumpy track. The small lane, concreted with slabs, climbed rapidly and steeply. Soon there was a cry of alarm from Caroline, looking over her shoulder.

They had a bird's eye view looking down on the coast road, and she had been able to see the police car pass the point where the Datsun had been forced off the road by Roly's gunfire. Moments later, she saw the single yellow track of the Datsun's remaining headlight start moving down the coast road again.

They had travelled barely three miles, with the coast road in full view, when she saw the police car, with the rapidly closing Datsun, turn around in the main road and drive back to where the little track wound up the hill.

"Roly," she cried, "they're onto us. They're following us up the hill." She had believed that there was no way to outrun them.

Roly, who had been driving without the aid of the headlights, and therefore, very much more slowly than he would otherwise have dared, cursed again. He flicked the roller switch to turn the headlights on, and changing down a gear, accelerated fast up the hill. The Moke had performed badly from being overloaded on the main, flat highway, but on this steep ascent, it was really telling. "Don't worry, darling. Just bear the chaos with me, and we'll get through it," said Roly, reassuring Caroline.

The engine really laboured, and time and again, Roly was forced to change down all the way through the gearbox in order to maintain even some sense of motion. The twin headlights of the police car and the threatening, The Cyclopean eye of the Datsun behind it drew ever closer.

With the pursuit barely half a mile behind him, Roly crossed the col at the top of the mountain range and started down the track on the other side of the island. Moments later, in an action replay of his earlier drive, the rain hit them. Once again, it was the ferocious, driving tropical rain of an Indian Ocean storm. The windscreen wipers were barely able to cope, and the headlights, which were pretty ineffectual at the best of times, merely created a wall of refracted light. Twice Roly bounced off the verge as he desperately tried to regain control of the bucking vehicle. A sign jumped out of the darkness indicating a hairpin bend, and Roly, recognising the start of the corner and knowing that he was driving too fast, whirled the steering wheel in the opposite direction to the turn and heaved on the handbrake. The back of the Moke, labouring under the weight of Nails and their luggage, spun viciously round, and Roly waited for the reverse of the turn to appear in his headlights before gunning the engine for all his life and dragging the little car round the corner.

As a neon sign glowed faintly in front of him, Roly hoped that the pursuing cars could not see the track of his lights through the rain and the night, so he heaved the car into the drive and cut the lights and the engine in the shadow of some trees. The rain continued to bucket down, and Caroline and Naylor sat huddled miserably in the open-topped vehicle. Moments later, the double headlights of the police car shot past them, closely followed by the Datsun with its single glowing orb.

Roly scrambled out of the driver's seat and ran up to the door of the guest house and leant on the doorbell. For several moments, there was no reply, so he tried again until, finally, a small, skinny elderly man with grey hair and a huge nose dripping wetly onto a desiccated-looking moustache opened the door. He

401

was virtually naked except for a pair of lurid, orange Lurex underpants. His skin had an unhealthy, yellowish tinge to it.

"Who you are? What you want?" he demanded querulously.

"Are you Josie's father?" Roly demanded. The old man just nodded. "She said that we could probably get a bed here," said Roly "the rest of the island is full."

The old man peered at him myopically. "What dat girl been saying?" he muttered to himself. "Ow many of you are there then?" he asked.

"Three," said Roly. "We need two rooms."

"Alright then," said the old man, "step inside. It'll be fifteen dollars – US, with breakfast." He cackled. "You interrupted me and me girlfriend." He leered. He grabbed two keys from the rack and handed them to Roly. "Your rooms are at the back there. If you want a drink," he nodded towards the corner of the room, "the bar's over there. Help yourself but write it in the book. I've got unfinished business." He cackled and scurried away.

"Just a second," called Roly, "have you got a phone? I've got a rather important telephone call to make to one of the other islands."

The old man pointed at the Reception desk. "Help yourself. Call away. You can't make any international calls if that's what you wanted. They're all blocked off on our exchange, but the island calls aren't a problem."

Roly went out of the hotel, where he found Naylor and Caroline, soaked to the skin, huddled in the meagre shelter of the porch of the hotel. He ushered them in and gave them each a key to their rooms. Caroline, trembling either with cold or from delayed shock, made a beeline for the bar and poured herself a stiff brandy. Naylor forced a smile out of himself as he said thinly, "I think I might make an exception in this case and have one of those too. Roly?"

Roly nodded and walked quickly out of the hotel door to recover their bags from the Mini-Moke. He brought them in and, dumping them on the floor, picked up the glass and savoured his first sip as he swirled the warming liquid around inside his mouth.

"I'm going to call Parviz," he said to Naylor. "I very much doubt that the phones will be tapped, and I think we need to take him up on his offer of help. It's in his interests to keep us safe, after all. There is a possibility that he will have us on the Shah's island."

"Good idea," replied Naylor. "I didn't enjoy that. The thing that is puzzling me is whether or not Van der Veden is involved in our problem. If he is, it puts our whole negotiation in a pretty parlous state. You might get Parviz's opinion."

Roly fished the business card with Parviz's local number on it out of his wallet and started to dial. The telephone was answered, and Roly, in French, asked for Parviz. A couple of minutes later and Parviz came on the line.

"I'm sorry to disturb you at this hour, Parviz," Roly said, "but we've got a problem and need your help. I

403

don't want to go into it too deeply for the moment, but Mr Naylor here is under a real physical threat, and I've identified one of Van der Veden's crew as the aggressor. I don't suppose we could impose upon your hospitality? I wondered if you might have room on the island for us."

There was a lengthy silence from Parviz, and then he said, "Yes, of course, Roly. I'll arrange for you to be picked up by boat tomorrow." He gave the name of a small fishing harbour on the western side of the island. "There's a café there called Michelle's," he said. "Be there at twelve hundred. I'll come and collect you. It's the boat we use for fishing, a forty-foot Bertram called 'The Butterfly', and I'll moor it at the main quay. Make sure you are there, please."

Roly thanked him and promised that they would be at the rendezvous but, suffering a trust crisis now, he decided to take precautions wanting to ensure that there would not be a reception committee waiting for them when they got to the village. As Naylor and Caroline prepared for bed, he told them that he would be leaving early and told Naylor that he would have to order a taxi to get them to the rendezvous on time. He would meet them at a small bridge, about two miles from the village, once he had had time to ensure that the coast was clear.

Apart from the Sterling, Bowen's backpack also contained two spare magazines, fully charged magazines, a pair of Zeiss binoculars, and an extremely high-quality, German-made image intensifier for night vision purposes with three spare batteries. He tested the scope before going to bed and

404

was impressed by the greenish image that showed up and thought it significant that it comprised more than just a minor element of the shopping list that Naylor and Botner had been discussing.

The next morning, as dawn broke, Roly was up without waking Caroline and walked quickly to the Moke, pausing only to help himself to a supply of Coca-Cola from the bar. It was going to be a long hot morning. He drove back over the mountain top and down to the coast road on the western side of the island. It took him about thirty minutes to get to the village, and he drove straight through it. Turning off the main road into a little track that meandered up through coconut palms. He parked the Moke behind a large breadfruit tree where it couldn't be seen and walked back, behind the village, climbing slightly through the coconut plantations until he found a vantage point from where he could see the harbour, the café, and the road snaking through the village. He settled down to wait. Taking the binos out of his rucksack, he deftly snapped the top off a coca cola bottle, using the cap of one of the other bottles as a lever and the ball of his thumb as a fulcrum to pop it off, and took a few sips.

The day's heat built rapidly, and although he was sitting in the shade, Roly felt the sweat starting to prickle along his back and on his brow. The village started to come to life, people setting about their daily tasks with a languid torpor that amused Roly. They didn't seem to have a care in the world. A couple of fishermen climbed into their small boats and set out to sea. Probably hoping to catch enough fish for the table for supper that night and perhaps a bit more to trade in the market for a few rupees. Enough, perhaps, for a bottle of coconut wine.

At about 10 o'clock, a dusty, yellow Datsun taxi, similar to the one that had accompanied Van der Veden's convoy to the Pirate Arms, pulled up at the head of the quay, and two white men got out. Roly lifted the Zeiss binoculars, and Peter Chesney's pale face and blond hair sprang into focus. Roly recognised the other man as one of the bodyguards who had been in Van der Veden's team. Grimly, Roly reached down into the rucksack, drawing out one of Sterling's magazines, and pressed down hard on the parabellum round at the top of the magazine to test whether the spring would feed the bullets firmly into the gun's chamber. Putting the binos down for a moment, he lifted out the pipe-shaped weapon and snapped the magazine into place.

He did not cock it and made sure that the safety catch was on as he knew that the Sterling had a notorious accidental discharge record, including a number of "own goals" in the British Army.

Chesney and his colleague had strolled out onto the quay and were now looking back at the village. Roly watched as Chesney pointed at the café and tapped his watch, and came to a rapid decision. Disengaging the magazine, he tucked the submachine gun back into his rucksack and slid down the slope, always in the cover of the palms and breadfruits as well as some heavily laden mango trees. Moving quickly, he approached the café and walked in through the back door, startling the jolly-looking Seychellois woman who was listlessly washing some dishes.

"Hello," he smiled. I'm sorry to startle you. I was up on the hill birdwatching," and he waved his binos at her.

She smiled. The Seychelles were an ornithologist's paradise. Tropical bird conventions were a regular occurrence in Mahé, so the excuse was pretty commonplace.

"May I have some cold orange juice, please," said Roly. She poured him a large glass from a big orange juice dispenser behind the bar and then went back to the kitchen to continue her washing. Roly placed himself beside the window where he could watch Chesney and the bodyguard. The two men strolled back along the quay, and after a brief word, the bodyguard climbed back into the yellow taxi and drove off. Chesney, whistling softly, strolled towards the café.

Roly quickly reloaded the Sterling and hooked back the cocking handle with the heel of his hand. The spring felt even lighter than he had expected. Checking the safety catch again, he flattened himself against the wall next to the door, praying that the café owner would stay in her kitchen. The door was a fly screen, and as Chesney unconsciously swished the hanging beads to one side, he felt the round snout of the Sterling against the back of his neck.

"Very gently, Peter. Hands against the wall. Feet apart. You know the form," threatened Roly.

Without uttering a word, Chesney turned and splayed his hands against the wall, spreading his legs at the same time. He was wearing a fawn-coloured safari jacket, and Roly could see the hard outline of an automatic pistol carried in a shoulder holster against the stretched material of the jacket. Roly reached under the jacket and lifted the Heckler & Koch automatic out of its holster. He knew that this pistol packed a big punch. As he continued to frisk Chesney down to the ankles, Roly could feel rather than see the ex-soldier tense slightly.

"Don't even think about it, Peter. This thing's on full auto. It'll cut you in half before you have even moved your weight to turn on me."

Chesney relaxed as Roly's frisking quickly revealed a small Smith and Wesson snub-nosed police special attached to Chesney's ankle. Removing this and satisfied that Chesney was now unarmed, Roly tucked the two pistols into his own waistband and gestured at Chesney to sit down opposite him at the table.

"I think it's time we had another little chat, Peter," he said. "Would you like a cup of coffee to go with that?"

Chesney didn't reply as Roly lifted his voice and called "Madame." The plump Seychellois poked her head around the kitchen door. "Two coffees, please," Roly ordered.

"Another bird man, uh?" She beamed at them and bustled into the kitchen.

Chesney, acutely aware that the Sterling on Roly's lap pointed directly at his groin, leaned back and waited for Roly to speak.

"Lovely islands, aren't they?" Roly opined. "It would be a terrible shame to bust up this peace and harmony with a little gunfight and people getting hurt. 'Topper' and your other mate were lucky last night. I only wanted to stop the vehicle. If there is any more unpleasantness, we'll take you out. Full Stop. Do you understand that? Or do I need to repeat myself to make it more clear for your trash-filled head?"

Chesney leaned back in his seat. "What on earth are you talking about, Roly?" He asked.

Roly laughed. "Don't bullshit me, Peter. I know full well that you and Bowen are under instructions to take Naylor out. I'm warning you that we are ready for you. We won't blink or hesitate in taking you out."

Roly was trying to give the impression that he was only one of at least a handful of security men looking after Naylor. Chesney leaned forward, causing Roly smartly to tap the barrel of the Sterling on the underside of the table and Chesney to sit up again.

"Last night," Chesney said, "Topper claimed that he'd met an old friend of his who was working for the police out here. He asked Van der Veden for a night off, which was agreed upon. This morning, Topper comes in with blood all over his face and a bloody great lump on his head, claiming that someone had tried to mug him. Van der Veden wasn't impressed, particularly as Topper needed to go and see a doctor. Van der Veden likes his bodyguards to be able to look after themselves

409

better than that, and I sent a telex off to the company asking for a replacement for him."

"Crap!" Roly snorted again. "You might have been a naughty boy, but Her Majesty's Government doesn't let expensively trained men like Topper go as easily as that."

Chesney paused and then remarked. "They nearly got rid of you, didn't they, Roly? Do you know anything about my family?" Remarkably to Roly, Chesney seemed to be going off on a complete tangent.

"No, why should I? Are you trying to tell me something?" responded Roly to what seemed like a complete irrelevancy.

"About seventy years ago," Chesney continued, "my grandfather, who was a hell of a lad with a hunting rifle, bought a chunk of real estate in Rhodesia outside a place called Fort Victoria. It's called Paradiso now. You might have heard of it?"

Roly knew it well. It was one of the two largest privately owned farms in Rhodesia. Bill Suto, one of Roly's closest friends, had been the Under Manager there before being called up into the Army to his National Service. The farm's revenues were huge, and Roly only knew that it was owned by an absentee landlord, the Earl of Kinlochnie. He said as much to Chesney.

"Yes," said Chesney, "he's my uncle. My father actually ran the farm for about ten years before he went back to England and entered Parliament. He's one of the most active MPs in the pro-Rhodesian lobby at the moment. He's also a director of a very large oil company. That's how he knows Van der Veden. He's the man who persuaded Van der Veden to go through with this deal."

He looked hard at Roly across the table. "If you're suggesting what I think you're suggesting, which is that Van der Veden, and we, as his bodyguarding team, are colluding with the British Government to kill off Smith's bankers and sanction busters, you're well off the mark."

Roly hadn't expected such a blunt statement, nor had he realised how much Chesney obviously knew about his employer's dealings.

"I found Topper lurking around the hotel gardens two nights ago with this," Roly tapped the submachine gun and then shoved it hurried back under the table as the café owner waddled in with their two cups of coffee. He waited until she had gone before continuing.

"How do you explain that?" he asked.

"Topper was slotted into the team at the last minute. Our regular man suddenly developed a bug of some sort." Chesney looked pensive. "Look," he said, "you can take it from me that any interference in this deal going through would badly affect my family, both in terms of fortune and future."

"Good God! Can you imagine what would happen to our farm, which by the way, will be mine one day if that murdering bastard Chitepo and his cronies got hold of it?" He paused. "Here's a titbit that might help you, Roly." He paused and sipped his coffee. "Van der

Veden is having a bad time at the moment. He has badly overstretched himself. He has done well out of the sanctions-busting, and he has done particularly well in his dealings with the South Africans. As a result, he's made a fortune virtually overnight. But about six weeks ago, he overstretched himself badly." Chesney showed a wry grin on his face. "He does get these occasional rushes of blood to his head. He committed himself to buying an oil refinery in Italy in order to store and process some of the crude that he was moving. There's been a shift in the oil price since, and he's finding himself rather out of pocket, to put it mildly."

Chesney leaned forward on his elbows and pointed a finger at Roly. "He's trying to bleed you blokes in order to replace the profit that he was going to make on the Italian job. If you play your cards right, you can get his price down. He's almost in the position of needing you more than you need him at the moment."

Roly whistled softly. That little gem of information, if true, was going to shift some bargain counters all right.

"Okay," he said, "if I believe you're not involved, what do we do about Topper?" Chesney looked grim.

"I'll handle that," he said, "Don't worry about Topper."

"Yeah, but there's another guy too," Roly said, "is he one of yours too?"

"No way," said Chesney. "I can account for all my boys last night except Topper. My bet would be on this chap being a spook attached to the High Commission here. If that's the case, then you've got a problem because he'll be able to call upon the help of the police."

"That's already happening," said Roly, "It was the local plod who set up the tail in the first place."

Chesney shook his head. "You're just going to have to find somewhere to lay low then."

"Well, I think I have already done that," replied Roly.

Chesney looked up in surprise.

Close gap

"You wouldn't, by any chance, be planning a short stay with a certain Mr Farukh Mehedi Parviz, would you?"

He saw from the expression on Roly's face that it had hit home, and he laughed.

"Oh, that's rich," he laughed, "That's bloody rich. That's where Van der Veden is at the moment. I'm here to meet him off the boat." He laughed again.

Roly looked at him speculatively. "Are Van der Veden and Parviz in cahoots then?" he asked speculatively.

"No, I don't think so," said Chesney. "Van der Veden is on the island because Mehedi Parviz is trying to trim the deal by getting him laid. Apparently, he trucked in a couple of high-class hookers from Hong Kong, and they're all out on the island having a good time. It won't get him far. Van der Veden is never influenced by that sort of thing. Use my information, and you'll get a lot further."

413

Chesney pointed out of the window where the Rolls Royce and Datsun were drawing up at the end of the quay.

"I've got to go now. That is if you'll let me. Don't worry about Topper. I'll handle him. See you again in a couple of days, perhaps."

He stood up and, nodding at where the Sterling was under the table, grinned at Roly and said, "You wouldn't have, would you?"

Roly held up the submachine gun. The cocking handle was fully back, and the safety catch was on automatic. Chesney paled and, still smiling, he sauntered out to join his colleagues, having retrieved his pistols from Roly. Roly unloaded the SMG, and walking out through the kitchen, paid the café owner. He trotted up the slope behind the village to his former vantage point and pulled out his binos from the rucksack. Peering out to sea, he made out the line of a graceful white motor yacht, powering its way through the blue ocean, heading towards the small harbour.

The yacht berthed, and Roly watched as Van der Veden was bundled into the blue Rolls Royce and driven away by his minding team. He wondered if he could trust Chesney or not and decided that he didn't have much option but that he would treat what he had just heard with some caution. In the meantime, he needed to remain alert himself. It was unfortunate, in the extreme, that Chesney had rumbled where they were going to be staying because, if he was "in it' with Topper, life was going to get very uncomfortable very quickly.

He watched as the yacht warped away from the quay and took off towards the open water. Through the powerful glasses, he could clearly see Parviz and an attractive-looking blonde girl seated on the bench in the stern of the boat. There was a fighting chair set up for fishing beside them.

He had about an hour to wait, so he opened a tepid Coca-Cola and continued to watch the village, looking for any signs of activity from the police or anything else that might arouse his suspicions. After about half an hour, when nothing else had happened, he reckoned that it was going to be safe and walked back to where he had hidden the Moke. Throwing the rucksack onto the back seat, he started up and swung back out onto the main coastal road. He stopped briefly at the café and asked the owner if he could leave the Moke there for a couple of days as he was going to stay on the islands with some friends. She smiled happily and readily agreed. He thanked her and then sped off up the coast road to the bridge and waited for Caroline and Naylor.

Crossing the bridge, Roly stopped the Moke just beyond, pulling off the road but making no attempt to hide it. He had picked this point not only because the bridge made an easy landmark for Caroline to find but also because the small hill next to it afforded a vantage point from where he would be able to see the coast road for a couple of miles as it snaked its way down towards the village. Slinging the rucksack over his shoulder, he sprinted to the top of the small hill and lay down just below the crest, with a clear view up the road.

There wasn't a great deal of traffic, just a couple of local buses and a few tourist vehicles. "Seems like a peaceful day today," he muttered to himself.

As midday approached, he watched as a garishly painted red and green car of indeterminate manufacture but with a large taxi sign on its roof drove towards him. He was more interested in any traffic that was following the taxi than in the vehicle itself, but the only other traffic on the road was going in the opposite direction. The taxi pulled up next to the Moke, and after one final sweep with his binoculars, he scrambled down the hill to the two cars. Naylor had climbed out and was, if anything, even more colourful than the vehicle he had just been riding in. He was sporting another of his Hawaiian shirts, even more vivid than the previous one, with white jeans and navy blue docksiders. The whole ensemble was topped by an awful pork pie hat and wrap-around dark glasses. Roly considered that the move from earnest banker to Marseilles pimp was obviously not as difficult as one might presume.

Caroline had her long blonde hair tied back in a tight ponytail. She looked pale and slightly tired as she climbed out upon Roly's arrival.

She had dressed sensibly for the trip in a red cotton shirt with a local batik design, which she had bought in the hotel shop, blue jeans, and sneakers. She could have been wearing sackcloth, Roly thought. She looked stunning under any circumstances.

He pulled the bags out of the boot of the battered old taxi while Naylor paid off the driver. They drove quickly back to the village and took the Moke up to the quay, where some old boxes and fishing nets were piled at the seaward end. Standing up in the driver's seat and looking seawards with the Zeiss glasses, Roly was able to make out the high white bow of the Bertram ploughing through the short swell towards them. Leaving Naylor and Caroline partially concealed by odds and ends on the quay, Roly quickly reversed back along the pier and swung the Moke behind the café. The landlady was sitting on the back doorstep, plucking a chicken, and happily waved him away.

Re-joining the group as the Shah's vessel made fast, Roly looked up and saw that Parviz was actually conning the vessel himself; there didn't seem to be anyone else on board. Certainly, there didn't seem to be any sign of the languid blond that he had seen earlier. Parviz brought the boat expertly against the side of the quay and shouted down for them to jump on board. Handing Caroline onto the deck, Roly quickly passed the cases over to Naylor in the stern cockpit and then leapt lightly on board himself, clambering up the ladder to the flying bridge to confirm that they were all there and ready.

"Bonjour," greeted Parviz as Roly struggled through the hatch. "Not quite what I was expecting. I didn't realise that you had a lady with you, and I take it that your colourful companion is our Mr Naylor?" He cocked a questioning eyebrow. "It's a good disguise. I wouldn't have recognised him." He paused slightly. "I'm not sure his mother would either!"

Somewhat awkwardly, Roly explained that Caroline was his girlfriend and that the Rhodesian authorities

417

had thought it prudent to send her along to give the group an aura of normality. Parviz had taken the big motor cruiser away from the quay, stern first, and now he deftly flicked the wheel to bring her head round to face the open sea and gunned the throttles. The big boat surged forward and was quickly on the plane, bouncing across the wave tops, her big Volvo diesel engines bellowing.

"I'm glad you brought the girl," he said. "Although the villa is secluded, we do have neighbours who might consider it singularly odd to have two more strange men as guests. Also, I have my fiancé staying, and the ladies can keep each other company." Roly wondered if the use of the word fiancé was a euphemism for a hooker from Hong Kong but decided to be prudent for the moment.

The Bertram cut easily through the rolling swell, and Roly realised that they were heading in the direction of a small island that he could discern slightly to the south of Fregat, the second-largest island in the Seychelles archipelago. As they scudded across the wave tops, Roly related his experiences of the previous evening with Topper and the Police. For the moment, he decided not to mention the meeting with Chesney. He would wait and see how events shaped before mentioning that.

"You did the right thing in calling me, my friend," Parviz said, "This Island was a private purchase by the Shah from the Seychelles government, and it enjoys diplomatic privileges. Even the police can't get you there. Van der Veden was my guest on the island last night when you called, which is why I was slightly slow to respond to your request. He is still being difficult."

Roly smiled to himself. The fact that Parviz volunteered such information made it easier to believe that Parviz was being open with him. Parviz suggested that Roly go down to the cabin and fix some refreshments for Caroline and Naylor. Perhaps could bring up a Coca-Cola for himself.

Easing himself down the ladder, Roly found Caroline sitting in the fighting seat, enjoying the sun and the short voyage. The swell was proving too much for Naylor, however, and he lay across the gunwale of the after cockpit, disposing of his breakfast in a noisy and unseemly fashion. He had lost his pork pie hat. "Thank God," thought Roly as he watched it bobbing in the waves in the distance, and he doubted that Naylor would need any refreshment as he collected a Coke for Caroline and Parviz each and a Seybrew for himself. After a short chat with Caroline, he climbed back up to the flying bridge as Parviz started to navigate the boat through the reef that guarded the pearly white beaches of the small island. A few minutes later, they docked at a small pier that jutted out from a rocky outcrop. An athletic-looking man in immaculate whites, who looked like an Arab, took the line that Roly heaved at him and made the boat fast.

Parviz climbed down from the bridge and nodded a greeting at a pale and exhausted-looking Naylor, who was sitting back on the bench seat, trembling and gasping with relief at the thought of terra firma again. Roly introduced Parviz to Caroline, and he bowed briefly over her outstretched hand in a charming old-world gesture of courtesy.

Close gap?

"Enchanté," he exclaimed, casting an appreciative eye over this stunning Rhodesian girl of Roly's. He had the eye of a connoisseur. Leaving the Arab to bring the bags, he led the party up a concreted walk and showed them into an immaculately decorated three-bedroomed guest house.

"I'll leave you two to freshen up, and when you feel like it, I think you will find that lunch is ready for us on the patio of the villa," and he pointed to another, larger villa about one hundred yards away. Roly and Caroline, feeling refreshed after a shower and some much-needed relaxation with the sense that a difficult forty-eight hours were behind them, strolled up to the main house, leaving Naylor to rest and recover on his bed for a few minutes. Parviz was there, standing with a drink in his hand on the marble-floored patio of the villa, overlooking a breathtaking, magnificent sweep of golden beach of a sandy cove with the island of Fregat clearly visible a few miles away.

Standing next to Parviz was a tall, elegant blonde girl, about the same age as Caroline, Roly felt. Although they were of the same height and their hair was the same colour, the resemblance ended there. She had the truly classical, beautiful features, married to the slender figure and narrow hips that would have done credit to the catwalk of the most discerning international couturier. Where Caroline's bosom and hips were full and rounded, Parviz's companion was

420

boyishly slender with small tight breasts and narrow hips leading down to long tapering legs. She was wearing a silk blouse, knotted at the waist and showing a tiny expanse of firm, tanned belly, from which her navel peeked cheekily. She wore figure-hugging blue trousers, bell-bottomed in the fashion of the times. Her narrow feet were poked into straw sandals, and she wore a thick choker of natural freshwater pearls.

Parviz spun round as he heard them step onto the patio, and welcoming them to the house, introduced his companion, "It seems you both have freshened up, huh? Meet Chantelle de Chenon, my beautiful lady." Knowing that Caroline spoke only schoolgirl French, at best, Roly was concerned that there would be a language problem. He need not have worried. Chantelle's English was perfect, slightly accented but with the rounded pronunciation of an English girl's public school. It turned out that she had spent a year at Priorsfield as an exchange student and another year with the art department at Sotheby's.

Roly recalled thinking during the business discussions at The Pirate's Arms that Parviz himself could understand more or less every word that was being spoken in English. Their time together at Aiglon had taught him that, and Parviz was now deploying his command of the language to charm Caroline verbally. Roly grinned in amusement, thinking back to some of the comments that Naylor and Botner had made, blissfully unaware that Parviz had understood every word.

Parviz led Roly over to a low bar at one end of the patio and nodded back to where the two girls appeared, already, to be deep in conversation.

"I don't think we better show those two in public, my friend," he smiled. "We'll be mugged, and they'll be mobbed." Roly laughed, nodding in agreement, "Absolutely not." The two girls were a breath taking sight, Chantelle, who wore her hair short, and Caroline, with her hair long and sensuous femininity.

For the next two days, they lived in the lap of luxury. Parviz was an attentive and gracious host, and the villa, which was tended by a small army of servants, was equipped with every amenity and luxury. The two girls rapidly became firm friends, and each day, Parviz took them all out to sea in the forty-foot Bertram, trawling the blue waters of the Indian Ocean for the great swordfish that lived there while Naylor relaxed on the shady veranda of the guest house, hunched over his figures, preparing a report on achievements to date.

After a brief discussion with Naylor, Roly decided to tell Parviz about the interlude with Chesney. Parviz had thrown back his head and laughed heartily.

"I knew that bastard Dutchman was being a bit too tough. There had to be something that was influencing him, and I know exactly what we can do about it." I'll enjoy this.

"What are you thinking, Parviz?" Roly asked.

"Well, my friend," replied Parviz, "the oil price is a very delicate little instrument. I think since it is our profit that is at stake, I might ask His Majesty to allow me to offload a little, just a little, more oil into the marketplace than we normally do." He smiled at Roly. "The law of supply and demand can do the rest. That little extra will dip the price. Not enough to hurt anybody, certainly not the big fish, but Van der Veden will panic. I think that the next time we meet the Dutchman, in a couple of days, we might just be able to get some juice out of that humourless little shit. What do you say?"

On the afternoon of the third day, Parviz had taken Roly to Victoria in the Bertram, delegating two of his Iranian bodyguards to make sure that Roly and Naylor had no interference. Roly met up with the courier from Salisbury and handed him Naylor's interim report with the revised figures that he had prepared, plus a brief update on 'things' that Roly had prepared for his uncle. Roly had telephoned Botner in Switzerland from the main post office and, using carefully coded language, had brought him up to date with the alteration in Van der Veden's position.

A strange intimacy had grown between Roly and Parviz. Despite two years age difference between them, they had enjoyed each other's company at Aiglon College in Switzerland. In particular, Parviz recalled Roly's swift action in diverting disaster when a helmeted motorcyclist had sought an earlier-than-planned visit to heaven for Hassan Fereydoun. For his part, Roly was able to thank Parviz again for one of the most memorable, fun, and informative weeks that he had ever enjoyed as Parviz's guest in Tehran in late 1966. Post Aiglon, Hassan had become a cleric and was becoming a political nuisance for the Shah's regime, and Parviz wondered whether troubled waters in Iran might have been calmer had Roly not been so quick to react that day.

So it was easy to develop their relationship. Parviz seemed to regard Roly as some sort of protégé, and the two of them talked at length into the balmy tropical nights. Both needed to look to very different futures; Roly because the tide of war in Rhodesia seemed to have turned, and Parviz because strikes and demonstrations in support of Ayatollah Khomeini's return and the Shah's overthrow were paralysing Iran.

A week later, the deal done, Roly and Caroline flew back into Salisbury. They had been away for a fortnight. It had been dangerous work, and Roly had felt satisfaction to have helped towards the positive outcome as well as refreshed from the subsequent few days with Parviz.

But returning to Salisbury felt depressing. Parviz's words were ringing in his head like an ongoing echo, warning him that there was no future for him back in Salisbury. ZANU and ZAPU were gaining traction in their campaigns, and Roly resolved that, for both their sakes, he and Caroline needed to look ahead to what their future could hold instead of staying stuck in the past.

Roly thought his old job at Caliph might be waiting and a swift call to DeLisle confirmed that they would be pleased to have him back. It was an anguished decision. As soon as Roly had things set up in London, Caroline would follow.

May 1980

Zimbabwe: Back to the Lion's Den

Brigadier Roland Spermot Dinks Flashman MC, DFC, rose from his bed, showered, and got into his swimming trunks and dressing gown. It was a Thursday in early May. The senior matron at Westridge Residential and Care Home and Roly's health mentor, Critchley, had poked her head round the door earlier to check on him. She didn't have to, she just liked to. In fact, they both liked it, and they had chatted, as ever. Critchley, an ex-QARANC, found that, because of his military background, Roly was about the only person at Westridge who was on the same wavelength, and she knew that his 69th birthday was imminent.

Ever since Roly's former batman, Brakspear, was exposed and incarcerated for fraud and theft – largely due to Roly's efforts – she had felt as though she had been lifted of a huge burden. God knows which prison Brakspear was doing his time in, but she hoped that he would never reappear in her life anyway. He had only been put away for a five-year term, and she reckoned that five years wasn't long enough for his particular crimes, taking advantage of public office to line his own pockets.

As Critchley strode out to carry on with her rounds, Roly wondered what he would do that morning. Kirsty, the curvy manager of the Wellness Spa, was having the day off, so Roly had got straight to the business of twenty lengths, and he was now back in his apartment, showered and dressed. It was already half past nine, and he decided to ditch breakfast. "I better buff my shoes though," he thought. He was due to pop in later to see his mother Anne, 95, who was in the Care Home part of Westridge, under Critchley's eye.

Roly had been looking forward to dinner that evening with Natasha, whom he had promised to take to The George & Dragon in a nearby village. They had become close over the last few months. He had even buried the hatchet with Natasha's sister, Lady Ponsonby, after an inauspicious start to their relationship. Before that, however, it was the opening day of the Lord's Test Match. Australia were in town, and he and Reggie had tickets for the Sunday.

"If England don't collapse, as usual," thought Roly. The play was due to start at 11 o'clock, and it was on the TV later.

Maureen, who cleaned his apartment for an hour, twice a week, was doing her stuff, and Roly had muttered, good-humouredly, that she better finish the hoovering before play started. Roly enjoyed her visits, but she did talk a lot. She had got into the habit of having a ten-minute coffee break during her sessions, sitting down in an armchair as if she owned the place. The ten minutes nearly always extended into twenty before Roly, seeing as it was becoming an expensive cup of coffee, found a means of suggesting that she might consider getting back to the reason for her visit.

"Oh, sorry, Mr Flashman. Doesn't the time flash by?" she would say, cheerily. "I'll just finish the dusting, and then I'll be off." This time, she rose, took the two coffee mugs to the kitchen, and was back with her duster to do the surfaces and was dusting diligently when she remarked, "What's this big white thing here anyway?" referring to a large oval object sitting in its stand on top of an inlaid chest of drawers.

"Christ, Maureen," thought Roly to himself, "Can't you see that the game's about to start?" But he couldn't say that, so he remarked, rather tersely, "That, Maureen, is an Ostrich egg. It simply reminds me of the time I spent in Rhodesia in the old days."

"Oi reckons oi could do scrambled eggs for about twenty with that one, Mr Flashman," she replied with a self-congratulatory, high-pitched giggle, but Maureen had got the message, and she left shortly afterwards, saying simply, that she would see him next Tuesday, to have a nice weekend and not to get up to anything she wouldn't do herself.

Roly had other ideas as he pondered the forthcoming evening with Natasha but later that afternoon, a couple of lunchtime sherries to the good, with the Test Match now in full flow, the exchange about the Ostrich egg must have stuck with him. Roly zizzed off, and his dream zoomed back to the day that the egg had come into his possession in the mid-eighties.

It had been a sad trip in May 1980. Caliph Security had been invited to attend the annual meeting of the Zimbabwe Agricultural Association ("ZAA"). Getting the farming industry's insurance needs in place required a bulk placement of their insurance requirements, and there were security issues to attend

427

to as well. Otherwise, the underwriters were just not interested, and even then, some essential covers were considered uninsurable in Mugabe's new Zimbabwe.

But there was more to it than plain insurance products. The white farming community looked as though they were going to be up against it, and Roly had devised a nascent plan to not only transfer the profit centre for their product out of Zimbabwe but to also start a new revenue source in Ghana with its tropical growing conditions, with Ghana becoming the hub for all their African operations in due course.

In fact, an incident had happened only two days before the meeting was scheduled when some of Mugabe's thugs had raided one of the farms, causing the staff to flee and leaving the owners distraught. The white farming community had, as usual, tried to come together in support, and the ZAA had had to defer Roly's meeting for a couple of days. So, rather than clicking his heels for forty-eight hours with the charming family of the flower growers that he was staying with, Roly's host had suggested that he take the co-pilot's seat with his friend Jerry who did safari charter flights to the north and west of the country.

It had been extraordinary. Roly had first arrived in Rhodesia in March 1978, just over two years earlier, towards the end of UDI. Since then, his feet had hardly touched the ground; long-range patrolling had ended in a major terrorist contact, followed, only months later, by getting shot in the thigh when his parachute had got stuck in a tree, and he had been left dangling there, unable to get free. After three months of recovery, he had then been sent on a cloak and dagger trip to the Seychelles, successfully concluded, but not before seeing the writing on the wall for Rhodesia's future and leaving.

So the frantic pace of events had limited Roly's chances of enjoying Rhodesia's delights to the full. He had never even had the chance to get to Victoria Falls, so the offer of a seat on this flight, picking up a safari party from the Bumi Hills safari camp on the edge of Lake Kariba, had seemed like a genuine windfall to see a bit more of the country.

Jerry, the pilot, was waiting for Roly as he was dropped off by his host at the entrance to the main terminal at Harare Airport. When Roly had flown in the previous day, he had noticed how different the atmosphere at the airport had seemed in the space of the few short months since he had left. The place already looked tatty. White faces were in short supply, and there seemed to be an abundance of staff with badges doing nothing much more than standing idle while their eyes were, doubtless, more active behind the dark glasses that they sported, and wearing ill-fitting dark suits which failed to hide the tell-tale bulges that concealed their owners' weaponry beneath.

More ominously now, as he stepped out of his host's car, was the presence of two goons who appeared to attach themselves immediately to Roly's tail. As they bypassed the normal routines through the airport, Jerry took Roly past the departure lounge and through the aircrew entrance and, leaving the goons behind, straight out onto the aircraft apron to an area allocated to the light aeroplanes used by the bush transport plane operators. Already, unknown to Roly, a photographer was capturing 'stills' of Roly, and his escort as Roly mounted the Britten Norman BN-2 Islander parked on the aircraft pan.

It could hardly have been less obvious to Roly that the passenger manifests of all inbound commercial aircraft were now examined at the Ministry for Internal Affairs as a matter of routine. For a couple of months since the election in late 1979, which brought Robert Mugabe to power, Jacob Nkala, so nearly killed by Roly's men some twenty-six months earlier in the Rhodesian bush, had been in a position of power and knew how to use it.

As the new Deputy Minister for Security, reporting directly to Mugabe, Nkala was already used to settling his master's scores as well as his own. His reputation was fearsome. Under Mugabe's authoritarian regime, the state security apparatus now dominated the country and was responsible for widespread human rights violations. Jacob Nkala had become a keen disciple, adept at the revolutionary socialist rhetoric that was Mugabe's trademark, and already blaming the gathering economic woes on Western capitalist countries.

High amongst his priorities had been to find the young British officer whom he personally blamed for the ordeal he had endured, first in recovering from the terrible injuries he had sustained in the Zimbabwean bush when his patrol had been ambushed by Roly and his platoon of the Rhodesian African Rifles and, secondly, for the opprobrium that his family had shown at the time for being an active ZANU resistance

430

fighter who languished between hospital and jail for the following 12 months.

Nkala was, in fact, just plain nasty, and he bore a grudge against everyone. His early enquiries had revealed that Roly had left Rhodesia before the independence of the new nation, and his chance for revenge would never happen. But it just had and when Nkala's staff reported the arrival twenty-four hours earlier of a man on his "wanted" list, it was an opportunity that he was not going to miss.

Roly strapped himself into the Islander's co-pilot's seat as Jerry did his pre-flight checks. It was to be a long day. If Roly knew what was in store for him that day, he might have asked Jerry to drop him off in neighbouring Zambia!

Jerry walked around the aircraft, climbed into the pilot's seat, and strapped himself in. He reeled off his pre-flight checks, automatically and thoroughly, by heart, with a keen eye honed by long practice. . After completing the safety measures, he contacted Air Traffic Control for start-up permission, started the engine, and taxied out to the holding point for the main runway.

He was a very experienced pilot; more hours than Roly, and all of them commercial or leisure.

"Flight controls; free and easy," he said as he manoeuvred the control column in all directions.

"Instruments and radios; set and correct."

"Fuel gauges and altimeter," he said, in a quiet voice to himself as his eyes darted across the array of instrumentation in front of him.

"Okay?" he said, turning to Roly "all strapped in? Let's go."

"Harare Tower. This is Islander 595. Request taxi over?"

"Islander 595 is clear to taxi," responded the Tower. "QFE is 1013 and wind North Easterly at 5 knots. Runway 35. Report ready at the threshold." The Air Traffic Controller's measured voice was always so reassuring.

Jerry taxied to the threshold of Runway 35, and after lining up and final clearance, he pushed the throttle forward, and they gathered pace down the runway with Roly, wearing his Rayban sunglasses, enthralled at the aircraft's momentum, almost as if it was projecting itself into the unknown.

At 70 knots, Jerry felt the aircraft seek to rise, and after suppressing the lift for a full ten seconds, he eased gently back on the column, and they rose gracefully into the air. Climbing swiftly to 700 feet, Roly breathed deeply as houses and roads dwindled into smaller perspective below them, and forgotten, but familiar flying sensations returned. As they cleared the outskirts of Salisbury, now known as Harare, Roly drew in the majesty of the cloudless sky and the Zimbabwean landscape below him. Jerry switched the altimeter to QNH, the regional pressure setting, and set a North Westerly course for Kariba, the vast lake lying on the border between Zimbabwe and Zambia.

"Just under the hour, I reckon," said Jerry.

"How long have you been doing this?" enquired Roly. Jerry hadn't realised that Roly was, himself, an experienced pilot, and as they flew northwest, the question gave rise to an exchange of their mutual experiences, the sense of freedom that flying afforded, and the joy of being at one with the elements.

"Fancy a go?" Jerry asked. The aircraft had dual controls, so Roly took over and was at once in tune with that feeling of delicate balance, reacting to the small wind shifts that he could sense through over two thousand hours of flying experience. "This sure brings back many memories, Jerry," says Roly. Jerry could see Roly's clear competence and enjoyment and encouraged him. They were about forty-five minutes into their flight when Jerry offered.

"See that cleft in the valley below us, Roly?" he said.

Roly looked down and could see what seemed like a small scar on the earth. He nodded to Jerry.

"Are you up for some adventure? Take her down, Roly. Perhaps 200 ft AGL and let's see where it takes us."

Roly reduced the throttle marginally, and they descended gently down to 200 ft, above a small river, noticeably dry for the time of year but still flowing. The banks on either side seemed to be rising as the river got larger, and its meanderings became a little harder to follow, but to Roly, this was flying as it was meant to be. Every so often, Roly caught a glimpse of movement beside the flowing water's edge, the

433

movement of one animal or another, and he sighed at the majestic scenery all around him. He surprised himself that he had spent all those months on patrol, mainly in Zimbabwe's easterly regions, and yet had failed to appreciate the full range of Zimbabwe's incredible scenery and varied wildlife.

"Concentrate, please, Roly," said Jerry. "This is the start of the Sanyati River, and it's about to become challenging. Please release the controls if I say, 'I have control'."

The river was now three times the width and its sides four times the height that Roly had first started to follow. 200 ft. above the river meant that the aircraft was now only just above the banks on either side of what was threatening to become a gorge, into which the river, previously meandering, was starting to plunge. This was challenging flying. Jerry was ever ready to take over but obviously comforted by the ease with which Roly was in tune with his surroundings. Soon Roly was flying the Islander in the ravine itself, turning in anticipation of the next bend and looking out for overhead obstacles whilst frequent reference to his instrumentation and tell-tale gauges told Jerry that here was a natural pilot with many hours of experience.

Below him, Roly could see from the white tips of the water that the river had become a free-flowing cauldron with rapids. The shallow valley had now become a high-sided canyon and flying within its grip was a test of any pilot's skills.

"This is fantastic," he said to Jerry. "Are you comfortable with this?" he added by way of reassurance that he was flying within his limitations.

"No problem," replied Jerry, "but I may take over in about 30 seconds when you find yourself overwhelmed."

Roly wasn't sure what he meant. Steep turns at 90 knots, of the sort that he was now experiencing in order to keep within the valley's confines, was the type of flying that gave rise to the "seat of your pants" sobriquet. It was two years at least since he had last flown himself. Steep left bank… steep right bank… steep left bank… and Roly was just imagining that the Hun might have been on his tail when they emerged from the canyon.

Roly was gobsmacked! Before him lay a scene of the likes that he would never, ever see again.

"I have control," came Jerry's reassuring voice before Roly, gasping in wonder, remembered where he was and released his grip on the control column as he stared at the awesome vista that had just unfolded.

Before them lay the vastness of Lake Kariba with Zambia on the opposite shore, many miles away, and below them, on the shores of the lake, were herds of what seemed to be every animal possible. Whole flocks of birds took off as the Islander flew over, and vast numbers of Zebra, Elephants, Giraffes, and Buffalo were everywhere to be seen. This seemed a true Eden.

"Sorry, Roly. Well done, but we can't stop. We're late at Bumi now. I hope you enjoyed that. Keep it to yourself, please; we've been well out of limits," said Jerry as he put the aircraft back into a climb and turned due west for Bumi, just five minutes away from their present location.

Landing at Bumi in a cloud of dust, Roly could see a reception committee waiting for them at the little hut that served as a shelter on the side of the runway. Turning round at the end, Jerry taxied back to the open-sided, atap-covered building and cut the engine. He was scheduled to pick up the same six French holidaymakers that he had brought up a week earlier, and they were waiting there, keen to ensure that they made their international connection back to France but less than eager to be leaving behind the marvellous experience of the last seven days.

Luggage loaded and passengers strapped in, Jerry repeated his 'walk round' and pre-flight checks, and they took off on the return journey to Harare, departing to the cheerful faces of the lodge staff, waving goodbye from the hut to their departing guests. The flight was uneventful, and Roly enjoyed listening to the French passengers' chatter excitedly in French about the unforgettable experiences of the previous week.

Roly and Jerry related flying stories to each other, and Roly, still awed by his emergence that morning from the mouth of the Sanyati River onto Lake Kariba, recalled a previous occasion when he had flown in a confined space and then emerged onto a wondrous sight. It had been in the mid-seventies, and he had been deployed on another flying tour in Northern Ireland. Low-level flying over the terraced ghettos of central Belfast had been a better way of reducing a helicopter's profile to the random IRA sharpshooter than any other; hardly classical airmanship but safer when traversing the city from the west to the base at Sydenham or nearby Palace Barracks at Hollywood. En route lay the Royal Victoria Hospital with a helipad on the roof, just west of the City Centre and about six stories high. On sunny days the nurses would sunbathe on the helipad at the top, and Roly recounted how he and his fellow pilots, when operational time permitted, would appear suddenly over the top to catch the nurses topless, squealing and reaching for their bikini tops. On one such occasion, one of his fellow pilots had even managed to blow a variety of folded clothing off the top of the building altogether, leaving the girls to return to duty after their lunch break with some explaining to do to their nursing hierarchy. In fact, the nurses enjoyed these occasions as much as the pilots.

Jerry related some of his own bush flying experiences, and as Roly listened to tales of what he might have liked to have enjoyed for himself, they arrived back at Harare all too quickly. The tourists' luggage was unloaded, and Jerry pointed out to them the way to the doors where they could check everything in for their return to Paris. Ten minutes later, with pitot head covers back on, chocks in place, and doors about to be firmly closed, Jerry noticed something white on one of the rear seats.

"Here you are, Roly. A memento, perhaps? I'm never going to catch up with those Frogs now. Pop it in your haversack."

An ostrich egg had somehow fallen out of one of their pieces of luggage.

Back at the terminal and vowing to meet again someday, Jerry said goodbye to a beaming Roly and walked off towards his crewroom to sign in on the aircraft log book whilst Roly went off towards the arrivals area where he thought he might find a taxi. It was only 2 pm, and he would be early back at his hosts' house. Jerry had been due at a meeting that afternoon, so he could not accompany him but had suggested that a quick trip down memory lane and, maybe, a beer somewhere might fit the bill.

"Why don't you take a taxi?" he said to Roly. Roly had planned to whip in to Meikles department store so picking up a gift for his hosts as well as a small detour to see how things were after his year and a half's absence wouldn't go amiss, he thought.

Roly mused how many other name changes there had been as the driver took him at a slow pace up Joshua Nkomo Avenue, heading north into town as they passed the old Falcon golf course on their right, where he used to play whenever the opportunity arose. The lovely purple Jacaranda blossom was out of season, sadly, and he was just wondering whether he would have time to walk around what was now called Harare Gardens when there was a sudden screech of tyres, and his taxi driver hit the kerb violently, and came to a shuddering halt, slamming into a street lamp post.

Roly was catapulted forward into the back of the driver's seat, hitting the bridge of his nose with great force, and a brief blackness, a temporary concussion, descended upon him. Coming to, a mere five seconds later, he could see that a large Datsun Utility Vehicle appeared to have forced them off the road whilst a large black Mercedes 4x4 with tinted glass windows had pulled up behind them to box them in. Roly was still shaking his head, groggily, when his door was yanked open, and a very large arm grabbed him by the lapel of his jacket. He was dragged onto the pavement before he had time to respond.

There was no point in struggling. There were three of them. Still reeling from the blow, his arms were pinned behind his back, shackled with plasticuffs, a hood put over his head, and without ceremony, he was bundled roughly into the rear seat of the Mercedes.

Within two minutes of the crash, they were back on the road, heading into town again. Roly was in the back seat with one of his abductors alongside him, the driver and apparent leader being in the front.

"Shit," Roly thought to himself, gathering his wits. "This does not look good. This feels like a regular kidnapping, and these guys don't seem to be about to take prisoners." He tried to remember the advice that Caliph gave their clients when they were asked to teach anti-kidnap measures.

Rule 1. Don't expose yourself to kidnap.

"Christ. What a fool I've been," he thought through the pain in his head. "I've come here to address

439

government interference in a client's affairs, and all I do is take a long jolly to amuse myself."

Rule 2. Make sure that your whereabouts are known to a third party at all times.

"Well, it's hardly a written schedule, but at least Jerry might remember what I had been planning."

Rule 3. The longer the abduction lasts, the less likely escape becomes but don't injure yourself in the interim. You might need to preserve your strength.

"Face it," Roly said to himself. "The longer this goes on, the less likely I'm going to emerge in one piece."

"So, Flashman, eh, so sorry about welcome, but our boss, he want see you," said the man from the front passenger seat.

"The man wants to talk, and he knows who I am," Roly thought to himself. "That's good. He might be the ringleader amongst this group. Probably pleased with himself, but don't give him the pleasure of a reply."

"You can hear me, Mr Flashman? I don't tink our boss am happy with you. What you done upset him, eh?"

Roly kept his counsel again. His non-reply seemed to irk his abductor, and he spoke to his colleagues.

"He not hold his tongue when Nkala speak him!" And they all laughed.

Instantly, Roly knew where he stood and the implications. There was no question other than he had to get out of that car before reaching wherever their destination was. He had heard of Nkala's appointment, and they had discussed the previous evening, at his host's house, the chilling tales of what was happening on outlying farms at Nkala's hands.

Thinking quickly, Roly started to make gagging noises under his hood, rocking his head back and forth whilst simultaneously shaking his own shoulders. It had the right effect. Worried that their prisoner might expire before delivery to their destination, the leading henchman indicated to the driver to slow down and turned abruptly to his colleague in the rear seat with an order.

"Remove da hood. Him sound like he bloody choking," said the man in the front passenger seat, twisting round, as Roly slumped, apparently unconscious, into the lap of the man in the back seat with him.

By holding his breath and simultaneously straining on his neck muscles, ably abetted by the glow of a day's worth of fierce African sun on his face, Roly managed to give the puce effect of a man suffering from a heart attack, spittle emerging from his mouth as he made guttural sounds while his body twitched.

"Ma God," said the boss, now worried that his parcel of goods would not get to Nkala in the condition that Nkala expected, and turning to the driver, he told him to drive straight to Harare Central Hospital, less than two minutes away.

"And take de cuffs off," he said as the Mercedes drew into the hospital's main entrance, blaring its horn to alert the reception at the doors to Accident &

441

Emergency. A stretcher trolley emerged quickly, and Roly, still gasping, was taken into the building whilst his abductors, after stating that they did not know who he was and had simply seen him fall on the pavement as they drove past, were told to wait outside.

Quick to assimilate his improved circumstances and with his abductors now out of sight, Roly's condition took an immediate turn for the better. He realised he didn't have long before they sought to enquire about his condition. Despite protestations from the attendant nurse, herself calling for help to restrain the patient, he sat up on his trolley and swung his legs to the floor at the same time as the duty doctor came into the cubicle into which Roly's trolley had been pushed.

Unbelievably, it was Johnny Oram, the same trauma doctor who had treated him after being shot two years earlier in the Rhodesian bush. The ensuing month under Johnny's care had meant that he and Roly had become firm mates.

"Bloody hell. Look what the cat's turned up!" said Johnny. "Shit, Roly. You don't look like a heart attack case. What are you doing here?"

Roly smiled grimly as he felt a huge relief come over him at the appearance of his old friend.

"You've got to listen, Johnny. I'm sorry, but this is no duff. I promise I'll catch up, but I have got to get out of here… and fast. Have you got a car I can have? And, by the way, there is nothing wrong with me!"

"Hey, c'mon," replied Johnny. "What the hell is all this? And what are you doing here? I can't just let you go. You will have been registered on arrival, and someone will want to know the outcome."

"Please, Johnny. I think you know me well enough. I'm not bullshitting. Mugabe's men are outside, and they won't wait long. I'm in trouble for no reason, and I need to get away fast. There is only one place I can go, and it's the UK Embassy."

"Oh.... Right," said Johnny. "How am I going to get my car back, eh? From memory, your driving is terrible, and you might have trouble getting there because the system has changed! I'll get someone to take you, and I'll sort out your goons in the meantime. It sounds as though they won't be too pleased!"

Thirty minutes later, and after leaving instructions with the nurse that the patient was not to be disturbed at any cost, Johnny was able to take Roly to the rear of the hospital, where a taxi had been arranged to take him off to the Embassy. He had had time to brief Johnny fully on what had happened. Sadly, it had already become an all-too-frequent episode in Mugabe's new Zimbabwe.

"Thanks, Johnny," Roly had said with real feeling. "If I get there, come and see me in London, won't you? I think it'll be on me, eh?"

Johnny undertook to inform Roly's flower-growing hosts, who arranged to get his small bag of possessions over to the Embassy, and after calling them personally to suggest that their next meeting might be in Ghana, Roly left Zimbabwe under diplomatic protection the next day. Throughout his ordeal, Roly had continued to wear his small backpack. Inside it, and undamaged, lay a medium-sized Ostrich egg!

Back in Westridge, Roly awoke with a start. He had drifted off in front of the box again and had missed the evening cricket session. England had made some progress after a difficult start and had reached 230 for 7. He thought he better hurry as he was due to pick up Natasha at seven o'clock. She lived about twenty minutes away, and there seemed time to have a quick sharpener in the bar before leaving. Kevin, the barman, was on duty, and Reggie was there, waiting for his wife. Reggie and Joanna were eating in Westridge's dining room that night.

"Whisky Pani," please, Kevin. "Actually, make that a large one, please."

"Yes, Sahib," responded Kevin, who liked playing the part of a liveried servant from Victorian Raj days.

"Bridge tonight, Roly?" said Reggie. "We're short of a fourth. Are you doing anything after supper?"

"Sorry, Reggie. I've got a date this evening. Doesn't happen very often at my age, so I'll need my wits about me. Why don't you see if Johnny is game?"

"No, he's not here tonight. I think it's a Squadron reunion or something. He's been humming the Dambusters March all day. It drove me potty on the golf course. If his bombing accuracy was anything like his putting, the enemy must have been pretty safe, I reckon."

February 2019

Westridge: An Evening with Natasha

Roly would remember 3rd February 2019 for a lot of reasons. It was the night that Natasha had invited him to dinner. He wasn't sure why he had felt so uncharacteristically nervous about going to her cottage, but the butterflies in his stomach had betrayed how much he had been looking forward to the evening.

It was snowing outside as Roly arrived by taxi at 7 pm at her 18th Century Cottage. The porch light glowed cheerfully, and Natasha was wiping her hands on her apron as she opened the front door.

"Ha-ha." She said conspiratorially, greeting Roly on the doorstep. "Welcome to my house, Roly. Come on in, now, before we both freeze." She wiped the front and back of her hands on the apron she was wearing. "Sorry, I was just finishing some crumble topping for our pudding. Ooh. I wasn't expecting this snow. It's quite nippy out here, isn't it?"

Stepping under the lintel of the heavy oak front door, Roly closed it behind him, and, as they kissed each other lightly on the cheek, he handed Natasha the bunch of roses that he had got in town that afternoon.

"I thought I'd bring this one too, darling," he said, offering the bottle of red wine, a good St Emilion that he had concealed behind his back with the other hand.

"Well, you shouldn't have. That looks lovely and extremely kind of you, Roly. And roses in winter! How does a glass of champagne first sound? I've got one in the fridge begging for you to open it if that's up your street?"

Roly smiled and removed his coat, draped it over the chair in her hall, and followed Natasha towards the subdued strains of some gentle mood music, stooping slightly as he bent his six-foot three-inch frame under the door into the beamed kitchen of her 18th Century cottage. At one end, Natasha had lit the fire to combat the chill of the evening, and a whiff of oak smoke mixed with whatever obviously delicious recipe Natasha was cooking up for their supper greeted Roly as he walked in to the room. As he popped open the bottle, he wondered to himself how some people just had the knack for getting everything right; the décor, the lighting, the colour, the aroma – all instantly putting him at ease.

Natasha was casually dressed in jeans with a cashmere jumper over a floral shirt. He knew she was in her early sixties, but she looked twenty years younger, wearing elegant earrings, a necklace, and jet black, shoulder-length hair, the same as he remembered from the early seventies, tied back by a colourful piece of material. As if she might not have had to make an effort for him.

"Shame about the tattoo on her inner thigh!" thought Roly as he remembered their first encounter in the potting shed at the Innes's house. But Roly's normal bravura was overcome by a strange nervousness.

"Your very good health Natasha," said Roly, as they raised and clinked their flute champagne glasses, "and how nice of you to have me over. February evenings in Westridge are a bit dull, so I need cheering up, although it's been an interesting day today. I had to give evidence in court!"

Natasha raised an eyebrow, and an enquiring look and smile came over her face.

"Oh dear, what have you been up to now, Roly?" she asked.

Roly laughed. "Just someone from the old days; my former batman," he replied. "Got his come-uppance at last. Always a sad creature and a lifetime of conniving and embezzlement has finally been revealed. His name is Brakspear. I expect your sister might have told you about him. It's been all the talk at Westridge since the police turned up, and he did a runner before they could arrest him."

"It was about six weeks ago. I'll tell you about it over sups."

Roly looked around the room. He noticed birthday cards on the wide mantelpiece.

"Hello," he said. "Someone celebrating something?"

"It's my birthday, Roly. Always worth forgetting, but the children wouldn't allow it, of course."

Roly wasn't aware. She sensed his discomfort, and patting him on the forearm with both hands, looked directly at him and smiled, saying, "Honestly. You shouldn't worry. Your being here is enough. Just don't forget it the next time, ha-ha."

It was at that moment, as he felt her hands on his arm that Roly knew what the outcome of the evening would be, as if they had been together for the last 46 years anyway and had no secrets to tell each other, their minds fused with the same thoughts.

How ridiculous! He felt like a teenager all over again. "Happy Birthday, darling," he said, and they embraced for a full two minutes as if frightened of letting each other go, butterflies fluttering in Roly's stomach.

"Ayeeee," cried Natasha. A small whisper of smoke was coming from the Aga. "Quick. We don't want to burn the supper!" She rushed to the Aga and took out a delicious-looking steak and kidney pie, the crust just turning the wrong side of golden brown.

"We won't want that just yet. It'll be too hot. Come and sit down over here," she said as she beckoned Roly to the two armchairs beside the fire.

Roly had the most wonderful evening. There was a lot of catching up to do.

He explained the Brakspear saga. Brakspear's Mercedes had been caught on the M4 cameras, speeding east towards London on the morning of his denouement. How he had got wind of the police presence, no-one knew. The Assistant Manager at Westridge was suspected, and further investigation revealed his involvement and the further extent of Brakspear's crimes.

Westridge had been just the tip of the iceberg. Seventy percent of the Care Homes within the Council's scope of responsibility had been coerced to buy their consumables from Cherry Products, 100% owned by Brakspear. It was a large operation, and Brakspear had been coining it in for a number of years.

The court proceedings had been clear-cut, and Roly had been called to give evidence. This time, Roly felt no sense of loyalty towards a fellow soldier. Brakspear needed to 'go down', and he gave a damning assessment of Brakspear's character. The hard facts of Brakspear's crimes could not be disputed, and Brakspear's defence counsel was unable to save him. A guilty verdict was returned by the jury, and the Judge sentenced Brakspear to 8 years at Her Majesty's pleasure.

"I expect you'll see it in the papers tomorrow, love. I just hope they keep my name out of it," said Roly.

Four hours later, and three courses to the good, they were still discussing their lives. Natasha's eyes stared wide in disbelief as Roly had gone through his military experiences and subsequent career in Insurance Claims investigation, itself real enough but doubling as a Case Officer for MI6. He could scarcely believe it himself; his love for flying, the disappointment of Northern Ireland, the war in Cyprus, the freedom of Belize, the plight of Zimbabwe, the close shaves, the villains, the City of London, Government workings, Seychelles skulduggery, and Triads in Hong Kong to name but a few.

The Tiramisu that Natasha gave him for pudding brought out all the incidents that Roly had endured over a tense three-year period in the Nineties in Italy, and, at moments, silence reigned between the pair as Roly reflected on the people he had known and lost and his loves.

He realised he was telling her more than he should. Somehow it didn't matter with this woman. She listened with sympathy and joy in equal measure .... and they laughed together at the impossibility of his close shaves.

"It must run in the blood," remarked Natasha. "What do you mean?" Roly replied.

"Well, I read the lot, Roly. Your friends in Aldeburgh told me who you were and about your grandfather. You owe me a few quid, actually. I went out and bought the whole blooming Flashman Papers series! And then you did a disappearing act. Thanks a bunch."

"Tell me about yourself, Natasha. I want to know about your life."

"I will, Roly, but not now. It might seem rather routine to you, but I have had a very wonderful life, although the last few years have been difficult. My husband, Peter, was taken from me too young, really. The children and I found it hard to cope initially, but life goes on. I've been very fortunate. Pete provided for us so well, and his legacy still does. The boys were educated privately and are now married with lovely wives and children of their own. We always had great holidays, and we have lived in only two very comfortable houses ever since we married. So I'm not complaining. In fact, I rejoice in my friends and good fortune!"

Roly glanced at the mantelpiece and the pictures of Natasha's family beside a lovely old antique clock.

"Blimey, Natasha. I've overstayed my welcome. It's half past midnight! Can I use your phone? I hope the taxis are still running."

"No chance," replied Natasha, "and anyway, have you seen outside? We must have had four inches of snow whilst you've been banging on! You'll have to stay here the night. Don't worry. I've got a bed made up, and I keep some spare shaving kit for the boys in case they need it."

A knowing smile spread across her face, and Natasha's eyelids fluttered. "Unless…. It's been a long time since my last cuddle," she added.

"Oh don't, Natasha. I swore to try and make a good impression. I told myself not to bugger this one up!"

For once, what happened to Roly that night wasn't a dream. They had gone to bed and made love and fallen asleep in each other's arms. It had been a long time for them both. He relished her warmth, and she, his security. For both, happiness was waking up and having someone to talk to.

The next morning, after showering and having a brief breakfast, Natasha suggested that they go for a walk in the sparkling sunshine. The trees were groaning from the weight of snow, and every now and again, one would release its load with a great whoosh. The snow-covered fields ran like an unblemished carpet of white around the edges of the woods, and Roly and Natasha had difficulty picking their way until, one hour later, they arrived at the pub where they had decided to have their lunch. The happiness of one was evident to the other, and as they talked here and there about everyone and anything, they laughed and laughed and laughed.

It was already three thirty when they got back to Natasha's cottage, and Roly settled down in front of the fire for another cosy evening.

"I'll have to pop off in the morning, darling," he said. "I've got the Knackers for lunch tomorrow. You know, that bunch of adolescents that I meet once a month. I've just had an idea. Why don't you take your sister out to the same pub? We've been getting along better lately, and the boys can seek to smooth the ruffled waters that they created last time their paths crossed."

The next day was Friday – Knackers day – and Roly had been looking forward to his session at The Jolly Roger. With Natasha's likely presence there too, he wanted to make a good impression, especially if she was bringing her sister, Jane Ponsonby, so he carefully considered what he would wear, electing for some mustard yellow cords and a short-sleeved sweater under a favourite sports jacket. It was always a careful process to avoid being dressed in the same deep pink trousers and stripy shirts as his friends. They just didn't know the impression that they gave other clients of the venues that they attended – buffers the lot of them!

Roly was quizzed and had his leg pulled about the court case. It had been in the local newspaper that morning. He was not to know that Brakspear would be out again within two years.

September 1980

Epilogue: London

It was a grey day in London's West End as the black cab, having fought its way through traffic from Euston, drew to a halt outside the main entrance of the American Embassy in Grosvenor Square. Its passenger, a short, powerfully built man with close-cropped reddish hair, dressed in a fading green blazer, denim trousers, and desert boots, sporting what looked like a regimental tie, paid the cab off and made his way into the foyer of the embassy. After frisking by the civilian security staff in the doorway, he made his way to the reception desk, where the US Marine guard, in full dress uniform, asked him his business.

He gave the marine his name, and without showing a flicker of recognition, the marine asked him to sign the visitor book. A couple of minutes later, a grey-haired lady emerged from a bank of elevators behind the reception and came over.

"Major Shacter?" she asked quizzically. He nodded his assent, and she continued. "My name is Anne. I am Colonel Lewis's assistant. Would you be kind enough to follow me?"

They took the lift to the second floor, and after walking down a carpeted corridor, she stopped and knocked at the door that they came to.

"Come in," came the cheerful reply from the other side. Ben Lewis's desk was neat and orderly, as you might suspect of a Colonel in the US Airforce; virtually clear of all papers but with a model of an F18 Hornet aircraft and a silver American football.

"Hi, Eric. I'm Ben Lewis," said the Colonel, introducing himself. They shook hands, and Lewis gestured to a couple of sofas beside a window overlooking Grosvenor Square. "Won't you sit down? How about some coffee?" That sounded good to Shacter, and the grey-haired lady left the room, closing the door quietly behind her.

"Well, Major. Thanks for the call. I appreciate the effort to come up here and see us. We are always interested in any ideas that might help secure the release of our boys in Iran."

Sitting back in his chair, he continued. "Perhaps you could start by telling me something about yourself. I don't even recognise the tie you are wearing!"

Shacter smiled and replied. "Well, it would be a toughie for most people. You can't get it in Savile Row because it's the tie of the Rhodesian African Rifles."

Shacter leant forward on the sofa, as if sizing up the Colonel and then started speaking. His voice was heavily accented, and the clipped sentences betrayed his Southern African origins. His square-jawed face remained expressionless, and by the slope of his shoulders, you could see that he was a man of considerable strength. Addressing the Colonel as if there was no difference in their rank, he said

"I think, Colonel, that my colleagues and I have been able to come up with a plan that might be able to spring your Embassy hostages in Tehran. You may or may not be aware that, throughout the recent Rhodesian conflict, we maintained fairly close links with the Iranian government and military."

"There was quite a lot of trade between us. From their point of view, it was oil and weaponry and the odd luxury. We used to ship them food and tobacco. A lot of the stuff was shipped by air by Air Transport Africa (ATA)." Shacter looked at the Colonel.

"Your guys used them too?" asked Lewis.

Shacter hadn't known this, but he could sense Lewis's underlying inference that such circumstances, were they known publicly, might be of some embarrassment to the US Government.

"Have you heard of the Selous Scouts?" queried Shacter. The American nodded his head. "And presumably, you have also heard of C Squadron of the SAS that was disbanded in 1953 and became the nucleus of "C" Squadron (Rhodesian) Special Air Service?"

The American nodded again.

"I served in the Selous Scouts and, before that, was a troop commander in "C" Squadron."

To many people, this may have sounded like a boast. From Shacter, it was just a flat statement of fact.

"I can assemble a team of about forty guys that I can get into Iran, all of whom would have seen considerable service with one of those two organisations. In my opinion, it would amount to the most battle-hardened and combat-trained Commando unit in the world."

At that moment, Anne came in with a tray, with a coffee pot, cups, milk, and sugar. The Colonel got to his feet and walked over to the desk, picked up a yellow pad of paper, and came back to his seat.

"Mind if I take notes, Major?" he enquired.

Shacter had no problem and nodded his assent as Anne poured two cups of coffee, placing one in front of each man, and left the room again.

"What do you want from us, Eric? Money?" Shacter looked at him steadily.

"Of course, there will be an element of money," he replied, "but this isn't our primary motivation. Most of the guys that would come on this trip are Rhodesians. They are stuck with Zimbabwean passports, and an American one would help their futures." Shacter put his cup down and sat back on the sofa, relaxing slightly.

"I will tell you frankly why we want to do this, Colonel. Firstly, most of the guys need a new home. We reckon that, if we do you a favour, you will look kindly on this. Secondly, we are going to need some cash to get going, not a huge amount but just sufficient to feel comfortable about getting started. Thirdly, we have got a score to settle. The crowd that is running Iran at the moment damaged some friends of ours, and we would like to help them."

458

He looked at the Colonel, who had been jotting down a few notes on his pad. The Colonel finished writing and looked up.

"Okay. So how would this operation of yours work?"

Shacter leaned forward again, one elbow resting on his knee.

"The Iranians have a major problem at the moment; a whole lot of American gear and, particularly, aircraft; helicopters, jets, and heavy transports which, for the best part of two years, they haven't been able to get any spares. Effectively, the Iranian air force is grounded. Your sanctions appear to have been rather effective."

Shacter looked down into his coffee cup as though seeking inspiration. Operation Eagle Claw, five months earlier, had failed in ignominious disaster.

"What we are proposing to do is to set up a Company in what is now Zimbabwe. You'll supply us with the spares that they need to get some of their aircraft airborne. Not the major stuff, not the Tomcats or the Phantoms, but the C130 Hercules and the helicopters."

"We'll airfreight the stuff in on ATA, just the way we used to. We have a friend who is still running ATA, the airfreight organisation, and he knows the form. He is still dealing with the Iranians on a trading basis. We've got a bunch of guys available to us who are competent on Huey choppers and also on the Hercules. We'll set them up in a workshop at a Tehran airport and start sticking some of the gear together. How does that sound so far?" enquired Shacter.

The American Colonel looked at him pensively and stroked his chin. "Difficult" was all he said.

"Yah, well, it was never going to be easy, was it? And you Americans have got a ten-month-old problem for which we are proposing a possible solution." Shacter reached into his pocket and pulled out a packet of cigarettes.

"Do you mind if I smoke?"

The Colonel shook his head in reply and raised his hand to refuse the offer of a cigarette for himself. Shacter lit up and, breathing the smoke through his nostrils, leaned back on the sofa.

"What we are proposing to do is to rotate the Commando unit through the workshop operation over a period of a couple of months, building them up gradually whilst maintaining engineering capability. The Iranians will think they are all fitters, but they will be 'subbing' for the main engineers. A couple of days before we go in, we will bring in the whole team as part of a major effort to get more aircraft serviceable."

"We'll have two of ATA's DC8s on the ground in Tehran, and we can hit the Embassy and get the people out fairly quickly. We are going to need some stuff like gas and silenced Uzi machine guns, but I can come on to the shopping list if we take this conversation any further."

"When we get the hostages out, we'll get back to the airfield in container trucks. We'll have to take care of the Tehran radar and any potential pursuit planes, but we will need some help from you. It's a long way to safety, so electronic intelligence from you guys, AWACS out of Saudi plus fighter cover as we get out over the Zagros Mountains."

The Colonel had said nothing while Shacter spoke but had listened politely and carefully. Shacter had very few illusions about what the Colonel's impression might be of ex-Rhodesian commandos walking in off the street with a hare-brained scheme. He reached into the pocket of his blazer and pulled out an envelope containing carefully folded typed papers.

"The detailed plan is here" he said. "It looks a bit hairy at first sight, but it is feasible; that is, with one particular group doing it. I actually think that we are probably the only outfit in the world capable of pulling this off."

Shacter stood up.

"I won't waste your time talking it through now. Have a look at the detailed plans, and you know where to get hold of me, if you like them. If I don't hear from you in the next two weeks, I'll take it that you are not interested. I'm not a salesman."

The American Colonel stood up and held out his hand. "Thank you for coming by," he said as he shook Shacter's hand. "It's an interesting idea, and your concern is appreciated. I can't really say what our reaction will be, but I'll certainly talk to some people about it."

He opened the door, and Anne was there, as if on cue. She accompanied him down in the lift and, after signing him out in the visitor's book, said goodbye.

461

In his office on the second floor, the Colonel had sat down at his desk and was reading through the ten, tightly typed pages of the outline plan. He picked up his telephone and dialled.

"Hi, Charlie. It's Ben Lewis here. How are you?"

There was a brief exchange as the two men went through the ritual small talk that often precedes a business conversation between two people who know each other well. Eventually, Lewis got to the point.

"Charlie. I wanted a favour. I need some information on a former Rhodesian soldier called Major Eric Shacter. He claims to have been in both the C Squadron of the Rhodesian SAS and, more recently, the Selous Scouts. We are trying to get a full bio on him. Can you guys help?"

At the other end of the telephone, in the offices of Century House from which MI6 operated, the man called Charlie reached into a filing tray on his desk and took out an orange file with the words 'Major Eric Shacter' written on it. He opened it in front of him as he spoke into the telephone.

Any particular reason for asking, old boy?"

"I don't think there's any harm in telling you, Charlie. Do you remember suggesting that I contact Roly Flashman a few days ago? Well, I did, and now this Shacter guy has offered his services to us for some analysis work in Central Africa. As you know, we are pretty worried about that region at the moment, and we are trying to find out just what sort of character he is."

462

At the other end of the telephone, the Englishman drummed his fingers pensively on the file in front of him. He did not, for one second, believe the explanation that had been offered to him by the American Colonel, but at the same time, it was hardly likely to be any of his business. If the Americans wanted to put an asset into Southern Africa, which was the natural area for Shacter to operate, that was their affair. Still, Shacter was an interesting one. He was one of the last Rhodesian officers to have been trained in Britain since UDI, and during the war years, he had visited the SAS at Hereford on a couple of occasions. He knew that Shacter often stayed at the Special Forces Club in Hans Place in London's West End.

"Ben," he said. "Curiously enough, I happen to have a file on the very man sitting on my desk at this precise moment. I'll get a copy across to you straight away. He might be pretty close to what you are looking for."

The American thanked him and put the phone down. The fact that his counterpart actually had a file ready to hand had surprised him and he wondered what the British interest was. Had Shacter already approached the British with a version of his plan? It made it all the more intriguing. What was their interest? He turned back to the typed pages, and after rereading them, he leaned over to the intercom on his desk and pressed a button.

"Anne," he said. "Get hold of Langley for me, will you please? When I go over Wednesday, I want to have an appointment with the Deputy Director. Could you get that confirmed for me?"

At the other end, Anne confirmed his request, and he turned back to the pages in front of him. It was a very detailed and daring plan. It would be interesting to see what they thought of it in Langley.

Shacter had another meeting later that day. He was due to meet with a former colleague in the Rhodesian African Rifles, one with whom he had had a transient relationship and whose reputation, he knew, was legendary. The young Brit had not been with them during UDI for very long but had, in the short space of a year and a half, built an extraordinary reputation.

For the last two months, there had been a lot of dancing about between MI6 and Shacter. Iran was a political minefield. Britain's historic role and the rise of Ayatollah Khomeini in exile ensured that it was so.

The ownership of the Anglo-Iranian Oil Company, the 1953 coup d'état of the Iranian Prime Minister and its support for his replacement, Mohammad Reza Pahlavi, whose mismanagement of what were intended to be reforms only led to further resentment, which meant that an economic contraction in Iran in the late seventies had laid the groundwork for a potential backlash against western imperialism which Khomeini had exploited.

Had it been the British Embassy in Tehran, rather than the American, that had been invaded, things might have been different, but reports of Iraqi troop movements on the Iraqi border amounting to a possible invasion attempt looked ominous, and the British had already taken the decision to, simply, encourage Shacter in putting his proposal to the Americans. They could not afford to be seen to be involved, but that did not mean that there was no advantage to be gained.

Without any property in London, Roly had acquired membership of the Special Forces Club. The club had served as the ideal location for Roly while he looked for a longer-term solution to his accommodation needs and while he settled back into a routine with Caliph, the small Lloyds Insurance Broker in London which had given him a home whilst he had been awaiting the outcome of his court-martial.

Re-joining Caliph had been a smooth process. Andrew DeLisle had hardly seemed to have batted an eyelid when he had made the approach, acquaintances renewed, and Roly was astonished when, without negotiation, he was offered a salary that doubled that which he was expecting as well as including him in the company's bonus scheme.

The Special Forces Club was intended by its founders to be a meeting place for both those who had served in the Special Operations Executive and for members of kindred organisations during the Second World War.

It was initially open only to ex-SOE agents and personnel, and to Resistance members from all over the SOE's areas. It is now a second home for ageing secret agents, veterans of the SAS, other special forces, MI5, MI6, and CIA officers and has expanded to include those who had served, or were serving, in organisations and units closely associated with special operations and the intelligence community, including high-threat bomb disposal experts and members drawn from the psy-ops community. Great stress is placed on the personal qualities of applicants, along with their technical qualifications, to ensure that the club maintains its reputation as one of the most discreet locations in London.

Three months after re-joining Caliph, having served her notice to Air Rhodesia, Caroline would join him, and they would set about the joyful experience of a young couple seeking a house and the furnishings to go in it. Meanwhile, Andrew DeLisle had been very happy to take Roly in again and gradually made him fully aware of Caliph's real raison d'étre as well as a hint that he was more involved with the British establishment than a mere director of a small City of London firm might be expected.

The grey area between overt and covert intelligence operations is often conducted so as to conceal the identity of or permit plausible denial by the sponsor. Caliph was a 49% subsidiary of a large multinational insurance broker whose services extended to Kidnap & Ransom Insurance. The necessity to resolve live situations and/or sometimes recover large sums of money or other high-value assets often meant for very dangerous situations which required a cool head. DeLisle would have taken Roly back anyway, but he noticed the difference that had occurred in Roly's demeanour since they had last met. His previously evident professionalism now had the edge of hard experience, borne out by two, recent, difficult assignments that Roly had already concluded, one involving the recovery of a pair of Van Gogh paintings and the other being a low-key hostage resolution.

The bottom then fell out of Roly's world. Caroline had been killed, inexplicably, in a car accident, whilst visiting her parents in Bulawayo, Zimbabwe. It hit him very hard. For the first time in his life, Roly had become committed to the dream of a shared future with the girl that he loved, and this cruel turn of events to disrupt his happiness with a girl to whom, only 48 hours earlier, he had waved goodbye at Heathrow Airport, drove Roly to near despair. Being able to immerse himself in Caliph's active cases had been a godsend.

Attendance at Caroline's funeral was just not going to be feasible. The other party in the accident appeared to have been attached to the Ministry of Internal Security and, possibly, an employee of Jacob Nkala, Roly's old bête noire. When DeLisle had sought to console him, Roly had spilled out his suspicions and fears to his boss, about his initial brush with Nkala at the ambush in which Nkala had only survived due to Roly's decency, the long-range patrols and the Seychelles episode and Roly had seen DeLisle's eyebrows rise in astonishment when he had mentioned the name of his friend Farukh Parviz.

"Now you're pulling my leg, aren't you?" said DeLisle censorially to Roly.

"About what, sir?" replied Roly.

"About Parviz. You mean... you're actually close mates with this guy?"

"Well. Yes, sir. We met in Switzerland many years ago, re-met in the Seychelles, a couple of years back, and have kept in touch ever since. In fact, I've seen

467

him a couple of times in London. He seems to have become a trusted face for the Islamic Revolutionary Council, which surprised me as he was close to the Shah. It's probably fair to say that we have a bond forged by having saved each other's bacon a couple of times," as Roly went on to explain what had happened at Aiglon and in the Seychelles respectively, "and Farukh knows how to survive. You couldn't exactly call him an Islamic zealot!"

DeLisle replied thoughtfully. "All right, but how come he has managed to survive the revolution so well? Just about all those associated with the Shah have been swept away. Some of them rather terminally! And stop calling me 'Sir'. I'm Andrew, okay?"

"Well, that one is not difficult, sir. I mean, Andrew. Whilst we were at Aiglon, we probably saved the life of a chap called Hassan Fereydoun, a fellow Iranian student who someone seemed to want to assassinate. The thing is that he is called something different now, Hassan Rouhani, close to Khomeini and has influence, having just been appointed to the Majlis, their parliament. Hassan is a pragmatist and has sought to maintain ties with the west by ensuring that Iranian patriots, even those that served the Shah, faithful to Islam but not zealots, continue to hold positions in government."

Roly and Andrew talked well into the evening. Two weeks later, Roly met up with Eric Shacter.

About The Author

An unusually varied career has meant that the author, Charles Pack, has been able to draw upon his many experiences, at home and overseas, in an eclectic variety of professions, as a soldier, banker, pilot, investigator, fruit processor, insurer, and event organiser (to name but a few).

Charles Pack's eloquent descriptive in **Flashman Rides Again** (FRA) is borne of personal knowledge of the places that Roly Flashman visits in his novel. FRA was conceived under pressure as homework at the Marlborough Summer School's "Creative Writing" Course and tasked to write the first three pages of his first novel (thanks, Fleur!).

It was easy to take inspiration from GMF's eponymous hero, Harry Flashman. Encouraged also by Bob Brightwell's marvellous accounts of Harry's Uncle, Thomas Flashman, Roly Flashman, his grandson, was born!

Charles Pack now lives in Hampshire with his wife (Fan), where their lives entwine with their family of three sons and their friends.